Presence

Laura
Wetzel

I hope you enjoy
the story!

Presence

THE STORY OF ADEL

LANA WETZEL

MORNING
SONG

Scripture quotations are from the ESV® Bible (The Holy Bible, English Standard Version®), copyright © 2001 by Crossway, a publishing ministry of Good News Publishers. Used by permission. All rights reserved.

Cover Art and Illustrations by B.D. Wetzel

Published by Morning Song Press

Paperback ISBN: 978-0-578-90670-6
eBook ISBN: 978-0-578-90783-3

In loving memory of my grandma,
Faye Elaine Heidel

TABLE OF CONTENTS

Prologue

Summer—1999

"Come on! Let's go! We have to leave soon!"

I hurried after the other children, my nine-year-old legs going as fast as they could to try to keep up. The hot summer sun shone down brightly on the field where we were playing. The dry grass crunched under my feet as I ran. Rebecca and Peter were already at the end of the long line of hay bales, trying to climb up the sides.

"Here! Let's jump on here!" Nate called as he scampered up the side of a hay bale about halfway down the line, then reached a hand down to help me up. We were pretending the large row of hay bales was a train, and we were sheriff and deputy, trying to catch a duo team of horse thieves before it was time for them all to go home for supper.

"Aha!" I hollered. "We've cut them off!" We leaped daringly from one hay bale to another in pursuit of the feisty outlaws.

The rich scent of hay surrounded us. The bright blue sky overhead contrasted with the dark green of the surrounding mountain range to create a lovely backdrop for our play. It was a *perfect* day, like so many before. *If only summer would last forever.*

As we were closing in on our soon-to-be captives, we heard their mama call out from across the field, "Rebecca! Nate! Peter! Time to go!"

"Aw, man!" I said as I plopped down on top of a bale of hay. "We were *so* close!"

"Come on," Rebecca urged, as she slid down and started walking toward the house.

"I wish summer wasn't so short," I complained as the boys and I followed along behind her. My young heart felt heavy. I knew the feeling well. Every summer about this time, I had the same old feeling. It was my last day on the farm, my last day with my beloved grandparents, and the last time to play like this, with these friends, until next summer, and a year was *so* long. I was glad to go home and see my parents again, but leaving behind a summer of such sweet memories was always hard for my tender nature, and it seemed to get harder with each passing year.

"Adel! My goodness!" Grandma smiled as we walked into the yard. "What've y'all been doing to get so covered in hay?"

I reached up a hand to feel the tiny bits stuck in my disheveled hair. I looked over at the others; they were covered in hay too.

Ms. Annie came over with little Marie on her hip and gave me a hug. "We're going to miss you, little honey! It's hard to believe summer's over already!"

I nodded. I didn't feel like talking. I felt an uncomfortable lump in my throat.

"Kids, tell her bye!" Ms. Annie continued. "We've got to get home and get supper going!"

The boys came over, gave me a hug, and said bye in a bashful, boyish way, and then Rebecca did too and said, "I hope you have a good year of school! Write me a letter if you think of it!"

I nodded again, then ran off toward the woods. I needed the solace of my secret place.

Through the woods I ran until, at last, I entered the magical room surrounded by mountain laurels, ferns, and soft green moss. I ran past the stone bench and crawled under the fronds of the weeping willow tree, leaning my back against the sturdy trunk. I wiped the back of my hand across my eyes and stared down into the cool, clear water of the mountain stream. I didn't know how to think through what I was feeling. All I could tell was that I was uncomfortable and unhappy.

Before long, Grandpa peeked his head into the secret room. He saw me sitting under the willow tree and came to join me. He sat down right there in the dirt beside me and put his arm around my shoulders. I wondered if he noticed that I'd been crying. I leaned into him and laid my head against his chest. Neither one of us said anything. We just sat there. As the sky began to grow dark and the song of the whippoorwills came out, Grandpa stood to his feet. "Come on, little un. We don't need to worry your grandma by being late for supper." He reached a strong hand down to help me up, and he didn't let go of my hand as we walked slowly back through the woods to the house.

When we got inside, Grandma had dinner on the table. Grandpa knew how to time it perfectly. She smiled warmly at me. "Go wash up," she said.

Grandma had fixed all my favorite things for my last day at the farm, even homemade sausage biscuits, which was my *absolute* favorite.

Grandma and Grandpa chatted while we ate, but my heart was still too full to say much or even listen well. I wished it was over already; I wished I was already home, in my own bed, in my own room, in my own house back in San Francisco. Then I wouldn't have to say goodbye.

After my bath, Grandma gave me a glass of warm milk and a couple of her homemade snickerdoodle cookies. She had some too. We sat at the table and ate our snack together.

"These are so good," I said between mouthfuls.

Grandma nodded. "I packed you some for tomorrow. After you finish that up, it's time for bed. We've got an early start in the morning."

I nodded slowly, staring down at my plate. Grandma wiped her hands on a napkin and stood up. She patted me warmly on the back and handed me another cookie before walking over to finish the dishes.

After I brushed my teeth and before crawling into bed, I walked over to have one last look at the night sky out of my bedroom window. It was a clear night. The sky was black like the ink of a pen. The mountains all around us were barely perceptible in the darkness. The millions of stars shone as bright as I had ever seen them.

I felt wide awake while Grandma was tucking me in and saying my prayers with me. She began to hum a little tune while she sat there on the end of my bed. I was anxious. My eyes were wide open; I knew I would be up *all* night. But the activity of the day and the soft and peaceful notes in Grandma's song slowly had their way with me, and my eyes grew heavier and heavier until at last, I was asleep.

ONE

The Funeral

Early Spring—2015

I stared down the open road before me. I could do this. I *was* doing it. The very act of moving forward would surely in itself give me the gumption I needed to go on.

My stomach growled. I hadn't eaten in a while. The blaring blue lights from the clock on the dashboard told me that it was past eleven o'clock, almost midnight, and it was still nearly sixty miles until the next town.

I glanced into the rearview mirror. Noah was sleeping peacefully, his chubby cheeks made chubbier by the position of his head in the car seat. His tiny lips were drooping adorably. It was hard to believe that it had been *eight* months since he arrived. Oh, how I loved him! It was mostly because of him that I pushed on with my decision to start this new adventure, to travel *all* the way across the country and attempt starting a new life. Just Noah and me.

My resolve wavered many times since we set out the day before yesterday, but I would not succumb to it. Whenever I thought of Noah, a surge of determination swept over me, warming me from my head to my toes. I did have a good reason to do such a difficult thing. His name was Noah. And he was my son. I would *no longer* sacrifice my life and my relationship with my son because I had been too weak to try anything else, because I didn't know any better, or because I hadn't been offered—been *given*—a fresh start.

A month earlier, I was standing with my family in the crowded room in the back of the church. The air was stuffy. The room was small. The noise was deafening to my sensitive ears. All the voices talking and talking—

People seemed to know who I was, and though I recognized several faces, I didn't remember their names. It was all so long ago.

I could feel my mom standing close by my side, her silky black dress swaying as she moved. Thankfully, she, Dad, Aunt Kate, and Uncle Alex didn't mind doing the bulk of the talking; I didn't feel like doing much talking myself. My heart was hurting in a way it had never hurt before. It was my first experience with death in such a personal way. When Grandpa had died six years before, I had been out of the country on a study abroad and missed the funeral. I had been so busy in those days.

But there was more to it than that. My heart was aching not just for what was lost but also for what would never be. I grew up spending my summers with my grandparents on their apple farm, Sweet Valley, in the Blue Ridge Mountains of North Georgia. Those were precious times in my life.

At home, I felt empty, alone, and in the way. But when I was at Sweet Valley, I felt loved and appreciated and *alive*. When I was about thirteen, my parents made the decision that I didn't need to go to Sweet Valley anymore. They said it was because we had other things we needed to do during the summer. Mainly traveling. But I always wondered if that was the real reason.

I kept the secret hope of returning to Sweet Valley one day to spend time with my grandma. I knew she was getting old, I knew that her heart had broken after Grandpa died, but I never went back to console her, to be there for her. Not even when I knew that she was growing frail. Not even when I was an adult and could have made the decision for myself.

Life was *so* busy. I was finishing up my degree at the University of San Francisco, and that's when I met Damian. We married after dating only a year. I was busy with work and married life. Then, with all the distractions centered around Damian leaving, and me with a child on the way—it was a lot. I always had the vague feeling that I needed to go back to Sweet Valley nagging me in the back of my mind, but I never went. And now it was too late.

It was a lot to wrap my mind around as I was standing there in the little country church, which had been home to my grandma and grandpa for so many years. All these people in the crowded room were their friends. These people knew my grandparents better than we did! It seemed strange to be the ones standing in the front, receiving the words of consolation.

Noah broke me from my reverie by reaching up a tiny hand and grabbing a lock of hair that was near my face. I gently pulled the hair from between his fingers and pushed it back behind my shoulders. I repositioned him to the other hip and glanced around the room.

There was yet *another* family walking through the doors. They slowly moved in our direction, stopping to talk with just about everyone on the way.

It still blew my mind that there were *this* many people in such a small town.

They finally made their way to us.

"Hi, Adel," said the tall, middle-aged woman. She had black hair that was beginning to gray, which fell down past her shoulders.

She must be the matriarch of the family, I thought.

"It's good to see you again," she said, and she hugged me. "I just wish it wasn't under these circumstances."

Did I know her? She seemed familiar. I tried to smile, but I couldn't. Her husband gave me a pat on the back, and then he and his wife moved down to talk with my parents. Next, their grown children stopped by. There seemed to be a lot of them. I assumed it was their children; they all came in together.

"Your grandma was a wonderful lady," said one of them. She was a woman who seemed a little older than me and had several small children clinging to her legs. Her eyes glistened as she spoke.

I wonder how she knew Grandma. They must have been close.

She hugged me tightly and said, "We're *all* going to miss her."

Then I noticed the man standing behind her. Was it her brother? Her husband? He was looking intently at me. His expression caught my attention but only for an instant. It was soon swallowed up by the other members of the family who came to pay me their respects. I moaned inwardly. *I'll be so glad when this is over.*

Our stay in Georgia was short. We were only there for the funeral. We didn't even go with Aunt Kate and Uncle Alex when they stopped by Grandma's house. Mom and Dad were anxious to get home, and Mom was especially uneasy about going back to her childhood home. "There will be plenty of opportunities in the coming months." She sighed. I could tell her nerves weren't up to the visit. The farm held so many memories for her.

By the time we arrived back in San Francisco the following afternoon, the funeral was just a blurry memory in my mind. A place I never wanted to revisit. There was no need. Now I just had to learn to cope with the feeling of longing that would never be satisfied, the longing for a place and a people that would never be mine again.

For about a month, life went on as usual. I had been living with my parents since my husband, Damian, left about a year before, but living in my parents' home had its effects. I had lived five years out of the house, and when I walked back through the door, I became the child again. Well, for the first time, really. I was only an object in their lives when I was young, something to feed their image. Sure, I had been taken care of, I suppose. I never went without food or clothes, but I rarely felt love or genuine affection.

Being empty nesters for several years had taught my parents what they had missed when I was a child. So when I came home, they accepted me with wide open arms and all their money. They *wanted* me there. They *needed* me there. But more than me, they needed *Noah*.

Mom began to wait on us, hand and foot. She was enjoying having a baby in the house. She was getting to be a mother, and in some ways, I appreciated the help. Noah nursed often during the night, making me extra tired during the day. It was nice to have extra hands to hold him so I could take a shower or a nap or just sleep in.

It seemed to me now that Mom was attempting to have back what she had given away so many years before. But this time, it wasn't hers to have. It was mine, and I struggled with this.

"Adel?" Mom said one day. "Adel? Where is Noah's sweater? We're going to visit Mrs. Sims, and it's chilly out."

"It's hanging on the rack in the foyer!" I called from the sofa in the living room.

"Got it. Thanks!"

As I heard the door close softly, something inside me cringed. I was painfully aware that Mom had just left the house with *my* son. She didn't even *ask* me if it was OK. And I had done nothing about it, yet again.

This sort of thing happened often. Mom would feed him, bathe him, and take him places without my consent. At first, I just went along with it. I didn't realize anything was wrong. But it had been a couple of months since I first began to notice the shift Mom was making from grandmother to mother. It started when I had the OK from his doctor to introduce cereal into his diet. I was excited about this milestone and hurried to the store after the appointment to buy some. But when I got home, there was already a box sitting on the counter, waiting for us.

My face felt hot when I saw some warming in the microwave. I felt—angry? That was an uncommon emotion for me. But angry it was.

"Hey! When did you have time to buy baby cereal?" I asked.

Mom looked up from her reading at the kitchen island. "Oh, I've had that for a while now. I figured he would be needing it soon."

"Oh. OK. Well, I bought some today too," I said, holding up the box for her to see.

"Oh, that brand isn't very good. I'm sorry, Adel. The one I have sitting on the counter there is the finest quality on the market. We want to give Noah the best of the best for his first food!" She smiled sweetly.

From that moment on, I began to be aware of all kinds of infringements on my personal rights as a mother. Sadly, I had not previously been aware of them and had even encouraged them at times. Like when I wanted to sleep in after a long night of nursing. But not anymore. From that day on, I began to take more initiative with Noah. He was my son, after all, wasn't he? Or was he? Was I even acting like a mother? Or was I allowing others to fill that role while I sat back and watched? The thought hit me like a ton of bricks. At that moment, I knew something was terribly wrong. I knew that something had to change. I wanted nothing more, in that moment, than to be ten thousand miles away from everyone, alone, with *my* baby. I would do whatever it took. Oh what a lousy job I had done at being a mother to this tiny, helpless little boy! But not now. I *would* do my best. I *would* raise my own child. God had given him to *me*. Not to anyone else. Not even to my parents. And I only had *one* shot at this.

It was a struggle. I wanted to be the one caring for Noah, but I was still learning what to do, Mom always seemed to beat me to the task, and whatever I did was never good enough.

Mom would say things like, "Adel, honey, that diaper is looking a little tight!" Or, "That pacifier you bought doesn't seem to be doing the trick, so I got him a new one." Or worse yet, "Adel, dear, it looks like Noah is beginning to get a diaper rash. Have you been using that special cream I bought you?"

It was a learning process. I still felt like I wasn't being the mom God made me to be. But I *was* trying. *And* I was praying. I learned early in life that whenever I had a problem, I could go to the Lord for help. I wasn't sure what kind of help he would be sending me this time, but I had faith that he *would*.

In late February, about a month after Grandma's funeral, my parents received some interesting news.

I had taken Noah out for a walk. It was the one thing I could be assured of being able to do *alone*. Just me and Noah. It was a time for solitude. For peace and quiet. Where I could hear the birds sing and think my own thoughts. When I arrived home, Cliff was there. He was a heavyset, middle-aged man with brown, gray-speckled hair. He was Dad's attorney, and he was sitting with Mom and Dad in the dining room. They had several papers spread before them on the table and were anxiously looking them over as we passed by.

"Hello, Cliff," I called as I carried Noah toward the kitchen in hopes of securing him a snack before he went down for his nap.

"Adel. Hi!" replied Cliff.

"Yes! Hi, Adel," Dad echoed. "Could you come in here for a minute? We have some things we need to discuss with you." He sounded unusual. Strained.

"So, I want to get right to the point," Dad began as I entered the room, a sleepy little Noah still in my arms.

"We are looking over Grandma Elaine's will. And," he said, looking over the rim of his glasses and down at the papers spread out in front of him, shaking his head in bewilderment, "apparently, she has left her *entire* estate to *you*."

"To *me*?" I asked in disbelief. "Everything? What does that mean?"

"Her home. The farm. All her money. Everything."

I was completely shocked. "But ... *why*?"

"Well, I don't know, Adel. She didn't say—but it's yours. It's all right here," he said, gesturing over the papers. "I can't understand why she would make a decision like this. Especially without consulting *us* about it. Now *we* must decide what to do with it all."

"Wow" was all I could say.

Mom was looking pale and withdrawn and said nothing.

"Well, it's going to be a lot of work. But after everything sells, you will have a good sum of money. Quite a large sum of money actually."

"Wait. What? Are you thinking of selling Grandma's farm?"

"Of course, dear. What on earth would we do with an apple orchard all the way over in Georgia? We know nothing about the business. We couldn't possibly take care of it. And renting it would be more pain than it's worth! The only option is to sell it. And as soon as possible before everything starts to decay. The house is old. I'm not sure how much it's worth, but it's situated on several hundred acres of good land, right in the heart of apple country. The established orchards themselves would bring a pretty penny. It will be an *excellent* inheritance for Noah."

"Well," I said, feeling a little indignant at the way Dad was talking to me and also feeling a burst of unusual confidence—it was all happening too fast. "I think if I am truly the rightful owner, I should be the one who decides what happens to the property. I will need to know more about it. And what all the estate includes. And then I think I will need some time to consider the options." As I spoke these words, I suddenly knew what I wanted to do. For a fleeting second, and for a second only, my strongest desire in the world was to move to the farm myself. Just me and Noah. *Alone.* As soon as the thought was birthed, the attacks began. It was so far away from my parents. I didn't know the first thing about operating an apple farm. How would I take care of and pay for it all? On and on went the questions, and I felt my face scrunch up in discomfort. It didn't take much to make me doubt the possibility and practicality of such a move. But still ...

The next morning, I couldn't shake it. I wanted to go. It was scary and intimidating. I knew nothing about farming, I knew nothing about living *alone*, but I knew in my heart that it was what we needed, Noah and I. He needed *me* to be his mommy. And I felt like it was nearly impossible for that to happen in my parents' house.

I was afraid to bring it up to my parents. They had a way of making me feel like a little child whenever I talked to them about important things.

I took a few days to mull over how I wanted to approach it. But finally, on a Friday afternoon, while we were sitting together at the dinner table, I felt the courage I needed.

"Mom, Dad, I have something I need to talk to you about."

"What is it?" Mom said, looking up from wiping Noah's mouth.

"I've decided to keep Sweet Valley. To move there myself."

The looks on my parents' faces were enough to tell me that this wasn't going to be easy.

"Adel," said my dad in his most patronizing voice. "I don't think that's a good idea. It's not worth the financial risks. You know nothing about apple farming. It would be better to secure the sale while it's most probable."

"So, you don't think I'd be there very long? That I'd sell it eventually anyway?"

"Of course! That's not the life for a girl like you! It just wouldn't work, Adel."

"Just what kind of girl am I exactly?" My face was beginning to burn.

"Adel, all I'm saying is that you were not brought up around farming. You don't know the business. It isn't an easy life, and considering you would be starting with an entire, fully established farm, it would just be a lot to take on. You know nothing about it!"

"I can learn," I said.

"Sure, you could *learn*. But learning how to run an entire farm isn't something that happens overnight. I'm sure there's a lot to it. It takes years of studying and being around the business to be able to handle something of that magnitude."

My mom leaned toward the table. "Besides, it's so far away from home—"

"I know."

"You would have no family nearby. No friends," she continued.

"Maybe no friends at first," I defended myself.

"Adel, you're just *so* young. You don't know how the world works."

So young ...

I had been away at college since I was eighteen. I had been married and divorced, and I had an eight-month-old baby. Maybe I wasn't as mature as I should be, but I wasn't a child!

"I just don't think this would be best. For you, for Noah," she went on.

"I'm sorry," I said. "But you were the ones who encouraged me to marry Damian. How well did *that* turn out? I don't think *you* know what's best for me and Noah!"

"Adel, there is just no use discussing this further," my dad interjected.

"That's fine. But my decision is made."

"You need to take some time to consider. To really think this through," my dad said forcefully.

"I *have* thought it through."

I got up from the table and took Noah out of his high chair. We were going for a walk—*again*.

Several days later, I brought it up to my parents for a second time. I wanted them to know that I was serious, that I felt like this was something I *needed* to do. I hoped they would understand, but I assumed they wouldn't. This time, my dad was prepared. He asked me to join him at the dining room table, and he brought with him a thin black folder and a pen.

"Look," he said as we sat down. "I have been running the numbers to determine how far your financial inheritance will get you, *if* you decided to go."

He set before me several papers with budgets and expenses listed out in graphs. I glanced over them. I already knew how much Grandma had left me. It seemed like a lot, but I knew that in reality, it wouldn't get me very far. I was still surprised by the results of Dad's calculations.

It seemed to him that I would need to either be profitable by the end of the fall season, or I would need to sell. I looked more closely at the numbers. Yes, he was right. If his guesses were correct, which they probably were—he was so good at researching and estimates—then I would need to sell early next year to avoid running out of money. The alternative would be to go into debt.

"Humm," I said as I looked everything over for a third time.

"What I'm saying, Adel, is that if you *do* go and try it for a while, then you will have a little less than a year to figure things out, assuming you *could* sell it at that time. Is it really worth the risks?"

I sat there, looking numbly down at the papers.

It's so soon. I didn't realize I would have such a short time to get the farm up and running. I had only the fall season to rely on.

"Just think about it," he said, and he gathered the papers back into the folder.

But Noah and I can't breathe *here! I need space! How hard can it be? To pick and sell a few apples?*

I sat up in my chair. "Thank you for taking the time to work out all those numbers. I really appreciate you doing that. It's definitely helpful to know how much time I'll have."

"So, you're going?" he said gruffly.

"Yes. I am."

"All right, then. Don't say I didn't warn you, Adel. It's going to be a hard road!" And with that, he handed me the folder and left the room.

TWO

Travels

Two days later, I met with Cliff at his attorney's office. I signed the papers and went back home to start packing.

No need to drag this out, I thought. *The decision is made. I might as well go as soon as possible, while my nerve is up.*

I waited until after church on Sunday, so I could say goodbye to my friends. They were all shocked and made me promise to keep up with my Instagram and Facebook accounts. Some even made vows to come visit me one day, though I doubted their sincerity.

Then I packed up my small Honda, and Noah and I started off to discover a new life. All I knew was that if I didn't go, if I didn't *try*, I would regret it for the rest of my life. What was the worst thing that could happen? That we hated it and moved back home? We wouldn't be any worse off than we were now. All I wanted was to bond with my baby the way I felt I wasn't. I felt too suffocated in my parents' home to be fully present with him. I felt too ill at ease to relax and be myself with him. I knew in my heart there was a closeness available to us that just wasn't happening. I longed for closeness. For bonding. Did it really require a cross-country move to be able to do that? Probably not, but it was the door that had opened for me, and it meant something to me that Grandma wanted me to have the farm. I had to go and try to find out why.

My head was full of these thoughts as I drove along the various highways between California and Georgia. At times, I felt excited about the adventure, and at other times, I felt the burden already too much to bear. I thought about returning to Sweet Valley, this time to find it barren, empty. The joyful life that had always filled its walls was no more. It would be a different Sweet Valley than the one I had known. Just how different I was yet to discover.

It was getting late. It was the third day on the road, and we had been driving in the dark for hours. I stopped at a red light. The light felt harsh on my tired eyes. I rubbed them with the back of my hand. Still harsh. Now blurry. *How much longer?* I whined to myself. I played some music on the radio to help me wake up. *Coffee. I need some coffee.* But coffee wasn't to be had until the next town, which was where I was planning to stay for the night. *I can make it.*

About thirty minutes outside of town, Noah woke up, and he was hungry. His cries soon covered up the sound of the radio. At least it kept me from dozing off. I contemplated stopping alongside the highway to feed him, but there were so many tractor trailer trucks, and the road was so dark; I was too scared to. I decided to see if we could make it to the hotel. *If only I hadn't used the last bottle!* I thought I had made enough to last this whole stretch of the trip. I had been wrong, and now I was paying the price by sharing the car with a hungry little boy, too young to understand the phrase "We'll be there soon." I felt sorry for him. I felt like a failure for not having planned accurately. My face held a decided frown the last twenty some odd miles of the trip, until we pulled into the parking lot at the hotel. When we got there, I was too exhausted to do anything other than feed my little boy in the passenger seat, which I quickly learned was more comfortable for that sort of thing than the driver's seat, and then check into our room, where we both crashed into the single queen-sized bed.

I woke to the smell of cigarette smoke and mildew. *Ew.* I was so tired the night before that I hardly noticed a thing about our room. Now I saw, in the morning light, that the room was small and basic, with a mini fridge and small table with one chair, and a dresser with an extra-large TV too big for the space. The wallpaper and furnishings were all outdated and dingy.

Well, at least it was only for one night, I thought. But despite the style and odor of the room, I was thankful for the decent night's sleep. I felt refreshed and ready for the last leg of the trip. By sundown, we would be arriving at Sweet Valley Farm, and I was ready.

Traveling with an infant is never easy, even with an extra set of hands. But tackling a cross-country trip single-handedly is a feat that ought never be attempted if there is any alternative.

I remembered my parents' expressions when I climbed in the car to leave a few days before. They were not the typical expressions of parents who were watching a child leave home, for a second time, in my case. They were tense. And cold. As if they were angry with me. I think they were. My mom and dad had reasons for not wanting to drive to Georgia with me. I was thankful they didn't. I wanted to be alone with Noah as soon as possible. Even though the trip was taking a lot longer than it could have, and even though there were moments when I wondered if I would lose my mind to the crying and fussing, it had mostly been a smooth trip. Noah was still little enough to spend much of his time napping. And if he was fed and clean, he was usually pretty happy. There were *those* moments—like when he had that blowout all over his car seat and when I accidentally pinched his arm with the seat belt. But overall, I was satisfied. We were doing it.

By now, we had about six hours left before we would be there. Again, my mind wandered to the lonesome scene. How would it be? The massive, ancient oaks in the front yard would be standing guard over the house, protecting it from outsiders. From what else? Decay? I had heard that Grandma hadn't been able to keep the place up the last few years. Would the house be showing signs of neglect? Would the yard be overgrown? I was worried about my abilities to clean up and take care of a house, especially one as old as that one was.

It was a two-story, traditional farmhouse, built more than one hundred years ago. It had white siding and heart pine floors and a large front porch that spanned the length of the house.

Grandma always kept a tidy house, neat and clean. The furniture always shined. The kitchen too. And the house always smelled *so* good. But not this time. This time, I knew that the familiar smell of Grandma's delicious cooking would be missing from my arrival. I would have to make dinner for myself.

Noah gurgled baby noises from the back seat, bringing me swiftly back to reality. I wished Grandma could have met Noah. She would have loved him.

THREE

Sweet Valley

We pulled onto Grandma's old country road about four that evening. My hands gripped the steering wheel tighter so that my knuckles turned white. The tires crunched over the gravel, making a sound that was pleasant to my ears. I remembered that sound well. Where I came from, there weren't many gravel roads.

Not far now, I thought.

We left the little town heading northeast and then wound and turned on mountain roads for several miles before reaching Grandma's road, which was in a valley of sorts. As we slowly drove along, I felt like I was in the middle of nowhere. Trees ... fields ... barns ... few houses.

The road seemed longer than I remembered it. I passed several overgrown cow pastures, with evergreen trees and shrubs growing along their fence lines, so that it was hard to tell if there was a fence there at all. The fields were mostly brown, with some new shoots of bright green grass beginning to show along the ground. The world was kind of gray, the last bit of winter still clinging on before spring burst forth in all its glorious color.

I passed a lightly wooded lot with a long driveway and a mailbox. The house was out of sight of the road. There was a rocky creek running through the lot, which meandered under a small bridge. It didn't have guardrails, so I crossed it carefully. Next, on the other side of the road, came a freshly plowed field, and beside it, a modest brick house, circa 1970, that seemed well kept and inviting. But then, there it was. Almost directly across the street from the brick house was Grandma's driveway.

The old red gate was closed.

I stopped the car and got out slowly, trying to take everything in. My stomach churned. I paused in front of the gate to have a better look around. The gravel driveway hadn't seen new gravel in a while, and there was grass growing knee-high up the middle and crouching in on the sides. On either side of the driveway was a large field full of apple trees that were just beginning to bud. The fields rose slowly upward into a hillside, and the apple trees stopped at the top of the crest, where the house sat, overlooking the farm. The old white farmhouse was surrounded by several large post and willow oaks. They must have been as old as the house. The two out front, one on either side of the driveway, were just as I remembered them. They stood to separate the orchards from the yard. There was still a tire swing under one of them.

I wonder if that's the same swing from when I was a kid?

The gate was locked the old-fashioned way, but I knew where the key was. I retrieved the key and opened the lock, sliding the chain noisily off the gate. I pushed the gate open, its rusty hinges squeaking loudly. I turned back to look up at the house again. The Blue Ridge Mountains rose up grandly behind it and on either side, giving the farm a breathtaking backdrop.

Here in the valley, it was peaceful and quiet. No cars passed me while I stood there looking around. No one interrupted my thoughts.

I breathed in deeply. The fresh mountain air mixed with the sweet scent of hay enveloped me.

I was *home.*

We slowly and cautiously made our way up the long driveway and pulled around to the side of the house, where Grandma's car was still parked. Grandma never had a garage. I guess I didn't either now.

I sat in the car for a moment to text my parents and a few friends to let them know I had arrived, then climbed out of the car and looked up at the old white farmhouse looming above me, the massive trees around it blowing stiffly in the breeze. It felt so strange. Everything was the same, but everything was *different*. The lights in the house were off. It looked sad. Lonely. Like I felt on the inside. All at once, I wanted to cry. I wanted Grandma to come smiling out the side door to welcome me. To embrace me. To comfort me.

Instead of crying, I turned to unbuckle Noah from his car seat. I grabbed my purse and diaper bag and headed for the door. I had been given a set of keys. I tried them until I found the one that worked. I swung the door open, took a deep breath, and walked inside. The air inside the house was stale, but the living room looked exactly the same as the picture in my memory. Grandma's pretty flora paintings still hung over the piano. There was still a stack of *Country Living* magazines on the coffee table. Oh, that coffee table—I had so many memories of meals eaten and games played on that coffee table. Grandma refinished it one summer when I was there. She let me help her sand and stain the old pine wood. It looked darker now and worn. But it was still the same old table. I smiled at it. Then I walked toward the little hall and the kitchen. But there was no delightful aroma to meet me in the hall. No delicious dinner cooking in the oven. No sweet, homemade dessert sitting on the counter to cool. It was all still, quiet, and lifeless.

The kitchen had been Grandma's hub. Her special place. She spent many hours puttering around her kitchen, making good things to bless her family. Cooking was a gift of Grandma's, and she used it wisely. To see the kitchen like this was more than I could bear. I sat down abruptly, right there on the old linoleum, with Noah in my lap, and cried. The sobs shook my shoulders. The fatigue of the long car trip and the emotions summoned by the sights and smells of the empty house overwhelmed me. I just sat there and held nothing back. Oh, how I longed for my grandma and grandpa! What on earth was I doing here? I didn't belong here! It was too much. Maybe everyone was right after all. Who was I to take my precious baby boy and bring him here to the middle of *nowhere?* Who was I to think that I, Adel Davis, could possibly come here, to this special place, and *not* be overcome by the past? I was *too* sensitive. Or maybe I cared too much. This was my grandparents' home. I didn't like seeing it like this. I wanted everything to go back to the way it was when I was a little girl! My heart ached. I held Noah tightly in my arms and rocked back and forth gently as I reined in my tears and tried to think. What was I going to do? We were so far from home. I felt so hopeless inside. So ... strange. Everything was wrong. I just wanted to feel better. I wanted some relief!

After a few minutes, I remembered how late it was. Sunlight was still coming through the kitchen windows, but I knew it had to be past five o'clock. Noah's bedtime would be soon. Then I knew what to do. Noah needed to have something to eat, and then I would set up his playpen so he could go to sleep. Yes. I had direction. I felt a little more at ease as I stood up and settled Noah on my hip. I took a couple of deep breaths and got to work.

I found my cooler in the back of the car. It was a large cooler and getting it into the house was interesting. I left Noah in his car seat as I half carried, half dragged it into the house. Then we ate a snack dinner of mashed fruit, apple juice, and arrowroot cookies. I supplemented mine with a little pack of peanut butter crackers. I held Noah while we ate. Focusing on him seemed to help keep my emotions in check. It gave me something to do.

Noah was settled and sleepy after his meal. I needed to finish unloading our things, at least the playpen, but he was ready to sleep *now.* If I missed this opportunity, he might not settle again for several hours. I put him back in his car seat as I unloaded the playpen and a few more things. As I pulled the playpen out of the car, I knocked over a box full of some of my favorite glass decor from back home. Some of the vases crashed to the ground, breaking into a million tiny pieces. *Oh!* I wiped an arm across my sweaty forehead. *Why now!?*

Cleaning up the mess took longer than I expected. Maybe I should have left it and finished unloading and setting up the playpen, because by the time I finished with both of those tasks, it had been a solid hour, and Noah was growing fussy.

"OK, boy," I cooed gently. "Here we go. Your bed's all made and ready for you. It's time to sleep now."

But he wouldn't have it. He continued to cry and fuss louder and louder. His eyes were glassy and tired. I decided to try rocking him in the living room while patting his back. He still continued to cry. But the volume and intensity grew gradually less and less until his eyelids closed and he nodded off to sleep. *Whew! It must be midnight!* I thought.

After lying Noah down gently in his playpen, I went in search of my phone. I checked the time. Well, it wasn't exactly midnight, but it *was* getting late. I stood there for a minute in the kitchen, phone in hand, wondering what to do next. I could finish unloading. It would definitely be easier while Noah was asleep. Yes, that's what I'd do.

The sun had fallen behind the mountains hours ago and left behind a dark unlike anything I ever experienced in the city. This darkness was consuming. It filled every nook and cranny and left nothing exposed. I saw it out the window, and when I opened the door and felt its full presence, I was intimidated. I searched for the floodlight switch on the wall and tried it. *No! The light must be burned out!* I cautiously took a few steps out into the night and was met with a humidity to which I was unaccustomed. Even though we were just on the edge of spring, and even though it was night, the air was dense and a little sticky. Why had I not noticed it before? I guess my head had been too full of other things. I noticed it now. But it seemed at peace with the gusty song of the crickets that filled the night around me. Somehow, they were in harmony with one another. As if they belonged together. The song of the crickets was loud, almost as deafening as the night was enveloping. But I didn't mind. I took another cautious step toward the car and stopped. I looked up. The sky was so black that the stars nearly jumped out of the sky and came right down into the yard. There were millions upon millions. I felt I could see them all. Clearly too. Then a gentle breeze ruffled the hair around my face. It was cool. I welcomed it. It belonged here too, with the crickets and the darkness, and the world of stars above me. Yes, I was *home.*

Four

Getting Settled

When the morning light filled my room, I woke and sat up in bed. It took me a minute to get my bearings. *Oh, that's right ... I'm at Sweet Valley.* I felt groggy. I rubbed my hands across my face and wiped at the corners of my eyes. I took a deep breath and looked around the room. I had been too tired after finishing up last night to really take in my new surroundings. The room was my mom's old room, made over as a guest room. I always stayed in this room when I came to visit Sweet Valley as a child. It seemed natural for me to stay in it now. The room had one full-sized bed with a high, creamed-colored metal frame. There was an old mahogany vanity and a matching dresser. There was a desk under the window and a small bookcase beside it. On the bookcase were a few books, neatly organized, and some wooden animals that Uncle Alex and Aunt Kate brought back from a trip to South Africa many years ago.

Just the same, I thought. It felt so strange to be sitting in that bed again after so many years, with the white and purple lilac quilt bunched up around my legs. I got up, listening to hear if Noah was awake. I heard nothing, so I tiptoed to his room to have a peek. I pushed the door open just a crack. He was still sleeping peacefully on his tummy, his little bottom sticking up in the air.

I tiptoed back and found my toiletry bag, then headed for the shower. As I passed by the only window in the room, I was caught by the view. I pushed back the lilac curtains and beheld with wonder the breathtaking view of the Blue Ridge Mountains. They swept out before me in grandeur and majesty, clothed in a blue-gray haze. Below them, settled over this little valley, was a dense mist. Cool and refreshing. I pushed up to open the window, but it was stuck. It had probably been years since it was last opened. I took one more look out of the window, and I saw down in the misty orchard a family of white-tailed deer. Several does and a couple of tiny spotted fawns. One of the does stopped grazing and lifted her head high with her ears alert, looking toward the house. Could she see me up in the window? The way she held her head was so graceful. She looked like a queen in sleek brown fur. I could have watched them longer, but I knew that if I didn't hurry up with my shower, I probably wouldn't get one at all. It was almost time for Noah to wake up.

I went to the bathroom and pushed back the shower curtain and let out a little scream! There, on the tiled shower wall, about at eye level, was a large brown spider with long, spindly legs and the shape of a violin on its back. I had never seen a spider like this one in my whole life. And I don't do spiders! I wished desperately for some other adult in the house who could handle this situation better than I could. But there was no one. So I hurried back to the bedroom and found one of my shoes. I closed my eyes and smacked the spider. Yuck. Its sticky mess was left there on the tile. After cleaning it up with a piece of tissue, I was finally able to get to my shower, and I appreciated it more than I had appreciated a shower in a *very* long time. After the shower, I was fixing my hair, and stopped to take a look at myself in the mirror. *Wow. It's been a while since I've really looked in a mirror!* I laughed. I had been so busy the last week or so with packing and then our long car trip, I had hardly taken time to care for myself. My slim frame looked a little more thin than usual, and my long, dark brown hair was in need of a trim. I leaned closer to the mirror. It's always strange when you see yourself after not seeing yourself for a while. I shook my head. There were dark circles under my green eyes. *I need to start getting better sleep*, I thought. *As soon as Noah can go all night without nursing!* I laughed again.

While I dressed and finished with my hair, I began to think more about Noah. I felt so inadequate to raise a child. What had I learned in my life? How to do well in school? How to pick out nice clothes? I learned that whatever my parents had was not for me. I wanted something different. Something deeper. Something real. Those kinds of thoughts always led to my feeling desperate. Noah was growing so fast! And now I had a house—a *farm*—to care for too. It was time to pray.

Lord, you know who I am ... what I am ... better than I do. You know how inadequate I feel. I want to be a better mom for Noah, I want to be a better homemaker, I want to be a better person, and to run this farm ... but, Lord, I don't know how! Will you help me? Will you show me how?

For breakfast that morning, we ate what we had for dinner the night before: crackers, bananas, arrowroot cookies, and some juice. We had already eaten the rest of our food. I would need to go to the store soon.

It still felt eerie to be sitting in Grandma's kitchen alone. It was too quiet. Too empty. I glanced around at the antique buffet that sat along the wall beside the old oak table. On top of it was a bowl of fake fruit, a beautiful glass cake stand, and a collection of tattered cookbooks lying flat. *Some of Grandma's favorite things ...*

Over on the counter, there was a knife stand full of knives, a coffee pot, a large cutting board, and not much else. *Someone must have cleaned up the house some after Grandma passed*, I mused.

As Noah sat in his high chair and nibbled on the rest of his arrowroot cookies, I began to cautiously look through the pantry and some of the cabinets. I saw some pots and pans, a colander, a blender, a sifter, and other things like that. The cabinets smelled a little like a pet shop. There was no food left in the pantry, and the fridge was empty too, except for a jug of water. I was thankful for whoever thought to clean it out. I shuddered to think what the house would have smelled like if no one had taken out the old food.

I also found where the silverware was and noticed that the old dishwasher was empty. I remembered the summer Grandpa bought that dishwasher as a surprise for Grandma. I was about eleven years old. Grandpa let me help pick it out. It was Grandma's first dishwasher; she had been so pleased. But it was old now. I wondered if it still worked.

After breakfast, I took Noah, and we walked around the rest of the house. The kitchen was at the back, and the kitchen door led to the small screened-in back porch and the patio behind it. Attached to the kitchen was the dining room. The front door opened into the living room. The stairs were in the living room, to the right of the door. They were narrow and steeper than modern stairs. Behind the stairs was the hallway where the stairs to the cellar were. Grandpa had someone build steps down to the cellar from inside the house many years ago. I knew that the old steps out behind the house were now boarded up and inaccessible. Down the hall from the cellar door was the bathroom and an old sewing room turned into a modern-day laundry room.

Everything was *so* dusty. There were cobwebs in all the corners and on the lamps and other decor. *This place is going to need a serious cleaning,* I thought. And in general, it just smelled musty. I had no clue how to get rid of that smell. But I knew how to dust. That wasn't hard.

I walked back up the stairs. There were three bedrooms: the one I was staying in; Noah's, which had been my aunt Kate's when she was a girl; and Grandma's room. The rooms were all large and tidy, though Noah's room had a few too many pieces of furniture now that I had set up his crib in one corner.

Grandma's room was hard for me to enter. It reminded me so much of her. The light pink walls. The Thomas Kincade picture of a bridge clothed in glorious light that hung above the bed. The floral bedspread. The pretty things she had collected in porcelain bowls on her dresser. The smell—Grandma loved roses. Her favorite perfumes were rose petal blends. Her bedroom still smelled of them. Everything looked in order. Then I noticed Grandma's Bible sitting on her nightstand. I remembered that Bible well. Grandma spent an hour each morning studying her Bible while she sipped tea at the kitchen table, and she read to me from it nearly every night while I was here during the summer. I caressed the black leather cover, then gently opened it.

"Elaine Adel Crawford." My heart came into my throat. I quickly closed the Bible and retreated to the security of my own room. I sat down on the edge of the bed, Noah still in my arms.

What am I doing here? I wondered again. And as I sat there, I began to feel a deep stirring in my soul. It was pulling me in. It was threatening to suffocate me. The house was *so* big, it was *so* quiet, and I missed my grandparents. I was *all alone.* A little streak of panic began to rise in my chest, growing rapidly. *I am all alone* ... I had never been alone in my life! And though Noah was with me, I still felt completely alone.

God, please hear me, I prayed. *Please help me. I don't know what I'm doing here. I don't even know if I should be here! But I feel alone, and I'm afraid ...*

I sat there praying and rocking Noah, and after a few minutes, I held him out a little so I could see his face, and he looked up at me with a serious expression. Then he smiled a big, goofy, toothless grin, which made me smile in return. In an instant, the fear began to lift. "OK, big guy," I said as I hugged him close. "What are we going to do, huh?"

As I sat there holding Noah, I remembered that we were low on food and it would be lunchtime soon. "I guess we need to get some groceries, don't we? Come on," I said, standing up. "Let's go find your shoes."

Twenty minutes later, we were driving down the bumpy gravel driveway, heading for the grocery store. As we bumped along, a thought came into my mind. "Be still, and know that I am God."[1] It was followed by "I will never leave you or forsake you."[2] It was exactly what I needed at that moment. To be reminded that no matter how alone *I felt*, I wasn't, and I never would be. My God was with me. My God cared about me. Tears pricked the corners of my eyes. *My God was with me. My God cared about me.* He cared. About *me.* He had shown me just then, by reminding me with his Word. Those sorts of small miracles never cease to amaze me.

I was suddenly thankful. A burst of praise leapt up into my heart,

---

[1] Psalm 46:10.
[2] Deuteronomy 31:6.

and I began to sing a hymn I learned as a child: "Blessed assurance, Jesus is mine. Oh, what a foretaste of glory divine. Heir of salvation, purchase of God. Born of His Spirit, washed in His blood." I started off shakily at first, but the more I sang, the bolder I felt. By the time I reached "This is my story, this is my song," I was belting it out at the top of my lungs!

I was thankful to God for showing me that he cared, and I was also thankful for whoever took the time to teach me those verses so long ago.

The only grocery store in town was a tiny Food Mart. We didn't even have Food Mart back in San Francisco, but I remembered liking this store when I was a kid, especially the gumball machines up front. Grandpa always happened to have an extra quarter in his pocket whenever he took me to get groceries.

We pulled in and I parked the car. *Wow,* I thought as I glanced around at the handful of cars in the parking lot. *I guess I will be one of the five people in the store this morning.* That thought struck me as funny and I laughed a little to myself.

We went in through the swinging glass door and took out a shopping cart. I buckled Noah into the seat.

There're the gumball machines! I noticed as we moved past the single row of shopping carts. *And yes, I do believe those old machines are the same ones!*

As I moved into the store, I was greeted by country music playing on the speakers overhead. The words "I'd start walkin' your way, you'd start walking mine, and we'd meet in the middle, 'neath that ol' Georgia pine" took me back to listening to country music while sitting with Grandpa as he worked on farm equipment in his old barn. He had loved country music.

The store felt quaint and old-fashioned, like stepping back in time twenty years. It was so small, much smaller than the marketplace stores I was used to back home, where one could buy just about anything they needed, from tank tops to iceberg lettuce. This store had only one purpose, to sell a few groceries. I could see all the aisles from where I stood near the produce department. There were no signs to tell what was on each row, and there was only one checkout counter, where a lady with a low ponytail and hot pink nail polish was punching in the prices of each item one by one. This was a new experience for me. It wouldn't take long to do our shopping; there wasn't much to choose from! It seemed too easy. Only, I wasn't sure what to get! Back home, I had only gone in the store for a few things here and there. My mom was the grocery woman in our family. I hardly ever needed to buy more than a day's worth of groceries at a time, even when I was married to Damian. He bought most of our groceries, and we ate out a lot. I wondered what we would need. Maybe I should have made a list!

I looked around. There were bins in the front near the produce that were full of discount items, Moon Pies and Honey Buns. The wooden produce shelves in the produce department were clean and tidy and filled with a small variety of fruits and veggies. I strolled through. I didn't have a clue what to buy. I didn't have a clue what to make for lunch when we got home!

Hmm ... these apples look good. And we could probably use some lettuce. Bananas! Yes, we definitely need bananas.

And so I strolled along, wondering about each thing I saw and debating about whether or not we needed it. In the end, we made it out with a random assortment of food, most of which Noah couldn't even eat yet. Thankfully, I did remember pouches and jars of baby food and arrowroot cookies. And juice, of course.

That afternoon, I began to get a little restless. Once Noah was awake from his nap, I decided it was time to get outside. It had been a while since we had taken a walk together. Thankfully, I brought my baby carrier, a gift from my aunt Kate, and this seemed like the perfect time to try it out. At home in San Francisco, I had mostly used the stroller for our walks, as the road and pathways were all paved. But there were no paved roads in sight of Sweet Valley Farm, and I feared the stroller wouldn't fare well on the rocky driveway. The carrier would have to suffice. Once Noah was strapped in comfortably, we headed out. *Maybe we can explore the yard when we get back*, I mused. We walked along the downward slope of the driveway and out through the gate onto the road, then headed left.

We wandered down the road, enjoying the sights and smells of the orchard, the fields, and woods, then stopped for a few minutes to enjoy the creek as it bubbled over piles of rocks under the bridge. The air around the creek was so cool and refreshing, the water so bright and cheery as it reflected up the bright rays of early spring sunlight. I smiled fondly down at the creek. When I was a kid, I claimed that creek as my very own, for along its banks was my secret place. My hideaway. It had been more than a decade since I last saw it. It was one of my goals for the spring—to find that secret place, though I was a little afraid that when I did find it, it wouldn't be the same.

We walked for longer than I anticipated, and by the time we made it back to the house, I was exhausted, and it was suppertime. We ate another light supper and spent the rest of the evening together in the living room, watching TV, and with me flipping through Facebook on my phone.

And so the evening passed away into night ...

FIVE

Of Mice and Men

There it was. That sound again. It already woke me up several times during the night, and there it was again! I looked over at my phone. It was three in the morning! I wasn't going to get *any* sleep if that sound didn't stop! But I didn't want to get out of bed. The room was so dark, the sheets so soft and warm, and I was *so* sleepy. And the sound creeped me out. It was a scratching noise. And to be honest, I didn't want to know what it was. I just wanted it to go away. But it didn't. It kept on and on, the sound coming closer to the bed. Finally, I couldn't take it anymore. I got up and ran to turn the overhead light on. I looked around the desk where I thought the sound might be coming from. I leaned over and pulled the chair back a little. Out ran a little field mouse, straight toward my bare feet! I screamed and jumped back in bed. It ran under the bed! *How dare he!*

My heart was pounding in my ears, threatening to jump right out of my chest!

How on earth am I going to get him out? I thought for a minute. Would a broom do the trick? Was there *stuff* under there? Would I have to move things around? I couldn't remember if Grandma kept things stored under this bed or not. The closest broom was in the closet in the hall. I decided that, despite my fears, I would *have* to go for it. I tiptoed quickly across the floor and out into the hall. I fetched the broom and tiptoed back to the bed, looking around on the floor for any signs of the little rascal as I went. *OK. Now what?* I decided it best to get it over with. So I stood up and peeked under the bed. There *were* things stored under there. Boxes and low plastic containers. Some old blankets. I started to slowly pull these things out, one at a time, slowly and cautiously. I just knew that he'd jump out at me at any minute.

After removing everything from under the bed, the room was a mess. But there was no mouse.

Ugh ...

I sat dejectedly on the floor next to the bed, shoulders sagging. *All that for nothing! I can't sleep in here now!* Then the thought struck me that maybe the mouse had left my room. He could have easily fit under the door. He could find me anywhere in the house. *And maybe there are more!*

In the end, I decided it best to stay in my own bed and to sleep with the broom next to me. Ha. Sleep. It was a long time before I got any. I lay there awake, listening for the sounds, for goodness knows how long. I never did hear anything else, and eventually I nodded off, because all at once, I was awakening to sunshine in the windows and the sound of Noah playing quietly in the next room. My hand was still on the broom.

My sole purpose for the morning was to go to the store and buy some mouse traps. I had never bought mouse traps before—I had never needed any—but I figured I could handle it. Better, perhaps, than chasing a mouse around the house with a broom! So, after a breakfast of cereal and mashed bananas, Noah and I headed out.

The midmorning light filtered through the tall branches of the trees overhanging the road, making beautiful, dancing forms of light on the bumpy asphalt in front of me. It was like driving through some story in a faraway place, with the boulders, ravines, and giant stone outcroppings bordering the road. Every now and then, I'd come across a little waterfall that came gently down over the outcroppings onto the shoulder of the road. I would slow down a little so I could get a better look. They were so cool and refreshing—*peaceful*.

I drove through a bend in the road and came face-to-face with eternity, stretched out before me in the form of a valley with giant mountain ranges stretched behind and to the sides of it. I don't know what the elevation was, but we were high up. The town down in the valley looked so small. There were pull offs beside the road where people could stop to get a better look. I stopped, despite the urgency of my errand. I didn't get out of the car; I just wanted to sit and look for a minute. I put the windows down and a breeze blew through the open windows and filled our car with clean, fresh air. The day was a little cooler than the previous. It was crisp and invigorating. The view was spectacular too. The sky was bright and clear without any clouds. And the farthest mountain ranges in the distance had a blue hue to them— almost purple. They contrasted with the browns, grays, and light greens of early spring. I could have sat there forever, feeding my soul on the beauty before me, but I knew it was time to go on to the store.

The sharp curves in the mountain roads always took me by surprise. I didn't know them well enough yet, so I drove slowly. We kept winding down and curving along the edge of the mountain until at last we arrived at the bottom and entered into the edge of town. We followed the main road over to Food Mart and parked the car.

As I buckled Noah into the shopping cart, I noticed that he was rubbing his eyes and looking around the store grumpily. *He needs an early nap today. Maybe he didn't get much sleep last night either!*

I picked out some more bananas and some blueberries and some vegetables for dinner for the next few days. Then we moseyed our way over the rest of the store, picking up some odds and ends and things I had forgotten the day before, like diapers and wipes and some more things we could eat for lunch. We made it to the checkout line when I suddenly remembered why we came. "The mouse traps!" I exclaimed to a startled Noah.

"Excuse me," I said as I quickly pulled our buggy out of line and headed to find the row with the mouse traps.

At last, we found them. Who knew they would be near the motor oil and lightbulbs? I was delighted to find a type of trap that I didn't have to set. These were *sticky* traps. They were supposed to lure the mouse over, and when they walked over the trap, they would stick to it, until, well, they died, I guess. I bought ten. I figured if there was one mouse, there were probably many more. It couldn't hurt to be prepared. I felt a little bad for not leaving any for anybody else, but desperate times call for desperate measures.

Our shopping trip took a lot longer than I anticipated, and we were hungry. Noah was making it loud and clear that he needed food fast, so I decided to feed him there in the parking lot. As I sat with him in the passenger seat, I looked around the shopping center and noticed a Mexican restaurant.

"Del Rio, huh?" I said aloud. "It's been a while since we've had some decent food," I admitted to a satisfied little Noah. Then I laughed. "Well, it's been a while since *I've* had some decent food!"

I decided we should try it, so after wiping Noah's chin and changing his diaper, we walked over and found a table. There were a few others dining at Del Rio that day. One, an elderly man in red suspenders, had just sat down before us. The waitress approached him, saying, "George! Where ya been? I haven't seen you in a while!"

"Oh, I've been sick! Been in the hospital nearly two weeks."

"Well, I knew something had to be up! It's not like you to not come see us for so long. Feelin' better?"

"Yep ... much better! Say, Darlene, d'you get a haircut? Your hair's lookin' different today."

"Sure did!" she said, cocking her head to the side with a smile, to showcase her new do.

My thoughts were suddenly drawn to the door, where a man had just walked in. He was in his mid to late twenties and had an air that seemed a little awkward or unusual, but I couldn't tell exactly why. Maybe it was that he was thinking too much about his movements as he walked across the room. He caught my eye and smiled. Then he came over and sat down at the table beside us.

"Hi, Darlene!" he called to the waitress, who waved her hello.

His unusual air caught my attention so much that I glanced over quickly to have a better look. He had sandy blond hair and bright blue eyes. He was well groomed, clean cut, and rather handsome. He seemed of medium height and stature ... Uh-oh! He looked up before I could look away.

"Hi," he said.

Now I have to talk to him!

"Hello."

Noah squealed loudly.

"And hello to you too!" he said to Noah with a laugh.

"I haven't seen you around," he continued. "Are y'all new in town?"

"Yes. We're from California. We just moved here."

"OK! Where in California are you from? I have some family that lives there."

"San Francisco."

"OK. My relatives live near Monterey. So, have you been here long?"

I was ready to order now. I had begun to realize that I didn't feel comfortable talking with men these days. Having been so recently married, and now *not*—I wasn't sure how to talk to a man who so obviously wanted my attention. I wasn't sure if I wanted to relax and get to know him or close off and be left alone. My feelings wavered and leaned mostly on the side of wanting to be left alone.

"No. We moved here just this week."

"You and your husband?"

He was getting personal.

"No. Just me and my son." I looked around for Darlene. Thankfully, she was making her way to our table. I kept my eyes on her until she arrived, and I gave her my order. Then I commenced chopping up one of our newly purchased bananas for Noah to eat and didn't look back up at the stranger in hopes that he would take the hint and leave us alone.

He didn't take the hint.

"Well, if you're new in town, you'll need to know the best places to go and where to avoid." He laughed as he said this. "I'm Julian, by the way."

"Adel. And this is Noah."

"Nice to meet you, Adel," he said with another handsome smile.

He sure isn't bashful.

Julian started telling me about the different restaurants in town. There weren't many, and from his descriptions and stories, it sounded like there were only three that were safe enough to eat at: Del Rios, JJ's Barbeque, and Subway. He was funny. I was pleasantly surprised by our chat, and before I knew it, we had our food, and then it was time to go.

"Well, hey," he said with a grin as we walked together toward the door, "maybe I'll see you around sometime."

"Maybe."

Back in the car, I tried to mull over what had just happened. It had felt a little like a date. It had been so long since I had been on a date. I didn't want to date anyone again. Probably never would. Though I had enjoyed talking with him and though he seemed nice enough, I hoped I would never see him again.

When we got home, I left Noah in the car while I unloaded the groceries. The winding road back up and over the mountain had lulled him to sleep, and I knew he needed it. He had missed his morning nap, and if he missed this one, there would be no getting him to sleep come nighttime.

I left the windows down so he could catch the gentle spring breeze that was blowing through the farm.

He was still asleep when I was finished unloading and putting everything away. *Hmm,* I thought. *Now what?*

I went back to the car and sat with him for a little while. I leaned my seat back and closed my eyes. I wouldn't sleep though. But I was *so* sleepy! The afternoon slump had hit me hard. I kept rubbing my eyes and yawning. *Ugh, I am totally going to fall asleep if I keep sitting here! I don't need to sleep! Noah will be awake soon.*

I decided to get out and walk around the yard.

Hmm, this place doesn't look too bad. And someone has cut the grass around the house! It wouldn't be this short if they hadn't. I wonder who did it?

I didn't know much about houses, but it seemed like this one was in pretty good shape. Better than I had anticipated. The paint seemed fresh and clean. The windows looked newish. The yard didn't look too bad either. Sure, there were places where the flowers were beginning to grow, and the weeds were keeping them company. Grandma *loved* her flowers. About as much as Grandpa loved his vegetable garden. I walked a little way around the house to see if the garden spot was still there. It was. The fence was still in its place, only instead of vegetable plants, it was full of tall brown grass and weeds, with small bare bushes in random places. *Are those herbs of some kind?* I wondered. The fence was overgrown with last year's vines, which were covered with dried leaves. It was a large garden plot. I wondered if Grandma kept it up after Grandpa passed away. She had always appreciated the bountiful harvest he brought in from it each season.

I walked back around to check on the still sleeping Noah and then over to the giant oak trees in the front, then over to the one that held the tire swing in its strong, massive branches. I smiled at the swing. I wasn't sure if it was the same one from when I was little, but it felt the same as I climbed on and pushed back with my feet against the dark brown dirt and leaves. I couldn't remember the last time I had ridden on a swing. I felt free. Yes, I was a little kid all over again! I hung my head back and pulled with both arms. I caught myself smiling widely as I swooshed through the air. Beyond the swing were the apple trees. Acres and acres of them. I wondered what the future would hold for those trees. What did it hold for me?

Once back inside, I let Noah play in the playpen while I put on some coffee. It was then that I noticed how nasty the counters were. Yes, *I* would have to clean them. It's shameful to admit, but I hadn't done much cleaning in my life; it wasn't necessary for me to. And now I was faced with the real concern that *I alone* was responsible for this house. It was up to *me* to get it clean and keep it that way. Was I up to the challenge? Maybe … I hunted down an old feather duster in the laundry room. Before I could dust the house, I would have to dust the duster! It was filthy! I took it to the patio and banged it over a large, empty flower pot until I felt it was clean enough to collect more dust, then returned to the house. I started in the living room and worked my way over the rest of the house. It didn't take long, and when I was finished, I was proud of myself. "No more cobwebs!" I said triumphantly to Noah, who was sitting in his playpen chewing on a rubber ducky.

I was motivated. If I could dust, surely I could sweep and mop, and ... my phone beeped. I walked over to the side table to see who had texted. It was Jessica, a friend from church back home.

"Hi, Adel! I hope you are liking your new home! We miss you guys!"

I sat down on the couch beside the playpen and looked down at the text. I would miss Jessica. We met only a few months before Noah and I left, but it was an instant bond. She was about my age and had two small children, and we both had degrees in middles grades education, which we hadn't used yet. Instead of pursuing our careers, we had both chosen to get married and start families right out of school. But she was still married, to a good man and a loving father. I tried not to envy her, but it was hard. They didn't have an elaborate home, but it was nice, and it was *theirs*, and they were a *family*. I texted her back to tell her that I missed her too and that she would have to come visit me sometime "down on the farm." After texting Jessica, I began to scroll through my Facebook feed and forgot all about the dirty house.

At dinnertime, we had a rotisserie chicken and some of the fresh food that we had picked up at the store that morning. Then Noah and I went on a walk down the driveway and back up through the apple trees. It was a lovely evening—still and peaceful, with some mourning doves singing their lonesome tunes in the background. The evening sky was full of color—oranges and various shades of pink. The sun was just beginning to slide down behind the mountains, taking the light with it.

On our way back up through the orchard toward the house, I showed Noah one of the apple trees up close and the tiny buds that were forming on its branches. The trees smelled sweet. Noah reached out and touched one of the tiny pink buds. He seemed to sense how delicate it was; he was so gentle with it. "That's a bud," I told him. "One day it will grow into a blossom and then into an apple!"

I glanced around at the acres and acres of apple trees that enveloped me. *All these blossoms will grow apples soon. What on earth am I going to do with them all?*

A crack of thunder peeled overhead. There were some dark, billowy clouds moving in from the west. We hurried back to the house.

After Noah was in bed that night, I pulled out the mouse traps. I set them in several places in my room and in Noah's room, and I put a few in the kitchen too, for good measure. Then I went to bed. I lay there for a few minutes, thinking of the day. I was still feeling unsettled and a little lonely. At night, I felt it the strongest—when the activity and noise of the day were gone away and I was left alone with the darkness and myself. My tired mind tried to go to places it shouldn't, places of fear and anxiety. I fretted over our future, running scenario after scenario through my head. I made up plans for getting the house in order, thought about money, and wondered what kinds of apples were growing in the fields. But it was all useless. It was all the workings of a tired mind. What I needed most was rest. And rest always came, eventually.

SIX

Sickness

I woke early the next morning with one thing on my mind: the mouse traps. I hurried to check the traps in my room. Nothing. In Noah's room, there was nothing. At last, when I checked the trap under the sink in the kitchen, I was satisfied. There was a mouse! But to my astonishment, it was *still* alive! The poor little thing was stuck fast to the sticky glue on top of the trap, and he was wiggling for his life. I didn't want to touch the trap. What if the mouse came off and bit me? That seemed unlikely; his whole left side was stuck in the glue. He wasn't going anywhere. Still, it seemed cruel to let him suffer like this. How long would it take? I thought about leaving him to die on his own. I shut the door on that awful sight.

Noah was still asleep. Maybe I could take the mouse outside somewhere. Maybe I could—finish it off? *Oh, this is just horrible! I* thought.

I peeked back inside the cabinet. It looked so wretched wiggling like that. *I wish I had found it dead! If only I hadn't been so keen to come check the trap first thing. If only I had waited an hour or two. Or set a different kind of trap! Oh, why does life have to be this way?*

I ended up deciding to get one of the brown plastic bags that was left over from the grocery store. I slid my hand inside, reached into the cabinet, and pulled the trap out. Then I slid the bag down over the trap so that now it was inside the bag. I carried it quickly out into the yard and over to the tool shed. I grabbed a shovel and set the bag on the ground. "I'm so sorry, little guy," I whispered. Then with one swift motion and my eyes squeezed shut, I brought the flat part of the shovel down hard on top of the bag. I did not open the bag. I just carried it over to the trash can and put it inside. With tears in my eyes, I put the shovel back in the shed and went back into the house.

It was a strange way to start the day. And as the day went on, I began to feel even more uneasy, and my stomach began to ache.

While Noah was taking his afternoon nap, I went outside to the small screened-in back porch for some fresh air. I looked out over the fields behind the house. The air was intense and still. The sky overhead was heavy with swirling, ominous gray and tan clouds billowing and rolling over the hills. The tension was great. The air was so thick it reminded me of when I was a kid playing pillow fights with my friends and a pillow was placed over my head. Under the pillow, it was hot, sweaty, and hard to breathe—suffocating. As I watched, a wave of cold air swept down off of the mountain behind the fields and flooded over the farm. The trees along the edges of the fields and around the house twisted and turned violently under the force of the wind. The movement of cool air was initially felt as relief, but it was followed by such a torrent of heavy rain that it made the clouds and the mountains behind them entirely imperceptible. The rain was intense. The wind had also become intense. Over in the fields, the rain had in minutes bent the tall stems of brown grass nearly to the ground. They looked beaten down, sad, and lonely, as if doubled over in pain. I felt for them. Indeed, the ache in my own stomach was growing steadily worse. I wanted to cry. The storm had brought with it feelings of such uneasiness. I felt unsettled; uncertain. What was wrong? I wanted to get away, to close out the uncomfortable feelings and the storm that raged.

I closed the door to the kitchen abruptly and went back into the living room. The air in the house was nearly as stuffy as the air outside had been only minutes before. I felt queasy. I lay down on the couch, its woven, nineties fabric scratching at my arms and legs. I pulled a light blanket over my legs and torso, a comfort to me, despite the stuffiness of the room. I lay there for some time. I was not sure how long. The pain in my stomach was growing steadily worse. *Where was the trash can?* My thoughts were fuzzy. But I needed the trash can. Did I have one? I looked around me. I got up and managed to make it to the bathroom before becoming genuinely sick. I wasn't in there very long before I vaguely became aware of the sound of Noah's playing, coming from up the stairs. He was awake from his nap. And I was sick. I was *very* sick.

My whole body ached, and there was a stabbing pain that began in my abdomen and radiated over my sides and back, and down into my arms and legs. I was weak and beginning to shake. My head pounded with the beating of my heart. I knew that I could not go anywhere. Definitely not up a flight of stairs. But Noah needed me. He would be getting hungry soon. *He will be OK for a little while*, I told myself. *I will feel better soon.* But I didn't. I don't know how long I was in the bathroom, I had lost all sense of time, but I realized after a while that I was not going to be feeling better any time soon. Noah's playing had turned to cries of loneliness and hunger. What was I going to do? I began to sob gently. *So, this is what it's like to be a single mom. This is what it's like to be alone. If I had just stayed home! If I had heeded my parents' warnings, I wouldn't be in such a mess! Someone would be there to care for Noah, and I could be resting quietly, alone in my bed ... Maybe my parents were right. Maybe this was too much for me.* I began to cry bitterly. I had failed. I had made a mistake. Now I was stuck far away from anyone I knew, all alone. And I was sick. Noah's cries became more intense. Oh no! My little baby didn't know what it was like to be left alone for so long! He sounded afraid. The stabbing pain in my stomach did not let up. But suddenly I was filled with a resolve to fight. I had to come up with a plan. Water. I needed water. Then I needed to go up to Noah's room and lay in there. I hobbled to the kitchen and found a glass. I also grabbed a full box of saltines. Then, with the blanket wrapped loosely around my shoulders and with a trash can, glass of water, and crackers in tow, I ascended the stairs, one painful and dizzying step at a time, and the storm raged on outside.

I was exhausted by the time I reached the top of the stairs, but I had done it. Next, on to Noah's room. There were red, wet streaks under Noah's eyes, which were puffy from crying for so long. He stopped crying when I entered the room, but his whole body continued to shake with silent convulsions. He wiped a little fist across his wet nose and looked up at me with a pitiful expression. He held up his tired arms for me to hold him.

"Hey, little man," I whispered. I leaned in to hug him and stroked his sweet, dark head. His hair was damp with sweat. I looked around me. "Mommy's going to grab some blankets. I'll be right back, OK?"

As I exited the room, Noah's cries picked back up. My heart hurt. But I couldn't hurry. I could only plod. And I plodded over into my room to grab the quilts off of my bed and two more blankets out of the closet. I dragged them back into Noah's room and haphazardly spread them out into a pallet on the hardwood floor beside Noah's crib. Then I lay down, opened the pack of crackers and I handed a few to Noah. He took them slowly, shakily. He began to nibble the crackers and then sat down in his crib. He seemed to be nearly as exhausted as I felt. It was then that I noticed Noah's sippy cup over on his dresser. Yes! A sippy cup! He needed that. *Thank you, God.*

About the time I stood up to get the sippy cup, I became violently ill. After the episode passed, I did, with shaking knees, make it over to fetch the cup, and thankfully, it was nearly full with water.

The virus lasted for the next few days. It was tough, but we made it through. I spent most of my time lying on the pallet on Noah's floor. The illness came in waves. In my moments that weren't as unbearable, I brought Noah out of his crib to nurse and play on the floor next to me. In the room, there were several boxes of toys that were easy for Noah to reach on his own. Cars, trucks, balls, blocks, and action figures. He mostly enjoyed dumping things out and attempting to put them back in, and he also enjoyed banging things on the ground and experimenting with putting them in his mouth. I watched him play, and time crept slowly on.

My pallet felt worse than a hospital bed. I'm not sure what was inflicting more bodily discomfort, the pallet of blankets or the virus!

I made it downstairs at least once each day to fetch more food for Noah. I still didn't feel like eating much. But at last, on the morning of the fourth day, I woke and opened my eyes to the sun shining brightly through the window, and the pain in my stomach was gone.

SEVEN

Good Neighbors

The rest of the week, I lay around the house and rested. I wasn't good for much else. I was so thankful for God's provision for us through our trips to the grocery store earlier in the week. If we hadn't needed to get the mouse traps, we wouldn't have bought enough food to get us through that difficult week. We would have been in real trouble, and I wouldn't have known who to call. That thought kept surfacing over and over as the week wore on. *I know absolutely no one here.* Grandma had lots of friends. I remembered meeting them when I was a child. But I didn't remember their names or where they lived, except the friends across the street. The Joneses. I couldn't remember their first names, and I doubted that they still lived there, and it felt strange to go hunting down Grandma's old friends. Still, just in case of an emergency, I was about to go looking through Grandma's old handwritten address book to see if any of the names popped out at me, when I heard a knock on the door.

That's strange, I thought as I went to peek through the blinds in the living room. There was an elderly couple standing there, and the lady was holding a small object wrapped in foil. I hurried over to the door.

"Hello," I said as I cracked the door open a little. "Can I help you?"

"Hi, Adel! My name is Doris Jones, and this is my husband, Ace."

Ace nodded respectfully toward me.

"We're your neighbors from across the street," she continued.

"I remember you! It's so good to see you!"

"We heard that you were to be coming soon. Saw you out walking in the yard the other day, and we just wanted to stop by and say hello and bring you some pound cake." She handed me the loaf wrapped in foil.

Doris was of small stature with short, curly gray hair and a pleasant, round face. She had bright and happy eyes.

Ace was tall, at least a head taller than his wife, and he was lean, wearing faded overalls and a baby blue button-up shirt. The skin on his face had the dark tan of a farmer and was weather worn, as were his arms and his large hands. He seemed reserved, but his eyes were kind.

"We were good friends of your grandparents," Doris went on. "You used to come visit with us when you were a little girl."

I nodded my head, and with a smile, I said, "I remember! You use to make the best blueberry muffins! Would you like to come in?"

We went into the living room and found seats. It was then that I realized how Grandma had strategically placed the couch and chairs in such a way that made it easy and comfortable for visiting.

"Have you lived here a long time?" I asked, though I knew they had.

"Heavens yes! Near-on forty years now." It was Doris that responded. "We moved here shortly after we married, back in seventy-nine. The place didn't look like much back then. Ace has done a lot to it over the years."

"It looks lovely now."

"Thank you." Doris looked lovingly over at Ace and patted his knee. He seemed the strong, silent type, and I liked him. There was something graceful and polite in his manners that was rare, and I appreciated it.

"We've heard a lot about you over the years," Doris continued. "Your grandma thought the world of you."

I felt myself smile.

"I thought the world of her too." I was not hardened enough yet to be able to talk about Grandma. Some tears seemed to be pushing themselves to the surface of my eyes, and I knew it was time to change the subject.

"What kind of cake did you say this was?" I said, wiping nonchalantly at my eyes.

"Pound cake."

"It's real good." It was the first time Ace had spoken since they arrived. It was then that I noticed the toothpick he held loosely in his teeth.

"I can't wait to taste it," I said. "My little boy will love it!"

Doris looked around the room, searching for Noah.

"Oh, Noah's still taking his nap. I'm sad he missed meeting you both."

"Well, that's all right. You can bring him by anytime! Our grandchildren are mostly grown now, and we don't see them much these days. We'd like to have a baby around. And you too! You're welcome to come visit anytime. And if you need anything, just let us know."

Ace nodded his approval. "Yes, just let us know."

They stood up to leave, and Ace shook my hand.

"Oh," Doris stopped in the doorway and turned back to me. "We'd also like to invite you to our church, Cherry Hill Baptist."

"My grandparents' church."

"That's right! We'd love for you to come visit us."

The thought of visiting my grandparents' church put a knot in my stomach, though I wasn't sure why.

Then they were gone. I plopped back down in an armchair with a sigh. *There, I'm no longer completely alone!*

The pound cake *was* good. *Very* good. I would need to get Doris' recipe. I would also need to learn how to make it. I knew *nothing* about baking. *Maybe Doris could teach me*, I thought, but doubts quickly took over and pushed the thought from my mind.

Noah stopped sleeping well at night about this time. He had always been a pretty decent sleeper, but not anymore. He started waking up about thirty minutes after I'd lay him down at night. Then it would take him a while to settle, and once he did, he'd only sleep for an hour or two. This went on night after night. I was beginning to feel it. I felt like my eyes couldn't see as clearly, and I started having headaches. But mainly I was just plain *tired*.

"Come on, boy," I coaxed at two in the morning one night. "That's enough now! Go to sleep." Noah peered back up at me with wide eyes. *He's not even sleepy! Here we go again ...* I spent the next hour rocking him to sleep. He was awake again at four. *What is going on!? Why is he doing this?* I was so groggy I could hardly stumble into his room and pick him up. I had recently moved an old recliner from Grandma's room into Noah's room for such a time as this. I plopped down in a daze and nursed him back to sleep. I woke with the morning light sometime shortly after six. Noah was sleeping in my lap. *Well, that was a short night!*

This became our new normal. I started getting used to the routine. My body was beginning to suffer because of it, but I didn't notice too much. Not yet.

One day the following week, I stepped outside to take a bag of trash to the trash can, and I left Noah in the high chair with some chopped-up fruit. There was a man riding a lawnmower across the yard over near the barn! *He must be the man who's been cutting the grass!* I thought. I guess he saw me standing there staring at him because he drove over to where I was and turned the motor off. He climbed off the lawnmower and came over to where I was standing.

He was dirty and sweaty and wearing old work clothes and large brown work boots, both of which were covered in bits of chopped grass and leaves. He was probably in his late twenties or early thirties. He was tall. Maybe six one or two. And he stood up straight when he walked. His gait was unhurried. He wasn't stocky, but he wasn't slim either. He had short, dark brown hair, about the color of mine. I couldn't see his eyes well enough in the glaring light of the sun to tell what color they were.

"Hello," he said, his voice deep and mellow. He paused. Then he continued with, "I'm Nathan Shepherd ..." He looked at me for a minute, as if that should have meant something to me. Then he continued, "I'm your neighbor. I live through the woods back there." He pointed in the direction of the trees behind the backyard, and for the first time, I noticed a trail leading into the woods. "I didn't realize you were here already," he said.

"Yes ..." I was a little puzzled.

"Another neighbor and I have been taking turns keeping the yard up until you got here. I just hadn't heard ..." He paused, as if remembering his manners. "It's nice to see you, Adel." He took off his work glove and offered me his hand. I shook it with my free hand, still holding the trash bag awkwardly with the other. He had a firm grip on my hand. It was a workman's hand. Well used and capable.

"It's nice to meet you, Mr. Shepherd."

He smiled a funny sort of smile. "Nathan," he said.

"Alright. Nathan. Oh! I'm sorry," I said, suddenly remembering Noah. "I would stay and chat, but I left my son in the high chair!" I hurried in the direction of the trash can and then back toward the screened-in back porch. "I'll see you around!" I called over my shoulder. "And thank you for keeping the place up until I got here!"

"Hey," he called after me. "Do you want me to go ahead and finish mowing since I already started? I don't mind. I had already planned to do that this morning."

"Sure! That'd be great, actually! Thank you!" And then I went back into the house.

Thankfully, Noah was still picking at the fruit on his high chair tray and didn't seem bothered by my absence.

I finished cleaning up the table and the kitchen and occasionally peeked out the window to check on the man on the lawnmower. He reminded me a little of Ace, though perhaps not as quiet. But his manners were slow and easy like Ace's. He was polite like Ace too. And I liked that I wouldn't have to worry about the grass again for the next couple of weeks.

I knew I had to start tackling some of the projects around the house soon before they got out of hand. I was having a hard time feeling like I was making any headway inside the house, and with it being spring and the weather so nice, I decided to get started on the yard. I couldn't afford a yard man, so it was all up to me.

There were already so many flowerbeds that needed to be weeded. Weeding the flowerbeds was something I used to help Grandma do in the evenings in the summer, when the heat of day had cooled off to a bearable temperature.

It was about ten o'clock in the morning on this particular day in late March, and I was ready to get started. I went to the tool shed and found some of Grandma's old work gloves. They were tan and well worn, and printed with pink and purple flowers. I found them on an old metal shelf next to some colorful ceramic flowerpots that were covered with dust. *The tool shed is going to need a good cleaning out too one of these days.*

The potting shed was actually an old smokehouse, probably built around the time the house was built, around a hundred years ago. Some time ago, someone, probably my grandpa, had turned it into a lovely tool shed and potting house, though it looked like it hadn't been used much in recent years.

I picked up Noah and went to the flowerbed in front of the house. There was a lot to do! I got to work pulling vines and weeds, and probably some flowers too. I had a hard time telling which was which! I worked while Noah scooted around on the ground by my feet. Occasionally, I had to stop and wipe some dirt out of his mouth. But mostly he was fine, and he seemed happy. Sticks and rocks would soon become his favorite toys, a preference that would last him for many years to come.

I worked hard until lunchtime, then stepped back to survey the fruit of my efforts. *Hey! That looks pretty good!* I thought. I had cleaned out the whole front of the house. Now you could more clearly see the boxwoods that lined the porch and the hostas that grew in front of them. There were some flowers, and there were also two pretty rose bushes, one on either side of the steps, that were beginning to bud. It looked like the roses were going to be a light shade of pink. Already, they smelled wonderful. So far, they were my favorite.

Though it felt good to have done something, I was beginning to get a feel for just how much yardwork there was left to do, and it was a little overwhelming. I wondered whether I should consider hiring someone to help, but I knew that in reality I didn't have the money. I would have to keep it up myself.

EIGHT

Lonely

During the following weeks, I spent more time than usual on my phone. I was curious what everyone was doing back home. Despite feeling that I had done right by coming here, and even though I appreciated my newfound independence, I really missed my parents. I also missed my friends. But it seemed that the only way to keep up with anyone was through Facebook, Instagram, and an occasional text message. Except for Mom, everyone was always too busy to chat on the phone, which was OK with me. I don't like phones anyway. I don't even care for the internet. Except for during those first few months, when it helped me feel connected to everyone when I was so far away.

I was always stopping in the middle of a chore to check and see if Betsey got that new job she had posted about. Or to see if Allison had ever come home from the hospital after her foot surgery. On and on ... it never stopped. But I was beginning to feel tired and lonely, regardless.

I tried to call Mom every few days to give her an update. But it wasn't easy. I always felt like whatever I was sharing was boring to her.

Or perhaps she was just unhappy with me for leaving, and being uninterested was her way of showing it. She had plenty to say when I asked her questions. But the questions never came in my direction. I was beginning to feel empty in the conversation department. And love Noah as I did, I was beginning to long for the company of another adult.

So far, our meals consisted mostly of hamburger helper and boxed macaroni and cheese. There were a few other things I was learning to buy, like hamburger patties and tater tots. But cooking had never been my forte. Not only that, but I had never really been allowed to cook while I was living at home. Mom was always so particular about her kitchen. Like the rest of her house, the kitchen was a place for display. It had an image that couldn't be disturbed, not even if the result was a batch of chocolate chip cookies. She would rather the cookies come from an easy-to-dispose-of plastic container.

When I moved to college, I did what everyone else did; I ate in the cafeteria and at the restaurants on campus. It was certainly easier that way. And then when Damian and I married—well, let's just say that my experiments in the kitchen were not always appreciated. So, I decided that cooking must not be my thing. But since moving to Sweet Valley, I had started wanting to try again. I wanted to *learn*. Anyone could learn to cook, right? With enough time and room for mistakes? So, I began looking through some of Grandma's old cookbooks. Some of the recipes looked intimidating. There was one for pancakes that didn't seem too hard. I tried it for dinner one night, and Noah ate them. He even seemed to like them. Maybe it was because of the syrup. But I was pleased, regardless. It emboldened me to try something else, this time a chicken casserole. I used canned chicken, rice, celery, and cream of mushroom soup. Only thing was I forgot to add the salt, and the rice burned. It didn't entirely burn—just enough that I thought I should use it anyway, and just bad enough that it made the whole dish taste horrible.

I leaned over the table and rested my head in my tired hands. *This is going to take a while.* I sighed.

One day a few weeks later, when the weather was nice, I decided to take Noah on a walk. I put him in the sling and started for the trail behind the house. If I remembered right, Grandma and Grandpa had owned the property behind the house for quite a way. *All the way to the creek,* I thought.

Once inside the woods, we left farm life behind us. We had entered the mountains again. The sights and smells of the farm were replaced with those of the forest. The pines, cedars, and hemlocks gave off a fragrant spring essence that was delightful. Growing on the ground under my feet were tiny purple flowers surrounded by their soft green foliage.

Then I heard a thumping in the trees, and at my feet a pinecone fell. I watched it roll to the side of the trail, then continued on.

After walking for a while, I found that we were coming to a clearing. *This isn't the creek ...* I continued on a little way until I saw that in the clearing there sat a house and a barn. Or maybe it was a workshop of some kind.

The house was a modest, two-story Cape Cod. It was painted dark blue, as was the workshop. They both had white trim and a gray metal roof that looked new. The yard was well kept, and the grass was cut.

This must be Nathan's house, I thought. *It must be his driveway that goes through the woods! The one by the creek! The creek ... where is it? How did I miss it?*

I turned around and slowly retraced my steps, trying to find where the trail veered off toward the creek. I never did see it. Eventually, I gave up and went back to the house.

That night, I was feeling especially lonely. I tried to call Betsey, my friend from college, but she was on a date and couldn't talk. Noah was asleep. I was sitting on the couch in the living room. I leaned back and propped my feet up on the coffee table. I sighed a deep and dissatisfied sigh. *Maybe I should watch a movie.* But what I really wanted was to *talk* to someone. I picked up my phone and fiddled on Instagram for a little while. Everyone seemed to be doing something. They were all smiles and good times, and I was sitting alone on the couch on a Friday night, doing absolutely *nothing.* I called my mom. We talked for a little while, but like usual, she didn't really seem into it. "Well, I guess I'll let you go," I said after a few minutes of especially awkward conversation.

But I wasn't ready for bed. It was still early, and I was feeling empty inside.

I ended up going to the freezer and pulling out a small container of cookie-dough ice cream before heading back to the couch to watch the entire Jane Austen's *Emma,* the *long* version. It was only interrupted twice by Noah's fussing, and despite the delays, I did finish it.

The next few days, I was in a funk. All I wanted to do was sit around and not do anything. I ate too much and played too little with Noah. I think he was picking up on my funky vibes because he started whining and fussing more than usual. That just made me grumpier. The chores weren't getting done, but I didn't really care. They would get done eventually.

I began to wish that Doris and Ace would stop by again. My first impression of them had been a good one. They seemed kind and considerate. They were older than my parents, but I knew that didn't matter when it came to friendship.

I wondered about them. I wondered what they did for a living. Farming, I guessed. I wondered what Doris did all day. I wondered about their church. I didn't feel ready to go to church yet. I just needed to get more settled in. Church would come in time.

I checked my phone again. Allison had sent me a text that read, "Christy's bachelorette party was *fantastic!* Wishing you were here!"

"Well, I'm *not* there!" I said aloud. "And even if I was, I don't think I'd agree with you!"

Allison's way of having fun was very different from mine. She preferred a lifestyle built on novelty and wild, new experiences, and that didn't suit me well at all. *What did I ever like about her anyway?* I wondered.

After a few days of sulking around, I knew something had to change. This wasn't like me at all, and for Noah's sake, if not for my own, it needed to stop. I decided to get back outside and go for another walk. We went down the trail again, this time stopping about ten yards before the trail ended. As we walked, I prayed and asked God for wisdom. I didn't want to be moody or sulky. But I didn't know what to do about it. I didn't know *why* I was moody.

Lord, please show me what I can do to make this stop!

Just getting outside seemed to help some, but I knew there was something deeper going on that wouldn't be fixed just by spending time outdoors.

On our way back toward the house, a new thought struck me. *Why don't I go visit the Joneses? Why should I just sit around waiting for them to come to me? I have two legs that work, don't I?*

NINE

The Joneses

The next morning, I put my thoughts into action. I put a cute little outfit on Noah, one of the many from Mom that he had yet to wear, and took a little extra time getting myself ready for the day. Then, after a breakfast of chewy granola bars and milk, we walked over to visit the Joneses.

Our driveway was long. I was thankful Nathan had also cut the grass down the driveway while he was here; otherwise we would have been walking up to our knees in it, and it was already beginning to get high again. *I'm going to have to learn how to mow, pronto!*

The pale tan and gray gravel crunched under my feet. The sun was already rising high in the sky. It seemed so warm for the first week of May! I didn't even need a sweater. I wasn't used to this, we were still getting temperatures in the sixties back home.

I stopped and looked carefully before crossing the road. There were no cars in sight. The road was pretty, I noticed. The bright green spring grass was adorning the shoulder on either side of the road, and some of the trees were leafing out and blooming in various shades of pink and white. Again, I had to stop and breathe in deeply before walking across the street. When we reached the Joneses' door, I suddenly felt a flutter in my stomach.

No turning back now, I told myself. *You will knock on the door!*

So I reached out and knocked.

Within seconds, Doris's friendly face appeared in the window.

"Why, hello!" she said as she opened the door. "Come in! Come in! It's so good to see you!"

"Hi, Doris," I said as we stepped into her living room. "We just wanted to stop by and say hello."

"I'm so glad you did! And this big boy must be Noah?" Then addressing Noah, she said, "What a fine big boy you are!"

Noah turned to hide his face in my shirt.

Doris went over to a basket sitting beside the couch and pulled out a toy truck. She brought it to Noah and said, "Here, would you like to play with this while your mommy and I talk?"

Noah looked at the truck longingly. Then he slowly reached out one tiny little hand to take it. He hugged it to his chest and put his face back in my shirt.

I laughed a little.

Doris motioned for me to sit at one of the couches.

"Would you like some tea or coffee?" she asked.

"Coffee, please."

"All right. I'll be back in just a minute."

While she was gone, I had a chance to look around the room. The carpet and the furniture were outdated, but it was all very clean and well kept. There were beautiful floral paintings on the walls, just like Grandma's. There were bookcases with shelves and shelves of old books. There were pictures on the shelves that showed a variety of different faces. I guessed three of them to be their children. A boy and two girls. There were pictures of the children at different ages. Then there were some wedding pictures. They looked like pleasant people. The pictures of one of the girls didn't seem to go beyond childhood. I wondered about that.

And I wonder where their children are now.

Noah was beginning to investigate the room a little too. He scooted over to the piano and crawled under the bench. That's where he was when Doris came back in the room.

She handed me my coffee and looked around the room. "Where's the little fella?" she asked.

I pointed to the piano bench.

"He-he-he! Let me show him something."

Doris went over to the toy basket and brought out a little, red, plastic barn.

That thing must be an antique! I thought.

She sat it on the floor in front of Noah and opened the little white doors. Inside were different kinds of farm animals and some little yellow fences. She pulled a few of the animals onto the floor for him to see, then came to join me on the couch.

"He will like that. All the children do."

He did seem taken with the new toy.

"So how are things? Are you all settled in?"

"Well, we're getting there ..." But I know the look on my face revealed the truth. I couldn't fake my feelings, even if I wanted to.

"Oh?"

"I have to admit that it's been harder than I ever thought it would be. We moved in with only a carload of stuff. Everything else is Grandma's. It's been a challenge to find where everything is and to figure out how we fit into it all. It just feels like I'm visiting, or like I'm living in someone else's house."

"Well, it's your home now. You will have to do what's best for you and your family, just like Elaine had to do when she first moved in. And sometimes that means cleaning out and starting fresh."

"Oh, I don't know if we need to do that! Grandma had so many nice things! Everything in that house is a memory to me."

Doris didn't say anything for a moment, but I could tell she was thinking.

"Well, it takes time to build a home. And lots of tears and sweat, usually. It may take a while before you feel like it's yours. But that's all right. The best things in life take time."

I smiled my thanks.

"So, what does Ace do for a living?" I asked, after taking a sip of coffee, the cup warm and comforting in my hands.

"We grow seed corn, hay, and sweet potatoes. And we still have a few cows. We've got men working for us. Ace just manages it all nowadays. Well, I wish he would, anyways. It's hard to keep him out of the fields. That's where his heart is, you know. Lives and breathes it. Would you like to come see?"

"I would!"

I picked up Noah, and Doris led us outside where the air smelled of soil and freshly cut grass.

Ace was riding a green John Deere tractor down the middle of one of the fields.

"See what I mean?" Doris said, her eyebrows raised.

I laughed. Ace looked so natural out there.

"This is where we will be growing the seed corn this year. Haven't planted it quite yet. He's gettin' the field ready for that now."

We slowly walked through the yard. I noticed what looked like a group of fruit trees. There was a white porch swing on an A-frame overlooking the field behind the house. I guessed that must be a place of solace and reprieve for the busy farmer and his wife. There was also a bench with a beautiful arbor. All around it were ferns and hostas, young and bright green. It was set in the shade of some large oak trees. There was sunlight shining down through the trees to rest on the seat and the arbor. It looked so peaceful that I wanted to go sit on it for a while, but instead I followed Doris over to the barn. The barn was painted gray, and though it had seen better years, it was perfectly adequate for housing the hay needed to feed their cows during the winter months.

After showing me a patch of tulips that were starting to bloom, Doris took us back in through the side door, into the kitchen. We sat at the table, and Doris brought us some homemade sugar cookies and a glass of ice water.

"Doris," I said after swallowing a mouthful of cookie, "do you think Ace would mind showing me how to use a lawnmower? I found a couple in the barn and one that looks newish. Nathan, through the woods back there, cut the grass a few weeks ago, but I know it's going to need it again soon."

"Oh, so you've seen Nathan? That's good. I reckon he will. He and Nathan have been taking turns checking on the house and yard since Elaine passed. That and anything else they saw that needed to be done. They haven't had much to do, though, with it being mostly winter. Yes, I'll ask him to stop by sometime this week."

"Great! Thank you!" I felt a little of the burden of yardwork lift, and it felt good.

Later in the week, I went to get more groceries and have a look at the town. I took my time driving through the various roads in Cherry Hill, trying to get my bearings. We drove up and down the roads, looking at the little shops and restaurants as we passed. There wasn't much to it, really—the one little grocery store, a few businesses and restaurants, and a few touristy shops surrounding a courthouse in the town square. There were lots of small churches, all with graveyards. And there were some ball fields where I remembered watching the fireworks on the Fourth of July. There was a Dollar General across the street from the ball fields. That was about it. But instead of feeling confined or disgusted by the size of the town, I felt comforted. This small town didn't overwhelm me the way that San Francisco always had.

We drove over to Food Mart, and as we were walking down the frozen food aisle, I noticed a man coming down the aisle toward us. His head was down, but I thought he looked familiar. Yes, it was the man from the Mexican restaurant when we first moved in. *Julian?* I didn't want to talk to him. I contemplated turning my head so he wouldn't see my face, or turning the buggy all together, but decided to be brave. It was too late anyway.

"Hello," I said as he looked up and caught my eye.

"Well, hey! Fancy meeting you again!"

"Julian?"

"Yes. Adel," he said confidently. "And how are you liking Cherry

Hill?"

"I like it" was all I said. I knew it sounded curt, but again, I didn't feel like encouraging this man's attention.

"It's a great little town," he went on.

"Yes."

"Have you been to the Trading Post yet?"

"No. What's the Trading Post?"

"It's a little store downtown, sort of like a general store. There are a couple of neat little places in the town square. Say, would you be interested in getting together sometime? I could show you around?"

"Well ... uh ... I ... I'm not sure I'm ready for that sort of thing. It hasn't been that long since ..." I shrugged.

"Yes, yes. I understand. Say no more! But can I give you *my* number, just in case you find that you *are* ready?"

I hesitated. I didn't really want his number. I hardly knew him. I didn't want to get to know him. But I also didn't want to be rude.

"I guess so," I said at last.

I entered his number into my phone.

"Have a nice evening," I said, and pushed our buggy on down the aisle.

For the first time since Damian left, I was beginning to consider if I was ready to see someone again. Julian was good-looking and seemed nice. He was apparently attracted to me. But for some reason, I didn't want to go out with him. I didn't even want to talk to him. There was something about Julian that I didn't care for. Maybe it was his forwardness. He seemed too confident in his approaches to me. But I also found it odd that he wore so many rings on his fingers. Large, silver and bronze rings. One, at least, was a class ring. I wasn't sure about the rest. And more still, my heart still felt a little numb. Cold. I knew it would be good for me to open up again. And every little boy should have a daddy, but still, I just couldn't do it. I couldn't call. I felt uninterested, but I also felt fear every time I considered it. Fear of the unknown. Fear that perhaps another relationship would end just as badly as the first. Fear of getting *close*.

TEN

Mowing

One morning in the middle of May, while Noah and I were playing on the living room rug, I heard a knock on the door. I jumped up to see who it was. It was Doris and Ace! I quickly let them in.

"Howdy," said Ace as he nodded respectfully to me. I loved how he did that. Such a simple gesture, yet it meant so much.

"Come in!" I said and made room for them.

Ace stopped in the entryway.

"Doris tells me you want to learn to mow?" he said, taking a toothpick out of his mouth so he could speak clearly.

"Oh! Yes, yes, I do! The yard is getting so out of hand!"

"Well, let's go," he said, replacing the toothpick and starting for the door.

I wasn't exactly dressed for yardwork. I was wearing a comfortable pair of slacks and a nice blouse. That was pretty much all I owned. Nice slacks and blouses and a few skirts and dresses. But I figured I should take Ace's help when I could get it, and I didn't want to make him wait.

"I can watch Noah for you, if you like?" offered Doris.

I gladly accepted her offer and followed Ace out the front door.

Once in the barn, Ace took his time looking over the three mowers. He tried out a couple, then settled on an orange Husqvarna. He drove the mower out of the barn and into the sunlight.

"Yep," he said. "This zero-turn should suit you fine. Never used one before, right?"

"No, I haven't."

"Takes a little gettin' used to. Not like a ridin' mower with a steerin' wheel. It's a different principle altogether."

I wouldn't have known, having never used a mower in my life.

He slowly and thoroughly walked me through the steps of operating the zero-turn. First, he showed me how. Then he let me practice. I sat down on the mower and cranked it, then slowly moved one of the handles forward. The zero-turn started to move. But not forward, in circles! Slowly, but circles just the same.

"Alright, alright," Ace was saying. "Bring the handles slowly back toward you."

I did what he said, and the mower stopped moving.

"Try again. This time, keep the handles even."

After some practice and lots of trial and error, I started to feel like I was getting the hang of it.

Man, I thought, *I sure am glad I asked Ace to show me how to do this! This is harder than I thought it would be!*

The noise was loud. The yard was bumpy. And grass clippings were shooting out all over the place. It was hard to make the mower go the speed I wanted. It seemed to want to go either too fast or too slow, and occasionally I still found myself going in circles!

He had me practice for a while, until he was satisfied.

"Alright!" he said at last, and waved me to bring it over.

"That'll do," he called as I drove the mower back into the barn and turned the engine off. I was sticky with sweat and covered in grass clippings.

I'm going to need some new clothes; these definitely won't do for this kind of work! I thought as I looked down at my lovely blouse, probably ruined.

Mom always had me dress well. We could afford the best brands, so that's what we bought. It also suited her style, to have her daughter wearing the nicest, most fashionable things. It was all I had known growing up. It was all I had owned. I realized quickly, after looking over my expenses, that I wouldn't be able to afford that kind of lifestyle anymore, and now I knew that the life I had chosen would demolish those kinds of clothes! I also felt a little out of place walking in the grocery store with what I owned. No one here dressed like that. I needed to find a new wardrobe, and soon.

"Thank you, Ace," I said as we walked back toward the house. The sun was now high in the sky. The shadows of the trees were short, and the day was getting hot.

"Anytime," he replied in his slow, easy manner. "You were gettin' the hang of it right well there at the end. Just takes a little practice."

"I plan on getting lots of practice over the next few days," I said, laughing.

"It's a noble thing, what you're doing," he said.

"What do you mean?"

"Learning what it takes to live here. Not being 'fraid to ask fer help."

I blushed a little at his compliment.

"Yes, sir," he continued, "it takes a heap a lot of helpin' each other to make it in this ol' world."

I smiled over at him and suddenly realized that I was walking with a friend.

"Oh look!" I exclaimed as I glanced up toward the house. "Doris has Noah sitting on the tire swing! Hey, Doris! Hey, Noah!"

I hurried over to them and watched as Doris pushed Noah very gently on the swing. He held tightly to the ropes, his eyes bright and excited.

"He wanted to come out and see what mommy was doing. I told him we could watch you right well from here."

I looked down and smiled. "Are you having fun, big guy?"

"Looks like you were getting the hang of it," Doris said to me.

"Yes, I think so." I smiled. "Thanks to Ace!"

"She won't be needin' me an' Nathan's help anymore. I think she's got it."

Soon, Doris and Ace were gone, and I was left with the feeling of having accomplished something. A small something but something nonetheless.

The following day, when Noah went down for his morning nap, I hurried out to put my new skill to the test. I was dressed in my least favorite clothes, just in case they were ruined like the ones the day before. The grass around the house had gotten tall. I went to the barn and backed the Husqvarna slowly out through the garage door.

I started off very slowly, maneuvering carefully around the bushes and trees in the front yard. It was getting hot, and the wet grass stuck to my pants and exposed arms. I cut for about two hours before I guessed that Noah would be waking soon. I put the mower away and returned to the house. Noah was still asleep, so I hurried to take a shower. When I looked into the mirror, I noticed that my face was bright red. Sunburned! The back of my neck and my arms were too. "Ouch!" I said as I carefully lifted my shirt up over my head. And I didn't even have any afterburn lotion!

The following week, I ran into Julian *again*, this time at the gas station right outside of town. It was after a long day of working in the yard, and I was exhausted. I didn't even try to pretend I wasn't. I'm terrible at pretending anyway. Julian didn't seem to mind, though, because he asked if I happened to be *ready* yet. He asked it kindly and with a sense of humor that I appreciated. He wouldn't be hurt by my no. But it did seem strange that I kept running into him. Was it fate? I wondered ...

We ended up standing in the parking lot talking for about twenty minutes before I finally gave him my number. What could it hurt? I didn't have to go out with him just because I gave him my number, and I politely told him so.

I started going to visit the Joneses every few days. I liked them both very much. Ace was usually busy outside somewhere, but Doris was almost always inside, and she welcomed my company with open arms. She included me in whatever she was doing. Sometimes it was preparing lunch or dinner; sometimes it was spot cleaning a couch or polishing a chair. Either way, I was learning something useful just about every time we went. She always kept her hands busy, and we talked while we worked.

Sometimes we would stay for lunch, and it was then that I saw that Doris also knew how to stop and rest. For a solid hour, Doris rested. She had her light lunch, then went to the living room to prop her feet up and read. Doris always had a book handy, and they were usually well-read and well-worn personal favorites.

"This book I just started," she said to me one day, "is just excellent. It's about Lewis and Clarke and the westward expansion. And all these things really happened! To real people, like you and me sitting here. Do you read much?" she asked me.

I shook my head. "Not since college. When I was forced to, I guess."

"Yep. It's too often the case. You just need a good book. Then you'd find reason to pick it up." She went over to the bookshelf and nosed around for a minute.

"Ah," she said, grabbing a book off the shelf. "Like this one. This'll keep you good company."

She handed me the book.

"*Jane Eyre*," I read aloud. "I know this story! I've seen the movie at least a dozen times!" I laughed.

"That may be, but there's nothing like reading the story for yourself. Why don't you try it? I think you'll like it."

"I will! I need something to do in the evenings these days. Thank you, Doris."

"Good! Then next time we meet, we can swap stories of what we've been reading." She smiled good-naturedly, but she was serious. I would start it that very night.

By the first week of June, I was tired of my phone. My online social life wasn't doing what it was supposed to, and I felt like I was spending too much time lingering online over absolutely nothing, time that should have been spent doing something useful. I longed for more than just pictures and tidbits of random information. I needed *life*. Real people in real time. I was finally beginning to see that and was willing to do something about it. My visits with the Joneses were good. I needed them and their company. I appreciated their kindness and hospitality. But they also whetted my appetite for more.

I felt like I had been scared of going to Grandma's church, ever since we arrived. It was hard to believe that it had already been three months! I didn't know why, but any time I thought of visiting, I was bombarded with a million reasons not to go, and it was always accompanied by a strange feeling in the pit of my stomach that I didn't like. It was an eerie feeling. Like something bad would happen if I went. It was just a vague feeling but enough of one that it made me a little nervous to go. But I felt that my faith had taken a back seat in my life since I had been here, and I knew that I needed more than to occasionally read my Bible or listen to an online service or podcast. I needed more in-depth study of God's Word, *and* I needed his people.

When I was with the Joneses, I was beginning to experience the joy and blessings of being around people who truly were Christ's hands and feet, and it was because of them that I finally decided to go to church. One day, Doris just came out and said, "A Christian girl ought to be in church, Adel. Who knows in what way the Lord might be wanting to bless her through his people? Or in what ways she's meant to bless them?" That made good sense to me, and those words became my sword of defense every time the attacks came, which they surely did.

I told Doris we would be there the following Sunday.

ELEVEN
Church

"Wow, where is *she* from?" I heard one of the teenage girls in the back of the sanctuary whisper when I slowly and cautiously inched down the aisle to find a seat.

"She definitely isn't from around here!" said another girl, giggling. "Look how short her dress is! Grandma is going to have a heart attack when she sees *that*!"

I felt that all eyes were on me. My face flushed hot. This was miserable. I had done my best to prepare for church, just as I always did at home. I wore what was fashionable and acceptable at my church back in San Francisco, but apparently that wouldn't do here in Cherry Hill.

I wonder where the Joneses are. I desperately wished I had come early to look for them. It had taken me longer than I anticipated to locate Noah's nursery room, and now I was a few minutes late entering the sanctuary.

Someone was playing "Come Thou Fount" on the piano.

I slid into a pew, and it creaked a little as I sat down. I was painfully aware of it. I brushed my hair back from my face. I looked around at the crowded pews. This country church with its rows of hard oak pews and stained glass windows was so different and so much smaller than the one I had attended back in San Francisco. It was so different that I had a hard time feeling like I was in church at all. I was used to a modern building, with seating for several thousand, mostly in the form of comfy chairs all linked together on the sides. Back home, we had a full band that played modern worship songs that were truly *amazing*. When the music started, the lights dimmed so that we could see the colorful lights dance across the massive curtains that hung behind the podium.

Though this church was full, there couldn't have been more than one or two hundred people, maybe less; I have a hard time with estimates. The stage was modest and made of light brown wood that hadn't seen any polish in a long time, and the only instruments were a guitar and a piano. Behind the podium was an old-fashioned choir stand full of singers in their robes, and behind them, there hung a wooden cross on the wall with a purple scarf draped over it. The room was bright. There were no special lights, just the ones that hung by chandelier overhead. There were no curtains. No band playing modern worship songs. All I heard that day were hymns.

I knew I had been to this church many times as a child, but I didn't recall ever feeling so out of place.

I had found a seat next to a kind-looking woman in her thirties who was holding a baby in her lap. She smiled warmly at me. That made me feel a little more comfortable but not much. I glanced up. There were still eyes on me. Some looked away when they caught my eye; others weren't as bashful, especially a young man with dark brown, curly hair and lively eyes. He seemed about my age. He wasn't bad looking either. But I tried to focus on the preacher, who was now approaching the podium.

The sermon was on Nehemiah and the rebuilding of the wall. The preacher approached it from the perspective of God rebuilding areas of our lives. I listened with interest. I felt almost as if the preacher was talking directly to me. I began taking notes in the margin of my Bible. I needed to remember this. When the sermon was over, I was still so deep in thought that at first I didn't realize that the lady beside me was trying to get my attention.

"Oh! Hi! I'm so sorry. I was just—" I motioned to my Bible.

"Oh, that's OK! I understand! I was just introducing myself. I'm Rebecca Blackmore. I don't know if you remember me from your grandma's funeral? There were so many people there. I know it's hard to remember everyone." She smiled.

"Yes, I think I do remember you! You had several children with you, I think?"

"Ha-ha, yes! We have four. This is Moses. Say hi, Moses!" She waved Moses's little hand.

"He's too cute. How old is he?"

"Nine months."

"Oh OK! So sweet! I have a little boy. His name is Noah. I left him in the nursery. I didn't realize babies were allowed in the service."

"Yes! You are welcome to do it either way!" She smiled again. "So how old is your little boy?"

"He's eleven months."

"OK! Well, would you like to come meet my other children?" Rebecca suggested. "They are all in rooms in the children's hall, and Noah's room is at the end. So, I can walk you there if you like?"

"That would be lovely! Thank you!"

I followed Rebecca through a crowd in the foyer toward the children's hall. We were stopped several times on the way by people welcoming me to church. There was Alice, Mr. Treadwell and his wife Ms. Jenny, and then there was a kind, elderly lady named Ms. Grace, who welcomed me with a warm hug and the comment that she had just left the baby room. "I'm the official baby rocker," she said with a laugh. "Your little fella and I got to be good friends this morning! He sat with me while he was warming up to everybody. He's precious!" Her kind and gentle heart were welcome to me, and I was glad Noah had such an experienced baby rocker to help look after him on his first day at church.

The children's hall was bright and cheery, with beautiful paintings of Noah and the ark, David and Goliath, and Jesus with Peter walking on the water painted on the walls, with verses painted in ribbons along the top and bottom.

The first door Rebecca stopped at was the third graders' room.

A little boy with a crewcut and a red buttoned-up shirt ran out of the room and hugged Rebecca. She laughed. "This is my son Randall. Randall, this is Miss Adel."

"Hi, Randall. Very nice to meet you!"

"Hello," replied Randall. His eyes were bashful and quiet, and he stayed right at his mama's side and kept his eyes on me while we walked to the next room.

"This is the first and second graders' room. Hi, Christy! Is Maggie Ann still in here? Oh, I see her. Hey, Maggie Ann! Time to go!"

Out bounded Maggie Ann, a cute little girl with blond pigtails and a swishy purple dress. She smiled a big, toothless smile up at me and said, "I lost a tooth last night! Guess what I got under my pillow? A dollar! A whole dollar!"

"That's very nice, Maggie Ann. My name is Miss Adel. I'm new here. In a minute, I'll introduce you to my son. His name is Noah."

"OK! How old is he?"

"He's a little baby."

"Oh! I have a little baby. He's my brother. His name is Moses. He has tiny feet."

"I bet he does." I laughed.

Maggie Ann began to twirl gracefully around us as we walked to the next room, where we picked up Allie, a very sweet and quiet little three-year-old girl with big brown eyes and dark hair like her mama's. She seemed a little small for her age. Her teacher lifted her over the half door and sat her on the ground, where she quickly reached for her mama's hand. She clung to it tightly while she buried her face in her mama's leg. Rebecca did not seem flustered by her child's behavior.

At last we arrived at the baby room. Noah was sitting on the floor with big red eyes and crimson cheeks. He noticed when I walked into the room and reached his hands out toward me with a very serious face, as if he might cry at any moment.

"He did very well today," said Mandy, one of the nursery workers in his room. "He cried and fussed some, but he was very snuggly and sweet.

Will we see you guys next week?"

"Yes, I think so," I said with a smile as I leaned back and looked Noah in the face. "What do you think?" I asked him. "Want to come back next week?" Noah just stared at me, his eyes still big and round.

"Thank you!" I called over my shoulder to Mandy as we walked out of the room and back into the hall.

"And this is Noah." I squatted down so the curious children could get a better look at the new kid on the block.

"He's cute!" Toothless Maggie Ann giggled.

Noah liked looking into the faces of the other children. He giggled back, which thrilled Maggie Ann. Allie bashfully came forward and fingered his tiny shoes.

"He looks a little like Moses," said Randall, who had not left his mama's side.

"Thank you for showing me around," I said as I stood up and turned to face Rebecca.

"Sure! Anytime. And seriously, I know that moving to a new place can be a challenge. If you need anything at all, just let me know. Here, let me give you my number."

I really appreciated her taking the time to help me feel welcome. I added her number to my phone and was saying goodbye when I heard a male voice behind me, speaking playfully with Maggie Ann. I turned and was surprised to see my new neighbor, Nathan. He had scooped up Maggie Ann and was holding her playfully upside down over his shoulder. She squealed delightedly in protest. He also seemed surprised when he looked up and saw me standing there.

My thoughts jumped to quick conclusions, assuming that Nathan must be married and that this was his family. He had failed to mention *that* when we met! *Well, our conversation that day had been short.*

Rebecca must have noticed my awkwardness and quickly went on to say, "Do you remember my brother, Nathan?"

Oh, her brother! I blushed a little and tried to think back to the funeral. There were so many people there, and I had been so out of it that day.

Rebecca didn't wait for an answer, she continued with "He's your new neighbor!"

I nodded hello, and Nathan smiled and told Rebecca that we had already met.

Rebecca's husband came up behind Nathan and scooped up little Allie, who was still hiding behind her mama's knee.

"And this is my husband, Jim!" Rebecca told me. "He and Nathan teach the high school Sunday school class. Jim, this is Adel!"

"Adel! So, I finally get to meet you! I've heard a lot about you over the years!"

"Nice to meet you!" I said, and wondered how he'd heard about me.

Jim, Rebecca, and Nathan began walking toward the door, and I followed them out.

"It's going to be a hot one. Feels like it might rain later today," I heard Jim saying to Nathan as we stepped out into the sunlight. Already, there was a heavy intensity looming over the crowd that had gathered in the parking lot outside the church. The air felt thick and humid.

As we walked toward the cars, I looked around for Doris and Ace, but I saw them nowhere. *Where are they?* I wondered again.

Soon we were joined by a few more people, one of whom was the curly-headed young man who had met my eyes during the service. He approached me and said it was good to see me again.

"I'm sorry, what's your name?" I asked.

"Peter Shepherd." He looked a little confused. "These are my parents—Annie and Robert?" He said it as a question, as if to remind me. I looked at them for a moment.

Annie was a tall woman with straight black hair mixed with some gray near the edges of her face. Her eyes were sharp, her countenance serious, but kind. She wore a modest gray sundress.

Her husband, Robert, was also tall and slim, with a head full of gray hair. His eyes glowed with intelligence. His air was one of quietness and gentleness. I liked him right away.

They both seemed so familiar ...

"Nice to meet you all." I nodded to them.

Wait ... Annie and Robert? I do remember Annie and Robert! They were friends of my grandparents! Their children—I looked around—*were friends of mine when I was a kid!* I hadn't recognized them! I looked over at Nathan. We had been especially good friends when we were little. He looked so different! But yes, it was definitely him. We hadn't called him Nathan though; we had called him Nate.

"Wait a minute!" I exclaimed. "I remember you guys! It's been so long! I didn't recognize you! I'm so sorry!"

"I wondered!" Rebecca laughed. "But I didn't want to ask you!"

"You all look so different! Except you," I said to Annie and Robert. "You both look exactly the same!"

Annie smiled and said, "It's been many, many years! I guess we can forgive you!"

"Thank you." I returned the smile. "I know you must have been at Grandma's funeral, but I was so out of it that day; I don't remember much of anything!"

"That's understandable," said Annie. "I think we were all a little out of it that day!"

Then she changed the subject. "So, you and my son Nathan are neighbors now."

"Yes, we met right after I moved in. Only, I didn't realize who he was." I glanced over at Nathan, who was watching us with an amused expression.

"And you already met up with Rebecca?"

"Yes! We sat together in church today."

"Good! Good! Our other two daughters are not here today. Ali manages a horse farm outside of town nowadays. She doesn't come to church much. And Marie, the bonus baby, is a senior in high school this year. She's usually here with us, but she's on a camping trip with some friends this weekend. How're you liking the farm?" she asked.

"Well, it's going to take some getting used to," I admitted.

"I imagine it will." She looked contemplative for a moment, then continued briskly with: "Well, I'd like to tell you about what we do on Sundays after church. The kids all come over to our house after the service, and we all just visit and eat. Ali usually comes too. Sometimes the kids bring their friends. Sometimes we bring *our* friends. I want you to know that you're invited, if it seems like something you'd like to do. No need to bring anything."

Her invitation was sweet and simple, and I felt obliged to her. If only she knew just how much I needed this.

"I'd like that very much!"

"Good." And it seemed like she meant it. "We eat at one. You can ask Rebecca to send you the address. I don't keep up with all that texting jazz. Or you can just follow one of us!"

Rebecca had walked up beside us and interjected with a laugh, "I better give her the address regardless, in case we lose her on Bear Ridge Road!"

Annie nodded and said, "OK then. Let's head out!"

Rebecca sent me the address. "There it is, but you are welcome to follow us. Where are you parked?"

I pointed out my Honda.

"OK, great! We're just a few cars down from you. That maroon van there. You might have to wait for us a minute." She laughed. "It takes us a little while to get everyone loaded! I'm glad you're coming, Adel!"

I walked to the car, feeling both happy and a little nervous. I was stepping outside of my comfort zone by accepting this invitation. But I knew I needed it—desperately.

One thing was for sure. I was glad I decided to go to church that morning.

TWELVE

The Shepherd Family

The Shepherds lived about fifteen minutes to the north of town, on top of a mountain. The roads leading to their home were winding and narrow, and the kudzu and other summertime foliage were beginning to grow thick along the edges of the road. The leaf coverage overhead was dense and dark green and dancing in the wind. Their home was off the road, like their son's, and it had a rustic feel to it. As soon as I stepped out of the car, I felt the call of the mountain on my soul. I looked around and saw a view to the left; it was of the valley below. The buildings all looked so small from up here.

That town must be Cherry Hill, I thought. *Wow, what an incredible place to live. I would love to see that view at night!*

Noah and I followed Rebecca and her brood over to the house. Nathan was just coming out as I walked toward the door. He smiled slightly and stepped to the side to let us through. It was a log home with a wraparound porch. The house wasn't huge, but it was ample in size to have raised five children there. Inside the vaulted living room, there were trophy deer heads on the walls, as well as some large fish and a stuffed bobcat! I looked around in amazement. Like the outside, the inside of the house was also made of wood. The entire house seemed made of wood!

I followed Rebecca into the kitchen and her three older children ran off to play. The kitchen smelled delightful. What was it? Chili? Stew?

Rebecca began icing a chocolate cake.

"Can I help you with anything?" I asked Annie, who was now busy shuffling around her kitchen.

"Certainly! Would you mind getting out some bowls? Up there in the cabinet." She pointed to a cabinet near the sink.

As I was getting the bowls out, she said, "I could also use some help cutting up the lettuce."

I was glad to help and have something to do with my hands. I set Noah on the floor by my feet. Annie handed him a plastic bowl and a couple of wooden spoons, and he was soon happily occupied.

While she was working, Annie was all business. Not many words passed between us. By the time I was done with the lettuce, Annie and Rebecca were also finished and it was time to eat.

Everyone gathered in the kitchen, and Robert blessed the food. He mentioned me in the prayer, thanking God for blessing them with the return of a friend. I almost cried.

The children all sat at the coffee table in the living room, and the adults sat at the dining table, which was set for ten. There were only seven of us today, though it was hard to count Rebecca— she spent more time checking on the children and meeting their needs than she did sitting at the table! Noah was in a high chair beside me. I guessed that it must be Moses's high chair, but his daddy was holding him today.

The stew was excellent. Annie served it with buttery biscuits and a salad tossed with tomatoes and cucumbers from her garden. I hadn't eaten a meal this good since—I couldn't remember when!

"Adel, do you remember Ali?" Annie said to me after we all had our food and were sitting down. "Ali, Adel," she said to her daughter.

Ali was in her early thirties. She was a serious type. She reminded me some of her mama, only not so tall, a little more intense, and a little less obliging.

"Hello," Ali said, nodding curtly in my direction. "So, where did you move from?"

"San Francisco."

"That's a long way from here."

"Yes."

"Has it been an adjustment, moving to Sweet Valley?"

"It has ..." but I didn't want to get into it. "I understand you run a horse farm?"

"Yes, Crestfall Equestrian, over in Ellijay."

"I love horses. I would enjoy coming to see your farm sometime."

Ali suddenly lit up. "Of course! You are more than welcome. You can come by for a visit, but we also do trail rides and lessons if you would prefer."

"Maybe we could all go on a trail ride sometime," Peter suggested.

"That sounds fun!" Rebecca said as she came back in the room from the kitchen. "It's been a while since Jim and I went riding!"

"Let's do it!" exclaimed Peter. "Next Saturday!"

"I can't next Saturday," Nathan said. "I'll be in Blairsville finishing up a project."

"Then we'll just have to go without you!" Peter said, his eyes teasing his big brother.

"That's fine." Nathan shrugged.

"No, we'll wait on you!" said Rebecca. "Would you be able to go the next Saturday? And, Mama, would you be free to watch the kids?"

They both answered in the affirmative. Then they remembered me.

"Oh! Adel!" said Peter. "We forgot about you! You're the whole reason we're going, after all! Do you have plans for the Saturday after next? We would love it if you could accompany us on a scenic trail ride through the majestic Blue Ridge Mountains." He said all this as dramatically as he could.

I couldn't help but stare at him a little wide-eyed.

"No, I have no plans," I said with a laugh. "And I would love to *accompany* you."

"Good!" Peter beamed. "So it's settled!"

Annie came over to me then, carrying a plate. "I just mashed up some avocado for Moses. There's plenty. Do you want some for Noah?"

"Oh. Avocado?" I hurried to think whether that was safe for babies. Noah hadn't eaten much other than prepared baby food and peanut butter and jelly sandwiches. And bananas, of course. It was a vegetable, right? Or was it a fruit? Either way, I figured it must be all right to let him try a little.

"Um, sure. I guess so!" I said.

She scooped some onto Noah's tray and went on to give some to Moses. Noah poked it with his finger. He tasted it. He poked it some more. Before I knew it, he had eaten the whole thing.

I'll have to remember avocado the next time I go shopping, I thought.

I was already feeling tired and my head was a little fuzzy. *I wish Noah would sleep better!* I thought. But despite my tiredness, I wanted to get better acquainted with this sweet family.

"What do you do for a living, Mr. Shepherd?" I asked.

"Robert." He smiled. It reminded me of when I first met Nathan and he corrected me in the same way. I blushed a little in embarrassment.

He seemed to notice my embarrassment and kindly added, "I'm a writer. I write mathematics textbooks. It's not an interesting job," he said with a smile, "but it pays the bills and allows me to work from home, most of the time anyway."

"I wish I had known you in high school." I sighed. "Mathematics is not my strong point."

"I think most people would feel more adept at math if it was taught to them correctly from the beginning."

He went on to explain some concepts that were a little over my head and told me how they were being taught incorrectly in most schools and in many textbooks. He explained a little about how his approach was more understandable—more comprehensible by a wider range of students. Though I didn't understand all that he said, I found the topic interesting.

I could tell Annie was wanting to have her say in the conversation. When the next break came, she jumped in to tell me what her two sons did for a living. Peter, the younger brother, worked for a lawn company that maintained the city and most of the local churches and businesses. Nathan was a carpenter, who focused mostly on cabinetry, but who also liked to make furniture on the side. He was also a certified electrician.

"And what do you do?" I asked Rebecca. Jim had just left the room to change a diaper.

"I stay at home with the kids. We homeschool."

"That's not very common where I grew up. Do you like it?"

"I do," she replied. "It's probably one of the hardest and one of the most rewarding things I've ever done."

Then the family went on to talk about what Marie might do some day. Annie turned to me. "Marie is planning to attend a nearby community college in the fall—for a degree in *English*! I'm not sure what she's planning to *do* with a degree in *English*! Teach? I can't see her teaching for the life of me, but you don't get a degree in English just because you like to read!"

"Maybe she'll end up a librarian," said Peter.

"Or an editor!" added Rebecca.

"Not likely," said Ali. "She's going to go off to college and meet some handsome guy and be married before the year is out. Then she won't care a hoot for school. You'll see."

"Well, I guess we'll have to. Wait and see, I mean." This time it was Nathan who spoke. He had been leaning back in his chair, listening quietly.

"What time is Marie supposed to be getting back today?" asked Robert.

"In about an hour," answered Annie. "Molly's bringing her home."

After dinner was over and the chocolate cake was eaten, everyone moved into the living room, except Annie, who was cleaning up the kitchen and who apparently had a rule that no one was allowed to help her. She wanted this to be a day of rest and refreshment for her family—and for their guests too, apparently.

I followed Rebecca into the living room. We sat together on one of the large brown leather couches.

"Where do you live, Rebecca?"

"In town. About three blocks from church."

"What does your husband do for a living?"

"He works at the bank. He's worked there about six years now. It's a good job. But it's not his dream. His dream is to be in ministry."

"Can't he do both?"

"Yes, he could. He does, some. He is a deacon, and he teaches the high schoolers' Sunday school class with Nathan, but I know his heart is to be a pastor again."

"Again? So, he has been a pastor before?"

"Yes. When we got married nine years ago, he was pastoring a little church in Braselton. We lived there for a few years. That's where Randy was born. But then we needed to take a break from that for a while, so he found this job at the bank, and we moved up here." She smiled, but her smile seemed a little sad.

"Did you enjoy the service today?" she asked me.

"I did! I was so glad I finally came. I've been here over three months, and I've had the hardest time making up my mind to go. But yes. I needed it. I felt like the sermon was meant just for me. When I get home, I need to read over my notes again."

"If you ever want someone to talk to about it, or anything else really, call me. You have my number."

"OK! I just might take you up on that!"

Nathan was sitting close to us, and I thought it seemed as if he had been listening to us talk. It made me feel a little self-conscious.

"So ..." I said, more quietly. "Where can a girl find some new clothes around here?"

Rebecca laughed. "Tanger Outlets," she said. "In Dawsonville."

"All right. Where's that?"

"It's east of here. About a forty-minute drive. Maybe I could go with you—show you where it is and show you some of the better shops? I need a few things too, and it'd be a good way to get to know each other better."

"Really?" I wasn't used to all this hospitality!

"Sure! It'd be fun."

"OK. That sounds great!"

"It'll have to be an evening or a Saturday, so Jim can watch the kids."

"That's fine. I'll have to bring Noah."

"Bring him along! He can help us pick out your clothes!" She smiled. Then Peter came in and sat down with us.

"So, how's the farm?" he asked me in an open and friendly manner. "Is Mr. Alan's old truck still broke down in the field behind the barn?"

"Oh!" I said in surprise. "I guess it is! I was wondering why there was a truck sitting out there!"

Peter laughed. "The truck broke down last winter when we were bringing in some firewood from a fallen tree on the other side of the field. It happened right before Ms. Elaine passed." He grew quiet. But then he smiled again and said, "It sat full of that old firewood for forever. Sometime in February, some of my buddies and I remembered it and went back to pick it up. Lots of people still use woodstoves here in the mountains," he explained. "So, we needed it! But we never got around to coming and getting the truck back in the barn! Sorry about that."

"It's really alright. I'm not worried about it."

"So, are you planning to harvest apples this summer?" he asked.

"I'm not really sure. I've been doing some research, but this is all totally new for me."

As I talked, Noah climbed over my lap and onto the floor. He rolled around at my feet and pulled at my dress. Then he climbed up into my lap and curled up. I could tell he was getting tired. I needed to go soon. But then Annie came in. She pulled up a chair and sat it by us on the couch.

She listened to me talk about my new life on the farm and lament the fact that my grandparents were no longer there to keep me company, before interrupting with, "Adel, we knew your grandparents *very* well. They were like family to us. And their family is our family. You are welcome here anytime. And if you need anything, you know who to call. Did you give her my number, Rebecca? But I *expect* you to come on Sundays, unless you have a good reason. You need it!" she said, pointing a finger at me in a teasing manner. "Being cooped up all the time isn't good for a girl! Or a baby!"

85

"I'd like that. Thank you for including me. Though we aren't cooped up *all* the time. Noah and I go on lots of walks." I laughed. "But since it's just the two of us now, it *can* get pretty lonely."

"Yeah, we were sorry to hear about your ex-husband and the way he treated you. That must have been really hard. Just know you are always welcome here. Scripture teaches that it's important to be in fellowship with one another, and in our family, we take that seriously."

"Thank you," I said. This was all so new to me; I wasn't sure what else to say.

"It's just so good to have you back with us, Adel! You're no longer the little girl with pigtails, pink bows, and a million questions. You're a mama now! Time does fly."

"Yes, it does."

"Ooh, I need to show you something!" she said, and she stood up and went over to the large bookshelf in the living room and took down a couple of photo albums.

She brought them over to the couch where we were sitting.

"This one is from VBS when you were about ten years old," she said. "That was an especially good year, and we had a girl take photos throughout the week. Here, see this one?" She showed me pictures of my younger self doing activities like singing, wood crafts, painting, and kickball. There were not many kids in the pictures. Maybe thirty or forty.

What a difference from the VBS at our church back in San Francisco! I thought. I had volunteered at our wild and energetic VBS while I was in high school, and though I enjoyed it, I always missed the slow, peaceful rhythms of the VBS at Cherry Hill Baptist.

I saw Rebecca and Ali. They seemed to be helpers or teachers. There was Peter, making silly faces and being a goofball. But where was Nathan?

In one of the pictures, all the children were standing together for a group photo. We were all wearing matching white shirts, on which we had painted "This is My Father's World" in big block letters. I looked more closely. In the picture, Nathan and I were standing side by side with our arms around each other's shoulders, and we were laughing. I stared at the picture for a minute. A flood of memories came washing over me.

We played together at church, VBS, and whenever our families were together, which seemed to be often. I had loved playing with him, more than with anyone else—until that summer when he seemed to change, when he didn't want to play anymore. I must have been about eleven or twelve. I remember feeling hurt. Sad. It's always hard to say goodbye to a friend.

I looked again at the picture, then glanced up at Nathan to see if there was any resemblance of the twelve-year-old boy with smiling eyes. He had the same dark hair, the same strong jaw line, and yes, the same quiet, thoughtful demeanor. It had been so long ago! It was hard to wrap my mind around the fact that we had once been friends! I tried not to think about it. I didn't want things to be awkward. He probably didn't even remember.

Annie had opened another photo album and was flipping through the pictures.

"Do you remember riding your grandpa's tractor in the Memorial Day parade? And Sunday afternoons sitting around under those big post oaks in your grandparents' front yard?"

I looked over at the pictures. "I do! Those were such sweet times."

"They were. You know, your grandparents were the ones who inspired me to start a Sunday tradition for my own family. It's why we still gather. It's good for us to be together. And to bring in friends." She smiled at me. She didn't seem as sharp when she was smiling.

"The boys always looked forward to your coming every summer. So did the girls, but they were just older than you, you know? But as soon as school let out for the summer, the boys would start asking when you'd be here. It was part of their summer routine!" She laughed. "Aww ... you're really little in this one! How old do you think you are?"

I glanced over at the picture of me snuggled in my grandma's lap, in a chair out in their front yard. "Wow. I don't know. Maybe five or six?"

I took the book in my lap and flipped through the rest of it slowly, thoroughly appreciating the step back in time.

Annie stood up and patted my shoulder before moving closer to hear what her husband was saying about a potential new youth pastor for the church.

Rebecca got up to check on her children.

Peter scooted a little closer so he could see the pictures. I was looking at a page that had another picture of Nathan and me. This time, we were younger and sitting together on a giant stack of haybales in the barn.

"You know," Peter said, leaning toward me and speaking quietly. "Nathan wonders how long you'll be able to stick it out at the farm. It's a lot of work for a city girl who isn't used to that kind of thing."

"Did he say that?" I felt my blood rising.

Nathan was still sitting close by, and I guessed he could hear us, yet he didn't step in to defend himself.

"I'm not sure he has faith in your being from the city. This is a different kind of life. It's a *hard* life. I heard a couple guys at church making bets on how long you'd be here."

I was indignant. How could they do that? And how could Nathan say such things? He didn't even know me anymore!

"Is that how you all feel?"

"No. I'm not going to judge a book by its cover. Or by its city of origin. I figure, if you're meant to be here, it'll work out. It *is* a lot to take on, though. Take it from me. I used to work there!"

"You did?"

"Yes, all throughout high school."

"Well, maybe you can teach me a few things then. I've got to start learning sometime!"

Peter agreed and heartily went on to explain some of the basic field practices of orchard maintenance—spraying and pruning and things like that. I wasn't sure I would remember much of what he said, but it gave me a start, and it also made me begin to feel overwhelmed. There really was a lot to owning an orchard!

While Peter was still deeply focused on explaining a technique used to treat fire blight, a new face appeared in the room. It was a girl, about eighteen. She was pretty, with the same dark hair as the rest of the family, though not as tall. *This must be Marie,* I thought. Peter noticed that he had lost my attention and glanced up to the doorway, where the girl stood talking to Jim. "Oh! Marie's back!" he said affectionately. "Hey, Marie! Come meet our company!"

Marie walked over to us, a bright and warm smile lighting up her face. "Hi, Adel! Jim tells me you came to church this morning! I'm so glad! And I'm glad my family convinced you to come join in our shenanigans today! It's so good to see you again!"

Marie treated me like an old friend. She had only been six or seven when I stopped coming to the farm. Did she really remember me?

"It's very good to see you again, too, Marie! You're all grown-up! Your mom tells me you plan to start college in the fall?"

"Yes! I'm super excited about it! A few friends and I are all going to the same school, and we will be able to live at home. This year anyway. We hope to get an apartment or small house together sometime, but not right now. I'm hoping to get a degree in English!"

"So your mom tells me." I smiled. "You must like to read?"

"I do! I love stories. Good stories! Living stories that encourage me to grow as a person."

"I'm just learning to like those myself!" I laughed. "Doris loaned me a book recently that fits that description."

"Oh? What book?"

"*Jane Eyre.*"

"Oh yes! That's a classic! One of my all-time favorites."

Just then, Noah let out a loud and demanding squeal to get our attention. It worked.

"So, who is this little guy?" Marie asked, crouching low to get on Noah's level.

"This is Noah. He's a little bashful." Noah had quickly hidden his face behind my leg and was shyly peeking out at Marie. He had a little smile on his face. He knew he was in good company.

Marie was soon called away by her parents to give them the rundown on her camping trip, and I was again left alone with Peter.

As I drove home that evening, I went over the events of the day. Overall, it was a very pleasant day. I had begun to feel a closeness with

Rebecca. She felt like a friend already. I felt like the Lord was beginning to answer my prayers in powerful ways. But there was one thing about the afternoon that was not pleasant, and I had a hard time getting it out of my head: The fact that Nathan didn't seem to care for me simply because I was from *the city*. He knew nothing about what I was like or what I was capable of! He had said no more than a word or two to me the whole day, though he was never very far away. Now I knew why. I fumed for at least half the way home. But before I pulled into the drive, I felt a sense of peace. It didn't matter what he thought. I would do my best regardless. His good opinion didn't matter. I would be myself anyway. I would be kind and courteous and give him no reason to believe he was right.

And I would show him I *could* do it. I *would* make it work!

THIRTEEN

Dancing in the Rain

On Wednesday morning, I went over to visit the Joneses.

Noah and I were sitting at the kitchen table while Doris bustled around the kitchen preparing some casseroles for the freezer.

"I went to church last Sunday," I said casually.

"Oh, you did?" said Doris, stopping what she was doing and turning to me with a smile.

"Yes. And I liked it. I'm planning to go back this Sunday."

"I'm so glad! It's a good mess of people we got there. None better."

"I didn't see you guys. Were you there?"

"No. We had to go visit Ace's mother. She had an episode the night before and wasn't doing too good. She's ninety-six years old, so we figure any day now, one of her spells might be the last. We like to be there for her when we can."

"Wow! Ninety-six!"

"And lord howdy she's got some stories to tell. You'll have to ask Ace to share some with you sometime."

"I will! I love a good story."

"He's got some of his mother that'd have you plumb tickled! She was born and raised in the backwoods mountains, a little north of here.

"Well," she said, wiping her hands on her apron and untying the string, "have you started that book I gave you?"

"I have, Doris! And you were right. I love it! I've been reading it in the evenings before I go to bed. Jane had such a sad childhood. It's actually made me cry a few times."

"You know it's a good story when it touches your heart."

As Doris walked over to hang up her apron, she took another off the hanger. "Do you need an apron? I've got so many hanging here that I'll never use." She held out a pretty blue and white apron for me to take.

"Sure! I don't have an apron. I don't actually cook much yet, but I really want to! Thank you, Doris! That's so sweet!" I stood up and took the apron from her.

What a special gift, I thought as I ran my hand over the simple design of the cotton fabric.

It rained for several days in a row, keeping Noah and me cooped up inside the house. I didn't realize how much I had grown to love our daily strolls around the yard, showing Noah all of the delicate beauty and nuances of nature. It was through these rambles that I really began to appreciate the beauty and splendor of God's creation, and in doing so, I was unknowingly learning something of the character of the Creator, something of God himself, and nothing less than praise can come forth when the first wild violet of the year is sighted! Or the first cardinal, with its striking red suit. Or the first field of wildflowers!

I was not aware of the names or habits of many of the birds or other wildlife we encountered on these walks, and was yet unable to tell the difference between a dandelion and a common daisy! But in my mind, an interest was forming, and my senses were being awakened to them. It had progressed to such a point that when the rains came and kept us inside for four days straight, I became irritable and moody at having *no fresh air*! I simply *had* to get out! So, I buttoned myself into a long crimson-colored raincoat and matching boots, slipped a warm jersey over Noah's chubby little belly, and picked up an umbrella that was large enough for the two of us. Then we proceeded forth—out the back door into a torrent of rain, out into a lake of a backyard, out under a shroud of thick gray clouds.

The rain came down heavily, but we weren't deterred. On the contrary, I felt a leap of joy in my soul as, together, we splashed through the muddy puddles that had formed on the gravel walk.

Noah clung tightly to my arms, as if for life. This was a new experience for him, and he didn't know what to make of it. His eyes were as wide as lollipops. He giggled nervously when I made a fuss about jumping into a particularly large puddle, and his heart beat faster as I began to swirl around and around with him in a waltz. I laughed aloud, and seeing me happy made Noah happier too; he let out a little squeal. I continued laughing and dancing and began to loudly sing the lyrics of "The Ants Go Marching." I had to sing loudly to be able to hear myself over the noise of the rain. We danced around the side yard, then around the corner of the house, only to be greeted by Nathan, who was also sheltering under an umbrella (minus the raincoat). He had apparently been on his way from his truck to the front porch and had stopped in surprise at the sight of us.

"Oh!" was all I could muster.

Nathan could not suppress a smile, though he seemed to try.

"Hi! We were just ..."

"Dancing in the rain?"

"Uh ... yes." I recovered some and managed to force a smile. "What can I do for you, Nathan?"

"Mr. Jackson said he wasn't able to finish replacing an outlet here yesterday." He had to speak loudly so I could hear him over the noise of the downpour.

I nodded in affirmation. "Yes, he didn't have the part he needed in his truck."

"That's right. He was supposed to come finish today, but he had an emergency job come up in a neighboring county this morning. Since I work part-time for Mr. Jackson, and since I live next door, he asked if I would mind finishing it for him."

"Oh. Well, sure! Thank you." I led the way to the covered front porch and set Noah down so I could shake off the umbrella and open the front door. "Come in!"

Nathan replaced the outlet while I made peanut butter and jelly sandwiches and Noah played in his playpen full of toys.

The unsafe outlet didn't take long to swap out, and by the time Nathan was done, I had some sandwiches ready.

"I just finished up," said Nathan, walking into the kitchen. "Is there anything else you need me to look at while I'm here?"

"No, that's it." I wiped bread crumbs onto my special new apron. "Thanks."

Nathan hesitated, then said, "OK, well, I guess I'll be going. Have a good day," and he started for the door.

"Well, hey!" I said, quickly following behind him. "I just made some sandwiches for Noah and myself. Would you like some too? I realize that you're probably here on your lunch hour ..." It was an effort to be kind and courteous.

He hesitated again, as if to consider, then turned back. "OK, sure. Thank you."

Nathan followed me back to the kitchen, where I quickly put together another sandwich, chattering some while I worked. He seemed a little surprised when I handed him his sandwich on a plate. *Maybe he was expecting to take the sandwich with him!*

"Oh, do you need to head out? I can wrap it in a napkin for you."

He hesitated again.

"No, it's fine. I've got a few minutes." He seemed a little uneasy.

I poured some glasses of lemonade and set them on the table with the sandwiches.

Nathan discreetly checked his watch and then slowly followed me to the table.

It may have been to thank him for coming in the rain on his lunch break to fix the outlet, or perhaps I made a place at the table for Nathan simply because I was thankful to have another adult in the house and wanted to keep him there as long as possible. I'm not sure I was aware of a motive. I just did, without much thinking and without considering what might be proper. It seemed like the polite thing to do, anyway, and it was my first attempt to show him my true self—my *capable* self.

"So, your mom told me you do carpentry work?" I asked, to break the ice.

"Yes." Nathan still seemed a little uncomfortable as he answered and sat down at the table. It seemed as if a bunch of thoughts were swirling through his mind. "I build custom cabinets," he continued. "for new construction mostly and some remodels. Working for Mr. Jackson is a side job."

"Oh, OK. Do you have to travel much?"

"Some but not far off. There's plenty of work for me to do around here."

I nodded and tried to think of what to say next. "Doris tells me that you spent a lot of time over here the last few years?"

"Yes, I did." He still seemed a little troubled.

Noah squealed from his high chair and began to babble something in Nathan's direction, distracting him from his thoughts. Nathan was delighted with Noah's attention and spent a few minutes carrying on with him before returning to more fully answer my question.

"Your grandma was a good friend of mine actually. Your grandpa too. They knew us from the time we were born, and our family stayed close to them over the years. As they were getting older and starting to have some health problems, they weren't able to get around like they used to. Especially Ms. Elaine, those last couple of years. So, I helped them out when they needed it."

"Oh." I looked up from breaking a piece of sandwich into smaller pieces on Noah's tray.

"I bought the house through the woods about a year before Mr. Alan died. I helped out while he was in and out of the hospital. After he passed, I helped Ms. Elaine with yard work and handyman projects, and she kept me supplied in good food and company." He smiled, but I thought I noticed a sadness in his eyes.

"Well! I have to admit that I'm a little jealous. I loved my grandparents. Better than anyone in the world—but I hardly ever got to see them. Living on the other side of the country makes that kind of hard." I laughed a little. "And my parents didn't make much of an effort."

"At least you were able to spend your summers here. Do you have good memories of them?"

"Oh, *yes!* I do! I loved my summers here! To be out of the crowded city, to be free to run and play and splash in the creek. We had all kinds of adventures. Grandpa was so much fun. And Grandma was such a kind, patient lady. She had such gentle hands! She was never harsh with me when I was little and I would mess up or break things. She loved to have fun too. Especially in the kitchen. I *loved* the smells that filled this house from the kitchen! Sometimes she would let me help cook. And she was always thinking of everyone else. Always taking things she had made to neighbors and people in need. Things like bread, cakes, homemade pickles. And she used to wake me every morning by singing soft, pretty songs."

"Your grandma had a wonderful voice. She used to sing in the choir at church. And while she was tending to her flowers."

"And while she was doing chores," I added.

"And while she was cooking," continued Nathan, and we both laughed.

After a moment of silence, Nathan grew sober again and said, "This is the first time I've been in this house, this kitchen, since ..." He shrugged, but I could tell he was struggling to fight back his emotions.

Oh ... so that's what's bothering him!

I spoke softly. "You and Grandma were pretty close, weren't you?"

"We were."

Here I paused for a moment, not really knowing what to say to comfort Nathan or myself, or how to approach what I wanted most to hear. Suddenly I was afraid that if I spoke, I might cry. Finally, and with some energy, I said, "Please, tell me something about her. It's been *so* long ... I was here every summer as a little girl. Up until, oh, about ..." I paused to think.

"About seventh grade," Nathan said.

"That's right, I was about thirteen. After that, we all got so busy. And my parents began to have elaborate plans for our summers. I begged them to let me come back, but it was hard to come down for only a week or two, and the rest of our summers were full. Seeing them on the occasional holiday was all right, but it wasn't the same as being alone with them all summer. I feel like I missed out on so much. As a high schooler and young adult. And now ..." I wanted to say, "It's too late," but I couldn't get it out. I turned my head away to hide the few tears that had escaped down my cheeks.

Nathan's brow was knitted in concern. He seemed to understand the loss of a beloved grandparent as well as a beloved friend. He had been around my grandma more than I had! Yes, he understood.

After a few thoughtful minutes of quietly eating, Nathan began to tell a story about "Ms. Elaine." A story about when she found a snake in the flower garden. It was a slow and thoughtful story—funny too. *He sure pays close attention to detail*, I thought.

"And after that, she never turned a flowerpot over, except with a rake," Nathan finished. I couldn't help but laugh a little at the end of the ridiculous story.

Nathan sat back in his chair and seemed satisfied to have made me laugh and to have lifted the mood of the emotionally charged room.

I began to relax. I was glad I had asked Nathan to stay for lunch. He was someone who understood what I was going through. Someone I could be comfortable with. Someone I could be myself with. A friend— almost. My comfortable feelings were quickly interrupted when I remembered what Peter had said. *Does Nathan really believe I'm incapable?*

We talked casually for a few minutes more, and Noah began to sleepily toss the remnants of his sandwich to the floor.

All at once, Nathan quickly looked at his watch and stood to leave. "I'm sorry to rush out, but I need to get back to work. Thank you for lunch! No need to get up," he said as I began to rise. "I'll let myself out." He carried his plate and glass to the sink and was gone.

I sat at the table for a while longer, playing with the leftovers on my plate, and Noah fell asleep in his high chair.

FOURTEEN

Blueberries and Baking

Rebecca and I were able to go shopping one afternoon the following week. I had no idea what kind of clothes to buy, and I was a little embarrassed to ask Rebecca what people in the country wear. So, I just did my best to pick out some things that seemed practical— jeans, tank tops, and jean shorts. I also tried to find some tennis shoes that were washable. I knew my shoes would be getting dirty on the farm. Over time, I would figure out what to wear, and these things would get me started. Rebecca held Noah while I tried things on. I tried not to take too long. She bought a few things too. Then, before heading back, we stopped at Starbucks to have some iced coffee. I bought a big chocolate chip cookie for Noah. It was such a treat to be sitting with another woman, enjoying something yummy, and talking girl things. I had missed this!

By the last Sunday in June, Noah was finally beginning to enjoy his class at church. When I arrived to drop him off, Ms. Grace was waiting at the door with open arms and Noah reached for her with anticipation.

After his hug he wanted down so he could crawl over to the bin of large plastic toy cars that the other babies where playing with. I smiled to myself as I turned to make my way to the sanctuary.

During the service, Nathan and his sisters Rebecca and Marie sang a song together. They sang "It Is Well." Nathan played the guitar and sang the melody. His voice was rich and clear and carried well over the sanctuary. His sisters sang harmonies to accompany him. It was beautiful. Their voices blended perfectly, like only the voices of siblings can. No one in the pews stirred while they were singing; everyone was captivated by the lovely music and the beautiful words:

When peace like a river, attendeth my way,
When sorrows like sea billows roll
Whatever my lot, thou hast taught me to say
It is well, it is well, with my soul
Though Satan should buffet, though trials should come,
Let this blest assurance control,
That Christ has regarded my helpless estate,
And hath shed His own blood for my soul
It is well, it is well, with my soul
My sin, oh, the bliss of this glorious thought
My sin, not in part but the whole,
Is nailed to the cross, and I bear it no more,
Praise the Lord, praise the Lord, o my soul
It is well, it is well, with my soul
It is well, it is well, with my soul

After church, we went over to the Shepherds' house as usual. I no longer needed to follow anyone; I now knew the route by heart. I passed an entire field of dainty Queen Anne's lace as I drove along Bear Ridge Road, their delicate white crowns bobbing gently in the breeze. It was such a pleasant drive. Most of the drives around here were.

And now I knew why this area was called the Bible Belt. Everywhere I looked, there were tiny churches nestled among the hills. I was beginning to feel like I knew the town a little bit too, like I belonged here, like it was becoming my home.

As we pulled into the drive at the Shepherds' house, we saw the kids playing with kickballs in the front yard. They ran squealing away from the parking area as we pulled into what had become *our* parking spot. Everyone seemed to follow that habit and parked in the same place week after week. *At least it eliminates the need to make a decision about it,* I thought.

Apparently, Annie had prepared a roast the night before and didn't have much need of Rebecca and me in the kitchen, so we stayed out on the expansive porch and enjoyed the view of the mountains.

Rebecca had a calm spirit. Nothing ever seemed to ruffle her. Occasionally, one of her children would come running up to her with some form of distress or other, and she always handled them with quietness and patience. I liked that about her. I hoped some of her patience and grace would rub off on me.

"Do you know, I have never grown tired of that view," Rebecca said to me, when she noticed how intently focused I was on the blue, hazy mountains in the distance, of which the porch offered an excellent view. "Mama and Daddy bought this place before we were born," she continued. "We spent all our childhood years here, at this house. And that view has remained the same throughout the years. It changes with the seasons, of course, but even then, it's the same old view. It's good for the inside of a person, isn't it?"

I nodded slowly, still intently focused on the distance. "Was it hard to move away? When you married Jim?"

"Well, I had been away at Emmanuel College. That's where we met. I was so focused on school and friends, and then Jim, that I didn't really notice it being hard. We married and moved to Braselton right out of college. So, I was gone for a while. And though I love the mountains, I don't need them the way Mama and Daddy do. And Nathan. I can come back and visit and be satisfied. I think it would be harder for them if they had to move. It's a part of who they are."

"Yes! I get that! Despite how hard everything has been, I feel more like myself now than I have since I was a little girl! I feel like the mountains give me life—or something." I shrugged.

Rebecca cocked her head to one side and looked at me kind of funny, and I wondered what she was thinking. But soon the moment passed and she changed the subject to more general things.

After a little while, Robert came out and took a chair near the swing. Rebecca went inside to check on the lunch preparations, and I moved over to sit on the swing. Noah was playing along the porch railing and reaching out to grab leaves off the bushes in front.

Robert, tall and slim with his gentle eyes and his slow, easy smile, was an object of interest to me. He always seemed to be tinkering with something—some small metal contraption that needed cleaning with a felt cloth, or he would take a knife and slide it down a small metal and plastic device that he kept in his pocket when he wasn't using it. He could do that for hours on end while everyone sat around and talked. He seemed to have no end of knives.

Both of his sons looked a little like him, in their own way, but Nathan was the most like him in personality as well as looks. He was quiet and thoughtful with the same slow and easy smile.

Peter was slim like his father, but looked more like his mother, except for the curly hair, which he didn't get that from either of his parents. And in personality, he was as different from his father as summer is to winter. Peter was active, noisy, and very cheerful, and he wanted the world to know it. He was always coming up with some game or grand idea for everyone to try; he was the life of the Shepherd household.

My attention was brought back to Robert, who was holding a small rectangular piece of wood. There was another just like it in his lap. He was using a small piece of sandpaper to smooth out the rough spots.

"What are you doing?" I asked, after watching him for a minute.

"This is a knife handle. I'm getting it ready to set."

"Oh. You're making a knife?"

"I am. It's a hobby of mine."

"What a neat thing to do! Do you sell them?"

"No, it's just for fun. I give them away to the boys and their friends. Annie has a couple she uses in the kitchen."

"How creative! I've never known anyone who made their own

knives. That's so impressive."

"Nah. It's just a learned skill like anything else." He smiled as he held up the smooth handle for me to see.

After lunch, everyone went back on the porch to enjoy the day. Robert brought out a banjo. His sons pulled out guitars, and they commenced playing. Everyone, even the children, gathered around them on the porch. They played "In the Garden," and Rebecca picked up the melody. She sang it slow and sweet, the sounds reaching far out into the still, evening light. Robert played lead, his fingers moving expertly over the steel strings. Both Peter and Nathan played rhythm and some picking. I could tell they must have played together a lot over the years; it all sounded so flawless. They played song after song, taking turns who sang, sometimes with harmonies, until at last, Robert said he was all tuckered out.

"My fingers can't keep up like they used to!" he said to me with a laugh. Then turning to his boys, "We don't practice as often as we should!"

"Well, play for me whenever you like! That was wonderful!" I said. I hadn't had that much fun in quite a while. "You used to play for us when I was little!" I continued.

"I reckon I probably did," he said with a smile. "That was quite a while ago. I'm surprised you remember."

Day slowly turned into evening, and little lightning bugs began to appear above the grass in the yard. The children were delighted. Soon they had several jars full, and they went around to each adult to show off their catch.

The hum of the crickets grew louder and louder, as did the talk and laughter of the Shepherd family. They seemed to enjoy one another's company so much. I longed for that—that sense of belonging. Though they were kind to include me, I still felt like an outsider, and I guessed I always would. At least a little.

After the music was over, everyone moved inside to play a game of

Pictionary. I stayed on the porch. Peter came back out; his face bright and cheery. "Are you coming? We need you! We're just about to start!"

I reluctantly followed him back inside the house, where the game was already spread out on the kitchen table. Games were not my forte. We didn't play many games growing up. But I took the seat he offered me, which was beside himself, and tried to figure out what I was supposed to do.

Throughout the game, Peter seemed to pay extra special attention to my turns, always defending me when no one could guess my picture and lamenting profusely when I lost.

The Shepherds were fun to play games with. They loved to laugh. It was catching. Even Ali participated and seemed to be enjoying herself. And by the end of the game, I was thoroughly enjoying myself too.

But then it was time to go. I couldn't believe how late it was. I'd been at the Shepherds' *all* day. Marie had taken on the role of babysitter, and had rocked Noah to sleep in an armchair in the living room, while the other children were watching a show.

Before we left, I had a chance to talk with Nathan as we were all sitting together in the living room.

"You all sang wonderfully at church earlier today," I said.

"Thank you. It's a wonderful song."

I nodded in agreement. "Have you played guitar long?"

"Since middle school." And after a pause, "Do you play?"

"No."

We sat silently for a minute. It didn't feel awkward like it often does when two people don't have anything to say to each other. But then I remembered something: "I grew up playing the piano. Mom said it was important to know music. But I haven't played in years."

"I bet if you sat down at a piano, it would probably come back to you. It's a lot like riding a bike. With a little practice, you'd probably be just fine."

"Grandma has a piano in the living room. It's just sat there since I moved in. Maybe I should take your advice to heart. I loved playing before life got so busy. Do y'all often sing in church?"

"Usually a few times a year. And sometimes at special events, like

Revival and the Christmas carol singalong."

"That sounds fun!"

"It is!"

We chatted easily like that for a little while longer, and then Nathan said, "Oh hey, I keep forgetting to ask you. There's a farm nearby that buys the hay from Sweet Valley, twice a year, usually the end of June and September, from the field behind the house. I know the guys pretty well, and ever since Mr. Alan died, Ms. Elaine has had me cut the hay and bale it for them. I'm sorry for not mentioning this before, but is that something you want me to continue?"

"Sure! I'll take all the income I can get! And you don't mind doing it? I'd pay you of course."

"No, I don't mind! The guys are friends of mine. No need to pay me. I just do it to help everyone out. They help me out sometimes too."

"OK. Well that sounds good."

"I'll probably start later this week."

"Alright."

But then it really *was* time to go.

Though I was exhausted and beginning to feel a little light-headed, it was hard to leave that night. I wished we could just stay and visit. Everyone was so relaxed, sitting around enjoying one another's company and some of Annie's delicious stove-popped popcorn. But instead, I scooped up the sleeping Noah and my bags and headed out into the dark night.

After seeing Julian at the gas station last month and giving him my phone number, Julian had gotten in the habit of calling me. It started out to be every once in a while but had recently turned into a call every few days. It was always in the evening, after Noah was in bed. At first, I tried to keep the calls short, just a few minutes, but as time went on, I began to enjoy our conversations. Just a little at first, increasing with each succeeding call. After being alone all day, it was nice to have someone to talk to in the evening. Someone I could share the happenings of the day with. Someone who seemed interested in what I had to say. Julian was a good listener. He didn't seem to mind when I rambled on about things. I also began to enjoy hearing his stories. He mostly talked of things from his past, rather than things that happened that day or week. But I didn't mind. His stories were interesting and fun. It made the time pass by more quickly.

After a few weeks of this, by the end of June, I agreed to meet him for a date. He was ecstatic. I was nervous. I didn't date much when I was young, and my one long-term relationship ended in a faulty marriage that terminated within a year. What a *storehouse* of anxieties I had! I *never* wanted to go through that again! I had actually planned to never marry again. I didn't want to risk putting Noah through the pain of divorce. He wasn't born when Damian left. If that were to happen again, he would now be old enough to feel the effects of it.

Julian seemed really interested in me, he seemed to have money, and he was handsome. And—he had asked. He had taken the initiative to ask a single mom out on a date. I was flattered, despite my reservations. I still felt like I didn't know him very well. But that would come with time, wouldn't it?

It hadn't been that long since Damian left. Not quite a year and a half. I wasn't sure I was completely over it. Not that I had any feelings left for Damian. My affection for him had ended when he refused to be the father of his unborn son. But the pain, the confusion, the wonderings of why it had happened. If I had done something wrong. I wasn't sure I had worked through everything yet. How could I move on when I wasn't at peace with what had happened?

And yet I *did* want to be married, despite trying so hard to convince myself that I didn't. I wanted to be married to the *right* man. Someone who would love me for who I was, *not* for what I could become, not for how I looked or for what I gave them. Someone who understood the innermost workings of my heart and chose to love me anyway. Someone I could be myself with.

"Julian," I said, in the conversation when I agreed to see him. "If we are going to go out, it's going to have to be relaxed. No pressure. I don't want to commit to being in a relationship. My marriage didn't end well, and it wasn't that long ago. I've got a long way to go before I would be ready for something serious. I just want you to know that up front, so you know what to expect."

"I totally understand. We can go as slow as you like!"

"I just want to get to know you," I continued. "And have fun, you know?"

"I get that. I really do. And I'm OK with it. I respect your need to go slow. I'll let you lead. But I also want you to know that I think the world of you. I feel like I've gotten to know you really well over the last few weeks, and I am committed to waiting. For *you*."

His words made me feel a little uneasy. Did he hear what I just said about taking it slow and not being serious? I guess he couldn't help how he felt, so long as he didn't pressure *me* to move fast.

Our first date was a picnic at Fort Mountain State Park. I left Noah with Doris in the morning and met Julian at a shop outside of town, which was on the way to the park. It felt strange to leave Noah with someone again. I hadn't done that since arriving at the farm. I had grown to need him as much as he needed me, and I felt the sting in my heart when I waved goodbye, but of all people, I knew Doris would take good care of him.

When I climbed into Julian's car, he handed me an entire pack of double stuffed Oreo cookies.

"I remembered you saying how much you liked them in one of our conversations," he said.

"Thank you, Julian. That was sweet." But inwardly, I wondered if it was necessary for him to give me an *entire* pack of cookies.

It was a nice day for a picnic, and we found a good spot in the shade, right by the lake.

"Those trees over there are just beautiful!" I said, as we propped back on the picnic blanket.

"Which ones?"

"Those over there!" I pointed across the lake to a group of trees that were covered in frilly, peach-colored flowers. They looked sort of tropical. Their reflection was a watercolor picture that only enhanced their natural beauty.

"Uh-huh," he said, but he didn't sound very enthusiastic.

As we ate, we hung out lazily on the picnic blanket, talking and laughing about random things.

"Would you like to go on a hike after we've finished eating?" I asked.

"Sure. We can pick up a map at the visitor's center."

I pointed out that there was a trailhead a little way from where we were sitting, but Julian still preferred to have a map.

We finished our lunch of sandwiches, potato chips, and La Croix and then drove over to the visitor's center. I wandered around the store while Julian looked at the map. He chose a trail that he thought would be good for us, and we started out.

So far, I hadn't been able to look at Julian very well, without his noticing. Now was my chance. He was walking just a little way in front of me. I could see him and his profile very well from where I was walking. His features were captivating. His expressions were bright. He had lively spirits. He reminded me a little of Peter in that way, but after being on the trail for a while, it became apparent that he was uncomfortable. At first, he seemed to try to hide it, but after a while, it was obvious that he was in some kind of pain.

"Are you alright?" I asked.

"No ... these shoes are rubbing me blisters!"

I looked down at the shoes. "Those seem a little big. Are you sure they're the right size?"

"I like to have a little room."

"Huh ... OK."

That's a little unusual.

"Well, you seem to be in a lot of pain," I said. "We can go ahead and turn back."

"I'm sorry. I wish I had worn different shoes."

"Oh, it's alright. I'm just sorry that you're going to have to deal with it until we get back."

To try to distract him from his sufferings as we made our way back to the parking lot, I began to ask him questions. I still didn't know much about him, though we had been talking for several weeks, and I wanted to be more intentional.

I began with, "So, where were you born?"

"Fort Worth, Texas. We moved here when I was six."

"How old are you, by the way?"

"Twenty-seven."

"Alright. Where did you go to school?"

"For college, I went to Georgia State. Where did you go?"

"I went to the University of San Francisco. My degree is in education, but I have yet to use it!" I laughed. "Where do you work?" I continued.

"Well, my dad owns his own software company. It has become a very successful business venture." He laughed, but I wasn't sure what was funny about it.

"Software is something I know little about," I said, "though it fascinates me. How people can turn numbers into websites that are capable of buying and selling things and hosting thousands of social profiles is beyond me."

Julian changed the subject to tell me a story about a dog he found while he was on a trip in France.

" ... And so, we were walking downtown to a little-known cafe that is just *amazing*, when we noticed a puppy sitting behind some trash cans. Someone had spray-painted him orange and purple and left him there to starve. He looked so pitiful ... all skin and bones!"

"So, what did you do?"

"Well, at first we tried to catch him with our hands. But he was a slippery little devil. We must have looked ridiculous chasing him all over the alley! Finally, we came up with a plan to corner him and catch him with a box we had found. That did it. We caught him. He was terrified. We took him to a local no-kill shelter and paid to have him fixed and cleaned up. We probably paid enough to cover his food for the next ten years!" He laughed.

"Awe! You guys probably saved his life!"

Julian smiled.

I enjoyed Julian's stories. They were such a diversion from the normal, everyday things.

On the way home, I asked if Julian knew the Shepherds.

"Why do you ask?" was his reply.

"Well, you seem to be about the same age as their eldest son, Nathan. I was just wondering if you two knew each other."

"We are acquainted." Julian smiled again. "In such a small town as this, it's hard not to know everybody. How do *you* know the Shepherds?"

"I met them at church. But actually, Nathan is my neighbor."

"Oh, I see." Julian frowned.

"What is it?" I asked.

His frown suddenly vanished into more smiles. "Oh nothing! Would you like to listen to something? I have a ton of music on my phone. You are welcome to look through it."

"Sure."

"Alright! Here you go," he said, handing me his phone.

We drove on to the tunes of one of Julian's favorite bands.

But after a few minutes, Julian said, "Every lady has a favorite dessert or special treat. What's yours?"

"Oh! That's easy for me! Cookies and cream ice cream! That's my one weakness."

"Cookies and cream! That's my favorite too! It's a sign. We must stop and get some on the way home!"

I laughed. Some ice cream after our hike in the hot summer sun sounded nice.

There was no ice cream shop in town, so we had to stop at Food Mart and pick up a carton. We took it back to the shop where we had met that morning. We sat in the car and shared it while listening to music from Julian's collection. While we ate, Julian spent time looking through the music on his phone, trying to find his favorite songs to share with me. I hadn't heard most of them. He seemed to have a large variety. Everything from rap to hard rock, to soul music, to a little country. I didn't notice anything Christian yet. I wondered whether Julian *was* a Christian. The thought had come to me a few times since we had started talking, but I hadn't been brave enough to ask. This seemed like a good opportunity, so I just blurted it out.

"Julian, are you a Christian?"

He looked up in surprise. "Of course!" he said, and went back to looking at his phone.

I didn't know how to go on from there. I fumbled around with thoughts in my head, questions I could ask.

"So," I said at last. "Where do you go to church?"

"My family goes to Friendship Presbyterian."

"I haven't seen that church yet. Where is it?"

"On the south side of town. Off West Main Street."

"Have you been going there long?"

"Since I was a little kid. And you must go to Cherry Hill Baptist. Isn't that where the Shepherds go?"

"Yes. I've been going there for a few weeks."

"And how are you liking it?"

"I love it."

That seemed to be the end of the conversation. It was also the end of the ice cream, so I told Julian goodbye and headed back to Doris's to pick up Noah. I had missed Noah while we were gone. I was so used to having him with me that now that we were apart, I felt like something was missing; the feeling had nagged at me while we were hiking. I wished that Noah could have come and enjoyed the hike with us. Maybe next time.

A couple of days later, I went to visit Doris. We spent the morning picking juicy, ripe blueberries. The bushes were heavy laden with berries. A "bumper crop" year, Doris explained. And she didn't want to waste a single one. Noah was beside us in the grass, with his own tiny bucket. Occasionally, I would give him a few berries so he could enjoy their sweet taste.

"Store-bought don't compare to fresh blueberries," Doris told me. I couldn't agree more. Besides, this was way more fun than walking through the produce department at the grocery store. A lot cheaper too.

After we had filled five large and sturdy plastic buckets, we took them inside to wash and freeze. Not all of them were to be frozen though. Two buckets were to be left out for baking and snacking on. Each bucket was at least a couple of gallons. That seemed like a *lot* of blueberries.

"What do you plan to make with them?" I asked as I poured another bucketful into the colander to be washed.

"Bread, muffins, preserves, and maybe a few pies, if there's enough."

"That sounds wonderful! Do you mind if I help? I don't have much experience in the kitchen, but I would love to learn!"

"Of course, dearie! You can help me bake today, and then maybe you can come with me tomorrow when I go to deliver some of what we made."

"Who are you planning to take the baked goods to?"

"Some friends of mine," was all she said. I knew questioning her was useless. I would have to wait and see.

After we finished washing the berries and storing some away in the freezer, Doris began to pull out baking paraphernalia—large bowls, measuring cups, spoons, and all the ingredients she would need. Then she found some recipes in an ancient-looking wooden recipe box with hand-painted forget-me-nots on the front. A wedding present from her mama, she explained.

"Alright now, you start with the muffins, and I'll make the bread," she said, handing me a recipe card.

I took the card gingerly and looked at it.

"Doris, I really haven't done much baking before."

"That's alright, dear. It's a pretty simple recipe. Just go right by the directions."

I did, and before I knew it, there were two large pans of muffins baking in the oven. I smiled proudly to myself and wiped my hands on my apron. Doris slid in four loaves of blueberry bread and closed the oven door. She checked her watch and set a timer.

"The muffins'll be ready in about twenty minutes," she said. "I've set the timer for the bread."

Then we got to work making preserves. This was especially interesting to me. I had never really thought about how jams, jellies, and preserves made it into the jars on the shelf in the market stores, but now I was learning firsthand. We had to boil a mixture of mashed berries, sugar, fruit pectin, and lemon juice in a large pan. After it thickened, we removed it from the heat to let it cool. Doris already had a counter full of sterile jars and lids sitting on a clean cloth. We filled the jars to the bottom of the rim and put the lids and rims on, screwing them on loosely.

"Screw them on just until they stop. Don't screw too tightly or they'll be too hard to get off after we can them."

As I finished filling the last of the jars, Doris brought a large pot full of water to a rolling boil. There was a metal liner in the bottom of the pot. She carefully slid some of the jars down under the water with a jar lifter. After just a few minutes, she brought them out again and set them back on the clean cloth on the counter. She repeated those actions with the rest of the jars while I made Noah a peanut butter and banana sandwich.

As we sat there and Noah ate, I marveled at what all we were able to accomplish in just one morning. It was only lunchtime!

When we left about an hour later, Doris gave me a couple jars of preserves to take home and a gallon-sized baggie of fresh blueberries. I was excited to try making something on my own with the blueberries. Maybe blueberry pancakes ...

FIFTEEN

Visiting

The next morning, Noah and I went to make the rounds with Doris. She had a group of people in the area she liked to keep up with and check in on every Tuesday, and she always tried to take them something. Sometimes it was specific needs she knew about. Other times, it was homemade goodies like we were taking today. I knew nothing about these friends or where we were going. Doris hadn't said much about it, but she was thankful for my company.

We set out in Doris's old Crown Victoria. It was a large car with a smooth drive. I tried to guess how old it was. Thirty years? Maybe more? But just like everything else they owned, it was well cared for and in good shape, despite its years.

The first stop was a house that was situated on a backwoods road east of town. It was a little house that sat at the very base of a mountain, and it was nestled in among a dense thicket of trees. It was small, probably only one or two bedrooms, and it seemed like it was in need of some major renovations. The roof was old and sagging and covered with last year's leaves. The front porch was screened in with a rusted screen that was hanging down in places. There were some holes in it too. The house seemed dark and foreboding.

We got out and approached the door, Doris carrying a basket with some of the baked goods and a few other things. I was surprised to see a large Cherokee rose covered in blooms at the base of the porch near the steps, where the sun shone down through the trees. I wondered if the birds had planted it. It seemed so out of place in that otherwise dismal yard.

Doris went up to the screen door and knocked a few times before opening the door and walking in.

We walked through the screened porch and over to the door of the house. I looked around at the messy porch. There were piles of things literally covering the porch—odd things, like a hairdryer, some old plastic bowls, stacks of newspapers, and a broken microwave. Everything was old and damp and dirty and looked like it had been there for a long time. I wrinkled my nose.

Doris knocked and then opened this door too. She called out, "Amelia? Amelia! We're here!"

I cautiously followed Doris into the living room. The smell was what hit me first. It was *horrible!* I was instantly afraid that something or *someone* had died in there, but Doris confidently went forward, continuing to call out in a friendly manner.

The room was tiny and crowded. The single couch was old and stained. There was also a recliner and some small tables. The tables were piled with junk—food and other random stuff; hairbrushes, combs, dishes, containers of various liquids and substances. But the smell ... I was beginning to feel sick to my stomach. How could someone live in these conditions!?

Then Amelia came into the room. She was elderly and looked much older than Doris. She was wearing a floral button-up nightgown. Her hair was gray and unkempt, and looked as if it hadn't seen a brush in days. Her face was haggard. Her eyes were sunken into their sockets and dull.

"Hello, Amelia. I've brought some friends with me this time." Doris hugged Amelia tenderly and motioned over to Noah and me.

Amelia came over to us. Her eyes haunted me. She looked longingly at my face, and then reached out an arm to pat my shoulder, her mouth moving as if she wanted to speak. Her lips were pale and thin; her face well-worn and wrinkled. It seemed that she didn't have many teeth, and no dentures either. I felt like I should reciprocate. I should show some sign of acknowledgment, of tenderness. I should take her hand or hug her like Doris did. But I couldn't. I had never been around someone like her before. I was a coward. My feet were firmly rooted in place. After she hobbled back to Doris, I hung my head down in shame. *How could I be so insensitive!?*

Doris led her into the kitchen, which was another example of what I had seen on the porch and in the living room, only worse. I tentatively followed, one slow step at a time. In this new and unusual environment, Noah was uncertain and clung to me tightly, his eyes big and round.

Once in the kitchen, Doris took to cleaning off the table so she could set the basket down. She showed Amelia the good things inside. There were blueberry muffins, preserves, cheese, bread, and milk. There were also some cups of applesauce and a few cans of soup.

Can this lady cook soup? I wondered.

Amelia seemed grateful, in her own way, for the things Doris brought. Doris went on to show Amelia where she was putting the things in the refrigerator and in the cabinet. Oh ... the smell! It was coming from the refrigerator! I almost threw up. I had to step back into the living room and walk briskly around the room to clear my head. After a few minutes, I peeked back into the kitchen. The fridge was shut, and the smell, not quite so atrocious. Doris was busily cleaning up the kitchen. Amelia seemed to be helping, slowly and painfully. It seemed that her body must hurt. She was so stiff and immobile. But she was doing it. She was taking a thing here and there and putting it into the cabinets.

Doris had the table completely cleaned off and wiped down. She was moving to the counters. I decided it was time to do something.

"Can I help wash some dishes?" I offered.

"Please" was Doris's reply.

I was afraid to set Noah on the dirty floor, but after a better look, it didn't seem *too* bad. I looked in the cabinets for a clean pot and spoon for him to play with, and then got to work. Doris brough the dishes to me, and I washed them. We worked for over an hour. While we cleaned, Doris chatted easily to her silent friend. But after a short time, Doris helped Amelia into the armchair in the living room. She took her a muffin and a cup of tea only warmed with tap water. I guessed it was so Amelia wouldn't burn herself.

Then she got back to work. After finishing in the kitchen, we moved to the living room. We worked quietly, only talking when necessary. With us working together, we got a lot done in a short amount of time. We were unable to get to the bedroom, but Doris did clean up the single bathroom.

I was beat. While she finished up, I decided to sit on the couch and try to be comfortable. I was holding Noah again. Noah was getting more comfortable in this new environment. He wanted down. I sat him on the now clean floor, and he crawled over to Amelia. He looked up at her and put a hand gently on Amelia's knee. He patted his little hand on her knee and kept gazing up at her with a smile. It seemed like he knew that she needed some love. Amelia looked down at him and laughed, a deep cackling laugh. It was the first sound I had heard her make since we arrived. Her lips were parted in a kind of smile. She reached an old knobby hand down to pat Noah's head. He giggled. Then he scooted on the floor back over to me.

It had broken the ice for me. If Noah could make friends with this lady, so could I!

"I hope you enjoyed your muffin as much as we enjoyed making them yesterday," I said.

I didn't expect her to talk back, so I just continued.

"The bushes were so full of berries this year. I guess the evening rains we've been having have helped. They were so plump and juicy."

"I'm 'bliged." It was said in a growly voice, barely perceptible.

Her voice pierced my soul. At once, I began to see her as a person. Just like me. Her heart, the heart of a woman. Her life, invaluable. She was precious, just like a newborn baby. Just like everyone ever made in the image of God. My heart began to be filled not with pity but with compassion and empathy. I did not feel sorry for her, but I suffered with her. I began to wonder what her younger life was like, what she had been. I wondered how she came to be living in this nasty old house at the base of a mountain.

As we stood to say goodbye, I stepped forward to gently hug the sagging shoulders.

"Goodbye, Amelia. I'll see you next time."

Amelia tried to smile again and nodded her head.

After we left Amelia's, we drove down another country road.

"Doris?" I said. "Who is she? Amelia, I mean. How do you know her?"

"She's my sister."

I stared out of the window in front of me in astonishment. A million thoughts were running through my head. *How? Why?*

But I didn't have to ask.

"Adel, Amelia has had a hard life. Our father was not kind. He mistreated us girls." She looked over at me. "Do you understand what I mean?"

I thought I did. And I was horrified.

"Amelia was gentle and kind. She was the middle sister. My older sister has been gone a few years now. But Amelia took the abuse the worst of us all. She went off and got married when she was only fourteen, to a man no better than our father. But it was all she knew. She married him because he went to church, and she thought it would be a better life. He ended up being a snake handler at a local congregation."

"A what?" I asked. Were my ears betraying me?

"A snake handler. It's an old Appalachian tradition for some churches. They catch venomous snakes, usually rattlesnakes, and then they have services where they dance and chant and hold these snakes with their bare hands. Even women. They base it on some verses in Mark that say that those who believe 'shall take up serpents'[3] and that they shall not hurt them. That verse has led some preaches to believe

---

[3] Mark 16:18.

that if they 'have faith,' then the snakes won't hurt them. That if they do get bit, which they sometimes do, then God will save them. They believe that if God doesn't save them, then it was their time to go. Amelia's husband ended up being a preacher at one of those churches. Amelia has such a sensitive nature; she didn't do very well in an environment like that. Her husband, Amos, died at thirty-six to a rattlesnake bite. Her congregation told her that it was God's will. It messed her up badly, and after that, she just wasn't the same; she lost what little meaning she had in life."

Doris was able to talk about Amelia without too much emotion, but I could tell her heart was broken.

"That was their house," she continued, "and she has stayed there ever since. The land was paid for long ago. She just stays home and wastes away; she doesn't like to go out of the house. We've tried to get her to move in with us a few times over the years, but she won't. I do my best to care for her. But you saw how it is. I get her groceries every couple of weeks and clean up some whenever I'm there. But there is only so much I can do."

I didn't know what to say. My heart was utterly broken for Amelia *and* for Doris.

Doris continued, more passionately. "At one time, she was *so* beautiful and had a good brain! She had so much potential! But she just couldn't handle all that life threw at her."

I shook my head sadly.

So far, I had only seen the beautiful side of these mountains. It was hard to imagine so much pain and suffering in the midst of so much beauty.

I thought through everything Doris told me as we drove along. There was so much to think about! I felt heavy. Burdened. Was there nothing I could do to help alleviate some of the suffering for Amelia?

We pulled into another driveway—gravel too. This house was also small and unkept, and it was dark inside, just like Amelia's had been. It had brown siding that was falling off in places. The yard was overgrown. Did someone actually live here? This place was eerie. Even more eerie than Amelia's. I didn't like it at all.

"This is Tanya's house," Doris said as she turned off the engine.

As I unbuckled my seat belt, Doris stopped me.

"Wait in the car this time," she said.

I nodded and wondered what was fixing to happen.

I watched as Doris got out and knocked on the door. It took the lady a long time to answer, but Doris waited patiently. At last the door opened, but just a crack. When Tanya saw that it was Doris, she opened it more widely. Tanya was probably in her seventies, though it was kind of hard to tell. She had long, stringy gray hair. Her eyes were those of a confused child. In her arms, she was holding a baby. A baby!? No ... it wasn't a baby! She moved it awkwardly to take the bag from Doris. As she did, the baby's head moved about in an unnatural fashion. No, it wasn't a real baby; it had to be a doll! The doll was large, about the size of a six-month-old baby. It had yellow hair that was stained and ratty and half torn out. The doll's face was cracked and broken. I tried to look closer, but then I had to look away. *This is horrible!* Part of me wanted to keep my eyes averted, but it was like a train wreck; I had to see! I glanced back up, half-heartedly. Tanya now had the doll cradled in her arm. She was holding a cup to the doll's mouth, as if to make it drink. Everything inside me revolted. I had to get out of there!

How much longer!?

Doris chatted with Tanya for a few minutes more, then reached over to give Tanya a hug. Yes, she even patted the doll on the head. Then she walked back to the car.

When Doris saw the look on my face, she shook her head.

"It's alright," she said.

I wanted to know more. "Was that a doll!?" I asked, incredulously.

"Yes." She sighed.

"Why does she do that!"

"Many years ago, she had a traumatic accident. I won't go into the details; let's just say it involved her only child, a baby. She lost her wits after the accident. She now thinks on the level of a very young girl. She can care for herself a little but not much. But she always carries that baby doll with her. She calls her Abby. She cares for it in her own way, like she would a small child. She truly believes she's real."

"How can she live all alone like this?" I said, motioning back down the driveway toward the house.

"Tanya has some family that cares for her regularly. But none of them care enough to have her live with them. They just do enough to get by." Doris took a deep breath.

"Tanya and I had been school friends. I was there for her after the accident, and I just never stopped visiting her over the years. I don't do much, but I like to know that she's alright just the same."

Despite knowing these things, I still felt eerie on the inside as we pulled the car out of the drive. I felt like we were leaving an entire world back there, a world unfamiliar and strange, a world I had never come into contact with before and one I was glad to leave behind.

From there, we went over to a mobile home community called Shoal Creek.

We stopped in at several of the homes. Each one was different, but the same in that these people were poor. They lacked things that I had always taken for granted, like decent clothes, toiletries, and food. Their houses were all cleaner than Amelia's place, but they were still dirty, musty, and hot. Most of them had opened windows, but there wasn't much of a breeze.

In one home, we found a girl about my age. She had three young children and lived alone. Her home was dirty and bare. I felt for her, especially being a single mom myself—only, in such different circumstances! She seemed anxious and scattered, but she appreciated the things we brought. Her children peeked at us from behind their mama's legs. They were so small and frail. Their eyes were dull, their noses snotty, and they all had dark circles under their eyes.

As Doris chatted with the mama and asked how they were doing, I kneeled down to the level of the children.

"Hello, there," I said softly. "Do you like blueberry muffins?"

They nodded.

"That's good, because we brought you some! We also brought some other yummy things, like milk. Do you like milk?"

They nodded again.

One of the little girls stepped cautiously toward me. She came over and looked at Noah.

"This is my little boy, Noah. He likes blueberry muffins too."

It was hard for me to imagine so much poverty right beneath our noses. It was always there. I had just never noticed it before.

"Doris," I said on the car ride home. "Does the church ask you to make these rounds? To visit all these people?"

"No. I just go on my own."

"I think it's wonderful. But why? Why do you do it?"

"These are just people that God has put in my path that I feel I ought to help. There's a heap more, just in Shoal Creek, that could use a lot more help than I can offer. But I have connections to all the people we visited today; I feel like they're my special assignment. Of course, if I see a stranger in need, I try to help them too. But there's only so much of me to go around, and Ace needs me too."

She does it just because she wants to. Because she cares. And she's happy to do it! Caring for these people seems to give her energy and life. I want that. But I already feel so overwhelmed with life! I'm not sure what I have to give...

SIXTEEN

A Visit from Family

The next day, I got a phone call from my dad. They were planning to come down for a visit. I was a little surprised but not much. I figured they would come down eventually to see how I was faring. I hoped they wouldn't be disappointed—or pleased, however I chose to look at it. They would probably be happy if I seemed overwhelmed and overworked. It would give them all the more reason to try to persuade me to go back to San Francisco, "back where I belonged."

Because of these feelings, I was a little anxious about their visit. And they only gave me a day's notice! I guess they figured I wouldn't have anything going on. They were mostly right too.

The main reason for their visit was to be there for Noah's first birthday, on Friday. I hadn't planned an actual party, but I did gather together a few things to celebrate the day, like streamers and some balloons. I even bought him a cake from Food Mart that had "Winnie-the-Pooh" on the top, with a big "one" underneath it. I bought him a few little gifts too. Despite my reservations, I *was* glad to have my family there to celebrate with us.

My parents arrived late Thursday evening and were planning to stay until the following Tuesday, when my dad had to be back at work. Noah was already asleep when they pulled into the drive that night. I tried to keep him awake, to no avail. They were disappointed not to see him, but I told them they could go in his room and peek at him while he slept.

It was good to see my parents again; it had been about four months since I left. A lot had happened since then, mostly inside of me.

They looked good. Like normal.

They put their things in their room, which was Grandma's old room, and came down to have some of the canned soup I'd heated up. Dad took a piece of garlic bread and dipped it into the soup.

"The house looks pretty good," he said, looking around him. He always went straight to the point. "How's everything been going?"

I didn't want to lie, but I also didn't want them to know the struggle I'd had so far, because no matter how hard it was, it was worth it. I never wanted to go back to California. I decided to shoot for middle ground.

"It's been going alright. A lot of work, you know. But it's been good. I love it here."

My dad stopped chewing for a minute to consider what I said. Then he changed the subject. "This old place looks just like I remember it. And it's been a *long* time."

I agreed with him. It did look the same. I hadn't been able to bring myself to change anything. This was still Grandma's house to me.

My mom was unusually quiet while we ate. I wondered what was going through her mind as she sat there, politely sipping at her cup of soup.

"On Saturday, I'm planning to go horseback riding with the Shepherds. Do you remember them?" I asked Mom.

"Yes, I do. They were at Grandma's funeral."

"Well, the last time I went somewhere, Doris watched Noah for me, but I was thinking that since you guys are here, you might like to. You know, to have some one-on-one time with him?"

"We certainly would!" Mom exclaimed. "Do you mean Doris Jones?

From across the street?"

"Yes. We've gotten to know each other pretty well the last couple of months."

"They're good people. Is Ace still alive?"

"Yes, and still farming!" I laughed as I pictured Ace in his faded overalls, sitting high up on his green John Deere tractor, clearing the fields. I just *loved* him.

"Who's that man mowing the grass back there?" mom asked the following afternoon as she looked out of the kitchen window.

I walked over to see. There were rows of neatly mowed hay stretching out across the field behind the house, in lines and ridges left by the tractor.

"Oh, that's Nathan," I said. "He's cutting the hay for some friends of his."

"Nathan Shepherd?"

"Yes."

"It's hard to imagine him being grown up enough to drive a tractor!"

"He's two years older than me," I said casually.

Mom shrugged. "Oh well." She turned back to the table.

I had decorated the dining area in blue and green streamers. There was a balloon tied to Noah's high chair. And there was the beautiful cake sitting in the center of the table. Noah was sitting in his high chair, trying to grab at the streamers I'd attached to the sides of his tray.

We sang "Happy Birthday," and I helped Noah blow out his candle. He sure loved the cake! He grabbed a big handful before I could pull it away to cut him a piece, but I didn't mind. It was his cake, after all! As I stood back and watched him eat fistfuls of cake, I thought about how big he was getting and how much he had learned. I was proud of my little fella. It seemed like only yesterday that he was a newborn, closely snuggled up in my arms, and now he was sitting up and feeding himself;

he was one! *It's all going by too fast,* I thought, and a little tear slipped down my cheek.

After I helped Noah open his presents, we all sat in the living room, watching him play with his new blocks and the battery-operated riding toy my parents had driven all the way to Dawsonville to pick up for him that morning. He couldn't figure out how to turn it on yet, but he enjoyed climbing over it and putting the blocks in the compartment under the seat.

I felt some tension beginning to arise.

"Adel," my dad began. "We think it would be a good thing for you to come home. It isn't good for you to be down here all alone."

Did they really have to do this on Noah's birthday?

I shrugged. "But I'm not alone. I know Doris and Ace, and the Shepherds, and I'm getting to know some other people at church. The Shepherds have invited me to go over to their house after church on Sundays. They remember me very well."

"That's not enough, Adel," mom said. "You need more than that. You need *family.* Trying to get this old place up and running by yourself is just too much. It can't be done, Adel. It will wear you out. You are already looking thin and run-down."

"I've already started, and I'm committed to doing this. I'm not backing out now. I'm doing fine. Really. We are doing *just* fine. And we're *not* going back." I got up and walked out of the room. I went out on the front porch to get some fresh air.

I knew they were going to do this! I fumed. *I wish they would just let me grow up!*

SEVENTEEN
Trail Ride

We all met at Crestfall Equestrian Center bright and early on Saturday morning. Crestfall Equestrian was at the end of a long gravel drive that was lined with Bradford pear trees. There were pastures on either side. The grass along the driveway was short and neat, and the fence was freshly painted. As I pulled into the parking area, I was immediately impressed with what I saw. I was expecting a small barn with a pasture and a few horses. I was met with an estate of an equine facility!

The barn was modern and quite large, and the grounds were expansive. There were several smaller structures on either side of the barn, one in the shape of a circle with high wooden walls and a cover over the top. I wondered what it was for.

There were beautiful maple trees and crepe myrtles in full and glorious bloom scattered here and there over the grounds. Then there was the arena. It was large and rectangular with a sandy floor and with a white horse fence for the sides. Inside the ring were several young girls riding over poles laid out on the ground. Their instructor was calling out instructions from nearby.

It was all so immaculate and clean.

The smell of hay and horses met me as soon as I opened the car door. It was a pleasant smell.

I walked over to join the others who had gathered just outside the main entrance to the barn.

Ali looked different out here. She wore tight-fitting riding clothes instead of her typical modest sundress, and she had her hair pulled up into a low ponytail near the base of her neck.

But what was even more striking than her change in appearance was her change in demeanor. Never super relaxed or comfortable at Annie and Roberts's, here she seemed to be in her element, her zone. She seemed almost happy! She was certainly more talkative. I felt that I understood her better now, and I liked her for it.

"OK. Well, I have a couple of hours before I am needed back here, if y'all are ready to head out! Y'all know what to do," she said, addressing Jim and Rebecca. I got the impression that they came riding often.

"Peter, you can ride Alexander this time. And, Nathan, you can ride Barre None. I'll show you where their tack is. Adel, I'll be back to help you in a minute."

They all walked off to fetch their tack and horses. I took this time to meander down the wide cement aisle of the barn and take it all in. On either side were stalls. Most had a nameplate on the door with a saddle rack hanging next to it. There were small tables outside of some of the doors, with grooming supplies and other horse paraphernalia gathered on them, some in dusty piles.

It smelled so good. Like leather. Hay. Grain. Shampoo. And horses ...

I stopped to take in the whole view. There was bright sunlight coming in through the back opening of the barn, which was wide, just like the front. The sunlight made silhouettes of several horse heads that had appeared over some of the stall doors. One of them whinnied. I smiled. I walked on down the aisle and peeked into one of the stalls. Inside was a dark brown chestnut horse with a long, flowy mane and tail. She turned her head to look at me and breathed out short and soft whuffs of air in my direction. Her eyes were soft and gentle and surrounded by thick, dark lashes.

I thought she looked delicate, like a girl horse.

"Hello there, girl," I said softly. I leaned back to check the nameplate. "Stardust," I said.

Stardust lifted her head to nuzzle my hands softly. Her velvety nose was warm, and her whiskers tickled my hands.

"I'm sorry, girl. I don't have anything for you." I wished I had brought a carrot or something.

She lifted her head to look at me again with those soft chocolate eyes, and my heart completely melted.

"Oh good!" I heard Ali say as she walked up behind me. I was a little startled. I had been so engrossed in visiting with Stardust that I had not heard her approach.

"I see you've found Stardust! She's the horse you're going to be riding today."

"Really?" I said. I was so glad. I felt like Stardust and I were already well on our way to being friends.

Ali walked into the stall and clipped a lead shank to Stardust's halter.

She led her out and handed me the lead. "I'll show you to the grooming area."

I had never led a horse in my life, and to be honest, I was a little nervous. Stardust was so big. I felt dwarfed standing beside her.

"Here," Ali said, noticing my awkwardness. "Hold the lead like this, near her halter. And keep your toes away from hers."

She walked back up the aisle toward the entrance, and we followed. Near the door were several stall-like areas that had chains hanging from high up on each side of them. We walked into one and turned Stardust to face out and then clipped a chain on either side of her halter. Then Ali produced a grooming bucket.

"Here, use this curry comb all over her body." She handed me a small, oval, rubber comb with tiny rubber teeth all over it. "Like this." She showed me how to move the comb in firm, circular motions.

After the curry comb, we used smooth, soft brushes to sweep across the hair and brush it flat.

"Go in the direction the hair lays—that's right." Ali then took another brush and quickly went through her mane and tale. She handed me a small, soft brush. "Move slowly on her face. Horses can sometimes startle when you're working with their head."

I stepped over to brush the short hair on her delicate head and muzzle. Her nose was a little concave before it came back out at the nostrils. Her face seemed the delicate face of a fairy-tale horse.

"What kind of horse is she?" I asked.

"Arabian. And probably the most gentle Arabian you'll ever see. Arabians are known for being flighty and easily spooked, but not old Stardust." She patted her firmly on the shoulder. "She's as dead broke as they come. She's the one we use for children and beginners. You'll be just fine with her."

Ali took a small tool and used it to clean out Stardust's hooves. I was impressed with how easily Stardust lifted her feet for this task. It was as if she knew exactly what to do.

Ali disappeared and came back with a saddle and saddle pad. She expertly placed the pad over Stardust's withers and slid it in place down her back. Then she gently laid the saddle on top of it. She reached under Stardust's belly and grabbed a strap and fastened it to the saddle on the side that she was standing on. "This is the girth," she explained. "It keeps the saddle firmly in place. And these are the stirrups." She slid the stirrups down their straps so that they hung down on either side of the saddle. She adjusted their length and then went to find the bridle. I watched as she smoothly slid the halter over Stardust's ears and off her head and replaced it with the leather bridle. Once the thin neck and chin straps were secured, she handed me the reins and said, "Walk on out into the yard. Rebecca's out there. She'll help you get settled while I get my horse tacked up."

Rebecca and the others were already in the yard. Nathan and Peter were in their saddles and riding off in the direction of a small field behind the barn.

Rebecca handed her reins to Jim and came over to me.

"Hi! How's it going?"

"Great!"

"Isn't Stardust a sweetie?"

"She is! She's just wonderful!"

"You've never been riding before, correct?"

"That's right."

"Come on, then. Let's head to the round pen. That will be a good place to get you started, since the ring is occupied."

I followed her over to the circular building I had noticed when we arrived.

Once my eyes adjusted to the low light inside, Rebecca showed me how to tighten the girth and mount. Stardust was not a big horse, but I still felt high up. Her movements were slow and steady, and soon I was getting used to the rhythm of her gait.

"Alright, when you want to turn, gently press with your outside leg and pull ever so gently with the reins on the side you are wanting to go. Yes, like that. You're doing great!"

Stardust was an intelligent horse. It seemed that she knew I was a beginner, so she was working with me, anticipating my clumsy cues. She was quick to respond, and soon I felt like we were beginning to work together as a team. It was exhilarating!

We worked on starting and stopping and making turns. Rebecca seemed to think I was catching on quickly. She had me try trotting in both directions. Stardust's trot was slow and easy, but it was still a little hard to get used to.

We stopped to have a water break and then meet back up with Jim.

Ali was leading a stunning bay gelding out of the barn. His tack was polished and clean, his mane neatly trimmed. He was the largest horse I had ever seen! Rebecca told me he was over sixteen hands. I wasn't really sure what that meant.

Nathan and Peter had returned from the field behind the barn.

Rebecca and Jim mounted their horses, and then we were ready to head out on the trail.

As we rode along, we formed a single file, with Jim in the front and Ali bringing up the rear. We followed Jim down a lane of grass that ran beside the pasture behind the barn. The sky overhead was bright and clear and sunny. The warm sun felt good on my face and the back of my neck.

In this wide-open space, the wind caught the horses' manes and tails and blew them gracefully about. The rhythmic clip-clop of the horse's hooves on the rocky soil and the gentle sway of the saddle were delightful to me. It was soothing to my soul.

We followed the lane to the end of the pasture and entered into a wooded trail. The trail was wide, probably kept clean with a tractor. The woods around us were in full summer regalia. The rain forest–like canopy overhead was a shield from the sun, except for tiny beams of bright light that escaped through gaps in the branches. These beams soared down and lit up the forest in a magical array of light. They rested gracefully over the ferns, buckeye, mountain laurels, and azaleas.

Occasionally, I caught the sweet aroma of honeysuckle—it was sweeter than any perfume.

Birds of various colors and sizes were abundant in the underbrush. I wished I knew what kind of birds they were. I recognized a cardinal, with his bright red coat standing out against the glossy green leaves of a mountain laurel. In one place, the birds were feasting on the berries of a small tree and hopping from one branch to another as they teased, scolded, or serenaded one another.

Chirrup chirrup, chirp chirp chirp. Chirrup chirrup, chirp chirp chirp.

"Those little birds with the yellow backs, what are they?" I said to Rebecca, who was riding not far behind me. She didn't answer. I looked back and saw that she was talking to Ali.

"Those are goldfinches," answered Nathan.

"Oh, OK. I saw three or four of them hanging out together back there. They're so pretty."

"Probably siblings learning how to fly."

"Oh, OK. Sticking together. I didn't realize birds did that sort of thing."

"Some do."

We rode on in silence for a while.

As we rode through an area with fewer trees and more sunlight, Nathan, who was riding in front of me, pointed out some wild blueberry bushes.

"Are they good to eat?" I asked.

"Yep. But they aren't as big or as sweet as the ones you've got."

"*I* have blueberry bushes?"

"You've got some between the barn and the hay field. About ten or fifteen bushes. They used to produce a lot of berries. They should be ripe now."

"Wow, I didn't even know that! I'm going to have to check that out when I get home!" I was excited at the idea of picking my own fruit. But it reminded me of Grandpa and his orchards. My face fell. Those orchards were my orchards now, only they were overwhelming to me, and I had no idea where to start. For some reason, the thought of just a few blueberry bushes seemed so much more doable.

So far, the horses had not been bothered by the birds or the terrain. They were hot on this midsummer day. Their necks were lathery with sweat, and it seemed like they were solely focused on taking the next step in front of them.

As we rode along, I was usually closest to Rebecca, who had taken it upon herself to keep up with me and make sure I was doing alright. Occasionally she would ask how things were going. I was completely enjoying myself! I had no idea riding horses could be so much fun. Or that from atop a horse, I could experience the world around me from an entirely new perspective. I saw things differently from up here. It was a new angle on a hiking trail, a better view of the mountains. I could ride forever! It would never get old!

As we ascended a woody knoll, I began to hear the music of a mountain stream. When we reached the top, we could see it down below on the other side. The small stream was bubbling down and over the rocks and fallen trees in its path.

As we began to go down the other side, I noticed a narrow ravine to the left. We had to go slowly, carefully, and keep as far to the right as we could to cross this part of the trail safely. All was going well, when suddenly Peter's horse, Alexander, began to twist and turn. He pawed a hoof high in the air. He snorted and stomped his feet. The horse had his ears pinned back against his head. "Whoa ... whoa, boy!" Peter soothed.

Alexander suddenly kicked out at Barre None, who was behind him. Thankfully, everyone had tried to back up a little to give Alexander space, and the kick was not successful. But then Alexander began to move backward, away from the trail! It was all happening so quickly!

"Whoa! Whoa, Alex!!" Ali shouted. "Kick him, Peter! Move him forward!"

But there was no moving Alex forward.

"A bee!" yelled Rebecca. "A bee on his shoulder! Slap it! Get it off of him!"

But it was too late.

Alex had gone too far and was now sliding backward into the ravine! As he slid down, his body twisted and turned so that when his feet hit bottom, he was parallel to the sides of the ravine. Peter was thankfully still on his back. But now all we could see were Peter's shoulders and head.

"Still! Still, boy!" Ali was saying calmly but firmly. She had dismounted and handed her reins to Nathan, who had also dismounted. The other horses were snorting and stamping their feet, their eyes wide and their nostrils flaring. All but Stardust. Stardust was standing calm and still with her head low and the reins slack in my hands. Her ears pricked in the direction of Peter and Alex.

Ali moved quickly to the edge of the ravine. She squatted down to have a better look. Jim and Nathan joined her. Alex was near panic at being stuck in the ravine. His large brown eyes were wide with terror. He snorted and whinnied. He tried to wiggle, but it was no use. The ravine was so narrow at this point that the horse's sides were touching on both the left and right. Peter's legs were trapped between the horse and the wall of dirt on either side. And he was stuck.

"Ow! My legs! I can't get them out!" he said, pain and desperation showing on his face.

"OK, Peter, listen to me!" Ali commanded. "Be still. We're going to get you out!" She looked around. I could tell that her mind was working a million miles a minute. What was she going to do?

Just then, Alex reared. Somehow the force of the upward movement released the tension on Peter's legs. Ali was quick to grab hold of Peter and pull him over to the bank before Alex had time to land. Nathan hurried to get a hold of Alex's reins. He kept the horse from bolting forward. By this time, Rebecca and I were both on the ground, standing as close as we safely could, our attention entirely focused on what was before us. Peter was lying on the ground beside Ali. She was looking him over and feeling his legs. His face was white and sweaty. He looked incredibly shaken.

Nathan and Jim were working with Alex. They were inspecting the bank and trying to figure out how they were going to get him out of the ravine.

I suddenly had an idea. I hopped back up on Stardust and rode quickly down the trail.

"Adel?" Rebecca called after me.

"I'm OK! I need to see something!"

When I got near the bottom of the hill, I climbed off Stardust's back and walked her through the woods to the left. If I had guessed right, the ravine would dead end into the creek. *Yes! It does! And the creek is shallow!* It would be possible for Alex to walk out through the water and step up onto the bank with no trouble at all. I quickly walked back through the woods to the trail, climbed up on Stardust, and trotted back to the group on the hill.

"Guys! The ravine dead ends into the creek down there! Alex can walk out. It's shallow!"

Nathan and Jim were both holding the reins now, with some effort because Alex was being incredibly difficult. Nathan looked up at me quickly, then down toward the creek. He said something to Jim that I couldn't hear. Jim quickly ran off along the side of the ravine toward the creek. He was looking down inside the ravine as he went. At one point, I saw him jump down into the ravine. What on earth? But then I saw what he was doing. He was moving fallen logs out of the way so Alex could make it through. By this time, Nathan had Alex slowly moving forward. I followed them. Nathan had a tedious task before him. The horse kept wanting to bolt forward, and Nathan had to keep him back with the reins above the horse's head. It was painfully awkward. Slowly they moved along, until at last they met Jim at the opening to the creek. Jim took the reins from Nathan, who was now exhausted. Nathan stumbled over to the creek, sat down beside it, and splashed cold water onto his face and hands.

Jim began to lead Alex back over to the trail.

I wondered whether Peter was OK. But before I turned to ride back up the hill, I turned to Nathan. "Are you alright?" I asked.

He nodded a tired and frazzled nod, and I went back up to join the others.

Apparently, Peter *was* injured, but thankfully it didn't seem that he had any broken bones. He couldn't stand though, and Ali and Rebecca were trying to decide how to get him back to the barn. We were a long way out.

Alex was a hot mess, and it seemed that he also had injuries—some cuts and small gashes on his sides, haunches, and legs. It was hard to determine just how severe his injuries were. There was no way Peter could ride him back. He didn't want to anyway.

"He can ride Stardust," I offered.

Everyone looked at me. The thought hadn't occurred to anyone.

By this time, Nathan had joined us back at the top of the hill, where Peter sat near the scene of the incident.

"Who would you ride? Not Alex," said Ali.

"I can take Alex." It was Jim speaking. "I'll lead him back. He and Abbot typically get along alright."

"OK," said Ali, still thinking.

"She can ride back with me," Nathan said. "Barre None is pretty gentle."

"OK, that's fine!" said Ali. And then to Peter, "Let's get you up on that horse and see how you do."

I hopped down and handed my reins to Rebecca, who was going to hold Stardust while Jim and Ali helped Peter get on. I felt so sorry for Peter. He was in a lot of pain. But somehow, he managed to sit without stirrups, in a way that was semi-comfortable. He held one of Stardust's reins and a large clump of her mane for support. Rebecca was to hold the other rein from atop her mount, so that Peter didn't have to worry about driving right now. It was going to be enough effort just to stay on the horse's back!

Jim and Ali returned to their horses, Jim taking Alex with him.

Nathan climbed back onto Barre None and reached his hand down to me. I slid my foot into the empty stirrup and swung up to sit behind his saddle. At first, I felt a little awkward. No saddle, no stirrups. And Barre None was *so* wide. How was I supposed to stay on? This was a whole new experience for me. As he urged his horse forward, Nathan said, "You're probably going to want to hold on."

I immediately knew why. As the horse swung forward, I nearly lost my balance and slid right off the other side! I grabbed at the saddle and then frantically wrapped my arms around Nathan's waist. Nathan pulled Barre None to a stop. I repositioned myself back on top of the horse and then held on tightly to Nathan as we moved forward again.

Our ride back was pretty quiet. No one really felt like talking. We were hot and tired and thirsty. We had been in the woods way longer than we had anticipated. The barn was a thankful sight to us all as we came around the last wooded bend and entered the grassy lane. The home stretch. We were almost there.

"It was nice of you to offer Stardust for Peter," Nathan said as we slowly swayed back and forth, back and forth across the sunny lane.

"He definitely needed her," I said.

"Yes. He's pretty beat-up."

"Do you think he broke anything? I know Ali doesn't think so, but he's in so much pain."

"It's hard to tell. We're going to have to take him straight to the clinic to get checked out. Rebecca and Jim are going to need to head back to their kids, so I'm going to take him. Would you mind helping Ali get the horses cleaned up and their tack put away?"

"I'd be glad to!"

"Alright. Thank you, Adel."

He turned his head a little so that I could hear him better. I could see the side of his face more clearly now. He was clean-shaven, and his dark hair was recently trimmed. For the first time, I was keenly aware of how handsome he was. His jaw was clean cut. His skin was smooth and tan, and his hair framed his face attractively.

"This was a traumatic first riding experience," he said softly. "I hope it doesn't ruin horses for you. Things like this don't always happen."

It was strange. Despite what had happened, I was in no way inclined to think ill of horses. Despite the accident, I had enjoyed myself tremendously.

"No," I said. "On the contrary, I would love to go riding again very soon."

EIGHTEEN

Sunday

I heard an update on Peter from Rebecca later that day. Thankfully, he didn't have any broken bones, but he did suffer from muscle and tissue damage and some major bruising. He was going to be out of commission for a couple of weeks. I knew that would be hard for him, busy as he always was with some project, scheme, or new idea.

Peter lived in town, not far from Rebecca. She was planning to pick him up after church on Sunday to bring him to their parents' house. She said his spirits needed it.

The Shepherds had the mind-set of the more the merrier. They were pleased that my parents were in town, and they generously asked that they join me in going to their house after church.

My mom knew Annie well. They were close in age and had gone to the same schools. The day was spent talking of old times and my mom asking, "What ever happened to the ..." and "What is so-and-so up to these days?" My mom and I had never talked about Sweet Valley Farm or Cherry Hill or about any of these people. It surprised me to see how interested she was. I didn't know she cared.

I sat with them, listening with interest. Dad had gone into the living room with some of the men. Peter, who was now in decent spirits despite being confined to the couch, seemed especially interested in talking to my father.

Annie pulled out several old photo albums and a box of yearbooks to show Mom some pictures of her old friends and stomping ground.

I enjoyed listening to them talk and hearing some of the stories that connected my mom to this place I had grown to love.

Sunday night, I got a call from Julian. He wanted to know if I would go to the Fourth of July celebration with him the following week. I told him that I was already planning to go with Rebecca and her family. He seemed to think they wouldn't mind if he came too, but I didn't feel comfortable inviting him to join us. Even though we had gone out once and had been talking on the phone regularly, I still felt like I hardly knew him. And actually, I was looking forward to spending that time with Rebecca and her sweet family. He acted a little overly sad about it, but I didn't give in; I had already given her my word, so I agreed to go with him another day the following week.

Doris and Ace had been absent from church that Sunday. They were rarely absent from church, so I called Doris that night to check on them. She said Ace hadn't felt well that morning, and they stayed home so he could rest. She said he was already doing much better, so come Monday, my parents, Noah, and I went to see them and take them some barbeque. Mom enjoyed getting to see and talk with Doris. Apparently, Mom looked up to Doris. That surprised me. Doris was very different from my mom in so many ways, but Mom seemed more relaxed and talkative with her than she ever was with me—and more than she had been all week, even when she had been at the Shepherds'. She even asked questions about Grandma in her last months. I didn't know she cared about any of that. She asked all about the farm. Why didn't she ask me? She also talked to Ace about his farm. She wasn't just being polite; she genuinely wanted to know.

All week, I'd been carrying a heavy burden regarding my mom. I had the feeling that there had been ill feelings between Mom and Grandma, but no one ever talked about it. It was only a guess. Thinking of my mom over the years and how distant she always was with Grandma made me wonder. Especially now after seeing her with Doris. I began to wonder if under all that callousness, Mom really did have a heart. Maybe she really *did* care. It was so good to see that side of her.

It was later that evening after Noah was in bed and while Mom and I were sitting quietly in the living room sipping tea that I decided to bring it up. I didn't feel like beating around the bush. "Mom," I said. "What happened between you and Grandma?"

"What do you mean, dear?" she replied, her tone tense.

"I'm not sure really. It just seems to me that maybe you two were not on good terms."

"Did someone tell you that?" she snapped.

"No. I just wondered on my own. You two never talked. You didn't really want me coming here ... not even when I was a kid!"

Mom stood up, suddenly flustered and angry.

"Adel, there are things in life that you just don't understand." She was treating me like a child again. "But you have *no right* to accuse me of anything!"

"I didn't accuse you. I just wondered."

"Your grandma!" She turned away from me. "Adel, these are things that I just don't want to talk about. Do you understand?"

"No, I don't. I feel like I have a right to know! She was my grandma, and *you* are my mother."

She was silent for a moment.

"Please, I just want to know."

She looked around the room, as if memories were coming back to haunt her. I saw tears glistening in her eyes and on her cheeks. She shook her head. "No. I'm sorry, Adel. But I can't." Then, with sagging shoulders, she turned away and went quietly up the stairs to her room.

They left early the next morning. Mom was still bothered by my questions the night before, I could tell. It made me sad. I knew something was weighing heavily upon her, and there seemed to be nothing I could do about it. She had shut me out. Actually, she had never let me in.

They were sad to leave Noah. They had treasured their time with him—more than they had treasured their time with me, it seemed.

I was sad to see them go but not because I would miss them. I was sad because I wouldn't.

Doris invited me to continue going with her on her Tuesday visits. I agreed to go, though my stomach still knotted up whenever I thought of Tanya and her doll.

That day, the plan was for me to help Doris clean up Amelia's nasty bedroom.

Amelia seemed to recognize me when we walked in, and she patted Noah on the back with a withered hand. The skin on her hand looked so loose.

"Doris," I said, when we were alone with Noah in the bedroom. "Do you think Amelia is getting enough to drink? Her skin looks like she may be dehydrated."

Doris paid close attention the next time she was near to Amelia. Then she told me that she agreed. We found a large cup with a lid. I went searching for a straw. At last I found a pack, in the back of one of the cabinets. I placed the straws in a large plastic cup and set it on the counter so Amelia could reach them easily. We set some clean cups on the counter. Then we filled her cup with water and ice and picked out a straw.

"Amelia!" said Doris. "Look what I have! I think it would be a good idea for you to drink more water, OK? I filled you up a cup full, with a straw. See? You need to drink at least a few of these every day. OK? One in the morning, one after lunch, and then fill it up again. Adel put some straws on the counter so you can reach them better. And we set some clean cups up there too."

Amelia seemed to understand. She took the cup and shuffled into the living room to sit in her easy chair.

"Good catch, Adel," Doris whispered as we got back to work in the bedroom.

There were stacks of newspapers as tall as me along one side of the bedroom. Stacks and stacks of them.

"Why are there so many newspapers?" I whispered.

"Amelia had to go without for so much of her life that she took to keeping things. Anything and everything. Even these old newspapers. She used to have a lot more than that! But about ten years ago, they caught fire and nearly burned the house down. Ace was stopping by to visit about the time it happened. He helped put it out before it got too far out of hand. But she still wouldn't let us get rid of the newspapers, even after that. Well, we did sneak some off," she whispered with a smile.

After Amelia's, I knew we would be heading to Tanya's house. I wasn't sure I was ready for that. Even though I didn't have to get out, it was still revolting to me to see Tanya with her doll. I didn't want to be a coward, but there was just something so creepy about it all.

I grimaced as we pulled into her driveway.

"I know it's hard. It takes time to get used to," said Doris kindly. "But Tanya needs love as much as the loveliest lady in the world."

Her words weighed heavily on me as I sat there in the car and watched. I wondered if Doris treated all people as kindly as she did Tanya. Actually, I knew she did. She didn't have preference for people. She treated them all the same, as I imagine the Savior did while he walked the earth.

NINETEEN

Fourth of July

"We're going to do something fun today, Noah!" I said.

It was the afternoon of July Fourth, and in the evening, there was going to be a parade down Main Street followed by fireworks at the park outside of town.

I love the Fourth of July! It's one of my favorite holidays. I love getting to celebrate our wonderful country and its heritage, but I also love the *way* we celebrate, especially in the town of Cherry Hill. The Fourth of July was one of my favorite days each summer as a child, because Grandma and Grandpa always took me to the parade and festival and then to the fireworks afterward. It was nearly the same every year, which was comforting to me, and it was always a day filled with fun!

The whole town would be decorated in red, white, and blue. The stores would all have their doors open wide and would be giving away free samples and goodies to those who passed by. There were patriotic hats, buttons, whistles, little notebooks and pencils, candy, and little American flags—anything that could possibly delight a child, complete with face painting and balloons.

Then there was the bandstand set up in the town square. They would have everything from patriotic country songs to brass bands playing the "Battle Hymn of the Republic." And of course, at some point during the evening, a lady would come on stage to sing "The Star-Spangled Banner." Everyone would stand and put their hands over their hearts while she sang, and at the end, everyone would yell and cheer and throw their hats high into the air. It was good old-fashioned fun, and I was looking forward to it immensely.

I planned to meet up with Rebecca and her family at five thirty. That would give us time to walk through town before the parade started.

I was delighted to see that my childhood memories had not failed me. The lampposts along the main drag were decorated in spiral red, white, and blue just like I remembered, and hanging across Main Street was a large banner that read "God Bless America." *Where else in the country would you see a banner like that?* I smiled to myself.

The town was abuzz with the gaiety of the day. Children were eating ice-cream cones and cotton candy, and their mothers and fathers were enjoying corn dogs and funnel cakes. The music was already playing. The air was filled with it. The mood was nostalgic. It had its effect. I began to miss the days of my childhood and my grandparents something terrible. They had always looked forward to this day as much as I did. I wished they could be there to enjoy it with me again as an adult. With Noah ...

"Adel! Adel! Over here!"

It was Rebecca! She was standing beside the steps to the courthouse where we planned to meet. She had Moses in the stroller. He and Randall were licking Ring Pops, and Maggie Ann had a blue stain all over her mouth. I guessed she must have finished hers already.

"Hey, guys!" I called as I walked up, pushing Noah in the stroller. "This is great!" I said to Rebecca. "Are you guys having fun?"

"Uh-huh! And we are fixing to go ride the ponies!" said an excited Maggie Ann.

"I'm too big to ride the ponies," declared Randall.

"I don't think you are, Randall, if you would like to," his mama replied.

"I'll just see." Randall was cautious. I knew he needed to check things out before he committed to the idea.

Just then, Jim and Nathan walked up. I didn't realize Nathan would be there. For an instant, I felt self-conscious. I wondered if I'd looked in the mirror before I left. Did my hair look OK? I couldn't remember.

Jim was holding Allie on his shoulders. She also had a Ring Pop, and a daddy-sized patriotic baseball cap on top of her head. Her light brown hair was pulled up in pigtails. She looked so cute sitting up there on her daddy's shoulders, eating that Ring Pop. But then my smile faded. In that moment, a longing deep inside me replaced my joy. I looked down at Noah. I yearned for him to have what Allie had, a daddy to hold him—but I wouldn't let that thought ruin my day! I looked up at Allie and gave her a big grin. "Are you enjoying that Ring Pop?" I asked her.

"Uh-huh!" She returned the grin.

After letting the kids ride the ponies, we wandered together downtown, looking into various shops, the kids collecting as many freebies as they could hold in their little patriotic gift baggies. *Not much has changed.* I sighed as we strolled along. *It's amazing how some places seem to get stuck in time.* But it felt like a good time to get stuck in.

As we sauntered along, I suddenly heard my name being called out.

"Adel! Hey, Adel!" It was Julian. He was walking with a couple of guys about his age, and they were coming our way.

"Hey, hey!" he said to me as they joined our group. He acknowledged the others with a nod.

"Hello, Julian," said Rebecca, but she didn't seem very excited to see him.

"Yes, hello, Julian," said Nathan. "Nice shoes."

I looked down at Julian's feet. Yes, they were the same too-large shoes from our hike the week before. I shook my head in bewilderment.

"What are the odds of running into you here?" he said to me, completely ignoring Nathan.

I thought it was a strange thing to say, considering I had told him only last week that I would be here.

They walked with us awkwardly for a few minutes, Julian and his friends talking, Rebecca and her family talking, and neither group really interacting with the other. I felt like the odd man in the middle, and it was making me incredibly uncomfortable.

Julian and his friends held a hushed conversation between themselves before Julian said, "We're about to go get some barbecue. Do you want to join us?" The question was directed at me.

I looked over at the others, pleading for help. But no, I could be strong! "Actually," I said, "we're waiting for the parade. It's supposed to start soon."

He seemed pouty but only for a moment. He was quickly back to his sunshiny self. "Alright! Maybe we'll see you around!" And they walked off in the direction of the food court.

Rebecca didn't wait long after they walked away before leaning close to me and asking quietly, "How do you know Julian?" I noticed that both Nathan and Jim had stopped talking to listen to my answer.

"We met at a restaurant in town right after I moved here. We've happened to run into each other a few times since then. We went out once, last week. But I don't really know him," I quickly added.

"Oh, OK." was all she said.

I glanced over at her. I glanced at the others. I noticed that Nathan looked at me for a moment longer than the rest. I wondered what he was thinking. When I caught his eye, he looked away.

"How do *you* know him?" I asked Rebecca quietly.

"We had mutual friends when we were growing up. He was always at the ballpark and hanging around downtown."

"Do you know him well?" I prodded.

"Well, it's been a while since I've really been around him ..." she answered slowly. "But when we were kids, he was a little odd ... not a bad kid, just well, unusual."

"Conceited and annoying," added Nathan.

"He may be just fine now!" continued Rebecca quickly. "Like I said, it's been a while!"

Then we heard the marching band's music coming from down the street. It was time for the parade! All the people hurried to line the streets and get out of the road. The children filed to the front near the edge of the street in hopes of getting some candy, and the parents stayed close behind them. Following the marching band was the fire truck. Noah and Allie didn't care for the fire truck; its loud siren was more than they could stand. Moses was good with it though. He was one of the most chill babies I had ever seen. Overall, the children *loved* the parade. Even Noah got excited when he saw the horses! He squealed and pointed to them with his chubby little arm.

"Oh no ..." moaned Rebecca when she saw the horses. "I think I've had enough of horses for one week!"

I laughed at her. I knew she couldn't mean it. I knew she loved to ride. But maybe having a brother seriously injured from one had given her a new perspective.

After the parade was over and the children had collected all the candy they could eat, we moved down to Subway. There was an incredibly long line that began outside of the building, but that's where we had decided to pick up our food for the picnic at the park. While we were standing there, in the crowd of hungry people, we chatted some about casual things.

"Are your parents coming tonight?" I asked Nathan, who was standing the closest to me.

"Yes, we're picking up subs for them too."

"Oh good! Are we going down to the baseball fields like we used to when we were little?"

"Yep!" He smiled as if his memories of the ball fields on the Fourth of July were as warm as mine.

After we received our food, we made our way down the street to the fields. Blankets already covered the dark green grass, but thankfully we found a spot near the back fence, in the second field we came to. We spread out our blanket, sat down, and began to eat.

The evening was beginning to fall all around us. The summer heat was lifting, and the night was crouching in. It wouldn't be long before the fireworks began.

This was my absolute *favorite* time—lying on the blanket in the grass with a full belly, listening to the music filter down from town to the ball fields. It was the perfect background music for what we were doing, and it was far enough away that we could still talk. I loved watching all the children run and play barefoot in the grass, waiting for the fireworks to begin, their glow-in-the-dark bracelets swirling.

I turned over on my stomach and rested my head in my hands. I gazed peacefully out into the field of waiting people. Noah climbed lazily over my back.

Ali came and joined us; it looked like she had probably just come from work. She was still in her riding clothes. We all sat together for a while. Nathan, Rebecca, and Ali chatted easily while I lay there and daydreamed.

A little time passed. Jim was playing Frisbee with the older children. Moses was in Rebecca's lap. She was still sitting with Nathan, Ali, Noah, and me on the large picnic blanket spread out on center field.

"Look at this! It's almost like we've stepped back in time fifteen years!" Annie said as she came walking up with Marie and Robert, who was carrying a red and white Igloo cooler. "I remember you all sitting there just like that when you were little! Minus the babies of course. Aw!" She came and sat down on the blanket while she made a face that showed that this moment was more than a little bittersweet.

"Do you remember how we used to catch literally *hundreds* of lightning bugs?" Rebecca asked me.

"Yes, and Grandma always brought some jars to keep them in! I would keep mine on my nightstand when I got home. I remember lying there in bed, watching one glow, and then another and then another. First thing in the morning, I'd take them outside and let them go. One time I forgot to, and they all died."

"We had that happen at our house recently," Rebecca said with a laugh.

Rebecca glanced over at Nathan, who had leaned back on his hands and was listening quietly.

"Nathan remembers!" she said. "He was the one who found the jar on Randy's floor!"

"Yeah. He'd probably caught a couple dozen. He was a little upset about that."

"He's such a tender heart," his mama said affectionately.

We quietly watched Jim and the children play Frisbee for a few minutes. Then I sighed. "I love the Fourth of July. It's probably my favorite holiday, besides Christmas."

"Yeah," sighed Rebecca, "me too."

"You guys are too sentimental," said Ali abruptly.

Nathan laughed. He had such a nice laugh.

That's when we heard the first explosion, far up in the sky. Noah took to my shirt as fast as lightning, his face buried in my lap.

The glitter and light of the first display was spectacular. The bright streaks lit up the night all around and blended in with the distant stars.

The two eldest Blackmore children squealed and ran to the blanket and plopped down beside us, big grins on their faces.

"Mama! I want my balloon!" said a breathless Maggie Ann.

Rebecca untied her red balloon from the stroller handle and handed it to Maggie Ann.

"I wanna give another little girl my balloon!" she said. "A little girl who doesn't have one!"

"OK, that's fine. What about that little girl over there?" said her mama.

"No! Not here! A little girl somewhere else! Who won't get to see the fireworks!"

"You're wanting to let it go?" her daddy asked.

"Uh-huh!" She nodded vigorously.

"That's fine," said Rebecca softly. "That's a sweet thought, honey. Go ahead."

Maggie Ann took one last long look at her balloon and then let it go while she exclaimed, "Happy Fourth of the Lie!"

We all smiled. Kids don't come much cuter than Maggie Ann.

"Alright, everybody!" said Annie, opening up the cooler. "Time for watermelon!" She started handing out slices of drippy red watermelon, starting with the children. The juice ran down their faces.

Everyone was mostly silent while we ate and watched the show.

For being a country town, they sure didn't skimp on the fireworks. The show lasted a solid hour, and the grand finale was exactly what a grand finale ought to be.

When the show was over at last, and all the people began to rush away to their homes and cars, we all just stayed on our blanket. The children were sleepily lying around in the laps of whoever would hold them, and the night was peaceful.

"No need to rush off when we'd just be sitting in traffic for half an hour. Might as well spend it here!" said Annie.

I couldn't agree more. I took this time to flip over onto my back, with one arm under my head, and rested a nearly asleep Noah up on my tummy. I looked up at the clear night sky above me. Heat lightning occasionally lit up the sky, making a silhouette of the mountains before it. The stars were so bright and dense, though not as clear as on the farm. I swore I could see the Milky Way swirling above and all around us. My hand came down and brushed the grass beside the blanket. It was wet with dew, and it smelled so sweet ...

Nathan poked me a little with his elbow. "Hey now, no falling asleep!" He smiled. "There's *no way* we could carry you *and* all of them back to the cars." He motioned to all the sleepy children.

I sat up groggily. "You're right," I said. "I was almost out!"

As we finally worked our way back toward the parking lot, the lights of the cars stuck in traffic mingled with the sounds of distant fireworks and the coolness of the night. I pushed a sleeping Noah in his stroller. I was tired and happy. It had been a good day.

TWENTY

Apples

The night for my next date with Julian arrived. I dropped Noah off at Doris's house and walked back across the street to wait for Julian on the front porch swing.

I was feeling kind of tired. Noah's poor sleeping habits had kept me up more than usual the night before. The swaying of the swing made me want to go to sleep. I stood up and stretched my arms up above my head and took some deep breaths. I looked at my phone. It was only four thirty. Julian wouldn't be there for another ten or fifteen minutes. It was then that I remembered the blueberries Nathan had told me about while on the trail ride. I decided to walk over to the barn and check them out. As I came around the back corner of the barn, I saw them. I didn't know how I had missed them before, except that I must have thought they were bushes like some of the other bushes in the yard. I hadn't gone close enough to them to see what they actually were. Nathan was right; there were maybe ten or fifteen large bushes, and they were covered in juicy berries.

I remember this! I remember picking berries! Grandma used to have a small

152

metal tin under the cabinet in the kitchen that she used for picking berries. I bet it's still there! I quickly ran inside to see. I had forgotten that I was wearing nice clothes.

After a little looking, I did find the bucket, and I hurried back outside to pick some before Julian arrived. I was just about to reach the barn when I heard, "Hey! What's your hurry?"

"Oh!" I was startled. "I didn't see you there, Julian!"

"So I noticed!" He laughed.

"I was just going to pick a few blueberries before you got here. But that can wait. Come on, let's go."

I was reluctant to set the bucket on the porch as we passed by it on the way to Julian's car. *I guess the blueberries will just have to wait until tomorrow.*

"So, what do you spend your free time doing?" I asked Julian as we drove along the highway toward Dawsonville.

"God of War," he said.

"What?"

"It's a video game."

"Oh, OK."

"Do you ever play?"

"No."

"I'll have to show you sometime."

"So is your house in town?" I asked.

"I actually live with my parents right now, to save money. They have a finished apartment in their basement."

"Oh, OK. That's a good way to save money. Are you planning to buy a house?"

"Sure. Someday."

We rode on in awkward silence for a while.

"So, you work for your father's company?" I asked, trying to think of something to say.

"Well, not exactly. Not right now anyway."

"Oh, I thought you said—"

"I *did* work for him," he interrupted. "But recently we had some disagreements about my job description, and he decided it was best for me to take a break from software for a while."

"Oh. I see. So, what are you doing now?" I asked.

"Job hunting, I guess!" He said it with a laugh.

"What is it you would like to do?"

"Well, what I would love is to find a way to not *have* to work. Not traditionally anyway. I know some guys who do it. They play video games for a living. They have these massive followings online who watch them play games, and they get sponsored for it. It's incredible!"

"Sounds like it," I said, completely unimpressed.

The date was mostly pleasant. Julian paid me a lot of attention, opening the door for me and assisting me with the chair at the restaurant, but I couldn't help feeling like his attentions were a little forced, a little put on. That feeling was balanced out by his good humor and lively spirits, and overall, it was a decent evening.

The next afternoon, I was sitting in Doris's living room, helping her fold clothes while Noah played with some old piano books that he had found in the piano bench. There was a lull in our conversation, and I looked up and noticed the pictures of the children hanging on the walls.

"Doris, are those your children?" I asked, pointing to the pictures.

She smiled. "Yes, those are my babies."

"Where are they now?"

"Well, Thomas is a lawyer in Gainesville. He's married and has two grown daughters. And Jennifer is living in South Dakota with her husband and five children, who are mostly grown now too."

"And that one," she said, pointing to the bottom picture, "is my Amy. We lost her a long time ago." She smiled sadly. I thought I saw tears in her eyes.

"Oh, I didn't realize ..."

"Oh, it's alright! It was long ago."

"Do you mind my asking what happened?"

"Not at all." She dabbed at her eyes with a tissue she had grabbed from the box on the bookshelf. "She was eight years old. We had gone down to a waterfall to play in the shoals at the bottom. People did that back then. She climbed up a little too far and slipped on a rock. She hit her head. She was my youngest. The baby. Those were hard days."

"I'm so sorry," I said. It sounded pathetic, but I didn't know what else to say. I had never been close to anyone who had lost a child before, and I didn't know what to do.

I noticed Noah playing down on the floor, his chubby little arms and legs working so hard to move him over the carpet. His eyes were bright and intent on the old piano books. He patted them with his hands and slid them across the floor.

I wondered what it would be like to lose a child—heart-wrenching. My eyes grew teary too.

Peter was feeling a little better the following Sunday, and though he still stayed home from church, Rebecca again picked him up and brought him to their parents' house afterward.

While we were sitting around the table, eating hamburgers and bratwurst with all the fixings, Annie started asking me questions about Sweet Valley.

"So, what are your plans for the farm?" she asked.

"Well, I'm not really sure yet. I'm still trying to get used to everything. I guess I would like to get it running again, but I'm not really sure how to make that happen. I have a lot to learn." I took a deep breath then continued. "And I don't have a very long time to figure it out before I would need to sell. I only have so much money to hold me over."

"Ah. I see. I wondered about that. Have you thought about loans? Have you noticed what the trees look like now? This week? Are there very many apples?"

"Yes, there seems to be a lot of apples."

"Do they look healthy?"

"Well ... I don't really know. I don't know what I'm looking for. I have a couple of books that I found on the shelves at the house, and I've been reading through them, but I haven't learned very much yet."

"Well, if you're going to harvest anything this summer, you are going to need to learn fast. It's almost time to be harvesting the summer varieties. And I know Alan and Elaine usually had a good crop of summer apples. Hmm ..." She thought for a minute.

"I could help," chimed in Peter.

"You're not really in a good place to do that right now," replied his mom. "She's going to need someone who can show her. Walk around the farm and point things out, like what equipment to use, you know."

"I can! I can help! I'll show you." He stood up from his chair at the table and walked slowly over to the counter and back. He did seem to be walking better. His gait was a little smoother than last week, and he didn't seem to be in as much pain.

"Well ..." said Annie. "Let's give it a few days. See how you're doing come Wednesday or Thursday. That'll also give me time to reach out to a few friends who might also be willing to help."

"You don't have to do that," I said. "That's a lot of extra work for you guys!"

"We're glad to help," they both said at the same time.

That must be a family phrase, I thought.

As we finished up our meal, I wondered why Nathan hadn't offered to help. Peter said he had also worked at the farm during high school, and *he* wasn't struggling to walk. Maybe it was because he thought of me as incapable—a city girl. Maybe he didn't want to encourage something I would eventually fail at. I decided it was probably best that he didn't help after all.

When Thursday rolled around, Peter was at the house, and Noah was in the sling. We were walking through the tall grass in the orchards, and he was telling me about the quality of the apples that were on the trees that year. Because the trees hadn't been tended to in a while, the apples were not high quality. They had spots.

"They're still good apples," he said, "just not produce quality. You won't be able to sell to the farm stands or the grocery stores. But the factories will be interested in them for making applesauce, apple butter, juice, and for baking ingredients."

"Oh, OK." I picked an apple and looked at it closely. It was a good-sized apple, though it was a little hard. And it was covered in small brown spots.

"They're not quite ripe. You have about two weeks, so the end of July or first of August. Do you have any ideas about how to get them harvested?"

"Not at all." I sighed. "I guess I could hire some people to come pick them. Are there agencies for things like that?"

Peter laughed. "No, not really. But I know some guys who would appreciate the extra money. How much would you pay?"

We chatted a little about the going rates of orchard work. Peter seemed so knowledgeable about the business. I guess that's what happens when you grow up in the heart of apple country.

After we decided on a good price, Peter said he would let his friends know. He told me that he would help too. He would help me keep an eye on the apples to know what day to start picking, and he would help with harvesting too, if he had recovered enough by then.

"Are you sure you're going to be up for all that?" I asked.

"Sure! I'm already much better. And by then, I should be as good as new." He smiled a bright and contagious sort of smile, and we walked on.

We had to check the orchard barns to see if we had the equipment we needed for harvesting—crates for the apples, ladders, clean buckets, and things like that. We had most of what we needed, though I would have a lot of cleaning to do between now and then. Everything was old and dusty. The barn for storing the newly picked apples was dirty too. It would all need to be clean and shining before we could harvest.

"You should also probably get the orchard mowed; it would be hard to pick in tall grass like we were walking through today. I bet Nathan would help you with that, if he's not too busy right now. He has an awesome tractor. And he also knows how to use all of these." Peter motioned to the several large tractors that were housed in the barn.

"Alright," I said as we started walking back toward the house. I didn't really want to ask Nathan for help, but I guess I had no choice. I didn't know how to run a tractor, and Peter hadn't offered.

I walked over to Nathan's house later that day, while my nerve was still up. The summer sun was high in the sky, though it was after six o'clock. The walk along the trail was so peaceful, and it smelled good too.

Noah was happily snuggled up in my front carrier, his little arms tucked in against my chest. He seemed sleepy already, though it was still over an hour until his bedtime.

"Don't go to sleep yet, little guy." I reached up and picked a leaf off of a branch above. "Here, look at this!" I said enthusiastically. "It's a leaf!"

Noah took the leaf and held it gently in his hand.

"Ahh ... this is so nice," I said, admiring the trail. "Now we are just going to have to find where the creek went!"

I wondered where the path to the creek was. I knew it was there. I had so many memories of afternoons spent alone down by the creek as a child. As we walked, I tried to keep an eye out for it but with no luck.

At last we arrived at the opening to the meadow. In front of us was Nathan's house. To the left was the shop, or garage, or whatever it was, and behind them both was a field. In front and along the driveway was the forest. I walked in the direction of the front porch. As we went under a large deciduous tree, I noticed little brown pieces of shell scattered over the ground. I reached down to pick one up. It was the shell of a nut. I looked around again and found a whole nut lying on the ground. It had several small black holes in it. It seemed lighter than a nut ought to be. I shook it—no sound.

Hmmm ... I wonder what kind of nuts these are.

We went on to the house and knocked on the door. No answer. I knocked again and waited a few minutes more. Still no answer.

"I guess he's not home, Noah." I was disappointed. "Oh well ... let's go back."

As we walked back across the yard toward the trail, I heard the faint sound of music coming from the workshop.

"Oh! So that's where he is. Come on!"

We walked over to the shop and knocked on the solid metal door. *Still* no answer.

"He must not hear us, but I hate to just barge in on him unannounced."

I stood there a moment, debating what to do. I really didn't want to have to come back again tomorrow, so I cracked the door open just a little and peeked inside.

So, it is a workshop, I mused.

Inside were several large benches with unstained cabinet doors resting on them. There were other benches housing saws and other machines I didn't recognize. There were cabinets covered in different kinds of tools.

For woodworking, I guess.

Nathan was learning over one of the benches with an electric sander in his hand. He was sanding the back side of a cabinet door. There was classical music playing loudly over a speaker in the corner. Between the music and the sander, there was no way he would hear us. Just then, he turned the sander off and stood up to examine his work. I took this opportunity to open the door a little wider. He noticed.

He was definitely surprised when he saw us standing there in the doorway, but he didn't seem upset. He took off his work gloves, left them on the bench, and dusted off his arms and pants. He walked over to turn the music down, and then he ran his hand through his hair as he slowly walked toward us.

"This is a surprise," he said, with a warm smile. "What can I do for you?"

Suddenly I felt a little nervous.

"Well, I ... um ... Peter came over earlier today and was helping me decide what to do about harvesting apples in a couple of weeks. He said you might be able to cut the orchard grass? If you're not too busy? It's almost up to my shoulders ... and I still haven't learned how to operate a tractor ... yet."

"Sure."

"OK ... great! Um ... thanks. Thank you." Why on earth did I feel so flustered?

"I'll have to do it a little at a time over the next week or so, in the evenings. Would that be alright?"

"Sure! That'd be just fine. Are you sure you have time?" I looked around his workshop. "You seem really busy."

"I am. But I don't mind at all." He smiled again. "I'll make time."

"Alright! Thanks again. Well ... I'm going to head back now," and I turned for the door. "Oh, wait!" I said, turning back. "I was wondering what kind of trees those are, growing near the house? The ones with the nuts?"

"They're pecan trees."

"Oh, OK. I saw them on the way to your house, and I was curious what they were ... I just wondered. Well, I have some growing in my yard too, and I wondered if that's what they were." I shrugged. "Well, goodbye!"

"See you later."

Once back out in the evening light, I felt more at ease. I kicked myself for stumbling over my words. I had felt so confident marching through the woods to his house, yet his presence made me feel shy and uncomfortable.

Nathan was true to his word. Several nights that week, he came and worked in the orchard. He usually came while we were eating dinner and was gone by the time Noah was asleep. It was a lot of work. The grass was tall and thick, but his tractor mowed it effortlessly—up and down, up and down the alleys in between the rows of apple trees. When the job was finally finished, it looked so good—clean and fresh and well taken care of. I was thankful. And it would make it so much easier to harvest the apples. It smelled heavenly outside too. I enjoyed the smell of the fresh cut grass while I sat on the porch swing and rocked. I had been doing that often, after Noah was finally asleep. I would slip out for just a few minutes and rock, with the porch light on but surrounded by the night. It was a good time for me to think, to reflect on the day or make plans for tomorrow. As I sat there, I often heard cows bellowing in the neighboring fields. I wondered if it was their dinnertime.

During the days that week, I spent my time washing all the crates and buckets and other equipment we were going to need to begin harvesting. Peter had been very specific with how I would need to clean everything and what cleaners I would need to use.

I also had to clean out the barn. It took a lot of soap and hot water and lots of elbow grease. It was hard work—made harder, I think, by the fact that I still wasn't getting much sleep at night. Each evening, I was ready for bed shortly after Noah went to sleep, and I was so tired that it was extra hard for me to tend to Noah during the night when he woke up.

Peter stopped by a few times over those last two weeks of July to check on the apples. Finally, by the first of August, the apples were ready! The variety to be harvested first was Detroit Red. We had an entire twenty-acre field full. Annie and I had worked hard to find a company that would buy the apples. They were going to use them for making cider, and they had given us a decent price, enough to help me order the fertilizers, sprays, and other things I would need for the coming year.

It was on a Friday that we got started. I was dressed in shorts and a tank top, and I didn't forget the sunscreen this time. Doris had agreed to watch Noah during the day while we were harvesting. She watched him a few times earlier in the week when I had needed to finish up some cleaning. After all that cleaning, my body was sore. Very sore. I wasn't used to that kind of work, especially for so many days in a row. But the work was just beginning. We had over two months' worth ahead of us, first with this field and then the other three fields as the varieties in each began to ripen.

Despite my discomfort, a thrill of excitement went up my spine as I crossed the yard and headed for the apple barns. Things were actually happening! I had gone from not knowing where to begin, less than a month ago, to harvesting apples for a deal with a legitimate company.

It was exciting!

Peter was right; he was much better when the time came, and after work, he would come help his friends and me with the harvesting. We worked all day Friday and Saturday, rested on Sunday, and then were at it again on Monday. By Monday morning, we were met by a drizzle of rain. It was the effect of a hurricane down off the Gulf of Mexico. We had been keeping an eye on it, hoping that it would stay on its predicted path, which would take it up the East Coast and not bring too much rain to our area. But things didn't go as we had hoped. The hurricane ended up traveling north through the panhandle of Florida and straight on up into Georgia. It was headed straight for *us*. That could mean torrential downpours and lots of wind, for a solid couple of days, at least.

The rain was light enough Monday for us to be able to continue picking. I was afraid that Tuesday would be too wet for us to work. The hurricane had now been downgraded to a tropical storm, thankfully, but Peter warned me that it could still cause some damage, especially to the apples.

Tuesday, it rained the entire day with a humid, drenching rain. I would occasionally go out on the porch and look out over the orchards with my arms crossed over my chest. I was beginning to get a little anxious.

Wednesday, it poured all morning, and during the afternoon, there was some strong wind but nothing terrible. The hurricane was a little to the west of us now and almost past. By evening, the rain had calmed to a mist again.

Good! I said to myself. *We made it out alright! Another day or two, and we should be back to picking!*

The air seemed especially stuffy as I got ready for bed, so I turned the air-conditioning down and went on to sleep.

TWENTY-ONE
Tornado

I woke in the night to the sound of banging—loud banging. It was coming from downstairs. I was instantly on alert and afraid. I checked my phone. It was eleven forty-five. I grabbed my robe and went cautiously to the top of the stairs where I could see the front door. Someone was knocking!

"Adel! Adel! It's Nathan! Wake up!"

I rushed downstairs and jerked the door open.

"What is it!?"

"A tornado." He seemed out of breath, as if he'd been running. "It's headed this way ... I figured you wouldn't know ... it being so late."

I stepped out on the porch to have a look at the sky, but it was so dark I couldn't see much more than an orange glow towards the West. But I could feel it. There was unusually high humidity for the middle of the night. And the air was eerily still. It was still misting. Nathan joined me on the edge of the porch.

"Hopefully it'll amount to nothing. It usually does. But better to know so you're ready in case it does get bad."

"Yes." I was beginning to feel a little uneasy. "Thank you for coming to tell me."

"I didn't have your number or I would have called. I already talked to Ace."

"How'd you find out?"

"After watching the sky this evening, I felt like I needed to stay up and keep an eye on things for a while. I was in my shop working on a project and listening to the radio. A few minutes ago, they said there was a tornado about to touch ground northeast of Ellijay and that it was headed this way."

"Oh!" I looked out again. As I watched, the trees started to sway in some gusty wind. The temperature seemed to be falling quickly. Within a minute, it began to pick up, the wind growing stronger and stronger.

"Uh-oh!" Nathan said, leaning out a little for a better look.

"What is it?" I asked in alarm.

"Nothing. I just should have hurried back. I think I may have waited too long."

"It's OK!" I told him. "You're welcome to hang out here until it passes." I was actually thankful to have another adult to brave the storm with.

We stayed on the porch for a few minutes longer, keeping an eye on the sky. The wind was beginning to tear through the trees around the house, twisting and bending their branches violently. Soon it began to hail, large nickel- and dime-sized hail. We were just about to go inside when a giant limb fell from one of the oak trees in the yard. It fell to the ground near the porch with a crash.

"We better head in!" Nathan said as he opened the door for me. "Go grab Noah and some blankets! Do you have a flashlight?"

"No, not that I know of. Just my phone!"

"OK. Then grab that too. Do you mind if I look through the cabinets in the kitchen for some food and water bottles?"

"No, go ahead!"

My stomach was in a knot as I quickly followed Nathan's directions and met him back in the kitchen. Noah wiggled for a minute when I scooped him up, but settled again and was now sleeping peacefully in my arms.

Nathan had found a grocery bag and filled it with things from the kitchen. By this time, we were beginning to hear a thunderous roar outside, as if we had a train right there in the yard! I was afraid. I held Noah tightly to my chest. He was still asleep. The house began to feel like chaos. I didn't know what to do. I looked around wildly. I wanted to hide somewhere. I was trying to figure out where to go when Nathan motioned for me to follow him and quickly led the way to the cellar door.

"Let's go!" he said, shining a lantern on the steps so I could see. I hadn't noticed his lantern.

At the bottom of the steps, he pulled the light string, and we found places to sit. It wasn't a comfortable place to be, but it definitely felt safer than up in the house.

There was nothing else to do but wait it out. The roaring sound wasn't as intense in the cellar as it had been upstairs. The air was cooler, too, but musty.

Noah continued to sleep in my arms. I felt impatient. I wanted it to be over already!

We didn't talk much while we sat there. We were both listening hard for sounds of what might be taking place up above.

My mind was running through everything that had happened so far, when I suddenly felt like saying, "Thank you. For coming, I mean."

"It's alright," Nathan replied. It was said more to comfort me than as a response to my thanks.

"Uh-oh ..." It was Nathan again, his eyes on the stairwell.

We heard wind rushing at the door to the stairs. It sounded like debris was hitting up against the door. *Somehow wind is getting into the house!* I felt a rush of fear sweep over me, chilling me to the bone.

Nathan grabbed my arm and quickly led me farther away from the steps and to the far corner of the cellar. We stood there motionless, listening, waiting. Then we heard it. A tremendous crash that radiated all the way down the frame of the house and to the cellar floor. It shook our very bones. I let out a little scream and clenched my eyes shut. When I opened them, I saw that the lights were out. Nathan had turned his lantern on. Then the door to the cellar was torn off, and the room became filled with violently swirling air and debris. Nathan stepped in front of me, and we both crouched to the floor. He hurried to slide some boxes in front of us. Nathan wrapped his arms around Noah and me so that, between us, Noah was sheltered.

There was some terrible lightning and thunder. I couldn't believe this was happening! I could hardly wrap my mind around it. All I could do was keep my head down, hold Noah tight in my arms, and pray. First in my head, then I began to pray out loud. "Lord, please make it stop. Please make this go away. I know that you are with us and that you will not forsake us ..." My voice faltered as another loud crash came from above.

Nathan continued, his voice calm and reassuring, "God is our refuge and strength, an ever-present help in trouble. Therefore we will not fear, though the earth give way and the mountains fall into the heart of the sea, though its waters roar and foam and the mountains quake with their surging. There is a river whose streams make glad the city of God, the holy place where the Most High dwells. God is within her, she will not fall: God will help her at break of day. Nations are in uproar, kingdoms fall; he lifts his voice, the earth melts. The Lord Almighty is with us: the God of Jacob is our fortress: Come and see what the Lord has done, the desolations he has brought on the earth. He makes wars cease to the ends of the earth. He breaks the bow and shatters the spear; he burns the shields with fire. He says, "Be still, and know that I am God; I will be exalted among the nations, I will be exalted in the earth." The Lord Almighty is with us; the God of Jacob is our fortress."[4]

Though the storm was still raging around me, I suddenly felt comforted deep in my soul. A wave of peace washed over me. Yes, our God was with us.

And our God was a *fortress*.

The whole thing happened in less than half an hour. As the noise and the wind began to die down, we relaxed a little. Nathan released

---

[4] Psalm 46:1–11.

his grip around us, and I relaxed my grip on Noah. I hadn't paid close attention to Noah this last little while, and when Nathan moved away from us to sit on a box close by, he smiled and said, "Look, he's still asleep!" And to my astonishment, he was! Noah had slept through the entire storm!

Nathan looked a little disheveled, and I can only imagine what I must have looked like. But it didn't matter. We were *alive*.

The wind was gone now, but we hung out in the cellar a little while longer. It was then that I was thankful for the supplies Nathan had gathered in the kitchen. We both ate a little and had some water from the bottles Nathan found in the cabinets.

My hand started shaking as I tried to drink from the bottle, and water spilled down onto Noah's blanket. I couldn't help but laugh. The release of the nervous tension that had built to extremes within me over the last hour. Nathan laughed a little too, but then he grew sober again. He looked thoughtful. Despite being disheveled, he still looked rather attractive, sitting there in the semi-dark. I looked down at the floor. *Now, of all times ... to be thinking like that!?* I scolded myself.

"I should probably go up first to see how bad it is," he said, after a minute.

I didn't want to be left alone in the dark cellar with only my phone for a light, but I knew there was wisdom in his words, so I nodded.

Nathan started moving things around to make a path back to and up the stairs.

He was gone for what felt like forever. Noah woke while he was gone. I nursed him, and he fell back to sleep. I was so incredibly thankful that no one was hurt.

At last I heard Nathan's footsteps on the stairs, and I saw the light from his lantern reflecting on the walls. I went to meet him.

"Well?" I asked anxiously.

"It's pretty bad."

My heart sank. "Really bad?"

"Yes."

"Oh." I said. I didn't know what to do. I just stood there on the bottom step, staring up at Nathan. Then quietly I said, "Can I see?"

Nathan considered that for a moment. At last he answered, "I think so. We'll just have to be careful. Are you sure you want to?"

"Yes."

"OK." He brushed a tired arm across his eyes, and led the way back up the stairs.

There were papers and magazines and other small things littered all over the hall at the top of the stairs. The door was hanging awkwardly on one of its hinges. It didn't feel like the same house!

We walked into the living room. The windows were broken. Glass was everywhere. Most of the furniture had been moved around and pushed up against the walls. The whole room was in disarray. I had to push broken decor and debris out of the way with my feet. My heart ached to see Grandma's things in such a state.

"The rest of downstairs isn't too bad. The worst is upstairs."

The worst? Isn't this bad enough?

I followed him up the stairs, pushing more stuff out of the way with our feet as we went.

At the top of the stairs. I saw my room. *Not too bad*, I thought. But then Nathan led me to Noah's room, which was above the living room. I stopped in the doorway and gasped. The whole room was *completely* demolished. It looked like a tree, or maybe several trees, had fallen through the roof and completely smashed the room. *The crash we heard ... Noah's room ...* At that moment, things began to get fuzzy, and I suddenly felt very cold. But I just stood there, stock still and motionless.

What on earth is happening? Is this real? Is this just some sort of ridiculous dream?

"Adel?"

I couldn't respond.

Nathan came over and put his arms around me and held me for a while. I laid my head down on his shoulder. It wasn't until I felt the wetness on his plaid cotton shirt that I realized I was crying. I wiped my eyes and looked around the room again. I needed to get away.

"I'm alright," I told him as I wiped a hand across my eyes and started for the stairs.

He led me back into the hall and down the stairs with one arm securely behind my back. I was glad he was there. He took us to the kitchen and sat me on the floor. Then he went and found some blankets and wrapped them tightly around us. I was shaking violently now.

"Are you alright?" he asked gently.

"Yes," I said, but I was beginning to feel extremely fatigued. "Are *you* alright?" I asked through chattering teeth.

"I'm fine," he said. Then he disappeared for a while. When he came back, he told me that Noah and I were going to be spending the night with the Joneses. He also said something about taking pictures of the damage and checking on the utilities, but I didn't understand what he was saying. I was getting *so* tired.

"What will you need?" he asked me.

"Just some diapers and wipes for Noah." I grimaced. "But they are in his *room* ..."

"Do you have a diaper bag somewhere?"

"Yes! In my room. In the closet. It should have some diapers and wipes in it."

Then he was gone again.

When he walked back into the kitchen holding the diaper bag, he found me in tears again.

"If you hadn't come, Noah ..." I broke into a sob.

"Shh. None of that." He reached down to put an arm around me again. "Noah is fine. So are *you*. Praise God for that." He tightened his grip around my shoulder for emphasis.

I nodded and tried to stop crying. But it was hard. Way harder than normal.

Nathan sat with me while we waited for Doris and Ace, neither of us saying any more.

It wasn't long before they arrived. Upon seeing the state of the house, they still somehow managed to appear calm and under control.

I heard Nathan talking to them in a low voice, and I saw Ace reach over and put his hand on Nathan's shoulder in concern. I heard something about "Noah's room ... symptoms of shock," and then he handed Doris the diaper bag. Both men helped me to the car. I was feeling so weak. Soon we were in the car, headed back across the street, leaving Nathan standing in the driveway looking after us.

Doris and Ace took good care of us.

We were settled into their warm guest bed almost as soon as we arrived. I was still shaking, but the warmth of the bed helped. Doris piled on the blankets. Noah and I were to sleep together. I wanted him close. I couldn't believe that he was *still* sleeping. *He hasn't slept this well since we got here!* I mused. *I wonder if it's because I've been holding him?*

I lay in the bed and heard the car drive back out of the driveway. Doris came in to bring me some tea. The scent of lavender filled the air.

"Where is Ace going?" I asked. I thought it was strange that he was heading back out in the middle of the night.

"He's going back over to help Nathan make sure there's no electrical issues with the house. Don't want a fire on top of a tornado!"

"Oh." It was then that I remembered leaving Nathan standing alone in the driveway at the farm. I was thankful Ace was going back.

My head was feeling so fuzzy.

Doris smiled at me. "Now drink some tea and get on to sleep. No more worrying about anything tonight."

TWENTY-TWO
Aftermath

The next morning, Ace came in while Doris, Noah, and I were sitting at the table having a late breakfast. I would like to say that I felt much better that morning, but I didn't. I felt *awful*. My head ached, and I was stiff all over. Thankfully, I wasn't shaking anymore.

I was *so thankful* for the warm bed that night and the good breakfast waiting for me in the morning. I hated to think where we would have been or what we would be doing if I hadn't come to know Doris, Ace, and the Shepherds so well.

When Ace joined us at the table, he seemed tired. He had been up much of the night.

"Nathan wasn't doing too good after we finished up last night," he was saying. "I took him home and told him to go to bed."

"Is he alright?" I asked, worry creasing my brow.

"I suspect so. I think things were just catching up to him. He'll be alright after gettin' some rest."

Nathan had seemed so calm and so strong. It was hard for me to imagine him not being able to handle what had happened.

"We looked things over best we could in the dark. Found some wires hissin' and sparkin' upstairs. Had to shut the power off. We pulled tarps over some holes in the room upstairs. Just to make do. We'll do it right this mornin'. Isn't much we can do with the tree still in there, though. We're gonna to have a full day today. Gotta get fueled up!" He piled his plate high with the pancakes Doris had made.

"You're gonna have to call your insurance company later on," he said to me, through a bite of pancake. "Nathan got some pictures last night. Should be enough."

We were getting close to finishing up with breakfast when Nathan appeared at the side door, which entered into the kitchen. He knocked.

"Come on in!" hollered Ace.

"I figured you'd be over sometime this morning, so I saved you some pancakes."

"Thank you, Doris," he said, but instead of sitting down, he looked over at me. I felt that he was assessing whether or not he thought I was OK. But then he asked, "How're you doing?"

I felt bashful under his gaze and looked down at my plate. "A little stiff. But OK. How're you?" I asked.

"Fine." He pulled out a chair, and Doris got him a plate. Nathan and Ace chatted some about what they had found and worked on last night and what the plan was for today. I listened quietly. It sounded like we needed a tree company to remove the tree from the house. I also needed to report the disaster to my insurance company. Then we needed to get to work lining up contractors and cleaning up the mess.

How on *earth* would we ever get that mess cleaned up? It seemed an insurmountable task!

"Was there any more damage in the area?" Nathan asked. "I saw that a tree fell on your carport by the barn," he said, addressing Ace. "Looks like your work truck is in bad shape."

I didn't even know that had happened! Doris and Ace hadn't mentioned it.

Ace nodded. "Besides that and some other minor damage, mainly to the shingles on the roof, we're alright. Escaped the worst of it. I drove down the road this morning to check out the rest of the houses. One or two seem to be pretty bad off. I stopped to check on everyone; no one was hurt."

"Thank the Lord," said Doris as she poured Nathan some more coffee.

Doris went on to tell us that our road was not the only one in the area that had been hit by the tornado. Apparently, it was more widespread. The Red Cross had been called in, and they were setting up a shelter in town for those who needed it. They would also be assisting with clean-up supplies and moral support.

"Did you have any damage?" I asked Nathan, as I leaned over to wipe syrup off Noah's chin.

"Not really. Just a couple downed trees and some limbs scattered over the yard. None near the house or shop, thankfully."

Nathan and Ace continued to talk a little while longer, and from time to time, I knew Nathan's eyes were on me. But I couldn't meet them. I still felt a little numb and wasn't sure I could handle any demands of my attention. After a few minutes, I took Noah from his booster seat and went into the living room. I let Noah play with the basket of toys on the floor while I lay down on the couch to rest.

After a few minutes, Doris came to join me. She sat on the couch opposite me with a book and began to read. I knew she was giving the men some time to finish their meal before cleaning up the kitchen.

Noah was happily playing with the old red barn and the tiny plastic animals that he had found in the basket. Occasionally. he would crawl over to me with some new animal he had found. "Gaa ... gaa ..." he would say, as he held the tiny animal up for me to see.

"Sheep. That's a sheep." I smiled. He scooted back across the floor toward the barn.

Eventually, Nathan and Ace joined us in the living room. I sat up to make more room on the couch, but Nathan sat down by Doris, and Ace didn't seem disposed to sit.

"I'm gonna go take a shower," Ace said to Doris. "I'm gonna have to head back across the street in a little while to get started."

"I'll ride back over with you when you go," said Nathan.

Ace nodded.

Doris stood up and put away her book. "Ace, would you mind helping me in the kitchen for a bit first?"

He looked a little indignant and didn't say anything, but he followed her out of the room.

"I'll help too, Doris," I said, and I started to stand, but she hollered back, "No, no, I think we can manage! You stay in there and rest."

For a moment we sat in silence, occupied by our own thoughts. What Ace said at the table earlier left me wanting to see for myself how Nathan really was. I glanced up a couple of times. He was sitting on the couch, with his feet propped up on the coffee table, watching Noah play. He did look tired, weary even. Like me, he was still wearing the same clothes from last night, which were wrinkled and creased from sleeping in them. His hair was a little tousled. But other than that, I could tell nothing.

"Nathan, Ace was a little concerned about you last night. Are you alright?"

He didn't answer right away, but I knew that sometimes it took him a minute to think through what he wanted to say.

"Well, I didn't get much sleep," he said at last. "I had some wild dreams ... but other than that, I'm fine." He tried to smile a little, as if to prove the truth of what he said.

Then I earnestly began, "I'm not sure how I can thank you enough—I don't have words—I don't know how you even thought to come warn us! But I'm so *very* thankful that you did ..."

He nodded, but seemed intent on watching Noah play on the floor.

"I owe you Noah's life, and possibly my own too! I spend half my nights in his rocking chair—"

His eyes came up to meet mine. He held my gaze for a moment. *What is he trying to say?* I couldn't tell. He never expressed those thoughts with words, other than to finally say, "You owe me nothing."

I sat back on the couch and took a deep breath. I was beginning to feel fatigue sweep over me again.

"I think I'm going to go put Noah down for his nap," I said.

"You should probably take one too."

"I will. After I call the insurance company. Do you have those pictures Ace was telling me about?"

"Yes. Can I have your number? I'll send them to you."

I gave him my number, and he sat there for a few minutes, focusing on his phone. I just sat there and watched him.

"There. All sent."

"Thanks."

I stood and went to clean up the toys Noah had been playing with. Nathan sat there, deep in thought. He seemed so serious and quiet. His silence never bothered me though.

"I hope you take some time to rest today too," I said quietly.

He slowly nodded.

I picked up Noah and started for the door. Nathan, rising up from the couch, met us on our way. He took one of my hands in both of his and pressed it for a minute, though he wouldn't meet my eye. Then he gave Noah a gentle pat on the back and headed out of the room, and I was left feeling incredibly blessed to have found such a good friend.

I did take a nap after getting Noah down and reporting the claim to the insurance company. When I awoke, it was well into the afternoon. I heard voices down the hall. I splashed my face with cold water and then followed the sound of the voices.

In the kitchen, I found a slew of people: Doris and Ace, Annie and Robert, Jim, Peter, Nathan, and several men I had never seen. They were all sitting or standing around the kitchen, some with coffee cups in their hands.

"We'll have it out by tomorrow afternoon," one of the men was saying. "Soon as we finish up at the Morris place, we can get started, probably midmorning tomorrow."

When Doris and Annie saw me standing near the door, they came over, their faces tense and fatigued. Annie hugged me tightly. "I'm so sorry, Adel. Good thing you both are safe. Safe and sound." She smiled a tight, forced kind of smile.

I nodded. I still felt groggy. I noticed that Nathan's eyes were on me, and he seemed tense too.

Doris walked away and came back with a cup of coffee for me.

"Thank you, Doris. I needed this." I tried to smile and lifted the cup to my lips.

"These fellows here are some friends of ours," she said. "They own a tree company, and are going to get the tree off the house tomorrow, if that's OK with you."

I nodded.

"They have to finish up another more pressing matter first—another house that was hit ..." She paused and looked at Annie, pain in her eyes.

Annie shrugged. "She's a grown woman. She can handle it," she said sadly.

Doris continued, "A house two roads over from here was hit pretty bad. A large tree fell. It was a family from church ... the Morrises ..." She paused again.

I tried to think who the Morrises were—then I remembered. It was a young husband and wife. They had a little boy in Allie's class, whose name was Felix.

"Their house was small. A tree fell on their bedroom. Felix was sleeping with them ..." Her eyes were now filled with tears. So were Annie's. I guessed the rest. My heart began to ache in a new way—a more *profound* way.

"None of them made it," Doris said with resolve, as she dabbed at her eyes with a tissue she had been holding. "Only the dog."

I suddenly felt sick. Horribly, horribly sick. I needed some water— ice water. That would help. I hurried through the crowd and over to the fridge and filled a glass with some ice and water and then went back to join Doris and Annie. "Would either of you like some?" I asked.

"No, thank you."

"Let's go sit in the living room," Doris offered.

I knew my face was evidence of the torment I felt.

We had been so close. Yet *we* had lived. *We* had made it. Why hadn't they? To think that the young life, only just begun, had ended so soon ... and the tiny little boy, Allie's age. My emotions had been through a lot over the last fifteen hours, and this was just too much. I had to find a box of Kleenex, quickly. Annie appreciated it too. She'd known the

Morrises well. Rebecca and the mother, Alissa, had been friends since they arrived in town a few years back. They were both pregnant at the same time, and had spent a lot of time together with their babies in the church nursery.

Our hearts were broken, and there was nothing we could do. Not really. We could send flowers to the families. We could help find a home for the dog. But there was nothing we could really do to help. It was too late.

"So, they are working on removing the tree now," Doris was saying to me. I was trying my best to listen, but it was hard.

"They hope to be finished by tomorrow morning. Then they'll start on your place by midmorning."

I nodded again, but it was hard for me to think about that at the moment. My heart was too full—too full of pain and sadness and confusion.

The tree was removed the following day, as planned. By the afternoon, it was time to start on the cleanup. Ace, Jim, Rebecca, Nathan, Peter, Robert, and Annie were all there to help me. A few of the guys I had hired to pick apples also showed up. Doris and Marie agreed to be official babysitters over at Doris's place.

In an effort to be prepared for the job ahead of us, we all wore long pants and gloves and closed-toed shoes. Some worked outside, cleaning up limbs and other debris. Others worked inside, sweeping up glass and trash that had littered the living room, hall, and the cellar floor. Noah's room had been roped off with orange tape due to being a safety hazard. The roof and attic above were smashed, and the floor was in terrible shape.

I was busy working in the living room with Rebecca and wondering at the things I found as I swept and scrubbed. Most everything was ruined, except for a few random things that were somehow miraculously untouched. Like a glass vase still setting on the bookshelf with a white fabric carnation in it. Or the one picture of Grandma and Grandpa at their wedding that still hung on the wall when all the other pictures had fallen and been smashed. It was going to be a ton of work. I wondered how we would ever get it all cleaned up. But I was *so* very thankful that I didn't have to do it alone.

Around lunchtime, Red Cross volunteers came by and brought supplies, food, and bottles of water. We were thankful for the reprieve. We sat on the porch and ate and rested a while. As we were finishing up, a miraculous thing happened: a convoy of trucks came rumbling up the driveway toward the house ... men from church! There were many I didn't even recognize! Apparently, those who had escaped the worst of the damage were out working to help those hit the hardest. They had formed several teams and set out in the direction of three different houses—mine, a house in town that had been hit hard, and the Morris place.

I couldn't believe it. It was hard to wrap my mind around. But I was *incredibly* thankful.

After lunch, several men who had experience with contracting securely covered the giant hole in the roof with tarps. I talked with them about rebuilding that part of the house. One of the men was a builder and said he would take the job but that it would be weeks before they could get started because they were already in the middle of several projects. I understood, and I didn't mind. I was just thankful to have already found someone who was willing to do it so I didn't have to think about it anymore.

After that, I joined a group of people who were cleaning up limbs and other debris in the yard. We talked while we worked, and one man even took to singing. As we worked, the crickets sang, and the robins fluttered about. Despite the storm, life did go on.

After a few days of working, Peter pulled me aside and informed me that the apple crop had been destroyed. The trees themselves were mostly OK, despite losing some limbs and a few trees, but the apples were not OK. Most had been blown to the ground in the storm ...

ruined.

I stared at him numbly.

I shook my head in disbelief. "Oh, well!" I said. I threw my hands the air in utter defeat and then slumped over to the house, numb. I sat down on the porch steps and pulled off my work gloves. I was *so* tired. We had been at this for several days, all day long, and I was beat. *And now this ...*

"You alright?" Nathan asked, coming up with a bottle of water in his hands and wiping the sweat from his brow.

"Peter just told me that the apple crop is ruined," I said dejectedly.

"Oh," he said quietly, and he came and sat down on the steps beside me.

I looked up at him. "I just don't understand ..."

"Me either," he said, shaking his head.

We sat there in silence for a several minutes, each lost in our own thoughts.

"Care to take a walk?" he asked gently.

I was startled out of my reverie.

"I'm sorry. What did you say?"

"Would you like to take a walk? It might be good to take a break from all of *this* for a little while." He motioned towards the house.

I felt so tired. I wasn't sure I had it in me to take a walk, but I *did* need a break.

"OK. I'm not sure I'm up for much of one though."

"That's fine. We don't have to go far." He got up and fetched another bottle of water for himself and one for me, and then we set off down the trail behind the house.

We walked slowly and didn't talk much. It felt strange to be back in the forest, in the world where things went on like normal. It felt almost like dream walking, and I was thankful not to be alone.

"There are just some things I don't understand," I said suddenly, when we were about halfway down the trail.

Nathan glanced over and then waited for me to go on.

"Like why ... why did *we* make it ... when the Morrises didn't?" My eyes stung a little as I said it. "Couldn't God have sent someone to save them too? Couldn't he have woken them up or something? Or made the tree fall another way?" I paused. "If he loves us so much, why does he let these terrible things happen?"

Nathan was silent for a moment. I could tell he was thinking.

"We have such a close-up view of life, Adel," he began slowly. "We can only see a tiny bit of what's in front of us, let alone what's happening in the lives of those around us. We see a little. We think we understand. But God is the only one who can see everything clearly, and he's in control. In the book of Job, God asks Job, 'Where were you when I laid the foundations of the earth?'[5] He describes his awesome power over the natural world ... He alone created it! His thoughts are not our thoughts, neither are His ways our ways. 'For as the heavens are higher than the earth, so are my ways higher than your ways and my thoughts than your thoughts.'[6] I have to draw comfort from that. I can trust that God knows what he's doing, even when it makes no sense to me. Even when it hurts ..."

It was then that I remembered that Nathan and Edmund Morris had been friends. They were hunting buddies.

I looked up at him. He truly believed what he said. He was hurting deeply for the loss of his friend. I could see it on his face, but his faith was not shaken because of it. He had full faith in his God, in his Savior.

He turned to look at me, to search my face. "He *is* working things out for our good, Adel. It just doesn't always *look* that way."

I nodded and stared at the ground in front of me. I was still deep in thought.

"It's probably time for us to head back," he said gently.

I glanced up; we were just reaching the edge of the forest.

"Wow, we came a lot farther than I realized," I said.

Nathan slid his hands into his pockets, and we walked slowly back toward the house.

---

[5] Job 38:4.
[6] Isaiah 55:9.

TWENTY-THREE

A Shepherd Family Gathering

Within two weeks, most everything was cleaned up and put back together. All the small projects had been completed, including all the trips to the dump, where we had to take all the ruined furniture and other trash and debris. It could have been hard for me to part with Grandma's things, but I had too much to think about to dwell on it for long. It would take much longer for the house to be reconstructed. The contractors were just getting started on it at the end of the second week.

Doris and Ace invited me to stay on at their house while Noah's room was being rebuilt—at least until the roof and floor were put back in. While I was staying with them, I spent a lot of time learning how a house ought to be run. Doris was an expert housekeeper. Her hands were never idle, yet she did her work gracefully. She hardly ever seemed hurried or harried or bothered by things, except when Ace was too late getting in for supper.

"Now he knows what time we eat, that man," she'd say. "It's been the same old routine for forty years! I have a mind not to tell him about that pie in the oven! It's what he gets for keeping me worrying about him."

I knew the real reason for Doris's anxiety was that she wanted to make sure he was OK. He wasn't young like he used to be. His movements were getting slow and tired. But he still kept working, right on alongside his hired help. Doris was worried that one day he might not make it back to the house. But he always did. And she always gave him the pie.

The Shepherds often included church friends in the gatherings at their house on Sundays, and since I was now staying with Doris and Ace, they were invited too. They gladly accepted. They had gone from time to time before I arrived at Sweet Valley, and it had been a while since their last visit.

It was a nice way to break up the week of thinking about the house. Those first couple of weeks after the tornado, I spent most of my time over at Sweet Valley with whoever was available to help with getting the house cleaned up. It was a long process, made much shorter by all the help we received from the men from church. I was so thankful for their help! It was nice, though, to go somewhere that the tornado hadn't touched and to think fresh thoughts with new faces.

The first Sunday that Doris and Ace came with me to the Shepherds' house, we all rode together in my car. Doris and Ace were right at home with their friends in the cozy mountain cabin. Doris got to work helping Annie in the kitchen, and Ace found Robert and the other men sitting out on the porch, sharpening their knives. He pulled an old Case knife out of his pocket and joined them.

A couple of Peter's friends were there that day, and they were all in lively spirits. It was interesting and a little entertaining to watch Peter with his friends. They joked with one another and goofed off constantly. They reminded me a little of some guys I knew from high school.

When we were all sitting at the table together during dinner, Doris began talking about her granddaddy. Peter had just finished telling us a story about how he had recently caught a snapping turtle while fishing for catfish in a friend's pond.

"When you mentioned catching that turtle down in the pond, Peter, it made me think about my granddaddy and how he used to go turtle grabbing, just to make ends meet."

"Turtle grabbing?" I asked.

"Catching snapping turtles with your bare hands. Usually along the edges of a creek bank or muddy stream. Granddaddy didn't make much money as a farmer in those days, so he and his boys'd go turtle grabbing. They'd face those snapping turtles on their own turf, braving the chance to lose a finger in the process! They'd slide their hands down under the murky water along the bank, or down in the mud along the bottom of the creek, and feel for the turtle's shells. They'd also search for underwater holes in the bank. Sometimes they'd have to stick their entire arm in the hole before they'd find one. Then there'd be turtle stew for dinner! They did it just to keep from starving. They lived a little south of here. I don't reckon you could do much grabbing in mountain streams, though I don't know for sure."

"My brothers tried it a couple of times," said Annie, "though they didn't have much luck or the guts to keep it up."

"I've heard it said that once a snapper bites, it won't let go 'til lightning strikes," said one of Peter's friends, whose name was Luke.

"It's not very bright to go sticking your hands in muddy water to try to catch a turtle that could bite your fingers off!" declared Marie.

"Well, people do interesting things when they're hungry," Rebecca replied.

"Some just do it for sport," added Robert. "It takes a certain kind of skill, grit, and patience to catch a turtle that way. Some do it to catch catfish and other things. Nathan, do you remember when you and Mr. Alan and I went over to Lake Nottely and you caught that whopper bass?"

Nathan nodded slowly with a smile.

"With your hands?" I gasped.

Everyone laughed.

"No, no," laughed Robert. "With a pole!" And to Nathan, he added, "That thing must have weighed as much as you did!"

"Y'all had to help me lift it into the boat. It almost pulled me in!"

"I bet that picture is still around here somewhere," Robert said as he stood up to go hunting for it.

"I 'member when you caught that 'un. He was a real *prize winner*," added Ace, his toothpick wobbling up and down as he spoke.

Oh, that toothpick. I smiled to myself.

Doris turned to me. "Did Alan ever take you fishing, Adel?"

"Not that I remember. We used to go on lots of hikes. That's what I remember doing with Grandpa the most. Hiking."

"We should go on a hike sometime," said Peter, looking at me.

"You should all go!" chimed in Doris. "I think it would be good for y'all to have a break from all the stress of the last few weeks. I'll gladly keep Noah for you, Adel, if you'd like to go."

"We could go to Crystal Falls," continued Peter.

I remembered Crystal Falls. It was a favorite hike of all the locals. Grandpa had taken me there a few times when I was a child. I couldn't remember where it was or much about it. I just remembered liking it. I was curious to see it again.

"That sounds fun!" I said.

"Are you *all* going to go?" asked Doris, but she seemed to be directing her question at Nathan.

"Sure! It'll be nice to get away for an afternoon."

"We'd love to as well!" Jim said, looking at Rebecca, who smiled and nodded her consent.

It was settled—we were to go the following Saturday.

Just then, Robert came back into the room holding an old photograph. He passed it around the table. It was a picture of Nathan when he was about seven or eight. He was standing in a Jon boat and holding up a large fish with the help of his daddy. In the picture, Robert seemed just as excited as Nathan. I smiled subconsciously at the picture. Nathan's smiling eyes, tousled dark hair, and faded jeans that were ripped at the knees were exactly how I remembered him.

"Your grandpa took that picture," Doris said to me.

I nodded and slowly handed the picture over to Rebecca.

Then Annie came into the room, bringing a black walnut cake with cream cheese frosting! It was a delicious cake, and our thoughts were redirected to the table. Annie was an *excellent* cook.

Peter was in such good humor that day, and his easy and friendly manners made it hard not to like him. He was friendly to everyone, but he seemed a little more than friendly to me lately. As the evening went on, he sat by me often and always tried to include me in the talk and jokes between him and his friends. It was obvious, and I was sure everyone in the room was aware of it. I wasn't sure what he meant by it, so I just tried to be friendly and polite in return. I wasn't interested in Peter. He was kind, and nice, and so likeable, but he wasn't what I would need in a man. I needed someone who was more established, someone who knew what they were about. Peter, though nice, seemed a little immature.

"Adel," Annie said, walking up to me later while I was sitting in a chair on the front porch, playing peek-a-boo with Noah and Moses. "Do you use vanilla?"

"Vanilla extract?" I asked.

"Yes."

"I do now," I said, thinking about the few times I had tried to bake things recently.

"Well, I just finished a batch. Would you like some?" she said, holding out a large brown bottle.

"I would!" I said excitedly. "So, you made this?" I looked down at the bottle in amazement. It looked familiar.

"Yes, I've been making our vanilla for years."

"She makes mine too," added Doris.

"Oh! So that's why I recognize the bottle! Thank you, Annie! This should last me a long time! Who taught you how to make your own vanilla?" I asked as Annie pulled a chair up next to mine.

"My grandmother taught me. She was Cherokee. She made most of her own things. Clothes, medicines, extracts, spices. She made everything from scratch."

"That's fascinating!" I said.

"She was a fascinating woman. Resourceful, too. She had to be."

We sat there on the porch talking for a while longer, but it was getting late. A mist was settling over the woods in the fading light. Over the dark shadow of the mountains, there was a hazy pink and orange glow where the sun had disappeared an hour before. It was time to go home.

The following afternoon, I was in the kitchen putting together something for dinner while Noah played on the floor nearby with some stuffed animals. He was trying his best to get one of his diapers onto a little stuffed doggie. I giggled as the doggie kept sliding away from him across the old, worn linoleum. "Here, let me help," I offered, and I wiped my dirty hands on a kitchen towel.

"Da? Da?" Noah pointed to the doggie.

"Yes, the little doggie?" I brought the pup over and sat it between us on the floor. Noah handed me the diaper, and I slid it in place on the puppy's bottom. "Here," I said, offering for him to secure one of the little Velcro straps. "Stick this down on that part."

He took the strap and tried to stick it in place.

"Here, now this one."

With a little help, he stuck that one in place too. Then he happily took the doggie by the ear and scooted across the floor to the cabinets. He stuck out one little leg and then the other, while he tightly gripped the doggie with his left hand and held onto the cabinet with his right. He pushed up. His legs were spread out at an awkward angle.

"Noah!" I cried. "Look at you! You're standing!" I hurried over and sat down beside him on the floor. Noah babbled out a string of baby talk that ended with a squeal. He bobbed up and down and smiled a big, gummy smile. He was so pleased with himself! I laughed. My little boy was standing!

TWENTY-FOUR

Crystal Falls

On Saturday, I left Noah with Doris and drove over to Nathan's house for our trip to Crystal Falls. The sun was just beginning to rise above the lowest hills as I pulled into his driveway. It wasn't even seven o'clock yet! *Why do we have to set out so early?* I wondered.

We were a large group: Rebecca and Jim, Nathan, Marie, Peter and his friends, Luke and Adam, Adam's girlfriend, Amanda, and me. We took two vehicles. I wasn't surprised to find myself between Peter and Nathan in the front seat of Nathan's large, gray pickup truck. Nathan was driving. Luke, Adam, and Amanda were in the back seat. Though we weren't going far in terms of miles, it still took about twenty minutes to wind our way up the curvy mountain roads.

There was music playing softly over the speakers:

Oh, I'm a world traveler
Pack your bags and dig down deep
Ride the storms and sail the seas
To the distant pole

I'm a world traveler
Into these uncharted lands
To blaze a trail in the vast expanse
Of the heart and soul ...

I listened to the words of Andrew Peterson's song and wondered what kind of adventures were ahead of *us*.

The last road we turned onto was a dirt road, well off the beaten path. We drove down it a ways, and then I let out a little gasp as I saw what we were approaching. The road ran *right through* a creek! Where there should have been a bridge, there wasn't! And to my surprise, we continued straight toward it! The creek was not small. It was a good-sized creek. It must have been several feet deep in the middle! Maybe ... it was hard to tell.

"It's OK. This truck can handle it," Nathan reassured me. Still, I pushed against the dashboard in front and shut my eyes as we splashed into the swirling water. Peter put his arm over my shoulders as we bounced roughly along. The powerful tires and motor of the truck propelled us wildly over the stones in the creek bed. We moved to the right, to the left, forward. At last we made it out on the other side. Peter did not remove his arm, even after we were safely on dry land. I made a fuss of brushing my hair back out of my face so that it was impossible for him to keep it there.

"Wow!" I exclaimed. "How deep was that?"

"A couple feet at most." Nathan seemed so calm about all of this. Everyone else did too, actually.

I quickly looked back to watch Jim's truck work its way over the rocky creek bed. It was wild! But apparently a very normal thing to do around here.

I settled back in my seat with a smile and waited for the next adventure.

A few minutes more brought us to our stop. We pulled off into a small gravel parking area; there was a green sign with an arrow pointing down the trailhead that read "Crystal Falls—3 Mi."

It felt so good to be in the woods. The deep summer canopy was thick and rich in color, shielding us almost entirely from the sun. I breathed in slowly and deeply. Yes, that smell the forest in the mountains had a smell that felt so clean and purifying. And the air in the mornings was so cool and crisp, a false security for what was to come later in the day, when the heat and the humidity were so unbearably hot and sticky. But it was pleasant now. Perfect for a hike. Now I understood why we had to leave so early.

The well-worn trail was made of dirt and rocks and exposed roots. Rebecca and her husband were walking together, talking and laughing as they went. They were an attractive couple by nature, but today it seemed especially true. They appeared to be hiking pros, even down to the clothes they wore. They seemed so happy and comfortable with each other and with themselves. There was an understanding between them that I envied. I secretly wished for a marriage like that.

My thoughts were interrupted by a ruckus up ahead and Luke exclaiming, "Lord howdy! Look at that!" He pointed to a spot on the left edge of the trail where a large snake was curled up, its mouth opened wide. Luke had been in front and had spotted him first.

"He was only about a foot from my leg!" Luke said with energy. "That sucker could have bitten me!"

I knew nothing about snakes. "Is it dangerous?" I asked.

"Only one of the most deadly snakes in North Georgia!" answered Peter.

"A timber rattlesnake," added Jim.

"Being curled up like that means he's ready to strike!" continued Peter.

From where I was standing, several yards away, I tried to get a better look. The snake was several inches thick. It was gray-brown with black geometric shapes on its back. It was curled up half on top of itself, its mouth open wide, showing the entire white inside and what looked like two large fangs. It hissed and rattled its tale viciously. Its coiled body reminded me of a compressed spring about to be set loose. A chill went down my spine.

Nathan took a step toward the snake for a better look and said, "He's not typically an aggressive snake. But he's mad. Anyone got a gun?"

No one did have a gun.

"If we leave him alone and walk around that way, we should be fine." He pointed to some large rocks we would need to climb over to pass by the snake safely. "We'll need to keep an eye out for him on the way back down though."

We all cautiously obeyed Nathan and climbed up over the mossy boulders to the right of the trail. We climbed along them a little way and then made it back down onto the trail. I was the last to go. The last bit of rock before getting back down onto the trail was slippery, and I wasn't used to this sort of thing. I began to slip downward over the damp moss and leaves, and my shoe got caught where two boulders came together. My body came forward, but my leg did not.

"Oh help!" I called out. But too late. It was an awkward and uncomfortable position to be in. "My shoe is stuck!" I tried to hop on one foot while I pulled with the other. In one swift movement, Peter was by my side, holding me by the elbow. But my shoe was free. I looked up. Apparently, Nathan had already loosened my shoe from the rocks. I wasn't hurt, only embarrassed. "Thank you," I muttered, and followed the others down the trail.

Everyone was a little unnerved by the sight of the rattlesnake, especially Luke, whose life had been threatened. He began to talk nervously and roll off silly banter even faster than usual. Peter and Adam joined in. Their silly talk seemed so out of place on this otherwise peaceful and picturesque mountain trail. I lagged behind the rest a little so that I didn't have to hear quite so much and so I could enjoy all the sights and smells of the things before and all around me.

"What're these heart-shaped plants growing beside the trail? The glossy ones?" I called out to the group.

"That's wild ginger," Rebecca said, slowing down so we could walk together.

"And these pretty ones with all the tiny leaves? These are just like something out of a fairy tale!"

"Those are Christmas ferns." Rebecca laughed.

We walked on in this way for some time, with me occasionally pointing out an interesting plant or tree, and Rebecca always knowing what it was. The noisiest of the group had migrated back to the front, and it seemed like Nathan, Jim, Rebecca, and I were getting left behind. I figured this might be because of me, so I tried to quicken my pace.

The trail wasn't exactly a walk in the park. It was long and rugged—and steep at times. Near a creek, the forest was dense with mountain laurel and rhododendron. There were soft pink and white blossoms on the branches of the rhododendrons. Their fragrance enveloped us as we tramped through. And as we walked along, we passed through a group of tiny purple butterflies, fluttering around near our feet. They gracefully danced together, looking so happy that I wished I could join them.

We followed the creek for a while until I began to distinguish through the trees the sound of roaring water. My pulse quickened. We were almost there.

We rounded a bend in the creek to come face-to-face with the majestic waterfall, forty or fifty feet high. It spilled haphazardly down over some boulders to make a tremendous splash at the bottom. The water down below seemed so peaceful compared to the violence of the falls above. On either side were some stone outcroppings and then the thicket of laurels and rhododendrons and a few fern-like mimosa trees.

Luke thought it wasn't enough to face danger just once in a day, so he and Peter decided to try climbing up the side of the waterfall. My stomach knotted up a little as I watched them climb. Rebecca shook her head and said something about them being too old for such foolery. But up they went, just the same. They made it safely to a ledge near the top. I began to feel a little jealous at their being able to see from so high up the waterfall, while the rest of us only saw it from the bottom. I made my way over to the thicket of shrubs, and I looked for a way up. There had to be a way!

"It's over here," Jim said, pointing to a narrow opening in the bushes.

"Thanks," I said, and made my way through the opening and up the narrow, damp trail to the ledge near the top of the falls. I cautiously made my way over toward Peter and Luke, who were standing a little too close to the ledge. I stopped before I reached them.

"Hey, hey! Glad you could join us! It's great, isn't it?"

"Yes!" I hollered back to Peter. The roar of the falls was nearly deafening.

After a few minutes, I had seen enough and wanted to see the bottom of the falls again. I made my way carefully back across the ledge and down the narrow trail. When I got to the bottom, I saw that Rebecca had spread out a picnic blanket on the dry soil beside the creek. She and Marie were sitting down together. *So that's what she had in her backpack!*

We all brought lunch and bottles of water, but before I could eat, I needed to be close to the falls again. They drew me forward like a bug to a light. Only this was good for me. I *needed* it. I went to the edge of the rocks at the bottom, where there was a railing that seemed to be the height of a horse fence. Jim and Nathan were leaning on it, talking. I went over and leaned on it too, and stared deep into the falls. The spray whipped at my face. There was something so spectacular about the falls, yet something peaceful too, like a lullaby lulling me to sleep. I could have lay down right then and there and slept like a baby. But the falls were also fierce and mighty, a force not to be reckoned with. The tension between the two was set. It would forever be that way. Both peaceful and energetic, beautiful and terrifying all at the same time. And I loved it.

As I stared into the thunderous billows of water, I couldn't help but remember the sad fate of Doris's little girl. My heart ached for her. She was so young ... And even though it was a long time ago, I knew that it was something Doris would never completely recover from. Her heart would forever be broken. Sure, she had learned to go on, to live life in some semblance of normal. But in her spirit, there was a longing for something that could never be replaced.

I was still deep in thought when I heard a laugh that shook me free from my reverie. It was Peter again. He and Luke had come back down and joined the crowd. Everyone was standing around near the railing or sitting on the picnic blanket. Nathan had scooted over to give them more room and was now standing very close to me, though he was looking the other way. I wasn't in the habit of noticing the physical presence of those around me, but for some reason, I was keenly aware of his closeness. He was leaning on the railing again, like I was, his arm nearly brushing mine, and suddenly, for some strange reason, I had the strongest desire to put my arm through his. To lean my head on his shoulder! What on earth was I thinking! I laughed out loud at myself, which, of course, drew the attention of those around me. I just shrugged at them and laughed again. I didn't even know how to explain myself, and I was too silly minded to make something up.

The rest of the hike was delightful, though the heat had come out while we were still at the falls. Soon we were all dripping with sweat. As we walked back down in the direction of the cars, I began to notice a buzzing sound coming from the trees.

"What's that sound?" I asked Nathan, who was closest to me.

"What? You mean the cicadas?"

"If they're the ones that sound like a group of tiny chainsaws, then yes!"

"You are very curious," he teased.

"Well, it's just been a while since I've been able to get out and really explore. A really long time, actually. I love it! I didn't realize how much I missed this." I opened my arms to the woods around us. "But I'm not sure I really noticed much before, back in San Francisco. There is so much to see!"

"Yes. There is always something new to see."

"Really? You and Rebecca seem to know so much about the woods already. How *do* you know so much? It must have taken you years to learn it all!"

"Our mom is a naturalist. She was born here in Gilmer County, and she learned a lot about the natural world from her parents and her grandma."

"Yes, she told me her grandma was Cherokee."

He nodded. "Mama uses a lot of the plants around here to make medicine for our family. She also sells to some of the shops in town. We grew up helping her collect and prepare the plants. You know, to make tinctures and salves, things like that. You should ask her about it sometime."

Nathan was always rather quiet and reserved. But this seemed to be a subject that he felt passionate about. His eyes were brighter and more expressive as he spoke, his voice livelier. He seemed proud of his mama.

"My brother and sisters and I also spent a lot of time outside by ourselves, exploring. And doing some learning on our own. Cherry Hill is a neat place to grow up."

"You and your brothers and sisters were very fortunate! To get to have a childhood like that, wandering around in the woods, being free. Is your dad into plants and the outdoors too?"

"Not as much. He likes to hunt. But it was mostly Mom and us kids. I do feel blessed to have had the childhood that we did. Not many kids get to have the kind of freedom that we had. We had our limits though, and we knew it. And it wasn't all great. We had our rough times just like any family."

"Did you play in the woods a lot? You know, camping, tree forts, and things like that?"

"Peter and I spent most of our free time outside. Dad taught us to hunt when we were young. And we liked to fish. We had some awesome tree houses. One is still standing on the east side of the property. Mama said she wanted to keep it around for the grandkids. They use it too! The older ones. They've made a nice little house out of it. It's been a castle and all kinds of things over the years."

"I know you make cabinets and furniture. Did you learn how to make other things? Like your dad and his knives?"

"Some. I feel like a man who can do a lot of things but none of them very well."

"I can understand that! I feel that way a little. Only I feel like I can only do a *few* things and none of them well," I tried to laugh it off as a joke, but I was serious. "I'm not sure I believe that though," I continued. "You seem successful in your business and as an electrician."

Instead of responding, he decided to change the subject.

"Have the contractors been able to finish all the repairs on the house?"

"Not yet. I had no idea construction work could take so long!" I moaned.

Nathan smiled the smile of experience and said, "Indeed."

"But tonight is my first night back in the house! I've really enjoyed my stay with Doris and Ace, but I'm excited to go home!"

"That's good! I'm glad to hear it."

We walked on in silence for a little while. Rebecca and Marie were having a serious talk about the less than desirable character of one of her beaus, and they didn't seem to mind that we overheard. Jim was walking with us. Peter and his friends were out of sight again.

It was interesting to witness this talk between sisters—the one obviously more experienced in life, and the other who respected her sister's opinion. Despite that respect, I could tell that Marie was struggling. It was hard to be a teenager. I didn't envy her, not for a moment.

Before we knew it, we were back at the parking lot.

"This was so much fun!" I said as we went up the last little hill and onto the asphalt.

"Good! I'm glad!" Rebecca smiled.

Nathan looked over at me. "Rebecca, Jim, and I go hiking regularly, mostly with the kids. Would you like me to let you know the next time we go?"

"I'd like that."

"Where ya been?" hollered Peter as we approached the cars. "We've been waiting here for *hours*! For real though, we're beat. And we need some food."

On the way home, we decided to stop at JJ's, a locally owned barbeque place. We took our seats. Next to me on one side was Adam's girlfriend, Amanda, whom I had hardly spoken more than a few words to. She hadn't looked in my direction all day. She seemed entirely focused on keeping the attention of the three young men with whom she had spent the whole course of her day. It was strange to me; she was supposed to be dating Adam, but it seemed to me that he received the least attention of the three. Peter, by far, received the most. By this time, Peter, who was sitting directly across from Amanda, seemed to have nearly forgotten me. He seemed pleased with Amanda's attention and I didn't mind at all.

Rebecca and Jim were down at the end of the table, and Nathan was on my other side. When I noticed that Nathan was beside me again, it reminded me of my silly thought earlier in the day, and I giggled to myself. But then I felt it again. *No way,* I thought. But there it was, just the same. I wanted to be *near* him. So instead, I fiddled with my napkin and sheepishly responded to any remarks that he made.

TWENTY-FIVE
The Creek

I awoke earlier than usual the next morning, thankful to be back in my own bed, in our own home. A mist from the mountains had come down and settled over the farm. It was like a cool and refreshing blanket had been placed over it, tucking it into its own little world. The edges of the fields slowly disappeared into the mist, leaving behind a world so fresh and new that I couldn't resist it. I slipped my shoes off at the back door and took off at a run, straight for the left field behind the house, where the hay was growing tall and thick. It smelled so sweet. I ran straight through to the middle of the field, where I spread my arms open wide and spun around and around. The grass was wet and cool on my feet. I stopped for a moment to take in the scene and breathe deeply. I felt so invigorated, so alive. Then I tore off back across the field toward the house. My clothes were damp and clinging to my arms and legs when I finally made it back to the porch. But I didn't mind. I was *exhilarated*!

Pancakes! I thought. *We're having pancakes for breakfast!*

My spirits were still high when we arrived at church a couple of hours later.

I was glad to be there. I always felt that the Lord was speaking to me during the sermons. The words were convicting, encouraging, and life-giving. I was so glad I hadn't continued to listen to the voice of fear that had been telling me not to go when I first arrived. That voice had gradually grown weaker and weaker over the summer, until at last, I didn't notice it at all.

The longer I went to church at Cherry Hill Baptist, the less I felt like a number and the more I felt alive, like a person ought to feel. It was true, when I stopped to think about it; all the years I went to church back home, I never knew half the people who attended, nowhere close. There were always people coming and going. No one seemed to stick around long. It felt *transient*. It made it hard to get to know people. The church was so large that even the small groups were twenty or thirty people. You may get to know a few people well over the years, but everyone lived in different parts of the city and had lives that varied so much from one another that it was hard to connect and do things outside of church. We did have some events, like social gatherings and community service work, but it wasn't much, and it didn't really feel like living. Here I was beginning to share a life with these people. We were *doing* life together. And it was beginning to fill a void in my life that I hadn't even known was there.

The following Tuesday, Julian asked me to go to the movies with him again. We had been going out at least once every week or two for the last couple of months, but I was beginning to grow tired of our dates. I tried it for a while, and it just wasn't working. But I had such a hard time telling people no.

I put on a blue and green sundress and some nice sandals. I did my long hair up with pins, leaving some cascading down my back. Before the show, we were going to Toni's, a nice Italian restaurant in a neighboring town, and I wanted to feel pretty. It had been a while since I had taken the time to do it right.

I slipped over to Doris's to drop off Noah.

"Woooeee!" Doris whistled when she saw me. "Where are you off to tonight?"

"Cartersville. Julian is taking me to Toni's and then to see a movie."

Doris gave me a disapproving look. She wasn't bashful with her opinion of Julian. Anytime I told her I was going on a date with him, she would give me that disapproving look and mumble something about time wasted. I knew I should ask her why she acted that way, but part of me didn't want to know.

"I'm sorry. I might be a little late tonight. The movie doesn't start until seven forty-five."

"I'll be up."

"Alright. Goodbye! Thank you, Doris!"

Most of the way there, we talked about the farm. Julian had all kinds of questions about it. He had suddenly seemed to take a new interest in the apple business.

"Are you wanting to have your own orchard one day?" I questioned.

"Perhaps."

Again, it was the same kind of movie and the same kind of restaurant. I just didn't care for horror movies. I had told Julian that many times. I had also told him that I didn't need to eat at an expensive restaurant. I knew he couldn't afford it. His parents must have been paying for it. I was glad when it was time to go home.

Wednesday afternoon, I heard a knock on the door. I was just getting dinner put away and was surprised to hear the knock. When I opened the door, I saw Nathan standing there, his hands in his pockets. He looked rather nice, standing there in the evening light.

"Hi, Nathan. I hope you're not coming to tell me there's going to be another tornado," I teased.

"Thank goodness, no. I actually came because I wanted to show you something. Do you have a few minutes? Well, more like an hour?"

"What?"

"After talking to you on the hike last weekend, and seeing your enthusiasm for the natural world, I remembered a place down by the creek that I thought you might like to see. Would you be interested?"

"I would! I've been wanting to see the creek! I haven't seen it since I was a little girl!"

"OK! Great!"

"Come in for a minute while I change my shoes and get Noah."

I ran upstairs to replace my slippers with some tennis shoes while Nathan made himself comfortable by playing with Noah in his playpen.

We set off down the trail as the sun began to sink low in the sky. We wouldn't be able to linger too long at the creek. We had only about an hour or so of sunlight left.

Noah was in the front carrier as usual.

We walked about halfway to Nathan's house when, for the first time, I noticed a small trail branching off to the right of the main trail. It looked freshly cut. *That's why I didn't notice it before! The trail had been overgrown!*

"I've been walking up and down this trail for months, wondering where this little trail was! And it was here all the time! I feel so foolish!"

"Not at all! It was pretty overgrown."

"This is so exciting!"

Nathan seemed pleased.

Noah reached for branches as we passed by and occasionally caught one.

Nathan noticed this and picked up a tiny straight stick off the trail and handed it to Noah. "Your first hiking stick," he said. Noah was delighted and held tight to that little stick for the rest of the trip.

As we meandered down the narrow trail, the air began to get cooler, the underbrush thicker and thicker. We went through a tunnel made from the low canopy of mountain laurels, which opened up to reveal a grassy meadow. It was lush and not very big. The meadow was surrounded by laurels and rhododendrons on three sides, making it like a little woodland room. The trees surrounding the meadow were ancient and large, towering above like a miniature rain forest. The evening sunlight filtered through the trees, casting glorious rays of colorful light down onto the soft grass below. On the fourth side of the meadow was the mossy creek bank, and below it, the glistening water bubbling gaily over the rocks and stones. Someone had placed a stone bench beside the creek. It looked old and worn but sound. Beside it was an ancient weeping willow tree. Its long, grassy fronds turned the scene into a magical fairyland.

It was Grandpa, I reminisced. *Grandpa set up the bench and planted the willow tree, a long time ago, when Mom was a little girl ...*

The grass was all freshly cut; the smell was sweet and delightful.

This seemed like every little girl's dream: a romantic place to come slip away to and forget the outside world, a place to play and pretend for hours on end. That's exactly what it had been for me, long ago. I didn't say much as I was taking it all in. I just wanted to remember and to enjoy it all to the fullest.

I walked over to the bench and ran my hand over the seat. Moss was growing all around the base and along the creekbank. There were ferns growing in clusters along the bank and on the edges of the meadow.

The creek was small, maybe ten feet across, and not very deep. The bank was low, only a step down. To the left, I saw a blue heron standing still, one leg down in the water. He saw me and slowly walked on down the creek.

The water looked cool and inviting.

I quickly pulled off my tennis shoes, rolled up my jeans, and waded into the icy-cold water. A thrill went up my spine. I shivered in delight.

I looked up at Nathan, who was watching me from the bank with amusement.

"Want to come in?" I asked. "It's really cold!"

Nathan laughed. It was good to hear him laugh.

He sat on the bench, took off his boots, and rolled up his pants legs. Then he joined me down in the creek.

"I used to come here when I was little!" I exclaimed. "Grandpa set up that bench and planted the willow tree! He would bring me here often when I was really little. Ouch!" I stubbed my toe on a small stone.

"When I got older, they trusted me to come here by myself. This was my secret place. My hideaway."

"Your grandpa was the one who first showed it to me too."

"Really?"

"Yes. When we would come visit when I was a kid, and then when I moved here, this became my thinking place, my place of solitude. My property comes to a point right there." He pointed to the edge of the meadow, on the right side. "When I bought this land, Mr. Alan said this spot was as much mine as his. I came here a lot at first. But after Ms. Elaine died, I just sort of stopped. The specialness was gone for me." He looked up at me intently. "But it's not anymore."

I lowered my eyes. Was the romance of the moment messing with his head?

I looked around and sighed. "It's hard to imagine that so much beauty can be all in one place!" I said, trying to change the subject.

"True." He was still looking at me.

"Come on!" I laughed and started wading down the creek. Nathan followed.

After a little while, I unbuckled Noah from his carrier and let him dip his toes into the icy water. He splashed and kicked and squealed with joy. *He's becoming braver*, I thought.

Before long, the sky began to grow dark, and the shadows of the trees grew long and thin. A reflection of the crescent moon appeared in the water near the shore, where it was the stillest.

"We better be heading back," Nathan said as he stepped back up onto the bank.

He reached a hand down to help me up. Why did things like that make me feel so strange? I would just as soon have kept my hand in his than let it go. But I didn't. I *couldn't*.

We each sat down on one end of the bench to put our shoes back on. I was glad he wasn't sitting too close. I let Noah play in the grass beside the bench while we tied our shoes. Then I sat up and took in the view once more. It was quiet and peaceful in the late-evening light.

"Thank you for sharing this with me."

"Do you think you'll be back?"

"Definitely!"

"Then I'll keep it cut for you."

"That's kind of you. Do you think *you'll* be back?"

"I think so." He said it with a little smile.

It would have been nice to stay for a while longer, but my better reason told me it was time to go.

When we got back to the split in the trail, we said our goodbyes and went our separate ways.

But then Nathan, who was only a few yards away, turned back and said, "Hey, would you like to go fishing sometime?"

I felt my face flush. I nodded.

Nathan smiled. "Alright. Maybe on Saturday?"

I nodded again.

"OK! I'll see you then." He gave me one last look before turning to continue on his way down the trail.

I turned, too, and began to walk, but my thoughts were not with my feet. They were about twenty yards behind me with a man who had just made my day.

TWENTY-SIX

Fishing

On Saturday, Nathan and I left about two o'clock. He picked me up at Doris's house, after I dropped off Noah. The front seat of his truck was manly but clean. I appreciated that he kept the music low so we could talk. It was country music. I recognized the words "write this down, take a little note, to remind you in case you didn't know, tell yourself I love you and I don't want you to go. Write this down ..."

I listened to the rest of the song while gazing out of the open window. The grass growing alongside the road was so tall I could have reached out and touched it with my hand. Rolling hills of pasture land passed by one after another. The grass in the fields was beginning to turn brown and made the air smell richly of hay. The sun shone down brightly on the scene before us. It was a *fine* day.

"So, where are we going?" I asked, when the song was over.

"You'll see ..." was all he said.

"Alright! I like surprises."

"Do you now?"

"Yes."

"Alright, then I should tell you that I have another surprise stop that we have to make on the way."

The surprise stop was actually a little store we came to as we left the fields and entered into the mountainous forest. The store was set right on the edge of one of those curvy mountain roads. Directly behind it was a river. It was called Cathy's, and inside were all kinds of neat things—mostly food related, like caramel popcorn, boiled peanuts, peanut brittle, cider, jellies, jams, and pickles, freshly ground corn grits and cornmeal, and many other delicious things. There was also a variety of camping gear and travel books and a collection of locally made handicrafts. There were bowls, wind chimes, scented goats milk soap, and crocheted washcloths made with organic homespun cotton. I enjoyed walking around with Nathan and looking at all the interesting things. I'd never been in a store quite like this one before. Then Nathan walked over to one of the shelves and picked up a loaf of bread.

"Ah, here it is! I was beginning to think they didn't have it."

"What kind is it?"

"Cinnamon apple."

I noticed a vanilla glaze on the top. "Yum," I said.

"Yes." He nodded with a smile.

We bought the bread and headed back down the road. A few miles more, deeper into the woods, we turned off onto a bumpy gravel side road. I was beginning to get used to these roads, and so far, it seemed like Nathan was a good driver, so I wasn't too worried, though the drop-off beside the road was hundreds of feet at times.

Finally we came to a stop. Nathan parked the truck on the side of the road, and we took the gear and picnic stuff and headed down a narrow trail. The early autumn day was unusually warm. It felt almost like a day in midsummer. The sky was mostly clear, with some fluffy white clouds dotting the blue here and there.

"Where are you taking me?" I teased as we walked along the wooded trail.

He hummed the tune from *Deliverance*, and I laughed.

"Almost there," he said.

I heard it then. The sound of water. Mountain water. There wasn't a sound like it in the world—crystal clear and calling. We followed the sound, and within a couple of minutes, we were met with a rocky sandbar and a river, which was about thirty feet across and didn't look too deep. There seemed to be no one else around.

"Is this *your* secret place?" I asked.

He nodded with a grin.

He took to getting his pole set up while I waded in the shallow water beside the sandbar, if you could call it a sandbar, with it being made of rocks and stones.

After he had his pole just right, he called me over to show me how to set up my pole. He asked if I had ever gone fly-fishing before. I told him that I had never done *any* kind of fishing before. He took his time explaining what each piece of tackle was used for and then showed me how to use the pole, putting the fly in and out of the water. It took some getting used to, but he was patient with me.

Nathan caught a trout not long after we started fishing. He told me we were only doing catch and release today, so he let the fish go.

After fishing for a couple of hours and neither one of us catching any more, we decided to have dinner. Nathan had made grilled chicken sandwiches, and they were *delicious*. Then came dessert: the delicious apple bread. I was genuinely excited about it.

He cut us each a piece with a clean pocketknife. I was thankful he didn't use the knife he'd used for fishing.

The cinnamon apple bread was gooey and cinnamony and oh so good.

"How did you find out about this stuff?" I asked between mouthfuls.

"My parents bought some from time to time when I was a kid. I've always liked it, so I just get some every once in a while, for a treat."

It made me feel special that Nathan wanted to share his treat with me.

After we finished eating, we just sat there on the picnic blanket for a while, talking about the places we'd been. The farthest he'd ever been from home was Texas, to visit family. The farthest I'd been was across the ocean. But we both had many stories to tell.

Even though I was enjoying our time together, I was having a hard time focusing. Despite my best efforts, I kept yawning and wanting to close my eyes. Noah still wasn't sleeping well, and I was definitely feeling it while lying there in the warm Autumn sun.

Suddenly Nathan got up and went over to his backpack. He took out a small blue and green bag, opened it up, and pulled out what looked like a parachute. He took out a thin black cord and tied it around a medium-sized tree, about five feet up. He took another cord and tied it around another tree, not far away. Then he attached the "parachute" to each of the straps.

"A hammock!" I said.

He had positioned it to be in line with the river but under a canopy of trees.

"Want to try it out?" he asked.

I nodded vigorously. It had been a long time since I had been in a hammock.

What a good idea, I thought.

I slid into the hammock, it swayed gently from side to side. "Ahh ..." I smiled.

Nathan seemed a little mischievous as he smiled down at me and said, "Enjoy yourself!" He gave the hammock a little push.

"I will!" I called back.

The day was warm for September. I was warm. My belly was full. *I felt full.* It had been a good day.

Thin beams of sunlight escaped through cracks in the fall leaf coverage overhead to rest upon my face. I closed my eyes to block out the sun and relaxed into the gentle rocking of the hammock.

When I opened my eyes, the light was no longer warming my face. The whole world seemed a few shades darker. The sun was now low in the sky.

I wonder how long I've been asleep! My phone was down on the picnic blanket. I had no idea what time it was.

I ran my hands through my hair a few times as I sat up. *I hope I look all right ...*

I scanned the shore for Nathan. He was standing up to his knees in the river and had just casted his line out across the dark water.

I bashfully approached him, stopping where the rocks rose above the shoreline. Nathan didn't take his eyes off his fishing, but he looked amused when he said, "Have a nice nap?"

I nodded, though he probably didn't see.

"How long was I out?"

"About an hour."

"Oh, I'm sorry."

"No worries. You probably needed it, and I've been enjoying myself." He reeled his line in and started wading back out of the water.

"Want to have another try?"

"Yes!"

We went over to the quilt to get my pole and a drink of water. Nathan was walking close to me, and now more than ever, I was aware of it.

As he put a new fly on my pole, he occasionally looked up and caught my eye. When he finished with the rod, he handed it to me with a look I found completely irresistible. He handed me the pole slowly, deliberately, still holding my gaze, his eyes asking me something ...

I felt flushed and conflicted. Part of me wanted to stay to find out what his eyes were asking me, the other part wanted to run. After a pause, I turned slowly away and walked back toward the water. I felt him looking after me for another moment before he followed me.

The shadows were getting longer. Night would be coming soon.

"We don't have much time before it gets dark," Nathan said, "but now's the best time to fish, so let's try for a little while at least."

The pull I felt toward him had been eased by activity.

I was focusing on my line when Nathan called, "Hey! You've got one! You've got it! Now reel it in nice and slow."

The fish flopped and splashed in defiance of being caught. I had to work at it, but I finally got him to the shore, where Nathan held him up for me to see. It was a spotted brook trout. He wasn't very big, but I was proud of him. Nathan slid the hook out with a pair of pliers and then gently placed him back into the water.

"Success!" I cheered.

"Success," he agreed.

As we drove along those backwoods' mountain roads on the ride home, we left the windows down so the wind could blow in our faces. It was dark now. The air had turned cool, but I didn't mind. I relished it as the wind whipped my hair around my face. I felt alive and free. The truck rumbled over the dusty gravel roads with precision. I felt safe. *Content.*

When we pulled into the driveway at Doris's, I turned to Nathan. "Hey, would you mind showing me your shop sometime? I've heard your mom and Doris and even Rebecca praise your craftsmanship so often that I've been curious to see what it is you actually do."

"Sure. I'm free Tuesday afternoon?"

"Yeah, that'd be great."

"Do you just want to walk over?"

"If it's not raining!" I laughed.

"Alright. Say four o'clock?"

"We'll be there! Oh, wait! Is it OK if Noah comes?"

"Sure, bring him along! We'll get him started early."

I wouldn't mind Noah learning a trade like carpentry, if he grew up to be something like Nathan.

I hopped out and shouted, "Good night!" through the open window as the truck rolled slowly away. I gathered up a sleepy Noah and our things and thanked Doris.

"Did you have a nice time?" Doris was all smiles.

"Yes..." Her unusually cheery demeanor made me blush in spite of myself. "Good night Doris!" I called as I hurried out the door and headed for home.

TWENTY-SEVEN

The Proposal

At about three fifty on Tuesday afternoon, we began our walk through the woods. As usual, I had Noah in the front carrier. Walking through the woods or around the farm was almost a daily habit of ours, and it felt natural to be heading out again, though it was nice to have a destination this time.

It was a bright and clear day without a cloud to be seen in the blue September sky. The leaves of the trees were hinting that fall was underway. A few leaves had already fallen to embellish the trail with their oranges and golds. A mockingbird was screeching somewhere nearby. Another was calling back.

I had never been so anxious to make our way down the trail. I wanted to be on time. I was afraid we should have left a few minutes earlier, but it was only two after four when we emerged from the forest and into the clearing near Nathan's house. The shop door was left open.

Nathan must already be inside.

We approached the door, and I could hear the music playing.

I poked my head inside and called out, "Hello!" But I didn't see

Nathan anywhere.

"Hey!" he said, coming up behind me.

"Oh! You startled me!"

"Sorry. I just ran inside to get some root beer. You want one?" he said, holding one of the bottles out for me to take.

"Sure, thank you! What a neat place!" I said, slowly walking through the door and taking in the scene before me. It smelled of fresh pine and sawdust.

"It's been many years in the works."

There was a large workbench in the center of the room, with one vice on the front and another on the end. Along the wall behind the bench were open-faced cabinets with an array of chisels, handsaws, and other tools.

To the sides of the larger bench were several smaller benches, all hollow underneath. On some of them there were large tabletop saws. Along the right side was a large assortment of wood of various shapes and thicknesses.

On several of the smaller benches, there were about ten cabinet faces lying flat.

"What's going on here?" I asked.

"Those are some cabinets I'm working on for a house remodel in Ellijay."

"Custom cabinets?"

"Yep."

"Wow! They're beautiful!" I said, noticing the attractive and solid design of the cabinets.

"And what's going on over here?" I asked, walking toward the tall bench in the center where several pieces of narrow wood were lying side by side.

"That's going to be a chair. I'm just about through with the details. I'll probably put it together in the morning."

"How do the pieces all fit together?" I asked, looking over the random assortment of wood lying on the table.

Within a minute, Nathan had the layout of the chair sitting before me.

"And this piece goes at the top," he said, gently laying the last piece in its place.

"Wow, that piece is really pretty. Can I see it?"

"Sure." He handed me the wood.

"Does it take a long time to make details like that?"

"I do it by hand, so yes, it does take a little while. Here, I'll show you." And he walked over to the cabinets behind us and took down a small chisel and mallet. He clamped the board onto the workbench and slowly and carefully chiseled away until a small rose appeared in the center of the piece, above the swirling lines of the previous design.

"There," he said, holding up the finished work. "I think I'm done with it now. After I'm through with the design, I have to sand it and make sure it's smooth, like this." He showed me how he gently sanded the wood by hand, then blew the dust out of the indentions.

He handed it to me for inspection.

"Beautiful!" I said. "Are you going to stain it?"

"Yes, I think I'm going to do this one a dark walnut. I keep all the stains over there," he said, pointing to a shelf filled with cans of stain.

What was most captivating was the detail of his work. It was intricate. Delicate. Beautiful. The cabinets seemed well made and pretty to look at, but this was something else entirely. I could feel his passion for his work. I could see it in the design, in the details, in the care he took—essentially, in the craftsmanship.

"This is just incredible," I said, running my hands over the finished piece. "How long did it take you to learn how to make something like this?"

"A long time. I started working with wood when I was fourteen. It took me about ten years to be able to make one like that."

"Wow," I said as I gently placed the piece back on the workbench.

I looked around. He had so many interesting things along the left wall of the shop. Antique signs and tools from long ago.

"Where did you find all these neat things?" I asked, pointing to the wall.

"Here and there. The mountains are full of off-the-wall junk shops where you can find interesting things."

"It's kind of like treasure hunting!" I said with excitement.

Nathan laughed. "Yes, I guess you could say that. There's a place not far from here that has some neat stuff. I haven't been there in a while. Maybe we could go sometime and check it out?"

"We should! It'd be fun!"

Nathan checked his watch. "I've still got some time; would you like to go now?"

"Sure! Only, I'll have to drive. Noah has to have a car seat."

Nathan laughed. "You're in luck! My truck is full of car seats! I always seem to have a niece or nephew coming along with me. But seriously, I have a couple in the back. They aren't strapped in right now, but you're welcome to check them out to see if one would work."

I thought it was funny that he had not only one but three car seats in the back seat of his truck. Apparently, they were family car seats that were shared between Ali, Nathan, Peter, and the grandparents. Nathan had taken the children somewhere last, and the car seats were still in his truck.

I checked to make sure I still had an extra diaper in the pocket of my carrier, and we were off.

We walked casually around the junk store, admiring some things and laughing at others. It was fun. Though Nathan was quiet, he had a good sense of humor. And he was the first one to point out and laugh at an old sign listing some outhouse rules. Time went on without us for a little while. We were lost in the worlds of days gone by—the smells of wood, leather, and old books. The old wooden telephones and record players, victrolas, and rusty farm tools were taking me back to places I had only visited in movies. Only this was real. These things had actually belonged to real people, long ago—people like my grandparents and their parents.

The prices of some of the things blew my mind. I had no idea old things, especially old, *rusty* things, could be so expensive! Neither one of us ended up buying anything. But it was worth going, just the same.

By the time we were ready to leave, it was after six o'clock.

"I'm getting kind of hungry," Nathan said, though he didn't look at me.

"Me too. Noah?" I said, looking down at him, who had been toddling along with us and holding my hand. "Are you hungry too, little man?"

He just looked up at me.

"I know it's getting late," Nathan continued, "but do you want to get something to eat before we head back?"

"I'd like that."

"OK." Nathan walked around the truck with us to open the door for Noah. He stood there while I buckled Noah into his seat. He seemed to be watching us absentmindedly. It didn't make me uncomfortable, though, like it would have if it had been someone else.

We ended up going to Del Rios. We didn't stay long, but we enjoyed it. As we were walking back to the car, Nathan slid his hand into mine, just for the thirty or so feet we had to walk to get back to the car. The gesture caught me off guard a little. I wasn't prepared for it, but I welcomed it.

On the way home, I received a text from Julian. It said he needed to see me tonight. Urgently. *I thought I wasn't supposed to have service out here! Why did I check my phone?* After some consideration, I decided to tell him no. I didn't want to see him anymore.

Nathan dropped us off near the side door to the house and slowly backed up and pulled away.

As the taillights were fading down the driveway, I heard my name being called out.

What! He's here!?

Julian walked around the back corner of the house from the direction of the barn.

Where is his car? I wondered.

"Adel!"

"Hi, Julian."

Julian was dressed nicely, and he seemed agitated. I wondered what was about to happen.

"Adel! I have something I want to show you! Come with me!"

"Julian, I don't ..."

"Please come! It's *very* important!"

He did seem agitated. I relented. "OK, just let me get our things inside, and then—"

"Adel, I just can't wait any longer! I've been here for over an hour already! And when I've got my mind made up ... I need to do this before I lose my nerve!"

Uh-oh ...

"Come with me!" he said, taking my hand.

"Julian? What are we doing?" I asked as he pulled me along behind him toward the barn.

"Shh! Just wait and see!" he said gleefully.

Oh no. This is worse than I thought.

I saw his car parked next to the barn door.

What in the world is going on?

Inside the barn, there was a table set up with glass lanterns around it, lighting the room with a soft yellow glow. The table was small and set for two. It had a white tablecloth and was covered in red rose petals. There was a bottle of champagne and a chocolate cake. It almost looked pretty, romantic even, except for the fact that I had no idea why it was set up in *my* barn. But then I began to guess ...

"Oh, Julian. That's pretty, but ..."

"Come inside! Come sit down!"

He ushered me to a seat with an air of pompous gallantry.

I sat. Noah was instantly fascinated with the chocolate cake and kept trying to reach across to the middle of the table to get at it. I was uncomfortable, but I tried to smile and be patient.

Julian sat down opposite me, only to hop up again and come instantly to my side. He went down awkwardly on one knee. "Adel," he said. "I have never met anyone like you." Despite my continual efforts, Noah had managed to reach the cake and brought back a handful of chocolate. "You are the most extraordinary woman I have ever met." Now Noah had managed to wipe some of the chocolate on my shorts. I only heard half of what he was saying. "... natural graces and extraordinary beauty."

"Adel, what I am saying is that I *love* you. I want to *marry* you. Will you consider taking my hand in marriage?" He pulled out the ring and held it out to me.

I glanced around the table for a napkin to wipe Noah's hands on while I racked my brain for what to say.

"Julian. You are such a nice guy, and you went to so much trouble. But I'm sorry, I can't marry you." Noah banged the table with his feet, knocking over the champagne bottle.

"I understand that you must have reservations after everything you've been through, but I promise that I will be good to you. I will treat you better than—"

I didn't let him finish.

"Julian, reservations aside, I *still* can't marry you. I don't think we would be good for each other. I don't think I could make you happy."

"Nonsense! You *already* make me happy!"

Well, that was the wrong route.

"I am happier with you than with anyone else in the world! I *need* you. You are good for me. I don't know who I would be without you."

"Julian, please stop. You're making me uncomfortable. I barely even know you!"

"We would live here and run the orchard, just like you dream of doing. I have everything worked out. Everything would be perfect, Adel."

I was beginning to lose my patience.

"Julian, I can't."

"I don't understand." he seemed exasperated now. "Don't you *want* a fresh start? Don't you want to stay here at the farm and get the orchard running again? Isn't that what you want? I can *help* you do that!" His face was getting red with anger. "Don't you need a father for Noah?"

That was it. I'd had enough.

"Julian!" I said firmly. "I need—"

"It's that other guy, isn't it? I *knew* nothing good would come of *that*!" Julian turned from me abruptly. He walked around to the side of the barn and leaned his arm on the wall, resting his head on his arm. He looked pathetic.

"How did this happen?" he moaned. "I know that if you think about it, if you take some time ..."

Between an overtired Noah pulling at everything on the table and Julian's persistence, I was about to lose it. "Look, Julian. I'm tired. I've had a very busy day. I'm ready to go inside now. I appreciate your offer. I'm flattered by it. But believe me when I say that I cannot accept it." I stood up and walked out of the barn, leaving Julian still leaning on the wall inside. He didn't follow me. I was thankful. I went inside the house, locked the door, and tried to forget that he may still be out there, hopefully cleaning up the mess in the barn. *What a waste of a cake,* I thought, and I shook my head.

That night, I lay in bed wondering about my day. What a contrast day and night had been.

TWENTY-EIGHT

Smitten

Julian called me several times that week, pleading his case. He was mostly polite. Apparently, in his mind, he had worked everything out between us to his satisfaction, and he believed that it was only a matter of time before I would see it his way. I tried to be patient with him. I didn't want to be rude, but I didn't know what else to say. It had been weeks since I had started trying to give him the impression that I wasn't interested. He seemed incapable or un*willing* to take the hint. And now this. I didn't know what else to do!

I was continuing to join Doris as she made her rounds each week. I had begun to feel like Amelia was a friend—a dear, old friend who spoke little and loved deeply, in her own way. I had even begun to get out of the car and speak with Tanya, though I would forever leave Noah in the car. Tanya didn't seem to understand much of what I said, but she would nod and smile a toothless smile. She seemed to sense that if I was with Doris, I must also be a friend. One day, when we arrived at her house, she greeted us at the door with a little basket. Inside the basket were some packs of candy. She gave us each a small pack of Skittles, smiling and nodding as she did. My heart grew a little softer toward Tanya that day as I saw a tiny glimpse of her soul and the affection she had for Doris, and now for me too.

The following week, there was going to be an extra gathering at the Shepherds' house on Wednesday evening to celebrate Ali's birthday. We arrived about five thirty. The night was falling more quickly as summer began to pass away. We had eaten, and it was getting close to Noah's bedtime, but I felt like we had a few more minutes. The evenings were so pleasant. Everyone was sitting on the porch, chatting casually about whatever was on their minds. Everyone seemed relaxed. Peaceful.

I was sitting on the floor of the porch with Noah, playing with some little cars, listening to the quiet chattering of the others and being lulled to a happy place by the rhythmic chorus of the crickets. I laid my head back on the porch railing and closed my eyes. Noah put a car in my lap. I laughed, took the car, and drove it up over his back and neck and head, then back down the other side. He giggled and laughed. Just then, Marie came over to ask if Noah could come have some cookies with the other children. She was turning into quite the babysitter. I didn't mind, of course. After Noah was gone, I closed my eyes again and listened. Jim, Robert, and Marie's friend Christina all soon followed Marie into the house, in search of cookies too, I guess. That left just me and Nathan on the porch. Nathan came over and sat by me on the floor. He took a toy car and rolled it back and forth over a wood plank.

"Enjoying yourself?" I teased.

"Yes, actually, but not because of the car."

He said nothing else and went back to driving his tiny car.

"What are you pretending?"

"Oh, I'm pretending that I'm driving along, sitting next to a beautiful lady. Going somewhere nice ... like Del Rios." We both laughed at the ridiculous turn of his story.

"But I don't really need to pretend," he continued. "I like where I am just fine."

"Oh?"

"Yes. I am already driving, sort of." He held up the car for me to see more clearly. "And I am already sitting next to a beautiful lady." He paused to look at me with that look I found hard to resist. He finished with "And I am already somewhere nice." He motioned around us.

I laughed. Sitting on the floor of his parents' porch wasn't exactly romantic, but it seemed to be tonight.

"So, you think I'm beautiful?" I asked mischievously.

"Incredibly so." He had leaned back on his hands with his legs stretched out and crossed in front of him. He seemed comical.

"You're being silly tonight," I said.

"I feel silly."

I couldn't help but laugh.

"Well, I'm glad you think I'm humorous. I try to tell you that I think you're incredibly and undeniably beautiful, and you laugh at me. This is getting nowhere."

I laughed some more. He was trying hard to keep a straight face. I had never seen him like this. I was enjoying it immensely.

"Well, I better not give you any more compliments then, because I don't think you'd take them seriously anyway." He shrugged and sighed dramatically but went on slowly with "Like how I love the way your hair falls across your face when you lean forward like that. Or how much I love the way you smile when you see something you think is beautiful. Or how much I enjoy watching you play toy cars with Noah ..." He sounded more sincere this time. I began to take him seriously. My heart beat faster. But then he quickly followed with "So, oh well! What are we to talk about then?"

"Let's talk about you."

"Me?"

"Yes. I want to know more about you. What it was like growing up here. What your favorite things are ... you know."

"Well, as long as you will sit here with me, I will talk about whatever you like."

"Good. Because I have lots of questions."

"Shoot."

"Where did you go to school?"

"I was homeschooled."

"Really?"

"Yes, before it was cool."

"I had forgotten that. Did you like it?"

"It has its pluses and minuses like anything else. But overall, I thought it was pretty good. I loved having the time and freedom to explore hobbies and passions outside of school. That's how I was able to apprentice under Mr. Holcomb and learn the craft of woodworking."

"What is your favorite thing to make out of wood?"

"Rocking chairs."

"Why?"

"They take time and focus and finding the right pieces of wood. It isn't easy to make a good rocking chair, but when I do, I feel like I've really done something."

"Mm ..." I said contemplatively.

"Next?"

"What's your favorite color?"

He laughed. "Green."

"Favorite author?"

"C. S. Lewis."

"Favorite band?"

"Too many to count."

"How many kids do you want to have?"

"Four."

"Me too!"

"Oh? Now I have a question for *you*," he said, leaning forward and looking me in the eyes.

I felt my face blush. "Yes?"

"Will you sit here and talk with me forever?"

I tossed a car at him.

Then we sat in silence for a few minutes.

All too soon, I heard a car engine turn on and realized how late it was—far past Noah's bedtime. The time had passed too quickly. But I wouldn't have traded it for the world.

Twenty-Nine

Cookies

The next day was Thursday. I woke up early and went over to Doris's for a morning visit.

"Doris, I woke up this morning feeling giddy and restless! I want to *do* something. *Make* something. Something crafty." I was sitting on the edge of the couch in Doris's living room, my hands clasped tightly together in my lap.

"I'm not a crafty person. I don't know where to start. What should I do? Help me!" I felt my eyes pleading my sincerity.

Doris laughed and eyed me suspiciously.

"Little honey, my goodness!" she said. "Calm down a bit first so we can figure out exactly what is going on here! Now, what's got you so agitated?"

"It's just ... I couldn't sleep well last night, I guess."

"Are you *sure* there's nothing *else* going on?" Her eyebrows were raised.

"I don't think so ..."

"Alright. Well, since you claim not to be crafty, which I heartily doubt, why don't you try cooking something? Something new. Maybe a cookie or dessert? I have plenty of recipes you could look through. Then, if you make plenty, perhaps you could share some, with Nathan, maybe?"

"Doris!" I felt my cheeks burn hot.

"Well, I just thought that if you went to the trouble to make something, and since he lives all alone and doesn't get many homemade treats of that sort, not since Elaine passed ..."

My happy agitation had turned to unbearable agitation very quickly. Part of me wanted to calmly and maturely take her advice and go make some cookies. The other part wanted to leave immediately and regret ever asking.

"Well, Noah," I said to my baby boy, once we had walked safely back across the street and were sitting at the kitchen table. "I guess we'll do it."

And we did, sort of ...

I looked over the recipes Doris had given me and found one that looked promising. I found all the ingredients and got to work. Halfway through spooning the cookies onto the pan, Noah began to fuss. I hurried through the last few rows and slid the pan into the preheated oven. Noah's fuss became a roar.

"There now. All done! Come on, little fella. Time for your nap!" I scooped up Noah and walked him upstairs to his room. We rocked for twenty minutes, but he continued to fuss and whine. "I think you're overtired. Go to sleep, Noah. It's sleepy time."

We rocked some more. Noah's wiggles and fusses became full-fledged cries again. My face began to feel hot. My whole body felt hot. The room felt small and stuffy. All at once, I smelled something burning.

"Oh no! The cookies!"

Down the stairs I ran, with Noah still in my arms. I reached the kitchen to find the room full of dark gray smoke. I ran across the room, wondering why on earth I hadn't left Noah in his bed. I put the now screaming Noah in his playpen, then ran to open the oven. Yes, there was fire. I stood motionless for a moment. *What should I do?* I looked frantically around. *Water! Yes! Wait. No, not water. This was an electric oven. Baking soda! Oh no! There was only a little baking soda left after making the cookies! What should I do!? A fire extinguisher! Maybe Grandma had a fire extinguisher!* I began to quickly look through the cabinets until I came to the sink. Looking under, I found the fire extinguisher. I yanked off the lock and opened the oven. *Oh no! I forgot to turn off the oven!* I shut the burning-hot oven door and leaned over to press the off button.

The smoke was so dense that I began to cough violently.

I reopened the oven and sprayed the flames until they were out, and then sprayed them some more. The fire was out and I felt my shoulders sag. I wiped a sweaty arm across my forehead and became aware that Noah was still screaming. He was standing in his playpen, looking over at me in fright. His face was all red and fatigued and wet with tears. My heart sank within me. *Was this worth it?*

"How could I do such a thing!?" I heard my voice say harshly. I shook my head in anger. Then I walked over to scoop up Noah. We went around to all the windows and opened them up.

"First thing tomorrow, we go buy a working fire alarm!" I told Noah as I pushed up the last window. All of a sudden, I felt fatigued and a little shaky. I walked back into the kitchen to double-check that the oven was still off, then went out onto the front porch to sit with Noah on the swing.

Later that day, after I had cleaned up the mess in the oven and wiped down the walls that the smoke had dinged, and after Noah had finally settled for his nap, I did finish cooking the rest of the cookie batter. This time, I stayed right by the oven and peeked in at the cookies every couple of minutes until they were done.

After they cooled, I sampled one. They were good. They were *very* good. *Thank you, Doris!* And despite the first pan being ruined, there still ended up being more than we could eat. Maybe I *would* share some. Why not? What message was it sending other than that of kindness toward a neighbor? Yes, I would do it! I looked through the cabinets until I found a nice little metal tin like the ones Grandma used to send me at Christmas, full of homemade goodies. This one was complete with a Christmas tree framed with a green wreath and holly berries. But it would serve the purpose.

After Noah woke, I changed and fed him, and we set off down the trail through the woods. I toted Noah in the front carrier as usual. We arrived in Nathan's backyard the same time that Nathan was coming out of his shop. He saw us approaching and slowly and self-consciously ran his hands through his hair a few times, then waved.

"Hi! I tried a new recipe in the kitchen today, and there was plenty, so I thought I'd share some!" I held up the tin for him to see.

"OK! Thanks! What is it?" He walked to meet us.

"Oatmeal chocolate chip cookies."

"Great! I love oatmeal chocolate chip cookies. Thank you!"

"You're welcome." I handed him the tin, with a bit of a laugh that made Nathan look at me curiously. *Oh, the mess it took to get those cookies made!* I said nothing about it though.

"Nice tin," he said, eyeing the tin with eyebrows raised.

"Thanks. It was my grandma's." I shrugged.

There was a moment of awkwardness as each of us was trying to decide what should come next. It was evening, and the sun would be setting soon.

"Well, we should be getting back," I said at last. "Have a nice evening." I turned to walk back down the trail.

Nathan followed.

"Do you mind if I walk back with you? I've been meaning to check on the hay in the lower field."

"Sure. But don't you think it'll be getting dark soon?"

Nathan looked up at the sky. "Yes," he said, smiling a very handsome smile. "But I'll be alright."

I turned away and felt my face flush as I became aware that I had been admiring his smile.

He came to walk beside me.

Like always, I was very aware of his closeness. I didn't mean to be awkward, but for some reason, it was suddenly hard to think. Hard to form thoughts into words, words into sentences. So instead, I just walked on silently down the trail.

The air in the forest was sweet. It smelled of hemlock and damp leaves. It was cool and moist, but all of this was lost on me. I was still too deep in thought.

After a few moments, Nathan broke the silence and asked, "So, are you still settling in well? Are you liking the farm?"

I almost jumped out of my skin. I had still been thinking of Nathan and the effect of his handsome smile ...

"What? Oh, yes. I think so ... I mean, I do love the farm. It's just, you know, a lot to get used to."

"Do you mean living in the country?"

"Well, yes. No, not exactly ... just, I don't know. Everything."

"It's a lot to maintain an old house, let alone a farm. Especially alone."

"Exactly! I didn't really get much experience with housework prior to coming here. Except when I was here during the summer as a kid. Grandma always had work for me to do when I was here, but that was all so long ago. I don't remember much of what I learned. At my parents' house, I never had to do much, you know? We had hired help who took care of everything. I didn't even need to buy groceries until moving here!"

"Wow," Nathan said with a teasing smile. I blushed again.

"But learning a whole new trade is something else entirely," I continued. "I know next to nothing about apples, and the more I learn, the less I feel I know! It's been so overwhelming. Peter helped some. But then the storm ..."

"You were very brave for coming here. Why'd you do it?"

Very brave or very impetuous ...

"Do what?" I asked.

"Why'd you come here?"

I was surprised at the question, and I felt like I only partially knew the answer. I trusted Nathan, but I still wasn't sure I wanted to get into how I felt while I was living at my parents' house. I wasn't ready. I wasn't sure how to approach it. So, after pausing a minute to think, I replied, "Well, to be honest, I'm not entirely sure. A lot of it has to do with my grandparents, I guess. I loved them very much. It meant something to me that Grandma wanted me to have this place. I don't know why she did, but it *meant* something to me. It made me sad to think of selling it without even *trying* to make it work and without ever seeing it again. I think it also may have something to do with my regret at not seeing them much over the last ten years or so. I want to make it up to them by keeping their place and their memory alive."

Nathan looked thoughtful, but he didn't say anything. I glanced over at him, hoping for his thoughts.

After a few minutes, he asked, "So you weren't just running away from home?" I stopped in the trail and turned to him. He didn't seem upset or doubtful of my good intentions. He had said it calmly and unemotionally. He genuinely wanted to know.

How did he do that? How did he know what I was thinking?

I tried to gather my wits. "Yes," I said at last. "I think in some ways, I was running away. But the other reasons are just as true, if not more true."

"You must have had good reasons for leaving."

"I ... I think I did ... though it's all still a little fuzzy to me."

"You'll work it out," he said kindly. "These things take time."

I paused to think. *Why did I come? And what is it about this place?* I knew deep down there was still more to my leaving than just Noah and my grandparents. And as much as I loved the farm, there was still more to it than that too. My whole life, I had always felt like something was missing. Something important. But I was never really sure what that was. I still wasn't sure.

"Nathan," I said. "I'm not sure of all the reasons for my wanting to come here. But I know that I was missing something in my life back home. And I think I'm beginning to find whatever that is *here*."

Nathan watched me silently.

"And I love this place! I loved it when I was a kid, and I still love it. I love the mountains and all the smells and the way the grass feels on the bottom of my bare feet. I love the sunsets and the stars at night, and the bright, hot sunshine on my face. I even love the humidity! I think ... Anyway, every day, I find I love it even more. It hasn't been easy. Sometimes it's been just plain horrible ..." I was thinking of the tornado.

"But I'm *trying* to make it work. I *want* to make it work, because, well, I love it!"

We were still standing in the middle of the trail. I could clearly see Nathan's face. He was still looking at me and I could detect an expression in his eyes that I hadn't seen there before. I couldn't identify it. He wasn't smiling, and he still seemed serious, but somehow, I felt that he approved of what I said.

After a moment, he motioned for me to walk on and said, "I think you'll be happy here, Adel."

It was all I needed.

Nathan changed the subject to point out a couple of songbirds we saw as we approached the green grass at the edge of the woods. We walked on and chatted easily for a minute more before Nathan stopped and said slowly, "Good night, Adel." He said it with more feeling than the words typically evoke. He stood looking at me with that same expression from the night before when he was telling me what he loved about me. It was something much deeper than admiration.

Then with a rueful smile, he turned in the direction of the lower field, whistling as he walked away. I watched him go. The sound of a barred owl filled the woods to my right. I barely noticed.

The sun was beginning to set, and the crickets were chirping a chorus from the thicket of the trees. The sound was growing more dim as the year wore on. I guessed it wouldn't be long before the air got too cool for the crickets. I would miss them. The dry leaves rustled in the breeze overhead. I felt change in the air.

I had such a mixture of feelings as we entered the house that evening. I enjoyed Nathan's company tremendously. Besides that, I felt comfortable with him. It had been some weeks since I had begun to think of him as one of my closest friends. I knew that much. But the uneasiness around thoughts of potentially falling for someone again were casting a shadow over my joy. I had been through all of that before. It wouldn't do. Most likely, he didn't care for me in that way anyway. But even if he did ... *worse* if he did ... I wasn't ready. Or was I? I had to get to the bottom of all this ... but later. I was tired, we needed to go to bed soon, and my back was sore from carrying Noah all that way. He was getting heavy! I bathed him and dressed him in a soft blue onesie covered in tiny little baseballs. Then we ate a light dinner and I tucked him into bed. He was out within minutes. I was so thankful. I needed some alone time, time to think. It was rare for him to go down so easily. He must have been exhausted from the events of the day. I anticipated not having long before he woke again, so I hurried to the porch swing. That was my favorite thinking spot. Only this time, I felt too restless to think. I ended up going to bed early too, only to toss and turn and wonder—my future seemed to be in the throes of a mighty sea. I was struggling with the farm. It felt like a huge burden on my shoulders, weighing me down, drowning me, but I didn't know what to do about it. Should I sell it? Or should I get some loans and fight it out? Should I move back to San Francisco? Or move somewhere else down here? And then there was Nathan—would he hold the key to my future? Or not? Would there be someone else? Or no one, ever? It was hours before fatigue finally won out and I fell into a fitful sleep.

The next morning brought with it the desire to see Nathan again. I was extremely curious to know what he was thinking. I was trying to think of a good reason to go back over to his house but could come up with nothing. At last I resolved to be patient and wait until Sunday when we would all gather back together again at the Shepherds' house. It would be hard, but I could be patient. It was Friday. Sunday was only two days away. Besides, I had no choice. Unless I called him ... no! I would rather talk to him in person.

Later in the afternoon, I noticed that we were getting low on a few kitchen staples and decided to run to the store. We left after dinner, about six o'clock.

We crossed over the river and entered the edge of town. We drove by a road that crossed Main Street, and I noticed Nathan's truck stopped at the light. As we passed, I looked hard to try to catch his attention and noticed a woman sitting next to him. I was so taken aback! I looked again, quickly. Yes, it was definitely a woman. And she was sitting *very* close to him. *Too* close ... and it wasn't one of his sisters! *They must be on a date!* I gripped the steering wheel a little tighter and drove on into the Food Mart parking lot. I pulled into a spot and turned off the engine. Then we sat. Noah kicked his feet and squealed out little babbling words, but I was oblivious to it all. *Well!* I thought. *At least I didn't have to wait until Sunday!*

THIRTY

Courtney

When Sunday finally rolled around, I was a little anxious. I wanted to see Nathan, but what about that woman? Church was important, and I wasn't going to miss just because of a potentially awkward encounter with Nathan. I tried to pull myself together, hoped for the best, and headed out. I decided to wear one of my most attractive dresses and spent extra time styling my hair.

Almost as soon as I entered the sanctuary, I recognized the woman who had been with Nathan on Friday night. She was standing with a group of ladies near the front of the church. She was talking and laughing and certainly seemed to be the center of attention.

I found my seat as quickly as possible. The normally comfortable pew seemed extra hard that day. And why were my knees so close to the pew in front of me? I felt hot and uncomfortable. I used my handout as a fan while waiting for the service to begin. Where were the Shepherds? I hadn't seen them yet. Oh, there they were, sitting up near the front. When the woman was through with her groupies, she turned and walked over to join them. She sat near Annie, and they started talking politely. *Who is she!?* I wondered.

After church, I drove anxiously over to the Shepherds' house.

As Noah and I walked into the kitchen, we were met by all the ladies standing around talking to that woman. That *woman!*

"Hi, Adel! Come in!" said Annie. "This is Courtney! She's an old friend of the family."

"Hello," I said curtly, with a nod.

"Hi, Adel!" Her voice was angelic. Her manners were soft and gentle. She seemed to be a country angel in cowboy boots and a flowy, short skirt. "I've heard so much about you! But it's nice to finally be able to put a face with the description."

"I'm sorry," I said. "What's your name again?"

"Courtney. Courtney Davenport. I grew up with the Shepherds," she said. "I've been out of town for a few years now. Man, it does feel good to be back!" She smiled around at everyone.

"I understand that you've moved into Ms. Elaine's old place?" she asked me.

Though she was polite and seemed nice enough, I was having a hard time wanting to talk to this woman. But I answered her anyway.

"Yes. I've been there since March."

"I was so sad to hear that Ms. Elaine passed away. I wished that I could have been here." She sighed. "My parents own Low Gate Farms off Highway Fifty-Two. It's also an apple orchard. Just like Sweet Valley. I've been off doing marketing and sales in West Virginia, but I've decided that it's not for me. *This* is where I belong. And I am so *glad* to be home."

She sighed again.

Alright, I'd had enough. I smiled politely and turned to walk out of the room and find Noah and the other children. I heard them laughing from somewhere in the house. But as I turned to walk out, Nathan came into the room. Courtney hurried over to him and took his arm. He looked a little surprised. She smiled up at him with her gorgeous blue eyes. She was stunning. Her blond hair was perfectly in place, and her features were also perfect, but her clothes had that rustic feel like the rest of the people in town. She was the perfect blend of beauty and country, and I was jealous. But I had seen enough. I turned away abruptly and went out the door.

My head began to ache as the day wore on. I hardly looked at Nathan the whole afternoon. A couple of times I thought he was trying to get my attention, but I ignored him. I also tried to stay out of Courtney's way, though it seemed almost as if she was seeking me out! I talked politely whenever she approached me and left her alone the rest of the time. I began to get exasperated by what I had seen and heard. I ended up leaving early. I needed to get away and have some fresh air and time to think.

The next day, the aches began. They started in my wrists and slowly spread to the rest of my body. My throat began to hurt, too, and before I knew it, I was sick in bed with the flu. I was sick the whole rest of the week. I missed the following Sunday at church and also the gathering at the Shepherds'. I was glad. I didn't want to go back. It wasn't pleasant for me to go there right now.

I hated being sick in bed, though, especially with Noah getting to the age where he wanted to get into *everything*. Once he found his legs, he took off at a run! I kept having to get up and get him out of the cabinets, the bathroom, off the stairs. Perhaps that's one reason why it took me so long to recover.

Doris stopped by a few times to bring us food and supplies. I was so thankful for Doris.

The next Sunday, I was feeling much better, but I decided to let the flu still be my excuse for not going to either church or the Shepherds'. I told Rebecca in a text that although I was better, I felt I still needed to rest and that I hoped she understood.

"I think I do understand ... feel better soon," her text said.

If only she knew.

Julian had backed off some, but he was still calling me. I only answered it sometimes and tried to keep it short. I told Julian I didn't feel like talking the first week I was sick. But after the fog lifted, I began feel lonely, so *I* called *him*. What a mistake. During our conversation, I mentioned Courtney Davenport and how we had met at the Shepherds' house.

"Courtney! Yes! She's been away for a while! How is she?"

"Just wonderful," I said.

"So, she and Nathan are a thing," he told me. "They started dating a few years back. It's hard to believe so much time has passed. Wow! But it's good to hear she's back around! Is she here to stay?"

"I hope not," I muttered under my breath.

"What?"

"I think so," I said.

After hanging up, I sat still in my bed and stared at the wall. I had made a mistake by calling Julian. I didn't want to hear what he had told me about Nathan and Courtney. I wished it unsaid. One good thing came from my calling him. I was now certain that I needed to close the Julian chapter of my life once and for all. No more leading him on and giving him false hope. I had always known he wasn't good for me, or I for him. And I didn't like the way he ignored Noah. But for some reason, I had led him along anyway, even after his proposal and my rejection. Shame on me! Early on, I thought that perhaps we could make it work, but work is what it would have been. And I believed it wouldn't have been worth it in the end.

It was cruel to lead a man on.

So I called him back, quickly.

"Hey, Julian. I'm sorry for calling you right back, but I need to tell you something."

"Alright."

"I'm sorry. I feel like I've been leading you on, and it's not right. When I told you that night at the barn that I couldn't marry you, I meant it. I really can't. And I'm not going to be able to talk to you anymore either. This is the last time I'm going to call you or answer your calls. I'm sorry. I just can't do this anymore."

Silence.

I think our conversation about Nathan and Courtney had given him a new ray of hope, only to have it immediately shut down.

"Fine. OK!" He sounded frustrated. Then he hung up.

I hated these sorts of things. It was one of the reasons I didn't date much when I was younger. I put my phone down and rolled over onto my stomach. I rested my chin in my hands. Life was so hard right now …

Over the course of the evening, Julian sent me eighty-six text messages. He poured his heart out in ways I didn't even know was possible. In creepy ways too. He claimed strange things, like my encouraging him in his faith. Without me, he would slip away again. He said that when he drove alone in his car, he often saw images of me in the sky above him. He said I was his reason for living. Each of these claims shook me a little more than the last. I had no idea that I could feel so little when he was feeling so much. I began to guess that he was a little unstable. Much of what he said didn't even make sense! I quit reading after message twenty-eight. I never responded to any of them. I was through.

The rest of the week dragged by. Even though I read two whole novels and even though Noah learned three new words, I still felt very *blah*.

The next Sunday, I was also absent from church and the Shepherds'. Later that day, I got a call from Rebecca. She said she needed to talk to me. Would I mind if she stopped by for a few minutes? Of course I didn't mind! I would be glad to see her!

"Hi, Adel," she said as she came cautiously in through the living room door. "How are you feeling? Better?"

"Yes, I think I've finally got my strength back," I said, though I knew I didn't sound like it. We sat on the couches in the living room, and Noah played with his toys on the floor.

"So, I've been wanting to talk to you. I suspect that there might be reasons other than the flu that have kept you away the last few weeks. Am I right?"

I just looked at her. Could I trust her? I wasn't even sure how I felt about anything anymore. I was all mixed up inside. I wasn't feeling like myself at all.

She took my silence as an affirmative and went on. "Well," she said. "I need to tell you what happened last week, at our house after church. Courtney came again. Apparently, she's been calling Nathan nonstop, wanting to talk and asking for his help. She actually broke down on the side of the road a few weeks ago, and he saw her and took her home. That was the first time they had seen each other in several years! Let me start over. So, Nathan and Courtney dated a few years back. Courtney broke up with him when she was wanting to move up north for a job and Nathan didn't want to go with her. It was hard on Courtney, but she left anyway. It didn't take very long for Nathan to see that it was for the best. After she was gone for a little while, he was convinced that he had never loved her. We were all glad. Though we grew up with her, and though we cared about her, none of us thought she was good for him. She's been gone for about three years."

I broke in. "Was that a Friday? That he found her on the side of the road?"

"I think so ... I don't really remember. Did you see them together?"

I nodded.

"Oh, Adel, I'm sorry."

"Go on," I said.

She took a deep breath and nodded. "So, apparently she had it in her mind to try to get him back. She has been doing everything in her power ... but, Adel, last Sunday at our house, after dinner when everyone was sitting in the living room, Courtney came over and sat *very* close to Nathan on the couch. He stood up and, in front of everyone, told her that he knew what she was doing and that it wouldn't work. He told her that he already cared for someone else. That stopped her in her tracks! She was flabbergasted! She didn't come back today. In fact, she didn't even come to church! I guessed that was why she was coming."

"Now, Courtney is a good girl, Adel. She has a good heart, I think. She's just a little needy. She didn't have a good home life, you know? Try not to think ill of her. All she knew was that Nathan was still unmarried. She didn't realize that his heart was engaged elsewhere."

She patted my hands, which were held together tightly in my lap.

This friend understood me. I didn't even have to say a word. I was so thankful for her at that moment.

"I hope you'll come back next week," she said softly.

After Rebecca left, I sat there on the couch, thinking. Rebecca had said that Nathan already cared for someone else. I knew what that meant. I knew it in my soul. But instead of feeling happy or excited, I felt anxious.

THIRTY-ONE

Dangerous

After talking to Rebecca, I felt like I should go see Nathan. While my nerve was up, I slid Noah into the carrier and set off to his house. The air was getting cool. The trail and surrounding woods gave evidence of the changing seasons. The leaves were turning vibrant colors of reds, oranges, yellows, and purples. They crunched under my feet as we walked along. When we got there, he didn't seem to be home. All the lights in the house were out, and the shop was locked up. He didn't answer when I knocked.

Aw, man ... I kicked at the dirt and wandered back to the house.

The next Sunday, I tried to arrive a little early to see if I could catch him before church. I didn't see him, not after church either. I did see Annie and Robert in the parking lot, who heartily encouraged me to join them at their house again.

I had to go. It had been three weeks since I last went to the Shepherds' house. *What must they think of me?* I wondered. *I'm sure they know why I've been absent. How incredibly awkward.* But still, I had to go.

I also had to run a couple errands before we headed over, so I told Annie that we would be there, just a little later than usual.

We arrived about three o'clock. It was a chilly day, and everyone was enjoying the warmth of the fireplace inside. When I walked into the living room, I saw Jim and Robert and the three oldest children playing a game on the floor. They stopped their game to welcome me warmly. Maggie Ann came running over to hug me. "I'm glad you're back!" she said. "Now that Miss Courtney's gone, will you stay?"

"Maggie Ann!" her daddy said sharply.

I knew my face must have given evidence of my embarrassment, but I just laughed and nodded to Maggie Ann. "What are you playing?" I asked.

"Candyland! Want to play? I just got Princess Lolly!"

"Oh! That sounds like fun! I'm not going to play right now though. Maybe in a little while."

"OK!" said Maggie Ann, and she ran back and plopped down on the floor beside her papa.

I put Noah in the empty playpen and went into the kitchen just as Nathan was coming up the stairs from the basement. He was the only one in the room. I wondered where everyone else was.

"Oh! Hi!" said Nathan. He was carrying a couple of rifles and a small leather bag. "I'm glad you're here." He smiled warmly.

My knees felt weak.

I had actually thought about things I might want to say to him once we were together again, but now all the thoughts left me. I didn't know what to say. I looked again at the things in his arms. "What are you up to?" I asked a little stiffly.

"I was just about to clean these rifles. It's been a while." He held one up as if I'd be able to see the dirt and grime he was speaking of. I took his word for it.

"Where is everyone?" I asked.

"Mom and the girls are downstairs looking through some old stuff in the storage room. They won't mind if you join them. Or you can sit up here and help *me*." He eyed me playfully. I caved.

"Alright! But I must warn you that I know absolutely *nothing* about guns."

"That's alright. You can just hand me the supplies."

He sure is in good spirits today, I thought with a smile to myself.

We sat and chatted about random things as he carefully showed me how to clean a gun. I was impressed with the craftsmanship of the rifles. I had never really looked at a gun up close, and I was finding that they were rather interesting.

"Sometime I'd like to learn to shoot," I said while looking down the barrel of the newly cleaned rifle.

Nathan laughed. "I'm sorry, but we can't let you do that! Because if we do, then you will soon be outshooting every man in town ... and how do you think they will take it? Not very well, I assure you."

I grinned at the compliment, even if it was in jest.

I also appreciated the fact that Nathan made no mention of anything that had passed over the last few weeks. It was as if it had never happened, and I was relieved.

After we finished with the guns and put them away, it was nearly dinnertime. I heard Rebecca, Ali, Marie, and Annie making their way up the basement steps.

"Hi Adel!" said Annie as entered the kitchen. "I'm so glad to see you! And to see you've been well occupied!" She smiled warmly and cast a glance at Nathan, who was busy putting the last of his supplies away.

They began to pull out the leftovers from lunch, as was the custom on Sunday evenings. I realized for the first time how hungry I was. *Wow, in running our errands, we forgot to eat lunch!*

I bet Noah was hungry too! I hurried to check on him in the living room, but he was still playing happily in the playpen, so I went back into the kitchen to help with the dinner preparations.

After dinner, everyone felt lazy. The men went into the living room to talk. The ladies stayed and relaxed at the kitchen table. The kids put on a movie, and even Noah curled up with Maggie Ann on the couch in the media room.

After a few minutes of talking, I got up to get some water.

Nathan saw me from where he was sitting in the living room. He came over to me and said quietly, "Hey, want to step outside for a minute?"

"Um … sure. Just let me grab my jacket."

We slipped unnoticed out the back door.

"Come on," he said as he led the way through the dark and across the yard.

He led us to the gazebo. It was chilly, but it wasn't unbearable. The view from the gazebo was spectacular. It was in the side yard, closest to the edge of the mountain, where you could see almost the entire night sky and the town down below, with its lights sparkling and twinkling in the crystal-clear night. It was spectacular! I leaned out on the railing and breathed in a draft of cool, crisp air and let it out slowly.

Nathan came and leaned on the railing beside me, only more closely than any time before. His arm was resting up against mine. I felt my face burn hot. I kept my head down so Nathan wouldn't notice how red it was, as if he could, in the dark.

The pull was there as strong as usual … stronger even. I leaned toward him ever so slightly. Then his arms were around my waist. He was holding me close. His hand went up behind my neck as he kissed me, soft and slow. Then he held me again, close up against his chest. I could feel his heart beating. His head was up against mine, his mouth close to my ear.

"I knew it was dangerous to be close to you," he said, with a hint of amusement in his voice.

I pushed back a little so I could see his face. Was he teasing?

He bent down to my level and looked me straight in the eyes. "But I *had* to. You were away *too* long."

There were no words for what I felt, so I just stepped a little closer and put my arms around him. I needed his warmth. Then I lifted my face to his, and he met me in another delightful kiss.

We lingered in the gazebo for a while, just enjoying each other's company.

Soon, we would be missed. Would it matter? Did I care if everyone knew what we were doing? I didn't really. I was OK with it. Let the world know!

"It's getting late," I said, my head resting on his chest.

"I guess we should head back in, but I'd rather not," Nathan said quietly.

I nodded slowly.

"I'm going to have a busy week with work, but I'd still like to see you?"

"Yes. I'll be around. Just call me or come over."

Nathan slid his fingers into mine and brought my hands up to his lips. He kissed them gently, then led the way back to the house.

On Monday, I was going through a box I had brought from home that was full of keepsakes. I enjoyed spending the evening looking through all my old treasures, reminiscing and daydreaming of days gone by. While I was looking through a small jewelry box of ornaments, I noticed my old purity ring. A Sunday school teacher from high school had given us the rings in tenth grade. I took the promise seriously and wore my ring religiously. I thought it had helped me to "save myself" for marriage. I thought it had worked. I was delighted to see it again. *Hey there, old friend! I think you're just what I need!* With my obvious attraction to Nathan, I thought that if we were to be spending a lot of time together, it might be good to wear my ring again. Without any more thought, I slid it on my ring finger and continued looking through the treasure box.

Monday and Tuesday went by, and I didn't hear anything from Nathan. I was OK with that. I knew he was going to have a busy week. When I hadn't heard from him by Wednesday night, I began to wonder if something was up. On Thursday, I texted him to ask if he still wanted to get together sometime, but there was no response. Something must be wrong. Did he regret spending time with me? Had he decided Courtney was the one for him after all? That seemed doubtful, but still

I wondered ... I became a nervous wreck as the week wore on. Fretful. Irritated. Clueless. I figured that if he were hurt or something, Rebecca would let me know. I heard from no one. My anxiety when Sunday finally rolled around was high. I wanted to go; I wanted to stay. I wanted to know; I didn't want to know. Out of habit, I went, but my head was scattered and unfocused. I hardly heard a word the preacher said. After the service, I picked up Noah. I still hadn't seen Nathan. Would I leave the church without seeing him? Rebecca and Jim and their four children were standing just outside the children's wing. I saw them and walked over. Rebecca's face seemed a little troubled when she saw me.

"Is everything OK?" I asked.

"Well, yes. I think so. Have you seen Nathan today?"

"No, I haven't."

"Oh. OK. Well, I guess we'll see you in a little while?" She tried to smile, but it was actually a question. What in the world was going on?

"Yes. We're planning to come today."

"Just the two of you?"

"Yes?" I was so confused.

Just then, Nathan walked up. He didn't seem like himself at all. His slow and easy movements were agitated and restless. Stress plainly showed on his face.

He didn't say a word to me. He looked confused and miserable.

"Alright," Rebecca said to me, though she was looking at Nathan. "See you in a bit." And they all walked off.

I felt almost sick. What was going on?

Between the stress of the last few days and Noah still not sleeping well, I had begun to feel lightheaded. My head had begun to ache too. I wasn't sure if I wanted to go to the Shepherds' today after all. But when I got Noah in the car and started to drive, that's where we ended up. Maybe Nathan and I would get a chance to talk.

I slowly and cautiously entered the house. The children were all wrestling with their papa in the living room. Everything seemed normal. I went into the kitchen where the ladies were getting lunch together. They seemed normal enough. Even Rebecca seemed to be her normal self again. I pitched in, and then it was time to eat. When everyone sat down, I noticed that someone was missing. It was Nathan.

Rebecca noticed my confusion and said, "Nathan had somewhere he had to go today."

"Oh, OK." My food was dry in my mouth. I'm sure it was good, but I tasted none of it. Everything went down out of politeness and from knowing that I needed food, whether I wanted it or not.

After lunch, I tried to act as normal as possible, but it was a struggle. I was fretting. I knew something must be bothering Nathan, but he wasn't here to ask. I didn't really want to ask anyone else. It was too personal. Our affection had not yet been publicly announced.

We ended up going home early, claiming a headache as my cause. It wasn't a lie either. I really did have a splitting headache. I was so thankful when we finally pulled into the drive at home and I could take some Tylenol and rest. Noah seemed sleepy, so we ate a light dinner and went to bed.

The next Sunday, I saw Nathan from a distance at church. He still seemed not like himself. I couldn't understand his mixed and muddled expressions. He was reserved, cold even. He would not meet my eye. It was painful to see him like this, his usual calm and relaxed self so uptight and tense.

He never came close to me, so I never had the opportunity to ask him what was wrong. It was more than I could bear. I wanted nothing more than to hear his voice and to talk to him. To figure out what the problem was. I wanted to call him. But we had never talked on the phone. It was one of the things I loved about him, that he preferred to talk in person. I felt awkward calling him, especially since our relationship had not really been solidified. He had a right to do what he pleased. If he wanted to tell me what was bothering him, then he would. My heart began to suffer though. It felt sore. Like it might be breaking.

I spent the whole next week throwing myself into preparations for our church's fall festival, which was to be held the following Saturday.

There was a lot to be done, with game making, cleaning, decorating, and cooking. I figured the best way to cope with everything was to stay busy. I was right. Staying busy gave me something productive to do and helped me keep my mind off of Nathan. At least during the day.

Besides, the festival sounded fun. It was something good to look forward to. I was *fine* going on my own! I didn't need a man in my life! I was doing just fine before all of this, wasn't I?

THIRTY-TWO

Fall Festival

It was the second Saturday in October. The day of the festival had finally come. It was five o clock, and I was dressed and ready, snapping the last few buttons on Noah's little blue overalls. My cheeks felt hot and my head was swimming, but I didn't stop to consider why; it was time to go. Noah's big, toothy grin as I scooped him up made me forget my weariness. I made my way down the steps and toward the front door, baby bag and Noah in tow. I reached over to the armchair by the front door to grab my purse, and we were out.

The afternoon was bright and warm, and the leaves of the deciduous mountain trees were literally bursting with color—the maples, a deep crimson, the oaks and poplars various shades of yellow and orange. The air smelled strongly of freshly mowed hay. I stopped to take in the view and breathe deeply. It all felt a bit surreal. My head was still swimming, my legs were a little weak, and my arms were heavy. I began to feel strange, as if I were only a spectator and not the one standing in the bright October sun, with the gentle breeze ruffling my hair. I shook my head and went on to the car and buckled Noah into his seat. I felt my forehead. No fever. No cough. *I'm not sick. I must just be tired. We don't have to stay late.*

The front of the little country church was a sight to behold. Adorning the entryway was a tastefully decorated arbor made of cornstalks and encircled with vines that were covered with fall leaves and tiny orange pumpkins. Hanging above the arbor on either side were two large glass lanterns, flickering with the soft glow of the candles inside. At the base of the arbor were piles of pumpkins and gourds of all shapes, sizes, and colors, such that you would only see in a small town in the country. Even more captivating than the church were the smiles and laughter of the chattering group of people standing around outside. The people at this church had a preference for visiting out of doors, in the parking lot or out in the little grassy area by the side of the parking lot, where the pavilion was. They filled up both places tonight, and they greeted us warmly as we approached.

Everyone seemed happy to be there. Genuinely happy. Like they were having fun in one another's company. Before coming to the town of Cherry Hill, most of the special events in my life had been a formality, not done because I *wanted* to do them. But with these people, I was getting used to what it was like to truly *enjoy* things. Even though the last month had been especially hard, I was still thankful to get to be a part of an evening like this. I waded through the crowd. *I'm just happy to be here tonight, with these friends.* Mr. Woodyard approached and shook my hand; his wife, Julia, gave me a warm hug. A little girl named Jenny ran over to pat Noah's arm and coo into his tiny pink face, which made him squeal delightfully.

Then I saw Doris and Ace. Doris waved at me and motioned for me to come to them. I slowly waded through the festive crowd and couldn't help but laugh a little as I did. I waved politely to Nathan, who was standing near the arbor, still looking serious and distant. He nodded back, but he did not come to me. To his left was Rebecca, who was tending to the injured elbow of a tearful Maggie Ann. The two younger children were looking on. Just then, Randall ran up, and I heard him exclaim, "Mama! They're going to have a *cakewalk*!" I had never seen him so animated!

"Mama" smiled gently and spoke something softly to her son, and I was forced by the crowd to keep moving in the direction of the Joneses.

From there, I could see the pavilion, which was decorated with orange and white streamers, balloons, pumpkins, and hay bales. Tonight, it served as the game area for the children. As the grown-ups put the finishing touches on the pavilion decorations and games, the children were taking turns going on a wagon ride around the field behind the church. I waved to the children as they passed by the crowd. Several of the children were holding little baggies of candy corn. A few others already had painted faces. They were such a jolly sight.

"Hi, Doris! Ace! How are you tonight?" I gave Doris a little hug and Ace a shake of the hand.

"We're doing just fine! But how are you?" Doris asked, holding me back a little so she could see my face. "You look a little pale. You feelin' alright?"

"Yes! I'm fine! I'm just a little tired, that's all."

"OK," she said, but she continued to eye me with concern.

"Well, we're about to make our way to the fellowship hall. We're supposed to help with the serving in a little while. What do they have you doing tonight?"

"I'm supposed to help with the ring toss!" I laughed. "And I better head on over there. I think it's about time for the games to start!"

There were all kinds of games set up for the children. There were ball tosses and ring tosses, a dunking pool with a clown sitting on a perch, and pools with little floating ducks, some of which had a special number on the bottom for the prize. There was a dart game where the kids had to pop a balloon and a funny game where the children had to hit one side of a small seesaw to send a stuffed puppy flying through the air in hopes of it landing in a barrel. And they had a special way of doing bobbing for apples, where the apples were hung by a string from the rafters of the pavilion. A fork was tied to the end of each string, and the fork was pushed into the top of an apple so that it was held in midair. The children had a ball trying to catch the apples in their teeth while they swung wildly through the air! And then of course, there was the cakewalk.

I held Noah while I worked our booth. It was a busy hour, and we handed out lots of prizes. It was fun, and I almost forgot about being so tired. On the way out, I let Noah choose a duck out of the tiny blue pool at Marie's station. His duck didn't have a number, but Marie gave him some candy anyway. Then we made our way over to the seesaw game. Noah had fun trying to lift the heavy mallet onto the end of the seesaw.

After the games were finished, it was time for the feast to begin. While the children had been playing happily and winning their candy and prizes, their mothers had been busy putting out covered dishes and desserts on long tables that ran along the front of the fellowship hall. The tables had white linen tablecloths that were sprinkled with fall leaves and decorated with colorful apples and pumpkins. The circular dining tables were decorated similarly, with the addition of a large candle in a glass jar sitting in the middle.

I had never in my life seen so much home-cooked food all in one place. The smell was heavenly! Macaroni and cheese, herbed potatoes, green bean casserole, sweet potatoes, ham, turkey, rolls, pumpkin pie! And homemade applesauce, apple butter with biscuits, apple cider, apple pie, apple tarts, apple strudel, apple bread ... There was way more than I could eat, even if I had an appetite, which I didn't. Even so, I couldn't help but fill my plate with a variety of things that looked oh, so delicious. There were two long lines, one running down either side of the tables. Everyone's eyes were on the food.

After filling my plate, I returned to the table I was sharing with the Joneses. Doris was holding Noah, and she seemed in no hurry to return him to me, so I ate a little. It *was* good. I ate some more. Before I knew it, my food was mostly gone. I had saved some sweet potatoes, green beans, and a little turkey for Noah to try. Before I reached for him, I took a minute to look around at the happy scene. The laughter. The happy voices. The simple love of just being together, all in one place. It spoke gently to my heart. I wasn't sure I understood it, but I knew that I liked it. All these people, of various ages, with different backgrounds and different families, different jobs, different economic statuses, some with heavy burdens, others just beginning on the road of life, all together in one place, putting their differences aside so they could just be together and enjoy one another's company. *Almost everyone, I* thought, thinking of Nathan. I loved what I saw before me. It made me feel warm inside, like I belonged to something good. This was a new and tender feeling for me. I relished in it, especially after the stress of the last few weeks.

"Adel, are you sure you're feeling OK? You aren't looking too good. Can I get you some more water?" Doris had handed Noah to Ace and was standing at my side, with her hand on my shoulder.

"No, no. I'm OK, thanks," I said, though I *was* feeling dizzy. "I'll go get some water, though," and I stood up and headed toward the beverage table, empty glass in hand. But as I weaved my way through the tables and chairs, the room started to spin violently. My legs grew very weak. I stopped.

"Adel?" I heard the voice but couldn't respond. I felt a strong hand on my arm, right before my legs gave way and I collapsed.

I woke up in a hospital bed. I was *so* groggy.

What am I doing here? What happened? I thought, but only for a moment. It didn't really matter. I was too tired to care.

Time passed where I was vaguely aware of nurses coming in and messing with my arms and blankets. Occasionally, I heard someone say my name, but it was all fuzzy and muted. I didn't like the sting I felt on the top of my wrist, but I had no strength, no will to resist. I had a vague sense that I shouldn't resist anyway. I needed to let the doctors and nurses do their work. I was also aware of a soft, gentle hand patting mine from time to time and a voice speaking to me, quiet and soothing, like a mother's.

I was just *so* tired. So very tired. I drifted in and out of this semiconsciousness for goodness knows how long. Maybe it was hours, maybe it was days. At last, by the mercy of God, I woke up feeling more rested, more refreshed. My eyes saw the world more clearly. I heard sounds more distinctly. That sound—it was a song that I heard, a hymn being hummed from somewhere nearby.

The room was dark and, except for the soft humming, quiet and still. I could tell from the bright slivers of light shining in from around the edges of the drawn curtains that it must be morning.

Morning.

All at once, I remembered the festival, the nurses, the hospital bed, and the soft voices soothing me. I sat up.

"Adel!" came that soft voice again. The voice was kind and motherly. "I'm so glad you're awake!" There was no anxiety in the voice, no alarm or fear, no excitement, just calmness and gentleness.

My eyes adjusted to the dark and I looked over to see Doris sitting restfully in a blue armchair beside my bed. She was knitting.

"Noah?" I asked, but my voice sounded strange and raspy.

"He's at Rebecca's house, and he's just fine."

"What time is it? What happened?"

"It's about two o'clock."

"Two o'clock? I slept here all night?"

"No, dear, it's Monday. You finally settled down for a decent sleep sometime yesterday afternoon."

"Oh!" I lay back down on my pillow, for the first time becoming aware of the dull ache in my head and lower back. It reminded me of when I had been in the hospital back home for Noah's birth. I rubbed my back with a grimace.

"What happened?" I asked.

"The doc says it was dehydration, something going on with your endocrine system, and exhaustion. Burnout. It made you quite delirious."

Burnout?

Doris continued. "The doc says this case was brought on by months or years of being past your limit. It doesn't happen overnight. Takes time to get to this point, and it'll take time to recover. Something about your endocrine system not working right. They wanted to keep you here so you could rest. You were pretty fitful, so yesterday they gave you something to help you sleep."

I tried to take this all in.

"Try to get some rest." She leaned over and patted my hand. "I'm going to head out for a little bit and give your parents' a call. And there are a few other people who are anxious to know how you're doing. I'll also let the nurse know that you're awake."

"Thank you, Doris."

I lay awake for the next couple of hours, trying to take Doris's advice to rest, but it was hard. My mind kept going to weird places, and I kept having to constantly bring it back to reality. That in itself was exhausting. But eventually Doris came back and sat with me the rest of the evening. She gave me an update on how Noah was doing. I was glad to hear it. I missed him.

"And you are beholden to Nathan for helping you when you fell," she said. "You'd have likely hit your head on that chair if he hadn't helped you to the ground, then you would have been in here for more than just exhaustion!"

Yes, I vaguely remembered that.

"He came with Rebecca, Ace, and I to the hospital that night. And when Jim came to take Rebecca home, he stayed to help with Noah. When we realized you were going to be here awhile, we decided it best for him to take Noah on over to Rebecca's. Thought her place the most fitting."

I nodded again. I thought it seemed a little strange for Nathan to help after the way he'd been acting the last couple of weeks.

Just then, the doctor came in. After looking me over, he said I was doing well and that I would be released the following morning. I was glad. I was ready to be home.

After the doctor went out, Doris turned to me.

"Adel, the doctor says that this will just happen again if nothing changes for you. You can't keep going on like you've been doing. You're going to need to rest. You're going to need to make some changes. You're going to need some help."

"What do you mean, Doris? What kind of changes?"

"That I don't rightly know yet. We've got to figure that out, and the sooner the better. I know that having a little baby is hard, especially alone. Keeping house alone is hard. Moving away from everyone you know. Moving to a place where everything is new. Trying to learn so many new things. Living through a natural disaster. All these things are hard. Takes some getting used to, but all at once like that! And then there's those menfolk. They won't leave you alone and give you a moment's breath! It's hard to be a lady and have to ward off constant demands of your attention."

"Yes, even Noah. He hasn't been sleeping well consistently since we got here. It's been horrible. But I don't really know what to do about it. I've tried everything."

"Could just be that he's extra tired too."

"Maybe."

"Anything else bothering you?"

"Well ..." I was debating whether or not I really wanted to go there. But my reserves were gone, and I was beginning to feel desperate, so I just plunged in: "I ... I'm *trying* to learn how to run a house. I'm *trying* to learn how to run an orchard. I'm *trying* to learn how to be a mom! I want to give Noah the very best. I pray about it, *all the time*! I try to listen to the sermons at church and take them to heart. I try *so* hard, Doris! But I can't seem to do anything right! I feel like everything is against me." Some tears began to slip down my face, but I didn't care.

"I wanted so much to be like Grandma ... independent and strong and capable. I wanted to keep her place up and keep her memory alive. To have a fresh start! But I just can't seem to do it! I have no idea what to do. I can barely get the laundry put away, let alone figure out all the finances and needs of an apple orchard! I want to. And I *am* trying! But I'm *so* tired! Everything is against me, Doris. I try, but everything I do fails! My marriage, the harvest, even the *house* was ruined!" The tears were falling freely now. "And ..." I couldn't continue. How could I tell her what was going on inside my heart?

Doris came over and sat beside me on the bed. She put her arms around me and rocked me gently like a little child. I laid my head on her shoulder.

"There now," she said. "What makes you think that the hard things you've gone through aren't God's way of answering your prayers? He knows how to use the evil things of this world for the good of his children."

He uses the evil of this world for the good of his children ... I stopped crying and sat up. What instantly came to my mind was Doris and all the evil she had endured in her own life. But to look at her, to talk to her, you would never know it. I wondered if it had taken time, God's grace, and those awful life experiences to help shape her into the amazing woman who sat there beside me today.

"Like he did for you," I whispered, and wrapped my arms around her neck, new tears falling afresh.

After a few minutes, Doris straightened up and said, "A lady has priorities, Adel. You have to figure out what yours are. You can't do everything. No one can. You're not superwoman after all. So, I think you need to do some soul searching to try to figure out what's important to *you*. What did the Lord Almighty make *you* to do? Then let go of everything else.

"And then," she went on, "then you can figure out how to do those things *gracefully* ... not *perfectly*. Do you understand me? We aren't meant to be perfect. We're just meant to do our best. My best is going to be different from yours. And the things I do will be different from the things you do. But to do them *gracefully*, which includes having grace for yourself while you're learning something new, letting Christ be enough for you, now that's where the joy comes from."

She left me with these thoughts. It was indeed something to think about. I had never gone there before. What *was* most important to me?

THIRTY-THREE
The Following Day

The next morning, Doris and Ace drove me home. It felt weird to be out in the sunlight. My eyes had a hard time adjusting to the light. I was thankful that I wasn't the one driving. I was thankful that I didn't have to do anything other than sit.

Once at home, I was made to go straight to bed. I felt like I would probably be OK to sit up, but I took the advice of my friends to heart and lay down in bed. Doris made some tea and put a soup on for dinner.

As I lay there, alone in my room, I remembered Noah. Soon Rebecca would be bringing him home to me. *I'm positive I will never let him out of my arms after what happened this weekend! What if something had happened to me?* As soon as the thought was out of my head, a wave of fatigue swept over me. *Wow. Doris was right ... I'm a little better, but I'm definitely not OK. What am I going to do?* I wiped a weary hand across my face. *It may take ages for me to be back to normal! How will I do it? How will I be able to take care of my baby? How will I be able to take care of myself? The house? The yard? Lord, please help me ...* More fatigue swept over me. I was feeling so overwhelmed. *Rest will help.* I settled down to try to take a nap.

The nap was successful though not very deep or restorative. When I awoke, a new thought was in my head. *Doris said I'd need help. That's it. I will ask for help. Doris will know what I should do. Maybe even Rebecca. They seem healthy, and they have more on their plates than I do!*

I began to be filled with a new feeling, very small at first. It was replacing the despondency and depression of the last two days. The feeling was *hope*.

My spirits certainly were not what they had been when we arrived in the spring. Though the slip was gradual, and I didn't notice it at first, I could tell now, when it was contrasted by the light I began to see at the end of the tunnel. The gleam of hope that perhaps things would be better soon. Perhaps, with the help of the Lord and some supportive friends, I *could* learn. Perhaps I could find my way out of all the muddled ideas and piles of work, accompanied by perfectionism and a weak will. *Please, Lord, please help me and please give me a second chance,* I prayed earnestly. *It may be like starting over again, this time on the inside, and I know I can't do it alone.*

The sound of voices and footsteps on the stairs brought me quickly out of my reverie and back into my cluttered second-story bedroom.

"Adel?" Rebecca's cheery face peeked around the door. Her eyes were bright and warm. She smiled at seeing me awake.

"Hey! We brought a little someone to see you!" Rebecca was holding Noah. She brought him over to me. He was all squeals and delight when he saw me, reaching with his chubby little arms for me to hold him. I took him and held him close. Then I tucked him into the covers. He laid his head down on my chest as if to say, "I have my mommy. Now I'm OK."

"Adel, he's just precious! You couldn't ask for a better baby. You've done such a great job with him."

I appreciated her words.

"How are *you?* Feeling OK?" She put her hand to my forehead.

"I'm fine. Just tired." I paused. "Actually, it might be a while before I feel 100 percent. Do you think you might be able to help babysit some?"

"Or course! Doris told us what the doctor said. We'd be happy to help! And the ladies at church have already set up a meal schedule so that you won't have to make dinner for a few weeks."

"Really?" My eyes were a little teary. "That's very kind."

I think Rebecca wanted to lift the mood, because then she told me some funny stories of things Noah and her children had done over the last few days. Nathan was mentioned in a couple of the stories. I wondered ...

"Was Nathan there this weekend?"

"Yes, he wanted to stay and help since Jim had to leave on a business trip first thing Sunday morning."

"Oh."

Rebecca looked toward the door and then back at me.

"What? Is he here?"

"Yes. Nathan?" Rebecca called.

Nathan came in but didn't seem to feel comfortable leaving the door.

Rebecca shook her head and smiled compassionately.

We heard some squeals from out in the yard.

I looked to the window in alarm.

"Oh! Ace is in the yard with the other children," Rebecca said, smiling.

We talked for a few more minutes before Rebecca said, "Well, we better head home so you can rest and get this little guy settled in." Rebecca leaned over to pat Noah on the back. He buried his face in my shirt.

Then I reached over and took Rebecca's hand. "Thank you, Rebecca. For everything."

She smiled affectionately and gave me a sisterly hug. "Adel, if you need *anything* at all, please call me."

"Actually, there is something ..." I looked over at Nathan, who was still standing awkwardly by the door. "I was wondering if Nathan would consider keeping the yard up for me for the next few weeks, until I can make other arrangements?"

At hearing his name and this petition, Nathan slowly approached the bed.

"I know you're busy, if you can't do it, I understand. If you know someone else who might ..."

Here, Nathan politely interrupted. "Of course I will."

"Oh good! Thank you." I held my hand out to him. He took it cautiously. "And *thank you* for taking care of Noah while I was at the hospital and over the last few days. I know you had to take off work to do that, and I really appreciate it. I know he was in good hands."

The coldness seemed gone for a moment. He was himself again. He leaned over and gave me a gentle hug while he said, "Anytime." He also leaned over to give Noah a little hug before standing up to follow Rebecca out of the room.

As they began to close the door, I heard Nathan speaking with some agitation. "And where is *he*? Shouldn't he *be here*?"

THIRTY-FOUR

Soul Searching

Doris stopped by regularly while I was lying around and taking it easy. She even offered to help put Noah to sleep for a couple of weeks, to see if that would help him get on a better schedule. It did help. After only two nights, he was going to sleep and staying asleep all night. I couldn't understand it, but I was glad.

"Sometimes it just takes a different face doing the work to get them to change their ways," Doris said. She continued to put him down for a few more days, just to make sure he wouldn't regress.

Before and after getting Noah to sleep, we had the chance to have some good talks.

I asked for Doris's advice. She encouraged me to stop work *before* I felt exhausted and to not worry about being perfect. "That's God's business," she would say. She also encouraged me to make a routine for our days, to keep thinking about my priorities, to seek God's wisdom and his presence more than anything else in life, and to pray.

"Pray about everything, Adel. Ask him for help with the littlest things. He cares! Ask him to show you your next steps. Ask him to lead you, to make the way clear. He says, 'Ask, and it will be given you.' Those words are promises. You can stand on them!"

Her words were a confirmation of some things I was already beginning to feel in my spirit. I knew frailty for the first time in my life, and it was scary. I wanted nothing more than to lean on my Lord and Savior. I was afraid to do anything else. I didn't know what the future would hold, but I knew that if I was close to him, I would be OK.

I began to notice a shift in my prayer life. I had always thought prayer was important, but now it was completely and utterly necessary for my survival, for my everyday life. I felt that I needed God at every moment. My very life depended on it. I needed his guidance, his comfort, and his care. I found I needed it as much as I needed air. As the days went on, I found myself crying out to God more and more often. Sometimes in pain, when I was conflicted about the farm and my future, or when I was thinking about Nathan. My heart still felt a yearning there that wasn't being fulfilled. Perhaps it never would be. And I needed his listening ear to poor out my heartache. I could tell him things I couldn't tell anyone else.

Sometimes I'd sing out in praise. The mountains around me were a glorious thing, made by his very words. So was the little red cardinal who liked to come sit on the branches of the leafless crepe myrtle beside the front porch and tweet to me his sweet morning song. And despite my overall fatigue and internal pain and confusion, those things still made my heart sing. My life became a prayer, and my life began to change.

Not that any of my circumstances changed for the better, but the way I looked at the world began to change. I began to see meaning in the littlest things. Washing the dishes, for instance. If I was doing them for the Lord, then they were a blessing to do, and I tried to do them well. I also began to feel free, like I was standing on my own two feet. I felt like I didn't *have* to do anything, not to be loved or accepted. God loved me *just* as I was. I didn't need the approval of anyone other than my Lord and Savior. The decisions I made were in regard to what I thought He would want, not what anyone else wanted for me or what I thought I wanted for myself. Because at the end of the day, I didn't really know what I wanted. Oh how I needed him to guide me! There was also a practical side to it. What were the simple truths I learned over and over as a child? Love God. Love your neighbors. Take the Gospel and preach it, teach it to your children, and on and on. These simple truths were what mattered most in life.

That's when I began to think more deeply about *why* I wanted the farm. Why did I really want it in the first place and why couldn't I just let it go? Why did I have to be everything for Noah? Why did I need to be perfect? A perfect mother? A perfect granddaughter? There were deep needs inside me that weren't being met before, that were suddenly beginning to be met. And *that* was freeing indeed.

If the simple truths I had learned were what mattered most in my life, then the huge decision of what to do with the farm suddenly wasn't so daunting. It didn't really matter. There was no wrong answer. I could try to stick it out, and that would be OK. It might be hard, it might not work in the end, but I was free to try. Or I could choose to sell and try again somewhere else. The Lord was concerned most about how I loved others and him—not about which house I lived in.

Annie stopped by a few times while I was recovering. She always brought me a delicious homemade soup with some biscuits or bread. She also gave me some supplements that would help me get my energy back and restore my worn-out endocrine system.

I was very thankful Annie took time to explain a little about what was going on in my body. I didn't know much about how the body worked or about what I should take. The doctor had said to rest and get rechecked in a month. But the fatigue I was dealing with was real. It was debilitating. I was finding it hard to do even simple tasks like making breakfast. I spent a lot of time lying on the couch watching Noah play.

"It's going to take time," she said to me one day, not long after I came home. "Healing doesn't happen overnight. And you're probably going to be more prone to colds while you're compromised, so I'm going to give you a couple things to help boost your immune system."

"I appreciate your help. I already feel like I'm beginning to fight off a cold!"

Didn't I just get over the flu!?

"No! Well, here," she said, handing me a small blue glass bottle. "That's elderberry syrup. Start taking it right away. A dropperful a few times a day. It's good for fighting off colds. It's high in vitamin C and things like that."

"Thank you, Annie. I really appreciate it!"

I wasn't prepared for the taste of the syrup. It was unique—spicy and sweet. "It's really not that bad!"

"Good! Try to get lots of rest the next few days. I'm going to have to head out. Rebecca and the kids are meeting me at that putt-putt place down in Ellijay! Don't want to be late! Take care of yourself, Adel."

Nathan was true to his word and came to clean up the yard. The first time he came was about a week after I came home from the hospital. I was still feeling weak, and I was also fighting off the cold. I watched him mow the leaves in the yard and then blow off the driveway around the house. Noah was taking his afternoon nap. I went out, wrapped in a blanket, and sat on the swing on the porch with a box of Kleenex. I knew I looked horrible, but it didn't matter. I needed some fresh air anyway.

Nathan saw me as he was walking back to the tool shed to put the blower away. When he was done, he stopped back by the porch to say that he was finished.

"Dank you," I said, my stuffy nose making it hard to speak.

Nathan was turning to go but stopped.

"You feeling alright?" he asked gently.

"Not really. I've caught a cold." My head was feeling kind of fuzzy.

"Can I get you something? Like some tea or something?"

"Um ... I guess so." I shrugged.

"Alright," he said, coming up the steps. "And you probably shouldn't be sitting out here where it's chilly."

"Okay," I said weakly as I followed him back into the house.

He disappeared into the kitchen, and I went and plopped down on the couch.

He returned a few minutes later with a cup of tea.

"Ginger honey," he said, handing me a cup. "Try to drink it hot."

"Alright."

He sat down on the recliner.

He still didn't seem like himself. There was more reserve than there used to be. His manners, typically so mild and easy, were still too tense, too forced. But I was feeling too yucky to talk about it.

"Do you have food for tonight?" he asked.

"Yes, someone from church brought some stuff last night. I've got a bunch of leftovers."

"Good. Is there anything else I can do while I'm here?"

I thought for a minute. My head ached ... "No, I don't dink so."

"Alright." He stood up to leave. "I'm gonna head out now. I hope you feel better." And he was gone.

THIRTY-FIVE

Quiet Growth

I was attempting to mop the floor one morning toward the end of October when I noticed a car pulling up the drive. It was a blue Expedition, and it looked new. I didn't recognize it. I watched as a man and lady got out and started walking toward the house, looking around them with interest as they went. They were young, maybe early to mid-thirties. They were wearing jeans and cowboy boots. I opened the door and greeted them as they came up the steps.

"Hello. What can I do for you?"

"Hi, Adel! Do you remember me? It's been so long! I'm your cousin, Christopher Atworth. This is my wife, Ashleigh. My parents are Kate and Alex Atworth." He had an open and friendly manner.

"Aunt Kate and Uncle Alex!" I exclaimed. "I do remember you! You all came to Christmas at Sweet Valley one year!"

He laughed. "Yes! That was us!"

"Well, come inside! I was just mopping, so the floor may be a little wet."

We walked into the living room and sat down. Noah was playing in the playpen. He looked up with wide eyes at our visitors.

"Hello there, little guy!" said Christopher. "What's your name?"

"This is Noah," I said proudly.

"We have a little boy about the same age!" said his wife. "Do you have other children?"

"No, it's just Noah and me. What about you guys? Do you have other children?"

"We do! We have four. Our eldest is eleven. Then we have a nine-year-old, a six-year-old, and Rhet, who is one and a half."

"Oh wow! Sounds like you guys are busy! It's good though, isn't it?"

"It is! We love it!"

"So," Christopher began. "I want to let you know why we're here. I don't like beating around the bush so I'm going to get right to the point. We would like to buy Sweet Valley!"

"You what!?" I asked in disbelief.

"We would like to buy this farm! We've owned and operated our own cattle ranch outside of Tulsa for many years now. We broke off from my parents' ranch and started our own about thirteen years ago, but we have always known that cattle is not our thing long term. We would like to do a different kind of farming. We were thinking fruit trees, pecans, or another similar crop. When Grandma passed away, we considered trying to buy the farm then. We love this area and the idea of owning a family farm, but we heard that it had been bequeathed to you. We also didn't have a way out of what we were doing at the time. So, we just sat on it for a while. Well ..." He stopped to take a breath. He seemed excited. "Well, we now have a buyer for our ranch. They want to take possession by February. We thought this seemed like a good time to make our proposal to you. We would absolutely love it if you would consider the offer! And in the end, if you decide not to sell, there will be no hard feelings! We don't operate that way. But we knew we had to ask you before trying to find something else."

I was dumbfounded. I was sure the shock was written all over my face.

"I know it's a surprise! We just found out our ranch is to be sold. We didn't even list it! A man came to us, kind of like we're coming to you ...

and now here we are! Would you consider it? Would you take some time and think about it?" He was looking at me earnestly.

I nodded slowly. "Yes," I said at last. "I'll think about it."

"Good! Good! Here's our numbers!" He handed me a sheet of paper with their offer and contact information handwritten on it in blue ink.

We talked for a while about Aunt Kate and Uncle Alex and what they were up to these days, but I was having such a hard time concentrating. All I could think about was, *"We would like to buy Sweet Valley ..."*

I offered them some lunch, but they declined, saying they had plans in town. And then they were gone, and I was left to my own thoughts. I closed the door behind them and headed straight back to the couch. I sat down slowly while looking at the names and numbers on the paper Christopher had left with me.

I told them I would let them know by the end of the year. That wasn't long. Just a couple of months. I had a lot of thinking and a lot of praying to do between now and then.

Ever since my stay in the hospital, Rebecca stopped by every few days to say hello and on Thursdays she would babysit Noah so I could rest. I still wasn't going out much—not to church or to the Shepherds'. I hadn't even needed to get groceries yet. Doris and Ace and other people from church were keeping me well supplied with food.

When Rebecca came to visit, she brought the children. They ran around the yard and swung on the tire swing while we talked. Sometimes she brought us muffins. Once she brought homemade chicken noodle soup. I enjoyed the treats, but more than anything, I enjoyed her company. It was so good to have a friend close to my own age who had young children, one who had been through the active ones *three* times already, and who *had* lots of wisdom to share with me when I needed it most.

Today we were sitting on the porch swing, watching the children play. The babies were toddling behind the bigger kids as they ran around the yard.

I was happy to know that Noah already had friends. He was lucky, because though they were far from perfect, the Blackmore children were still some of the best-behaved children I had ever seen. What good examples for my little fella! He looked up to them already. He followed them around and tried to keep up. He watched everything they did and tried to copy it in his own sixteen-month-old way.

"I'm so thankful we are friends with you guys. You have such a lovely family, Rebecca ... you really do."

"Thank you!" She smiled.

"And you and Jim—you both seem so perfect for each other. And *so* happy. I envy you sometimes."

"If you only knew!" Rebecca laughed.

"Knew what?"

"The ways we've dishonored each other. It puts us to shame!"

"No way! Everybody has issues sometimes."

"Well, that's true. But I don't want you having us up on a pedestal! I'd rather you just know the truth. We're good enough friends, aren't we? You won't think any less of us if I share something personal?"

I looked at her curiously and leaned forward to ask in a low voice, "What happened?"

"You know how I told you that we moved back here about six years ago? Closer to seven now, but anyway, we moved back, and Jim quit preaching because he had an affair with a lady in church who was getting some counseling from him. Randy was just a baby."

"Oh wow. I had no idea ..."

"Yep."

"How ... how did you get past that? What happened?"

"It was rough. My initial reaction was to give up on him and turn in. I despised him because of it. I wanted nothing to do with him, and I didn't want him around. I needed some time, so I came back here with Randy. I was pregnant with Maggie Ann ... go figure. We stayed with my parents for a few weeks. Mama talked me through it. She and Ms.

Elaine, they talked life back into me. They told me our marriage was worth fighting for. That Jim was a good man, and even good men mess up sometimes. I didn't want to hear it. I didn't want to believe it. It took some time, but after a while, I agreed to talk with him. I drove down to Braselton alone. When I saw him there, standing on the steps of our porch, looking so miserable and wretched, my heart softened toward him, just a little. He *was* sorry. He wanted to do whatever it took to make things right. I told him that things would never be what they were but that I'd consider working it out with him. My heart was still so crushed though, Adel. I figured all joy in life was over for me. I felt like I couldn't trust him anymore."

"That must have been so hard!"

"It truly was ... but he wanted to make it work, and in the end, I did too. So, we went to counseling together for a while, and honestly, I think that was the best decision we ever made. They taught us how to make our marriage healthy again and how to keep it that way. Looking back, I don't think our marriage had ever been healthy, but we started learning how to meet each other's needs better and how to respect each other's boundaries. We started spending more time alone, away from the kids. In the evenings at least, when they're all in bed. We try to have date nights and movies nights."

"And going hiking and horseback riding," I added with a smile.

"Yes, and things like that! It's been a long road. Sometime along the way, I found I *was* able to forgive him, somehow, by the grace of God. I am happier now than I've ever been, and Jim is too. It really was a miracle. I know there is no guarantee it won't happen again; it very well could. But by God's grace, I pray that it doesn't. I pray for protection around us both, all the time."

"Wow, Rebecca. What a story! I can't believe you guys went through all that. I can't believe you're still married! Happily married?"

"Yes. Happily married."

I sat, deep in thought for a minute. Then I looked over at Rebecca and said, "You know, in my marriage, I was the one who wanted to make it work. I was willing, but *he* wasn't."

Rebecca put an arm around my shoulders.

"It takes both of you being willing to fight like mad to make it work," she said. "There was nothing you could do about that. You can't *make* someone ..."

I nodded. "At the time, I was so hurt. I couldn't understand what was wrong with me. I figured *I* must have been the problem or he would've wanted to stay. But I see it all more clearly now. We were *both* part of the problem. My parents were the ones who encouraged our relationship. At church, he was a different man than he was at home. They liked his money and his credentials, so they thought we were a good match. Well, they were wrong. I didn't have what it took to stand up and decide for myself what I wanted, so I just went along with it. And then, when he wanted to leave, I wanted to make it work because I didn't know what else to do. He had an affair, too, you know."

"No, I didn't know that."

"Yes. Right before I found out I was pregnant. And when I told him that he was going to be a father ..." I paused. It was so hard to say it. I took a deep breath. "When I told him he was going to be a father, he didn't care. He wanted to leave anyway. But looking back now, I'm kind of glad he did. He wasn't a good guy, Rebecca. He was into all kinds of bad stuff. I'm sad for Noah though."

We both looked out into the front yard where Noah was bending down to pick up acorns, his little bottom sticking up in the air.

"At least you won't have to worry about that anymore," said Rebecca. I wasn't sure what she meant by that, and I was about to ask when Allie fell down and skinned her knees something fierce. We took her inside to be tended to, and then it was time for them to leave.

THIRTY-SIX

Engaged?

The next Sunday I felt well enough to return to church and to the Shepherd's house afterwards. It felt strange to be back, but good too. Nathan was there that week, but he had yet to look at me. Tonight, his reservation and coldness seemed to be what it was before my collapse. I longed to know why.

I guess it was because we were finally in the same room together, but I began to feel a tension between us like I hadn't felt before, and I didn't like it. After sitting alone for some time, in the same room, without a word passing between us, Nathan, his features obviously fighting for calmness and control, got up and walked outside. Like a horse following his master, I stood up and went outside too. I found Nathan down on the patio behind the porch. He was leaned over on a railing, looking out into the dark night. The air was crisp and cool. Nathan didn't see me follow him, but he seemed to sense my presence as I drew near, and he turned toward me. In the light from the porch, I could see that he looked tired, defeated. His shoulders sagged, and his expression—was it sadness? He wasn't trying to fight his emotions anymore. It was obvious that something was terribly wrong.

In alarm, I walked quickly over to him and put a hand on his arm.

"Nathan," I said quietly. "What is it? What's wrong?"

He forced a smile but said nothing, then turned to look back out into the night, almost as if to shut me out.

I gave him a few minutes, but it was apparent that he was suffering under some heavy burden, and that he wasn't going to tell me what it was. I could bear the silence no longer.

"Nathan?" I urged. My voice sounded strange in the silence of the crisp autumn evening.

Nathan turned back toward me. He forced another smile.

"I'm alright," he said, but he looked me in the eyes for the first time when he said this, and then he didn't look away. Neither did I. I held his gaze, questioning him, pleading with him. Finally, he took a step toward me and gently placed a hand on each of my arms. He pulled me toward him ever so slightly, still holding my gaze. I thought he would kiss me, but he didn't. His expression had changed though, to one I had seen many times when he was looking at me. I hadn't seen it in a while, and I felt the full effect of his expression this time, though I had often tried to ignore or reason it away in the past. He smiled genuinely down at me and wiped a stray strand of hair out of my face. His hand slid back down my arm, warming my whole body. I felt frozen in place and in time. I wanted whatever this was to last forever. To never end. I wanted to be *near* him. As close I could get. But my feet didn't move.

Our breath made a mist in the air around us. I'm sure it was getting colder, but I couldn't tell for sure. Nathan rubbed his hands gently up and down my arms a few times, and I felt a tension between us again, but this was the old kind, and it was good. But then he stopped. He was no longer looking me in the eyes. He looked miserable again and turned away. He began to walk slowly off the patio and out into the yard, toward the cars. Again, I felt a pull to follow him. It was just like Mr. Rochester and Jane in the book Doris had loaned me. It was as if there were an invisible cord attached somewhere underneath his left ribs that was attached to a similar place in me. When he walked away, my heart ached. It *had* to follow, so I ran after him.

"Nathan!" I yelled. "Stop! Please stop. Wait!" I was out of breath a little as I ran into him in the dark beside the house. He caught me with both arms and held me back a little. It was hard to see his face in the dark, but I knew he was looking at me intently.

His hands went to my face, my hair. Again, I thought he would kiss me, but again, he didn't.

"Adel," he said quietly, though firmly, and he took a few steps back. "We can't *do* this. You're engaged!" He seemed to waver between coming back to me or turning to leave. Then he stopped and said, "*Please* don't marry him."

Then he just stood there, as if waiting for my response.

What!?

I stood stock still, trying to wrap my mind around what he had just said.

Then he came close and took me gently by the arms again so he could see my face more clearly in the low light. "I don't understand this at all," he said slowly. "I don't know why I feel the way I do, but I *do* feel it, Adel. I can't keep going on like this ... trying not to care. I *love* you." He lifted his hands to brush back my hair. He gently stroked the side of my face.

My legs were shaking a little in the cold.

"*Engaged?*" I whispered. "Where did you hear that?"

"I ran into Julian back in September." As he talked, he turned and took a few steps back and ran his hands through his hair. "After you came back that Sunday. He led me to believe that you were engaged. I didn't know whether to believe him or not. It didn't seem likely to me. But when I saw you the following Sunday at church with the ring on your finger ..." His voice trailed off. "I was *so* confused! I'm *still* confused."

I held up my left hand. What little light there was reflected to show the thin band of silver on my ring finger.

Oh, what trouble you've caused! I cursed the ring.

"*This* ring?" I said. "*This* ring is from a Sunday school class in high school! My teacher gave them to the girls to remind us to stay pure until marriage. Well, I used it the first time around, and I thought it had helped." I paused to take a breath, to steady my voice. "So, I thought I would try it again. Nathan, Julian *did* propose to me, but I'm *not* engaged to him. I told him no. Repeatedly. He lied to you! He lives in his own little world where he believes whatever he wants, regardless of how other people feel!

"Oh, this ridiculous ring!" I took the ring off my finger and threw it into the night. "I put that ring on because of *you* ... not *Julian!*"

Nathan stood there in the dark, unmoving. I wished so much that I could see his face more clearly. What was he thinking?

After another moment, he said through clenched teeth, "I have a right to pummel Julian ..." He walked slowly toward me again. "But I won't."

He took me in his arms and held me for a long time.

"I should have come and asked you," he said after a minute. "It would have saved us both a lot of trouble."

It was true, he should have. But it didn't matter now. None of it mattered anymore. He was *holding* me.

I never wanted to move. I *finally* felt at peace. I was free to be happy. *Completely* happy. I had felt little pieces, little snippets of happiness when I was on the mountain trails, at the farm, with Doris or with Nathan and his family over the past few months. Now my happiness was complete. I rested there and let him hold me. I wondered what was going through his mind, but I didn't ask. I didn't really need to know. I knew enough. I knew that he loved me.

THIRTY-SEVEN

But Where Is Home?

We walked back into the house hand in hand, and from that moment on, Nathan and I were nearly inseparable.

"Finally!" was the general consensus of the room when we walked inside, which was followed by "What took you so long?" and "I knew it was only a matter of time!"

We sat together on the couch. We sat together while we played Monopoly. And when it was time to go home, Nathan left when we did. He wanted to follow us back, to make sure we made it safely. I think the stress of the previous months had facilitated a need for caution and for togetherness for us. Whatever we did from then on, we wanted to do *together*. We saw each other every day, mostly at the farm in the evenings after Nathan was through with work. He would walk over and eat with us. On Wednesday, he wanted to take me out on an actual date. I was a little bit thrilled. He wouldn't tell me where we were going and referenced what I had said in the past about liking surprises.

I dressed in my favorite green dress and messed with my hair for about an hour before I felt that it looked *just* right. Then I waited for

Doris to come. She offered to watch Noah at our house so Noah could go on to sleep. She imagined we might be a little late getting back.

Doris arrived and got busy with putting Noah into his PJs. She was all smiles over the development between Nathan and me, and this time I didn't mind it.

Then I saw truck lights coming up the drive. My heart skipped a beat. I grabbed my purse and jacket and went to kiss Noah. "See you later, big guy! Bye, Doris!"

I met Nathan as he was getting out of the truck, and he held me and kissed me, and then we figured we better get going or we'd never end up going at all!

I hopped into the open door, and Nathan shut it behind me. It was getting chilly, and I was glad I brought my jacket.

We drove along in the dark, listening to some quiet music on the radio. I was so thankful that Nathan felt comfortable with silence between us. We both just sat there, relaxed and happy and enjoying the moment.

"Check Yes or No" by George Strait came over the radio.

I propped back, listening, and stared out into the dark fields and forest as we drove along. When the song was over, I turned to Nathan.

"That song made me think of when we used to play together when we were little."

"Yep."

"I didn't realize who you were when you came over to mow the grass that day."

"I know."

"We used to call you Nate!"

He laughed.

"When did you start going by Nathan?"

"In high school. I just liked the sound of it better."

"Hmm ... I have good memories of playing with you."

"Good guys and bandits ..." Nathan grinned.

"Yes! Those were the days!"

About that time, we arrived in town. Nathan drove his truck over to Del Rios.

"It's not sushi. Do you think it'll do?"

"It's *perfect*." I said, smiling my approval.

After dinner, we got back in his truck and drove down Highway 15, then turned onto a side road. It was then that I saw where we were going. It was an old-fashioned outdoor theater!

"I thought Cherry Hill didn't have a theater!" I exclaimed.

"Well, if Julian told you that, then he was wrong."

I poked him in the ribs, but was too excited to think any more about Julian.

We pulled in and paid for our tickets at the drive-thru booth, bought some popcorn and drinks, drove over to find a spot, and turned off the engine.

"What's the movie tonight?" I asked.

"*Back to the Future.*"

"I haven't seen that one in forever! This is going to be fun!"

Nathan glanced over at me longingly. I unbuckled my seat belt and slid closer to him, and he put his arm around my shoulders. I was thankful that his front seat was a bench seat.

The movie was good, but the company was better. I wasn't ready to go home, but the theater was closing soon. We didn't want to get towed, so we cranked up the truck and headed back.

I was still sitting next to him, and he still had his arm around me. He drove back slowly. Probably as slowly as he legally could.

The nearly full moon was bright in the sky above. There were no clouds, only the moon and zillions and zillions of stars.

"When did you know you loved me?" I asked as we inched along.

"I don't know ... probably about second grade."

"You're teasing!

"No, actually, I'm not."

"You really loved me all the way back then!?"

"Yep. In a boyish kind of way, I guess."

"I never knew that. Why?"

"I don't know. You were pretty. And kind. And you seemed to like me too, which never hurts. When you were here as a kid, you were like a bird let loose from its cage, wild and free. I loved that about you."

"Then why did you stop talking to me? After a while, it seemed like you didn't want to be around me anymore."

"You were a beautiful girl, and I was a teenage boy. Around the end of middle school, things just got awkward for me. It seemed strange to play like we used to when we were younger and oblivious to the world. I didn't know how to go from being childhood friends to being anything else. We were still young. Too young to date but too old to not feel what I was feeling. When you came down that summer, I just sort of kept my distance and tried to act like a man, but you still had my heart. Each year after that, we just sort of grew apart. The magic of childhood was broken, I guess. Then you stopped coming altogether. I missed you. I thought about you over the years. Ms. Elaine often talked about you. I never would have told you this before, but I think one of the reasons she wanted you to come back was so we could meet again. I never expected to see you, though. But then you came for Ms. Elaine's funeral ..." He stopped for a minute, then continued. "You were always a pretty girl, Adel. But when I saw you that day ..."

"And to learn that you were moving here? I was trying to prepare myself for someone entirely different. I wanted to protect myself. I didn't know you anymore. You could have been anything. At first, I thought you *had* changed. But you hadn't. I slowly began to see that. I didn't really feel like I had a chance though, with Peter and Julian both vying for your attention. Deep down, I knew neither one of them would be good for you. I just hoped and prayed you would see that too."

"And I did," I interrupted. He leaned down to kiss me. Thankfully, we were on a straight shot of road.

I was slowly taking in everything he had just told me. It seemed like a fairy-tale story. Like something from a movie. Did things like this really happen? It seemed to be happening to me ...

"What about you?" he asked. "When did you know?"

"It's been such a gradual thing ..." I smiled. "Though I think there may have been a little something already there when you came walking across the yard toward me that day, covered in grass clippings!"

He chuckled. "Yeah ... that wasn't exactly my idea of a

reintroduction."

"Oh, I didn't mind!" I snuggled up against him. "However we got here, I'm glad."

"Me too."

"Why didn't you ever get married?" I asked. "I mean, you probably could have had your pick of the girls in the county."

"I heard the mermaids singing each to each. I did not think they would sing for me."

"That sounds like something from one of my literature classes in college."

"It probably is."

"I'm not sure what it means ..."

Nathan laughed. "I don't know. Chasing after girls wasn't really my thing. I had other stuff to do, and I didn't really think I'd find anyone. I did have one long-term relationship, but that wasn't a very good experience."

"Courtney."

"Mmm ... I'm sorry that happened, Adel."

"I'm not. That's how I learned you really cared about me."

Nathan shook his head and pulled me a little closer.

We drove the rest of the way in silence.

The next few weeks were happy bliss for Nathan and me, and when Thanksgiving rolled around, Noah and I went with the Shepherd family to celebrate at their grandparents' house, the Shepherds senior. They lived about an hour away in Dahlonega. Nathan, Noah, and I rode together in Nathan's truck. We arrived a little earlier than the rest of the family. The Shepherds lived in a small brick home with a modest yard, but the yard was beautiful! It felt like we were pulling into a park. The bare flowerbeds were lined with stones. There was a deck and gazebo, birdbaths, wind chimes, and a paved walkway that ran the length of the yard. Though everything was on the tail end of the fall color, it still truly felt like I was walking through a park to get to the back door, where Nathan was leading us. We were greeted at the door by an elderly couple who were both in their eighties. Despite their age, they seemed to be in good health and spry. They welcomed us warmly, me especially. They took turns giving us hugs and were immediately taken with Noah, rubbing his back and taking him by the hand.

"So glad you could join us today! It's so nice to meet you!" said Mrs. Shepherd as she led the way into the kitchen. "Come and sit down with us for a spell before we're bombarded by the rest of the family!"

We followed her to the kitchen table. As we passed by the stove, I noticed the expansive array of food that spanned the entire length of the counter, plus the stovetop. Everything was covered, so I couldn't see what was inside, but it all smelled *so good.*

"Here, we brought this," I said, handing a pan full of brownies to Mrs. Shepherd.

I practiced a few times before baking for this special event. I wanted to make sure I had the recipe down pat before feeding my creation to strangers. I was still a little nervous handing the brownies over to her; I hoped they turned out alright.

"Oh! That's great! Let me set it on the dessert table!" She moved past the kitchen to another room and quickly returned to meet us at the table, where Mr. Shepherd was already sitting down.

"Please, sit down!" she said, motioning to the table. "Nathan, my boy, it's *so* good to see you! How's the business these days?"

"Fine! I'm finishing up a big project in Low Branch. Then I'll be able to take a break for Christmas."

"That's good to hear!" she said. Then turning to me, "Tell me a little something about yourself. I've already heard a good bit. Nathan's pretty good about keeping up with his ol' grandma and grandpa—but I'd still like to hear it from you."

I told them a little of my story, with Nathan adding a detail or compliment here and there.

Mr. Shepherd was listening with a smile as we talked.

When we had reached present day, and the story around my purity ring and Julian's proposal, and at last our love for one another, Mr. Shepherd took me by the hand and said, "True love is a special thing. Nothing like it. It can outlive whatever life throws at it. We're a living, breathing example of that. Been married sixty years this past April. We've gotten to the age where every day is a gift, and there's still no one else I'd rather spend my time with." He looked over at Mrs. Shepherd, who smiled warmly at her husband.

"But you got to guard it, protect it!" he added firmly.

Nathan reached under the table and took my other hand and gave it a squeeze.

"Well, true love or not, we've got a feast to make ready!" said Mrs. Shepherd as she rose from the table. "Everyone will be here shortly, and I've still got a few things to set out!"

Mrs. Shepherd was right; soon the family started trickling in. Robert was apparently one of seven children! I stood amazed when I heard that this was their childhood home. It couldn't have been more than three or four bedrooms!

Soon I was surrounded by many unknown faces. It seemed that each of Robert's brothers and sisters had several children of their own, and a couple of them also had children! I was surprised this many people could fit in one little house. They didn't, really. Many ended up eating at tables spread out on the beautiful back deck. It was a pretty day—a nice day for eating outside.

I began to feel a little overwhelmed by all the noise and movement inside the house. They were pleasant people; I just wasn't used to such crowds, especially in small spaces. So, after Mr. Shepherd blessed the food, we took ours outside too.

The food was wonderful—all the Thanksgiving favorites: ham, turkey, green bean casserole, sweet potato souffle, cheesy potatoes, mashed potatoes, baked beans, rolls. There was even a sweet potato pie, which was entirely new to me.

We sat at a table with some of Nathan's cousins. They were a jolly lot and spent a little time teasing Nathan about me. He didn't seem to mind.

After we ate and were sitting around talking, I ended up next to Mr.

Shepherd. I was thankful for this opportunity to ask him about his yard.

"Are you the one who keeps up this beautiful yard?" I asked.

"Yep. Keeps me going."

"It's just lovely," I said, looking around at the delicate beauty of the yard. "It feels just like we're sitting in a park!"

"Well, thank you." He smiled. "I do it for my lady. She likes a pretty yard. She tells me what she would like, and I try to figure out how to do it. Most of these things were built a while ago though." He motioned around to the gazebo and walkways.

"You must be in really good shape to keep all this up!" I laughed. "We have a lot of flowers and things at our farm, and it's been a struggle for me to keep up with it all!"

Mr. Shepherd smiled and nodded. "Yes. But you're young and busy with that little one of yours. When you're as old as me, it's good to have something to do. Something to keep you busy. Something to keep you going."

I thought I understood that and nodded slowly.

I liked Mr. and Mrs. Shepherd so much! They were intentional with their family. When they were talking to someone, they always looked them in the eyes, giving them their full attention. They were kind. And Mrs. Shepherd was such a good cook. Her food was as delicious as the yard was beautiful.

Before we knew it, it was time to leave. We drove back, full and content and a little sleepy.

"You have a wonderful family," I said to Nathan as we drove along. "You're really fortunate, you know? Not everyone has what you have."

Nathan seemed thoughtful. He didn't say anything, but he reached over and slid his hand into mine.

A few days later, on a cold and windy afternoon in late November, Noah and I were hanging out in Nathan's workshop. He had the heater on, and it was warm and cozy inside. Nathan was working on a rocking horse for Noah, and we were sitting on the floor, over to the side near the heater. Noah was playing with some odds and ends and leftover pieces of scrap wood, and I was watching him.

Nathan was leaning over his workbench, focusing intently on some small detail with a chisel. He glanced over at us sitting there on the floor. He smiled contentedly and continued working.

"Adel?" he said after a few minutes, his voice calm and easy as usual. "Hmm?"

"Have you thought about what you're going to do with Noah as he gets older and you're trying to run a business?"

I sat there a minute, watching Noah play. I had done a lot of thinking lately, but *that* thought hadn't come to me yet. I couldn't keep asking Doris to watch him. She had her own busy life to live. I knew that she didn't mind watching him occasionally, but every day? While I tried to run an orchard?

"No" was my reply. "I've haven't really thought about that. I know I can't keep asking Doris; she already has a lot to do."

"Would you consider a daycare?" He kept his eyes on his work.

"I'd rather not, if I can help it."

"A nanny?"

"Maybe ..."

"Mmhmm." He seemed to be really focusing on some small detail in the wood.

I still sat cross-legged on the floor, casting my eyes first to Nathan, then to Noah, then back to Nathan.

"You know, I'm not really sure that I want to run the orchard at all."

Nathan stood up in surprise. "What!?"

"Yes. I'm not sure it's how I want to spend my time. My relationship with Noah was one of the main reasons why I came here in the first place. I didn't tell you that at first. I was ... I don't know. I just didn't feel comfortable telling you. I've had a hard time working through it all in my mind, but I feel like I'm getting the bigger picture more clearly now. Back home, I felt that I was just a child in my parents' house and that Noah was their child too. I felt like my relationship with him was slipping away before my very eyes ... and I was giving him over to someone else to raise. In my soul, I knew that I didn't want that for us. For him but for me too. So we came here, to be alone. To be together. And it's been good, Nathan. It's been *so* good. I don't want *anything* to take that away again ... not even Sweet Valley." As I said those last few words, I felt a choke in my throat. I stopped talking to prevent myself from crying.

"I don't know what else I'd do, but a cousin of mine has already made me an offer for the farm, a couple of weeks ago ... and ... I'm considering it."

Nathan was staring at me, eyes wide, not saying a word.

I looked down at the floor.

"What you did was a very brave and noble thing," he said at last. "Staying home with Noah would be a very noble thing too."

"I'd love to, and I could for a while, because the farm is worth a lot of money, but long term, I'm not sure how it would work."

Nathan was silent and slowly went back to working on the rocking horse.

After a few more minutes, I noticed that Noah was rubbing his eyes and not really playing anymore.

"We're going to have to head home soon. Noah's all tuckered out."

"Alright. Let me put these things away, and I'll be ready."

I helped Noah clean up our spot on the floor and then scooped him up.

"Can we see?" I asked.

"Sure. It's not finished yet, but it's getting close."

We walked over to the bench where Nathan had been working. Lying there on the table was a rocking horse, just the right size for Noah. It wasn't entirely finished, but the body was mostly put together, and the face was etched into the wood with beautiful design.

"It's wonderful!" I said as I ran my hands slowly down the smooth wooden face and neck.

"How you can take a piece of wood and turn it into something so lovely yet so practical is just beyond me! It's a calling, I think. Something you were born to do. Otherwise, it wouldn't come so naturally."

"It's something I *love* to do, anyway. There's no way to accurately describe how I feel when I see the wood taking shape and becoming its own unique creation. It's satisfying on a very deep level. I'm thankful that I'm able to do what I love for a living."

As Nathan drove us home, I was silent. My head was full of orchards and children and rocking horses.

THIRTY-EIGHT
A Christmas Visit

The first week of December, I got a call from my parents. They wanted to come down to visit again. I told them that I'd planned to visit them closer to Christmas, but they said they were going to be traveling to visit my dad's side of the family the week of Christmas and that this would be a better time for them. I was brave, and told them that if they were coming to try to convince me to come back with them, they were wasting their time. They assured me that wasn't the reason for the visit, so I agreed that they could come.

The day before they arrived, I was at Doris's house helping make peppermint bark to give as Christmas gifts to the ladies of the rounds.

"Doris," I said as I hammered a plastic baggie full of peppermint candies, breaking them into tiny pieces, "my parents are coming for a visit. I wish they wouldn't. I just want to be left alone!"

Doris was silent for a moment. She seemed to be deep in thought.

Then she turned to me. "Adel, do you ever wonder what's come between you and your parents?" she asked kindly, while continuing to stir a potful of melted white chocolate.

"It's the way they treat me. Like I'm still a child! Yet they never appreciated me when I *was* a child! They don't even care about *me* at all. All they care about is *Noah*."

"Be wary, Adel. That sounds like bitterness. The broken relationship between your mama and Elaine can very easily be passed down to future generations."

I stopped hammering and looked up. "What do you mean, Doris?"

"Some things happened long ago that caused a rift between your mama and your grandma, I think you know what I mean."

I nodded.

"Ill blood of that nature can easily slide down into the unsuspecting children, grandchildren, great-grandchildren, and so on."

"I don't understand," I said. "What kind of things happened? I knew that my mom and grandma didn't have a good relationship. They never did. But anytime I ever mention Grandma, Mom closes up."

Doris looked at me long and hard.

"I really want to know! If there is anything that could help heal the gap coming between my mom and I, or protect me and Noah from suffering the same fate ... I will do whatever it takes!" I was earnest.

Doris stopped her stirring and turned to face me. "I don't know if it's the right thing to do or not. Seems a little like gossiping to me. But if it could help ... They're your family. I guess it can't hurt for you know." She paused a moment to collect her thoughts, then began. "About the time your mama was starting junior high, a good friend of hers was very unkind to her. I don't remember the particulars, just that it wasn't good. Then her whole group of friends joined in. It made your mama very upset, but she kept it mostly to herself at the time. Elaine was busy working the farm, it was a *lot* of work, but during this time, she was even more busy because she was having to care for *her* mama, who had just had a stroke and was slowly on the decline. She wasn't there for your mama the way she could have been. But your mama began to change. She began to believe the lies of the enemy, that she was alone, that no one cared about her, and she began to turn bitter.

"She couldn't understand why her friends were being so mean. She couldn't understand why Elaine wasn't around. It was true that your mama needed her, but what was Elaine to do? Her ma needed her too. She *was* trying to keep a balance. I remember. She tried to spend time with your mama and aunt Kate. But it was never enough to satisfy your mama. She already had it in her head she was being wronged in some way. Your mama started to look for friendship from a different crowd. A wild crowd. She began to turn from the ways of her upbringing and to the ways of the world. It broke your grandparents' hearts. They tried to talk to her, but she blamed them for her own bad behavior. After Elaine's ma finally passed, she had more time to give. She tried to work things out with your mama, but in the end, she rejected the truth. She turned from the faith her parents worked so hard to instill in her and went off to marry your pa. Your mama wanted to get as far away from here as she possibly could. That's how they ended up in San Francisco."

I listened to all this with wide eyes. None of it surprised me. But it was still intriguing to *finally* know the truth.

"So *that's* why she didn't want me spending time here during the summer! But why on *earth* are they going to church back home?" I said warmly. "They go every Sunday! *Religiously!* But they never talked to me about the Bible. Or their faith. They knew I got saved at VBS that year when I was twelve, but they never asked me about it. Everything I know is what I've learned in church and from reading on my own! Why do they do it? Why do they go?"

"That I don't know, Adel. It surprised me too, when I first heard of it. At first, I think Elaine had her hopes up that they had a change of heart. But after a while, she sensed nothing had really changed. And there was certainly no reconciliation between the two of them," she added sadly.

"My dad's business ..." I said slowly. "We started going when my dad started his new job. His boss went to our church ... and a few of his coworkers! Maybe *that's* why."

"Could be."

"So, what about passing down all of that?" I asked with energy.

"Not all of *that*," Doris said firmly. "You're not your mama! You've chosen a different path for your life, a better path. What I was talking about is the hurt and the anger. And the unforgiveness. You're starting to feel some of the feelings your mama felt toward her mama. I see it. Only yours are more justified. Still don't make it right though, to go on that-a-way. No matter what wrong she's done you, don't go getting all bitter and bent out of shape. The Lord can bring healing—to you, if not to the both of you."

I continued to stare at her.

"What I'm saying is that the change has to start with *you*. You don't have to carry on the anger and the hurt. You can give Noah something better! You can talk to your mama. Tell her how you feel. She doesn't have to reconcile with you. She doesn't *have* to do anything! Then move on. Choose to forgive her. Lay it at His feet."

"It's just so *hard*." I shook my head.

My expression must have told Doris how I felt, because she said, "Oftentimes, the truth hurts, Adel. But it's got to be said, just the same. When truth is told, healing can begin. Without truth, there's no healing. Talk to your mom. Do your part and *try* to make amends. Amends don't always happen, especially not right away. But talk to her, *try*. Then you can go on and be *free*. Free to live without guilt. Free to be who God made you to be. You don't have to carry it on, Adel. You *can* teach Noah a better way. The way of forgiveness and grace."

An hour later, Noah and I walked back home. Noah was getting so big. He walked along beside me, holding tightly to one of my fingers. I noticed the crunch under my feet as we walked in the dried grass along the driveway. The ground was a little frozen. I zipped up Noah's coat. The wind was getting chilly and bitter. I glanced around at the rows of trees on either side of us, their barren branches moving stiffly in the breeze. The leaves were all fallen to the ground around the base of the trees—a blanket for the cold winter to come. I wasn't used to winter. In San Francisco, we didn't have winters. Not like this. It would take a little getting used to, but I didn't mind it. The more obvious change of seasons was welcome to me.

My parents came. They stayed just a few days, and as I expected, most of their energy was focused on Noah. They lavished him with gifts. They lavished him with their time and affection, and they practically ignored me. I was fighting the temptation to be angry with them, but I was mulling over the things Doris had told me, and I had been praying about it, *hard*. I didn't want this for Noah. I didn't want it for my mom and me. But I wasn't really sure what to do about it. *Lord, help me love them ...*

Nathan came over and spent the day with us on Saturday. I was curious to see how they would like one another. Nathan was the same with my parents as he was with everyone else, which I appreciated. My parents seemed to make an effort to be cordial.

By their last day, I knew I had to say something to my mom while it was on my heart and while I had the chance. My dad had taken Noah into the living room to play after dinner. Mom and I were alone.

"Mom," I said, while I washed the dishes. It was so much easier to talk while my hands were busy. "I need to talk to you about something."

"Oh?" She looked up from her phone.

"Yes. I just want you to know that when I left last spring, I didn't really understand all of the reasons why I needed to come here. I didn't know what would happen when I got here, but I felt like I needed to be Noah's mama alone. By myself. And I was having a hard time doing that when I was living with you. I felt suffocated."

"Adel!" she said as she stood up from the table. "What on *earth* are you talking about?"

"I felt like you needed him. You needed him to be your child. And he wasn't yours to have."

"This is just ridiculous! Of course that's not true!"

"Mom, please listen to me! I'm trying to be honest with you about how I feel!"

"We would *never* try to suffocate you ... or make you want to run away!"

"I just want you to listen to what I'm saying."

"You know, I was right!" she continued as she paced about the kitchen. "This place *was* too much for you. It landed you in the hospital! When will you see that enough is enough? That it isn't worth it? Give it up, Adel!"

"Mom, please don't distract from what I'm trying to say! I *want* to try to work things out with you—to get along better—"

"That's why I never wanted you to have the farm," she interrupted. "I *knew* what it was like! I knew it would steal your life away."

"Just like it did Grandma's?" I asked.

Mom stopped pacing and looked up sharply.

"She *loved* you. She wanted so bad to be close to you ..." My eyes were stringing with tears of grief.

"Enough!" she snapped. She had her hands up at her temples and was pacing around the kitchen again.

"I'm not saying it was easy," I continued.

"I said *enough*!" she shouted.

I gave a little start at the sharpness in her voice, and turned back to the dishes. We were getting nowhere. I remembered what Rebecca had said about not being able to force someone to change, and Doris had said only to *try*. I couldn't force her. So, I wouldn't.

Mom had stopped pacing and was standing next to the table, staring blankly down at the red-and-green checked tablecloth. She looked tired. Worn. My heart softened instantly. She was *my mom*. "I just want you to know that I care about you," I told her softly. "That I love you. And that I'm glad you're here."

Mom looked up. She just stood there, not really knowing what to say.

"Oh," she said awkwardly. "Me too." And she slowly walked out of the room.

They left the following morning. We were standing in the yard, and I was holding Noah in my arms. We were dressed for church and bundled up in our winter coats. Nathan was there to see them off and drive us to church.

Neither said much in a way of goodbye, but before walking to the car, Mom gave me what felt like a genuine hug. The first I could remember. My eyes stung smartly as I turned back to join Nathan.

Nathan put his arms around my shoulders. "I love you," he said warmly. "Come on." And he gently led the way to his truck.

THIRTY-NINE

Home

It was the night of the Christmas carol sing-a-long at church. The sanctuary was crowded to the brim with people dressed in their festive holiday best. The room was glowing from the merriment of the evening. There were holly wreaths on all the doors and a series of candles lit in the front of the sanctuary, on either side of the stage. Nathan was leading the carols, and the congregation was singing with more gusto than usual to the tunes of "Go Tell It on the Mountain" and "Hark the Herald Angels Sing." There was clapping and stomping, and everyone was singing at the top of their lungs.

He's so incredibly talented, I thought as I watched Nathan humbly and effortlessly lead the congregation. *He would've really been something at the churches back in San Francisco. He probably could have made a career out of it.* Yet here he was, in this little country church, in the middle of nowhere. *Here,* he was invaluable. *Here* was where he belonged.

He led us in "O Come, O Come, Emmanuel" and then ended the night with "Joy to the World." Everyone truly gave their best on that last song, and I wouldn't have been surprised if they'd heard us singing in the neighborhood two roads over.

After the carols were over, we all filed into the fellowship hall. Many had brought desserts to share, and now was the time to visit. The people at Cherry Hill Baptist *loved* to visit. We hadn't been in the room long, and I was talking with a group of women from a Bible study I had recently joined when Nathan came up to me and said, "Come on! There's somewhere we need to go. It's OK. Doris has Noah."

He seemed excited. Maybe a little nervous. I wondered what was up.

We drove along the roads that took us back to our road, but instead of pulling into my driveway, Nathan pulled into his. We drove down the long-forested drive, until at last we came to the opening. Nathan parked the car in front of the house. The porch lights were on, as well as the lights inside. It looked pretty, sitting there in the dark.

He turned the engine off.

We sat there for a minute.

I looked over at Nathan.

"What is it?" I asked.

"Adel, I know it isn't Sweet Valley, it never could be, and that you may need some time to think about it … but …" He paused. He was nervous! I tried not to smile, but I couldn't help it. He continued, "Would you consider letting *this* be your home?"

My eyes got wide.

"You don't have to answer tonight," he said.

I laughed in spite of myself. Nathan seemed surprised, confused even. He didn't know what to think!

"Nathan." I grabbed his hand. "I don't *need* to think about it! I know what I want. Yes! Yes, I would love to make *this* my home!" I said, gesturing toward the house.

"Really?" He seemed doubtful.

I had a hard time containing my excitement. "I've been doing a lot of thinking since we talked the other night, and I'm sure! I'm *absolutely* sure! I already set up an appointment to talk to my cousin! I didn't know for sure what the future would hold, but I knew in my heart that it was time for me to move on from Sweet Valley."

"Adel, wait. Let me explain better," he said. "Noah was the main reason for your coming here, but I know he wasn't the *only* reason. I know how much you love the farm."

"I do!" I said, nodding vigorously.

"I think I could probably find a way to make it work," he said. "I think we could do both my carpentry work *and* the apples, if that is what you really want. We could get some business loans, hire a manager, but it just seems to me that your heart isn't really in it?" He looked questioningly at me.

I sat there in the semidarkness, on the bench seat in his truck, staring out the window at a beautiful life.

"It's not." I sighed. "I tried it, and it's not that I *hate* it, but at the end of the day, I would just rather do something else."

"Like what?"

"I don't know. Learn how to cook?" I laughed.

"And besides all that," I said, scooting closer to him in the seat and leaning my head on his shoulder, "I love watching you work, Nathan. And I love the things you make. I think they're just wonderful, and I want to be a part of *that!*"

Nathan wrapped his arms around me and held me for a few minutes.

"So," he said softly, his face up close to mine. "You're *sure* you're not just doing this because of me? Because you think it's what *I* want?"

We sat there silently for a moment, while I tried to form thoughts into intelligible words.

"Yes," I said at last. "I loved the farm as a child because I was *free*. I wasn't the one having to run everything. I thought that perhaps Grandma knew something I didn't, that I would be like her or something. I thought maybe that was why she gave me the farm, because she believed I could do it."

"I think you could."

"Maybe so, but I can honestly say that I don't *want* to. The thought of selling it makes me feel free, like a heavy burden has been lifted, and I haven't even sold it yet! I love the farm; I think it's beautiful and magical and a wonderful place to grow up. But there is so much more to an orchard than its beauty. I'm not interested in spending my time, my *life*, on such a huge commitment. It doesn't come natural to me.

"And you know?" I continued. "I didn't really know what was important to me before. But once I started thinking about that, after I was in the hospital, it didn't take very long for me to see what matters most in my life, and apples just aren't part of it. I think it was pride, my keeping at it for so long. I was trying to prove something to myself, to people at church, even to *you*."

"To *me*?"

"Yes. When Peter told me that you wondered how long I'd be able to stick it out, that was a challenge for me."

"Yeah ... I shouldn't have said that."

"It's alright. I think I needed to be encouraged to do it for a while anyway. I learned a lot through the process."

"True."

"Nathan, *people* are what matter! *You*. Noah. And Doris and the ladies we visit. I want to spend my time with *you*, not running a farm. And a house is just a house! I finally understand that! Sweet Valley is special because my grandparents lived there. It will always be special to me, but I don't have to *own* it. My home will be wherever *you* are. And if this is where you say home is, then I say yes!"

"Well good!" he said, sitting up and facing me with a smile. "Because I wanted to go ahead and give you this." He held out a silver ring, its diamonds glittering in the pale light.

I held out my hand, suddenly quiet and still. He slid the ring on my finger. I held it up for a better look.

"It's beautiful," I whispered.

Nathan sat there, looking at me looking at my ring while sitting there in his truck, in *our* driveway.

"I talked to your dad when they were in town," Nathan told me on the drive back to church. "I was planning to wait until Christmas, but once I bought the ring, I couldn't." He laughed. "It was burning a hole in my pocket!"

"Well, I'm glad you didn't wait. That was *perfectly* romantic."

I held up my ring again and smiled.

"And you know what?" I said.

"What?"

"All the things I love most about the farm I will still have! The mountains, the mist, the fresh air, the wild animals."

"The creek."

"Yes! The creek! Noah will get to grow up playing in that creek!" A sentimental smile lifted the corners of my mouth. "I'll have to tell Christopher that the area around our special place isn't for sale. I think I'll keep that part."

"Good idea." He smiled.

"And I bet Christopher will let us visit! I don't know why he wouldn't! It'll be the first time I've ever lived close to family. I wonder what that's like."

Nathan laughed. "It's got its pluses and minuses like anything!"

When we arrived back at church, most of the congregation had gone, except for the few people who were anxiously awaiting our return.

"Well?" demanded Peter as soon as we were out of the car.

The others all walked up expectantly. It was Doris and Ace and the whole Shephard family, including Ali. I felt jittery, and my face flushed as I held up my hand so they could see the ring.

"Yeah! Congratulations! Finally!" they cheered. We were hugged and kissed and patted one another on the back.

The children were not about to be left out of this joyous occasion; Maggie Ann hurried over and wrapped her arms tightly around my legs, and even Randall gave me a little hug.

"We'll celebrate with the leftover brownies and punch!" exclaimed Rebecca, and she hurried off to get them ready. The others followed. The noise died down, and the stillness of the night crept back around us.

Nathan put his arm around me, and we walked over to Doris, who was holding a sleepy Noah. I took him gently. He laid his head down on my shoulder and rubbed his eyes. Doris smiled warmly at us and then walked away to join the others.

"Noah," I said quietly, after Doris was out of hearing. "Nathan's going to be your *daddy*."

Nathan was just standing there, hands in his pockets, quietly taking in the scene. Then he came over and gently put his arms around us.

And then it happened, as if by some supernatural force—in that moment, we became a *family*.

Next summer, in between bouts of morning sickness, Nathan and I hung a tire swing in the pecan tree beside our house, so that Noah and his new baby sister could swing on it together in the years to come.

I hope you enjoyed the book! For updates on new releases subscribe at...

LANAWETZEL.COM

Would you please consider recommending the book to a friend and leaving a review on Amazon?

https://www.amazon.com/dp/0578906708

Made in the USA
Columbia, SC
24 August 2021